I0614454

The Riddle Key

by

Jane Drager

This is a work of fiction. Names, characters, places, and incidents are either the product of the author's imagination or are used fictitiously, and any resemblance to actual persons living or dead, business establishments, events, or locales, is entirely coincidental.

The Riddle Key

COPYRIGHT © 2017 by Jane Drager

All rights reserved. No part of this book may be used or reproduced in any manner whatsoever without written permission of the author or The Wild Rose Press, Inc. except in the case of brief quotations embodied in critical articles or reviews.
Contact Information: info@thewildrosepress.com

Cover Art by *RJ Morris*

The Wild Rose Press, Inc.
PO Box 708
Adams Basin, NY 14410-0708
Visit us at www.thewildrosepress.com

Publishing History
First Crimson Rose Edition, 2017
Print ISBN 978-1-5092-1621-5
Digital ISBN 978-1-5092-1622-2

Published in the United States of America

"What in the world is he talking about?"
she complained. "He has to be talking about another Marina Cavanaugh, because I haven't the slightest idea what this means." She paced the room, one hand on her hip, the other in her hair.

Three clues, all pointing to Marina. He pursed his lips. "Which book was it in?"

She whirled to grab the book and read the binding. *"The Art of Marquise Gelt."* She flipped the pages and gasped. "Jon, he's talking about diamonds! The book's dated 1907, but look, Roger's note mentions the cuts." Extending the book, she showed him the page. "That's what this list means, diamond cuts!"

He flew around the desk, took the book, and flipped to a page illustrating the cuts. "Well, I'll be damned. The money's in diamonds, and Marina Cavanaugh holds all." He turned to her and peered.

In a gesture of surrender, she elevated her hands, palms up. "I do not know anything about your brother or diamonds."

Jonathan reread the note. "I'll show this to Farnsworth." He looked upward. "The book came from the top shelves, right? Why hide a note so high? Why not in his safe?"

Praise for Jane Drager

"Jane Drager has proven herself to be a first-class author! Her first book, *SECRETS BY NECESSITY*, launched her writing career and got me hooked. She followed with *ASK NOTHING IN RETURN* and *INFINITE CHOICES*, combining romance and mystery into one fascinating package. I am so anxious to read her next book!"

~*Daryl D.*

~*~

"*ASK NOTHING IN RETURN* is a fantastic story with plenty of twists. Was so good, I couldn't set it down and read it in eight hours. Wish I had a man like Sam to come home to every night!"

~*AnnMarie D.*

~*~

"I enjoyed *SECRETS BY NECESSITY* so much that reading it was the only real thing I accomplished today."

~*Kat O.*

~*~

"Jane did it again with *INFINITE CHOICES*! She has a wonderful knack of getting you involved right from the 'get-go.' The suspense never deviated. Loved it!"

~*Brenda P.*

Dedication

To my husband,
for his encouragement
and continued support.

Chapter One

Marina Cavanaugh flopped onto the lounge sofa with a huff and let her body collapse. Finally, a break. A reprieve from the morning chill of the warehouse to the warmth of the break room. What she wouldn't do for a nice, hot cup of coffee, but the pot was empty, and she had no gumption to get off her butt to fuss. Besides herself, only four employees worked in the Billingsley Auction warehouse, and they were busy unloading a truck at the dock while allowing in more of the blustery March winds to circulate.

Whoever made the claim about winters being slow months should have their lips sewn together. She had cut and unpacked more cardboard boxes today than the entire past month and had sore hands and feet as proof. Per her usual, she wore her jeans and sweatshirt under an oversized coverall, the kind that gave her an Amos-down-on-the-farm look. But the garment had a twofold purpose. One was to allow extra warmth while working in an area too large to heat, the other to protect from dust and dirt.

The boxes had contained the treasure trove of a wild hunt through the backwoods of Maine and Vermont, her latest jaunt to accumulate objects for auction. Two items in particular should fetch a hefty sum—a Tiffany lamp from the early part of the nineteenth century and a British tea set with a Queen

Victoria inscription. Both were well worth the ensuing blisters forming on her palms. Of course, if she wore gloves more often, she wouldn't have nails that frightened a manicurist into early retirement. Unfortunately, gloves had a tendency to walk away on their own. The same for her eyeglasses. The old put-them-down-and-can't-remember-where scenario.

She grasped a red apple from the end table and took a big bite before stretching her legs across the sofa cushions, throwing back her head onto the arm while chewing. Despite the fatigue, she felt blessed. She had turned a hobby into an exciting career, traveling the world with all expenses paid, always searching for that one special item to make a collector drool. Mrs. Dorothy Billingsley was a gem of an employer, and after three years, Marina Cavanaugh had turned into the company's main buyer.

"Dr. Cavanaugh?"

Her back was to the door, and Marina wanted an interruption as much as she wanted head lice. She spoke over her shoulder. "I just sat down. So, whoever you are, I'm not moving. If you want to talk to me, you'll have to come over here." She took another bite of her apple.

A man approached, his tall form appearing from the left.

Holy shit, the man's an Adonis! She nearly choked on her apple.

He wore an Armani suit of gray, impeccably tailored with a silk powder-blue tie tacked with a diamond stud. He carried a black wool overcoat draped on one arm which indicated he'd come from the business office. The girls upstairs kept the heat on

2

furnace blast.

His expensive suit was in direct contrast to the starkness of the lounge with its yellowed appliances and metal tables and chairs. This man was dressed for a plusher environment, not this hodge-podge room of second-hand furniture. The sofa had a used-and-abused look with worn leather armrests and indented cushions, but everything was clean. Visitors were rare, and she preferred the solitude rather than the hustle of the front office. Slowly, she lifted her head to scan him more fully.

He shifted his feet. "You *are* Dr. Marina Cavanaugh, right?"

Short, light brown hair fell to the side of his forehead while pale brown eyes surveyed her with caution...well, maybe annoyance since she stared up with the surprised wide-eyed expression of a kid in a toy store.

A wealthy man rarely entered the warehouse, especially one who had the handsome looks to stop a woman dead. They stayed in the office with her boss and a cup of coffee while a subordinate trudged through the warehouse world of boxes and packing material. She swallowed quickly and somehow found her voice. "Can I help you?"

His gaze narrowed. "You can confirm your identity before I ramble like an idiot. Are you the *Antiques 101* author?"

"That's me."

"I'm Jonathan Blandish. Your boss told me I'd find you here." Stepping closer, he extended his hand. "Please don't move. I wanted to meet you in your own environment."

Great. She had a chance to chat with an attractive man without an auctioneer babbling over a loud speaker, and here, she wore her frumpy coveralls, no makeup, and her hair resembled a post-cyclone hit. *So much for first impressions.*

She shook the outstretched hand and resisted the urge to yank him onto the sofa...until the gold wedding band sparkled from the overhead lights. She never had trouble arousing the interest of a man, but single, handsome ones with money were few and far between. "Mrs. Billingsley should have called, Mr. Blandish. I can easily run to the office instead of you finding your way to the warehouse." Not to mention give her enough time to readjust the large hair clip holding her wild mane away from her face. Ordinarily, she'd have fixed her hair before flopping onto the sofa, but her objective had been to get off her feet, not to look beautiful for the men in the warehouse. She'd been unpacking boxes since seven this morning and missed her morning break. With lunch still an hour away, she deserved a much-needed rest. Reluctantly, she released his hand. "What can I do for you?"

Before answering, he threw his overcoat on one of the table chairs and grabbed another, placing it alongside and, with his hand, dusted crumbs from the seat before slipping onto the cushion. "I understand you're the best antiques appraiser in the City of Boston."

Mrs. Billingsley again, bragging about her young appraiser. *I really must talk to the woman.* She shifted on the seat. "Depends on who you ask. Some people think I'm still in diapers and too young to know anything." His mouth attempted an I-don't-have-time-for-humor smile, polite but strained. Typical businessman. Time was money. Like she gave a shit.

"Did you know my brother, Roger Blandish?"

She bit into her apple and chewed while scanning her memory banks. "Can't say the name is familiar."

"He died two months ago. I haven't done anything with the contents of his house, because frankly, I won't know an antique from a piece of junk. I need an expert who knows what she's looking at." He unbuttoned his suit jacket and leaned back, revealing a belt buckle of gold. "I've already talked to your boss. If you agree to have a go at his stuff, you can place the entire contents of his estate for auction with this firm."

Why would her boss send her top appraiser to a home when several others were equally qualified to handle the job? She inspected her apple. "Mrs. Billingsley rarely does estate auctions, Mr. Blandish." She bit the apple and pushed the food to the side of her mouth. "How did you convince her?"

"A sixty-forty split with her receiving the sixty."

She stopped chewing and stared. "That's very generous. Why?"

"I don't need the money, but I must finalize his estate." He tilted forward, his posture on the rigid side. "I also agreed to pay your salary. I don't know how long you'll take, but I'm willing to pay five thousand a week."

This time, she choked on the apple and threw her feet to the floor in order to lean over and cough off her head. He scraped his chair backward as if she was about to hack up pneumonic plague onto his nice trousers.

"I'm sorry I startled you, Doctor. I assumed a woman in your position was used to large checks."

"Yeah, doling them out when I conduct purchases for the firm, not receiving them." She blinked the tears from her eyes and cleared her throat. "You're not talking pocket change, Mr. Blandish."

Placing both hands on his knees, he drummed his fingers while his head tilted slightly to the side. "I'd want a commitment to a time line, of course. Three weeks should be sufficient. I expect a detailed printout of the contents plus their approximate value."

Through her blurred vision, she took in the gold Rolex watch, the diamond-studded cuff links protruding from the jacket sleeves, and the blue silk handkerchief to match his tie. The man had way too much money to throw around. "Not to change your mind or anything, but do you realize you're paying me fifteen thousand for three weeks of work? Are you crazy?"

One brow rose with a quiver. "I'm perfectly sane. I see nothing wrong with paying for the best. Your boss certainly agreed."

"Of course, she agreed. You're presenting quite a profitable venture. And for the record, I haven't decided."

"That's why I made the salary attractive. The money should entice you. You'd be a fool to refuse."

Her back stiffened. "Oh, would I now? I don't have any heavy debts hanging over my head, and my needs are small. I've no reason to jump at your offer."

"Except to deprive your boss of her sixty percent. I want you or no deal."

Her mouth fell open. "That's blackmail!" How dare he be so presumptive. She should tell him to shove his offer up his anus. She leaned forward and peered. "I don't like being forced into something, Mr. Blandish.

Nothing triggers my Irish temper faster."

With a huff, Tony from the front office rushed into the lounge carrying a large box. "It came, Dr. Cavanaugh. I know you wanted the delivery right away." He placed the box at her feet, breathless. "And here. I collected these on my way." He dumped a handful of eyeglasses into her lap and left.

Marina put one pair on the top of her head. The rest she placed in a pocket.

Blandish stared. "How many glasses do you need?"

"Quite a few. I keep losing them." She glanced at his widened gaze. "They're the drugstore variety, not prescription. They help me see fine lines or damage on an object." She slipped a hand into a back pocket and withdrew a knife.

Openmouthed, he backed farther away, his chair legs screeching on the linoleum floor. "That's a switchblade!"

Oh, good grief. "No, this is a utility knife. They're designed with a two-finger folding mechanism." She demonstrated several times, opening then closing the blade. "See? No effort whatsoever. Best investment I ever made. Hold my apple for me."

Slapping his mouth shut, Blandish blinked at the half-eaten apple she'd thrust into his hand while she cut the tape securing the box. She'd waited a week for this parcel and prayed some delivery person hadn't tossed it like a football.

"A lot of packages come from around the world," she explained. "The contents are protected by layers of whatever is available. Cloth, rope, paper, you name it. My knife never leaves my side, because when I need to cut something, I can never find anything to use. I drive myself nuts and waste a lot of valuable time." She folded the knife and replaced it in her pocket. "My knife is like my credit card. I don't leave home without either one."

He jerked his chin toward the top of her head. "Yet, you lose your glasses."

She shot him a sheepish look. "Strange, I know." She opened the box. Styrofoam popcorn welcomed the escape and poured onto the floor. She frowned at the mess. "I guess I should do this over a trash can." And wait to investigate the contents, perhaps give him a few minutes to wrestle with her Typhoid Mary cough and Jack the Ripper knife since he sat looking a little stunned, sort of a wowed expression that almost made her laugh.

****

Jonathan watched her fuss with the popcorn and wondered what the hell he'd gotten into. She was nothing like he expected. Her profile on the Billingsley Auction website showed a photo of an attractive woman, but he anticipated an uptight PhD with polished fingernails, sitting at an office desk, not this beautiful woman with a long mane of auburn hair. A large rhinestone hair clip held the strands in place, and her face had no more than a glancing blow of makeup.

She jammed the Styrofoam into the box and closed the flaps. "Thanks for holding my apple." She grabbed the fruit from his hand and took a bite.

Since the apple caused juice to drip onto his skin, Jonathan wiped his hand on his trouser. "I want you to start tomorrow."

While chewing, she returned to a sitting position on the sofa and leaned on her knees, her gaze cautious.

"Are you asking or demanding? Either way, I haven't agreed to go."

Never one to let anyone get the upper hand, he leaned forward, matching her posture. "I'll increase the ante. Seventy-thirty. This way, your boss will kick you out the door."

Marina crunched on the apple and chewed then leaned back with one brow arched. "Why me? I'm not the only antiques appraiser in Boston."

"But you are the best. I wouldn't be sitting here if you weren't."

Marina stood to toss her apple core into the trash. While turning back, her foot nudged the box, and more popcorn floated onto the floor. She sighed, kicked the Styrofoam to the side, and retook her seat. "I'll make a deal with you, Mr. Blandish. I'll check to see if you're legit. If I'm satisfied, then I'll check your brother's address for nearby hotels. At the salary you're paying, I'm aiming for a first-class establishment with all the amenities assuming, of course, his house isn't around the corner from our warehouse."

"Fair enough. You'll have roughly an hour's drive on a bad day, which is more traffic than distance. On a good day, you'll make the trip in forty-five minutes. The house is located in the Boston suburbs, but you won't need a hotel. My brother lived alone and never married. His housekeeper can ready a room and also stock the refrigerator so you'll have food to eat. To save time, I have the address and key with me." He took a business card and a key out of his pocket and held them on his open palm.

She took the card and key, glancing at the address.

"My brother was in the process of refurbishing his

old house so you might enjoy the antiquity. The housekeeper lives in the development across the street, and a gardener works the grounds a couple days a week. I live with my family ten minutes away. If you stay on the premises, you'll finish the job a lot faster."

She chewed on her inner lip, clearly undecided. When she finally looked up, their gazes met, and his breath hitched. Her eyes had a deep, chocolate hue, like molten fudge, ready to be poured onto a big bowl of ice cream.

"I can't start right away, Mr. Blandish. I have commitments for the next two weeks."

She'd agreed to accept. *Mission accomplished.* "All right. I've waited two months. I may as well wait a little longer." He stood, replaced the chair to the table, and grabbed his overcoat. "You'll find a lot of information about me online. My brother, Roger, lived a quiet life so you won't find much about him. Neither of us have personal info posted, only business."

With a grunt, she stood and tugged on the coveralls. "My publisher detailed my entire life. I'm sure you've acquainted yourself."

His lips curled with a smile. "I saw the biography. The most surprising was your earning a PhD at age twenty-seven. That's quite an achievement, and to be considered the best in the field at age thirty is impressive." He pointed to the card. "If you have any questions, you'll find my cell number on the front." He slipped on his overcoat and fussed with the collar. "On my way out, I'll tell Mrs. Billingsley about the seventy-thirty split. Hopefully, my brother has a few items worth your time and effort." He pointed to the card. "Call me with a start date, and I'll inform the housekeeper."

Jonathan Blandish stopped in the doorway and focused on her oversized coveralls. Her choice of garment hid any recognizable shape and made her look like a clown without the big, red nose.

"I'll call you, Mr. Blandish."

Her voice broke his trance. He nodded, turned, and left. *I think I just made the biggest mistake of my life.*

Chapter Two

Marina stepped from her red SUV and zipped her jacket to the neck. The wind bit her exposed skin like a sand blaster, swirling her mane in every direction, and sending a shiver straight down her spine. Early March hung onto winter with all its might, not giving an inch to the impending spring. Even the gray clouds overhead threatened to release a blanket of snow, despite the forecast calling for clear weather.

She had often wondered why she stayed in New England to establish her career. Her home state of North Carolina had a milder climate. A snowstorm in Charlotte meant an inch of white fluff and created total panic. Before the first snowflake hit the ground, schools and businesses rolled in the sidewalks whereas two feet in Massachusetts hardly generated a yawn.

But she'd never return home. Not to Charlotte anyway. Farther south was an option, but after studying for her doctorate at Brown University in Rhode Island, she'd gotten used to the inclement weather of the northeast corridor. With her PhD in hand, she migrated to Boston, which seemed the natural path to take because she wanted to freeze off her ass. Although, she never could build a proper snowman. The poor thing always fell over sideways with the tree-limb arms positioned like he was waving for help.

The drive to Roger's house had taken a mere forty

minutes, a lucky break considering the mid-afternoon traffic. Like in any sprawling suburb of a big city, strip malls dominated the landscape along with multiple fast-food restaurants, the kind where buildings sprouted overnight. One blink and—ohmygosh—a new place to eat existed.

Roger Blandish's neighborhood was probably the last farmland still available in Boston. One side of his two-lane highway was open fields, the other side housing developments and shopping centers. With the house standing before her, she'd swear time had bypassed his property. Not a mansion by any definition of the word, but simply a large structure in a common saltbox design built with red bricks, positioned on a hill and surrounded by open fields of dormant weeds. A nineteenth-century dwelling at a guess, two stories plus an attic—judging from the number of windows. A nondescript farm house brought into the twenty-first century with the addition of new vinyl windows and a sturdy front door.

Two concrete steps led onto an open wooden porch. The porch flooring was replaced in spots with new pine boards, unpainted showing old and new. A railing with freshly-painted white spindles enclosed the entire area. No chairs for relaxation nor flower baskets to add color. Nothing much of anything. Definitely not an inviting house. The entire property lacked personality and warmth.

The front door opened. A woman stepped onto the porch, clutching her arms tight to shield against the cold. She was as round as she was tall with short, dark hair and deep-set dark eyes.

Marina glanced at the woman and climbed the two

steps. "Are you Patti?"

A smile spread onto her lips. "Yes, Patti Gleisberg. You must be Dr. Cavanaugh. Please come in. The air's colder than normal today."

Patti was pretty in an odd sort of way, even though her eyebrows resembled floor brooms. She barely had a neck to put a necklace around, but her smile was bright, which stretched her flawless skin across high cheekbones.

They entered a parlor—a dark, dismal room about as inviting as a rat hole—brightened only by the daylight seeping through the front windows. A blend of black-and-brown paneling gave the room the appearance of a cave, and Marina half-expected to see bats escape through the open front door. The paneling was the 1960s style where everyone and their mother covered the walls with cheap sheets of colored plywood, because manufacturers jammed the craze down everyone's throat. Unusual to see in this day and age with such a wide variety of colors from which to choose.

The living room—if she could use such a general term—stretched from one end of the house to the other with a hardwood floor of unstained pine, varnished to a glossy finish. A staircase stood on the left wall and a fireplace on the right. The room's dimensions were twice as long as wide, its odd size made worse by a sofa and two end tables sitting in the middle of the floor. This atypical position blocked a direct path into the dining room, and instead of facing the double windows for a view of the street, the sofa faced the front door, a location so peculiar she couldn't help but stare.

The furnishings were Queen Anne style, another

oddity to add to the list, especially for a bachelor. Generally, men liked the heavier masculine look of large, solid pieces, not the dainty appearance of simple curves and cabriole legs. Yellow brocade upholstery on the sofa's thin cushions gave the impression of an elderly aunt's version of luxury and looked about as comfortable as a bed of nails.

Two parlor lamps rested on mahogany end tables at opposite ends of the sofa. The lamps were the gray-flowered, pot-bellied monstrosities popular in the early part of the twentieth century. Ugly as all get-out, but they fetched a couple hundred bucks each at auction. A wing-back chair was positioned near the fireplace. Why was questionable since the hearth showed no evidence of being used.

Apprehension flooded her veins. She had the unmistakable urge to bolt, to retreat to the outside and take a deep breath, remind herself that a world full of color and light was only a footstep away. The rest of the house couldn't be as dark and gloomy as this one room, right? What if it was? What would she do?

"Let me take your coat," Patti said, extending her hands. "The closet's over by the archway, but Roger preferred to use this coat rack by the door." She draped Marina's jacket on a rung. "I understand you're here to assess the contents of the house?"

Shaking away her apprehension, she forced a smile. "Yes. How many rooms are we talking?"

"Well, as you can see, the parlor leads to the dining room with the den and sunroom on opposite sides. Three bedrooms are upstairs, two furnished. Another flight of stairs leads to a walk-in attic, unfinished, and the house has a full basement, also unfinished. Roger doesn't have a whole lot of stuff. He's only had the place for five years, and I've been with him from the start. I live across the street toward the rear of the development."

Patti had referred to her late boss in the present tense, as if he floated around the house in ghostly form. From an anthropological standpoint, this wasn't unusual. Several cultures practiced similar rituals and never spoke of death until months and sometimes years later. Here in Boston, however…a trifle disconcerting.

"Come into the kitchen, Doctor. I've got coffee on."

The dining room came right out of the 1950s with a chandelier made of green-stained copper. As they passed through a wide archway, Marina paused to rub her fingers along the surface of a heavy mahogany dining table, happy to see the finish in such excellent condition. Six matching chairs surrounded the table—two with armrests, four without—all with the Queen Anne style to the legs. The suite should create a bidding war at auction. Otherwise, the dining room reflected the mood of the parlor with the same dark paneling covering the walls. No warmth or personality. Again, an unstained pine floor. Without the benefit of rugs, everything echoed—their voices and footsteps, even their clothing rustled too loud.

As Marina entered the kitchen, she sucked in the aroma of coffee. And bright lights!

Patti reached for a mug from an overhead cabinet and poured. "Cream is in the refrigerator, sugar on the table. I stocked the freezer with prepared meals. All you have to do is heat them in the microwave. If you need anything, just ask. I can pick up something at the supermarket."

"Thanks, Patti. I should be fine." She took the offered cup and strolled to the refrigerator for the cream. Coffee wasn't the same without cream, and she poured a hefty dollop. While taking a slow look around at her entry into the twenty-first century, she released the tight hold on her muscles. At least, the kitchen had warmth, both in air and atmosphere, with none of the darkness so predominant in the outer rooms. "The kitchen's new."

Patti nodded with a quick grin. "When I first started here, I cooked on an old avocado-colored stove, which thankfully, broke down completely. The whole kitchen had avocado appliances and no lighting. I told Roger if he wanted me to stay, then he had to do something with this kitchen." Her face beamed. "I now have the brightest room in the house."

And had a woman's touch with frilly curtains and colored plates hanging on the walls along with teddy-bear canisters and a red rooster clock above the door.

"He also renovated the bathroom upstairs," Patti continued. "Plumbing and electric throughout the house. The mandatory code stuff. This here—" She opened a door showing steps leading into a black void. "This is the basement. The doorway over there—" She pointed across the room. "That's the mudroom, an old term for storing muddy field boots. The outside door leads to the garage. Do you want to see your room?"

Gee, can't wait. Marina swallowed a big gulp of coffee before placing the mug on a counter. "I'm ready."

Patti led the way to the living room where she threw a switch for a light at the top of the staircase. A narrow flight of steps stood before them, its width slightly wider than Patti. They ascended the uncarpeted stairs, their shoes echoing and filling Marina with a sense of dread, for the same brown paneling lined the wall all the way up. She'd stayed in some rundown places in her life, mainly throughout her college years, but never in a house this dark. The only upbeat point was cleanliness. Not a dust ball was in sight.

At the top of the stairwell, she looked around at the odd emptiness to the hallway. Though the walls were wide, no pictures hung on the dark paneling, no little table with a bowl of flowers to break the monotony, not even an open door to allow light from a bedroom window. Two doors on the right, three on the left with only one light hanging overhead to brighten the way. "Were any photos on the walls?"

Patti's head shook. "Roger wasn't sentimental, and he hated cluttering the house with unnecessary objects. This way, Doctor."

Marina touched the wall, hoping to see the color rub off onto her fingertips. "I've always hated this dark paneling. Is it in the bedrooms, too?"

"Yes, everywhere. One of the prior owners installed it, and Roger saw no need to change. He liked dark for some reason."

"How about you?"

She glanced over her shoulder with a smile tugging the corner of her lips. "I'm only the housekeeper who gets paid to do a job." She swept with a circular motion at the floor. "He had the rugs ripped out before he moved in. Dust triggered his allergies. You'll see an occasional throw rug. Like alongside your bed and also in the bathroom. Here we are." She opened a door and stepped into a bedroom.

Marina's heart sank. A room straight out of a nun's convent stood before her. Single bed, easy-to-assemble chest of drawers, small mirror tacked to the wall, no closet, no chair, an oval wastebasket by the door…wow. A lamp stood on a nightstand by the bed, the only light in the room. A small throw rug was positioned alongside the bed in the proper spot for kneeling. This prompted a quick glance for the cross at the head of the bed. *I gave up a first-class hotel for this?*

"Roger's room is across the hall." Patti gestured with a thumb over her shoulder. "The bathroom is the next door over. Adjacent to your room is another bedroom used mostly for storage, and then, at the far end of the hall are the steps leading to the attic. You'll need a flashlight for both the attic and basement. We keep one in the kitchen you can use." She stepped into the hall.

Not having the least desire to be left alone, Marina followed.

Patti pointed toward the lone light overhead. "Even though Roger had the whole house rewired, he never added extra lights. So, some of the areas are pretty dark." She approached the staircase. "If you need help with anything, you'll find my phone number on the refrigerator door. Mr. Blandish still pays me to serve as the housekeeper, so I'll be in every day, rain or shine. Do you have any questions?"

Yes, why am I here? Marina shook herself and, with a knuckle, tapped the wooden banister tacked to the stairwell wall. "Give me a little history about the house."

Patti led the way down the staircase. "I understand this building was a parsonage built somewhere in the 1850s. Baptist, I think. The church was destroyed by fire about a hundred years later. The property became a farm after that, but the church cemetery is still accessed by a side road. Hardly anything was added to the house except for the sunroom. That's my favorite spot. The room's bright and airy, and the double doors open to the rear of the property." She approached the front door and paused. "You, of course, need to wander and familiarize yourself with the layout. It's not complicated." Stretching, she grabbed her coat from the rack. "Do you want help with your luggage?"

"I travel light, Patti." She looked around, hesitant to ask such a worldly question. "Did Roger have a computer?"

"Oh, sure." She gave a curt nod. "In the den—that's the door on the left in the dining room. Why?"

"I work with a laptop. Mr. Blandish wants an inventory printout so maybe I can use the printer."

"Probably. The machine's fairly new." She slipped on her coat and opened the front door. "Call if you need me. I'm a little bored without Roger barking orders, but don't call too soon. My cell phone is acting weird. I'm heading to the mall for a new one." She opened the door then quickly turned back. "By the way, Roger has a really nice brass bed. He and—"

Patti paused with her hand on the doorknob, her gaze distant. Within seconds, tears moistened her eyes.

Recognizing the signs, Marina jolted, realizing the woman cared for the eccentric bachelor, dark environment and all. "I'm sorry for your loss, Patti."

Patti glanced at Marina with a faint

acknowledgment and left.

Before deciding what to do first, Marina returned to the kitchen for a fresh cup of coffee. She hadn't seen a sniggin' of comfort in the house. The furnishings looked about as appealing as cactus cushions. Lack of rugs made the rooms feel cold, and the darkness... Of all things, the darkness. She might have to sleep on the kitchen table.

Jonathan Blandish had given her a three-week timeline. Her estimation was one week tops. Although, the lack of good lighting would hinder the process, unless she carried the items into the kitchen for inspection. Sleep, eat, work in the kitchen. She'd been through worse.

The aroma of brewed coffee calmed her nerves, and Marina sipped while allowing her gaze to take in the surrounding renovations. The cream appliances gave the room warmth, a necessity in such a stark house. The cute curtains hung over the sink windows with pale beige paint on the walls to complete the homey appearance.

Besides the outside exit leading to the garage and the opening to the mudroom, three doors were part of the kitchen. Walking to the first to investigate, she opened a small door which opened to a half-bath with modern toilet and sink. The next revealed a walk-in pantry almost empty, and of course, the third led to the basement. The latter could wait for a nice, bright sunny day, assuming the basement windows weren't boarded over to block the light. For the hell of it, she checked the sturdiness of the kitchen table...just in case. Lengthwise, she'd fit perfectly along with her blankets and pillow.

Her original misgivings about this assignment had doubled as she wandered from the kitchen. Roger Blandish wasn't an antiques collector. What she'd seen was ordinary, the common variety stuff found at any garage sale. So far, only the dining suite would pay for a single week of her salary.

Although, she shouldn't jump to conclusions. Several times in her career, she'd come across a pleasant surprise, like the day a Ming Dynasty jade owl fell on her head and into her arms. Mrs. Billingsley was ecstatic, not because of the ten stitches in Marina's scalp, but because the owl was worth four hundred thousand bucks. She doubted Roger had anything extraordinary, certainly not worth paying an appraiser five thousand a week, but time would tell…if the darkness didn't drive her stark raving mad.

What irked her more than her bleak surroundings was Jonathan Blandish's insistence on Marina Cavanaugh, even though her name wasn't well known within the industry. All right, she'd written a layman's reference book that sold well at the bookstores, but she hardly considered herself at the top of her field, especially for a man with the money to pay for the *crème de la crème*. At this point, he was overpaying for her services. Any estate appraiser would suffice, or better yet, erect a big tent and have an estate auction right on the premises.

Maybe she should talk to Mrs. Billingsley about the last option.

The web had revealed the barest of information about Jonathan Blandish. Like he told her, no personal data appeared except his age—thirty-five, but his business side was impressive. Jonathan Blandish owned a property development company worth millions, the biggest, privately-owned enterprise in Boston.

Roger Blandish had even less info on the web. His brief obituary popped onto the screen. Sudden death at the age of thirty-seven. No specifics given.

Ah, well. Time to grab her gear from the vehicle and make the best of her depressing situation. She placed her mug on the end table by the sofa, grabbed her jacket from the coat rack, and stepped outside into waning daylight.

The stone-covered horseshoe driveway added nothing to enhance the front of the property, a utilitarian place to drive-in and drive-out. No edging to give it shape nor any bushes or trees to enhance the perimeter. A plain, dreary exterior to match the depressing interior.

Apprehension returned. The place, the entire property, was too damn dismal. Bad enough Boston hadn't seen the sun for four days, but her psyche screamed for bright lights. After this job, maybe a quick trip to the Caribbean would settle her nerves.

A dog barked from somewhere in the development across the street, a big dog from the sound, the kind who'd tear off a leg and use the tibia bone for a toothpick. The houses were typical split-level, built too close together to pad the developer's multi-million dollar bank account while people erected fences to create the illusion of privacy. Roger's porch offered the best vantage point to watch the world go by, high on a hill, like a king on a throne presiding over the constituents. So far, the open porch was the only positive weighed against too many negatives.

Seconds later, a man meandered from the right side

of the house with a rake over his shoulder. He was an older man, late fifties with balding salt-and-pepper hair, wearing brown work clothes tattered at all four cuffs. He smiled, displaying teeth more sideways than forward.

"Evening, ma'am. I'm Karl with a K, the gardener. Patti said she was expecting an appraiser."

"Marina Cavanaugh." They shook hands. "You have quite a lot of property to maintain."

He glanced toward the house. "That I do. Ten acres to be precise, including the cemetery and around the lake. This is the slow time of year, though. Nothing wants to grow. I come a couple days a week to rake leaves and whatever." He nodded toward her opened hatch. "Do you need help with your luggage? I'm about to quit for the day."

The man leaned on his rake, not looking the least bit anxious to leave. "Thanks, Karl, but I'm fine. Do you live on the premises?"

"Nay. Got an apartment twenty minutes away. Suits my needs. My van's parked around the other side of the garage—if that's your next question—in its usual spot. Like Patti always parks by the mudroom door. Easier to unload groceries."

"I guess she walked over today. I didn't see any car when I drove in."

"Yeah, she does that a lot, more than ever with Mr. Blandish gone. Neither of us know what we're gonna do." He lifted the rake onto his shoulder. "If you need help with anything, give a holler. I've a strong back."

"Thanks, Karl, I will."

With a wave over his shoulder, he disappeared around the side of the house.

She grabbed her suitcase, laptop in its case, and her acoustic guitar, also in a case. She never went anywhere without her guitar, her favorite traveling companion, good for the long, boring hours of being away from home. Not like she was Maria Von Trapp and broke into song on a whim, but people had remarked on the pleasantness of her voice. Never anyone who could offer a recording contract, of course. The singing PhD. With a bemused shake of her head, she locked her SUV and returned to the house.

Once inside, she placed her luggage by the door, turned the bolt, and then yanked on the knob to check for security. As darkness approached outside, the gloom increased tenfold inside. The living room desperately needed lights. She hung her jacket on the rack and clicked on the two lamps alongside the sofa. The light produced hardly brightened the far corners, leaving too many shadows for her imagination. She peeked over the lampshade at the top of the bulb. A forty-watt. Sparse furnishings, limited lighting. The man had been a modern-day Mr. Scrooge.

A switch by the front door activated an overhead light for the entryway. She left it on along with the staircase light. A hot fireplace would be nice, but with her luck, the chimney was sealed shut to prevent drafts. She made a mental note to ask Patti about it in the morning.

Should she go around and check all the doors and windows? "If I don't, I won't sleep tonight." She started with the front windows. Cheap-ass curtains hung on rings, the bargain basement variety where one wash turned them into strips of rags. She checked the window locks then jerked the curtains shut for privacy.

A faint flash of light caught her eye as she headed for the dining room. The living room lamp caused a reflection somewhere above the fireplace where several figurines decorated a stone mantel. Her gaze instantly drifted to a large framed portrait...*whoa!*

Now, *that* was a significant find. The wood frame of beautifully carved black walnut had to be as ancient as the house. It hung on a red brick face that served as the backdrop for the fireplace wall with bricks layered from the hearth to ceiling, the only wall in the house not covered with paneling. The portrait, however, was unremarkable. The artist had simply painted a woman dressed in Victorian-era clothes—black dress, white collar, hair in a bun. Folk art from long ago and positioned too high to spot a signature. The frame, though, with its intricately cut flowers and stems, could fetch a nice price at auction.

But a reflection had caught her attention, not the portrait. She studied the figurines, four in all, a set of nude women in various poses standing among bushes, like Eve waiting for Adam. The stone mantel was higher than normal, way above her eye level, so she inspected the interior of the fireplace and found the hooks used to hang cooking pots. The hooks explained the height because even on tiptoe, she couldn't see behind the figurines. Reaching, Marina lifted one of the statuettes to check the bottom. Made in China. *Worthless.* She picked up another and gasped, her grip tightening.

A miniature camera stared back, wedged into the clay foliage at the base. Cameras were not uncommon in her line of work, but here in this sparsely furnished house? Why? More importantly, who?

All right, let's analyze this logically. Patti, Roger, or Jonathan?

Roger protecting his precious heirlooms? A ridiculous notion. Forty-watt bulbs in the lamps and an expensive camera on the mantel? A dichotomy for sure. *No, not Roger.* Marina stood on tiptoe to run a finger along the mantel. As expected, clean as a whistle. Patti's height prevented her from reaching without a step stool, but with a dust wand, she might clean around the figurines and never once see the camera. So, Patti was not completely eliminated, merely less suspicious. That left Jonathan Blandish, the most likely suspect. Tall enough to set his toy wherever he wanted, wealthy enough to buy the best. The question was why?

Marina wandered into the dining room and threw the switch for the chandelier. The little tear-drop bulbs flickered like candle flames and provided barely enough illumination to see the surface of the dining room table. *A flashlight, that's what I need.* She ran to the kitchen and rummaged through one drawer after another until she found the one Patti mentioned.

Returning to the dining room, she stood in the archway, hands on hips, gaze surveying the meager furnishings. "Where would I hide a camera?" The chandelier? No, the view should cover as wide an area as possible. The china cabinet then. The tall piece had several nooks and crannies.

Marina placed one of the dining room chairs near the cabinet and stepped up, swinging the flashlight beam from one end to the other and caught the reflection. Bingo! In the wood along the top edge, she found another camera wedged between a section of carved flowers. Even with a chair, Patti could never reach so high. She'd need a ladder, and again, that brought Jonathan's height to mind. *It ain't looking good for you, Jonny baby.*

On a lark, she ran to her bedroom and turned on the lone light by the bed. No reflection caught her eye, but if a camera covered the room...

Hmmm.

In the far corner, a vase of artificial flowers sat on a corner shelf. This was within easy reach so she used the flashlight beam to reflect the lens and found the camera within a fake rose. In her bedroom of all places. *Of all the perverted...*

Hot blood coursed through her veins. Shaking, she grabbed the vase with every intention of smashing it on the floor but stopped, arms and vase overhead.

Cameras in the living and dining rooms and now the bedroom. Why? *Should I gather them and flush the lot down the toilet or wait?* Since she'd already made up her mind to leave, she turned the rose to face the wall and tucked the camera close to the corner, nearly toppling the shelf off its loose hinges.

One more room for the hell of it. After a few steps down the hall, she entered the bathroom, flipped the switch for the light, and looked up. Her hands curled into tight fists. This one was more obvious, but how many people inspected a light fixture when using a bathroom?

No wonder Jonathan Blandish had insisted she stay in the house. He'd see her undress, bathe, and shit on the john. A blatant invasion of privacy, and the idea caused a shudder to ripple through her body. Was he watching now? If so, he had to realize she was madder than a hornet.

She ran downstairs, grabbed her jacket, and opened the front door only to see Jonathan standing on the threshold with his hand poised to knock.

Well, I'll be damned.

Without another thought, she slapped his handsome face.

Chapter Three

Jonathan staggered, hand clamping onto his cheek. His eyes protruded so wide she swore he'd pop them from their sockets.

Marina wouldn't give a damn if he fell flat on his ass. He owned the house and could put cameras anywhere he pleased, but she refused to be suckered into his sick game. She grabbed her luggage by the front door and, using her suitcase as a shield, pushed past him and into the night air.

"Wait a minute!" He caught her arm and spun her to face him. "What was that about?"

She yanked her arm from his grip while resisting the urge to swing her laptop at his head. "You know damn well what I'm talking about. Your game is over, Blandish."

His gaze turned to ice. "I haven't the foggiest idea what you're talking about. So, before I call the cops to have you charged with assault, I suggest you give an explanation."

Playing coy. The oh-I'm-so-innocent scenario. With the use of her key fob, Marina popped the hatch to her SUV and threw in her suitcase, but the guitar and laptop she handled like two babies, even throwing a blanket over them to hide them from prying eyes. She slammed the hatch shut then turned to confront him. "Look, Blandish, I'm used to working with cameras on my back because I handle expensive antiques, but I will not be your porn show!"

He gaped. "What *are* you talking about?"

"The cameras, damn you! Even in the bedroom and bath. You must be Boston's biggest pervert." She headed for the driver's side door.

He caught her wrist, his expression like granite. A narrowed gaze sliced her in two. "Show me."

His grip was strong, his anger very real, and an internal alarm bell sounded. But she wasn't one to frighten easily, not after a lifetime of abuse. She jerked her wrist free. "You know where they are. I'm not going back." She grabbed the car door handle.

"Doctor...Marina, please." He slapped his palm onto the door's frame, preventing her from opening. "Show me."

His voice had lost the edge of anger and now held a plea that stopped her. She met his intense but bewildered gaze, and an uncertainty flooded her mind. She had the unshakable sense that something was wrong. What wasn't he telling her? Were they his cameras? If not, whose?

Of course, they were his. Who else but the new owner would install cameras to protect his brother's precious possessions?

"Marina...please."

Something in his voice... A desperation? She wasn't the most astute person on the planet. If she was, she'd have figured out what her boyfriend was doing in his spare time before being clued in by a friend.

She studied the man whose gaze had softened but not enough to hide the sharpness. He was on the alert, far beyond spying on an antiques appraiser. The only way to prove guilt or innocence was to go along and test his skill as an actor. But was she safe to be alone with him in that forsaken house? He could be a rich, perverted psycho. Just because he had money…

"Doctor?"

The streetlights revealed just enough of his face to show the sincerity of a pleading gaze. Her gut said to trust him. "Oh, what the hell?" She led the way into the house and marched straight for the fireplace then pointed at the figurine.

He grabbed the statuette for a close inspection, and his face hardened even more—if that were possible. His cheeks flushing to a deep red, he pried the camera from the base. "How many did you find?"

"Four so far."

Palming the device, he gritted his teeth. "Whoever planted them knows they're discovered."

"Yeah, no shit. That's why you became suspect number one when you showed at the door. I figured you were watching a monitor somewhere close."

"Not me, Doctor. I had no idea these *things* were in the house." He stared at the camera in his hand, brows creased into a frown. "This has a microphone included. Expensive gadgets. I wonder how long they've been installed?" He looked around the room, his gaze darting in every direction. "Maybe Patti has an answer."

He took his cell phone from his breast pocket, dialed, and paced before the sofa, glancing occasionally in Marina's direction.

Had he really dialed or merely pretended for Marina's benefit? Again, for what purpose? What the hell was she missing?

Moments later, he disconnected and held the phone

at arm's length. "Her phone's not working. Not even for voicemail."

"She said she was heading to the mall for a new one." Even *that* sounded contrived. The whole damn scenario might be a calculated plan between Jonathan and Patti.

Frowning, he returned the phone to his pocket. "This leaves me with no choice. You're staying in my house."

Her muscles tensed. *Like hell*! "No, thanks. I'm heading home. Find yourself another appraiser." She hurried for the front door.

"Please, Doctor, I need your help."

"Spying won't win me over, Blandish." After yanking on the knob, she swung the door open and stepped outside.

He followed, his long strides placing himself in front of her so he could walk backward. "I had nothing to do with the cameras, Marina. You have to believe me."

She stopped and huffed out a breath. "Why should I? How do I know you really called Patti?" She stuffed her hands into her coat pockets. "I don't know what's going on, Blandish, but I smell a rotten fish." She maneuvered around him and reached her car. "You don't need an antiques appraiser. From what I've seen, an estate appraiser will do. Save yourself some money." She opened her car door.

"Roger told me to contact you."

She whirled to confront him, eyes wide, her loose hair slapping her face. Was he pulling her leg? Why would a complete stranger leave such a request? She tucked a dangling strand behind her ear. "Explain."

"I found his note folded inside your *Antiques 101* book telling me before I did anything, I was to study you closely."

Her brow arched. "He probably meant the book."

"No, I'm positive he meant you." He cocked his head. "Very positive."

"But that's ridiculous." She stepped away from her SUV and slipped all ten fingers into her hair and tugged. After dropping her hands, she sighed heavily and turned back. "I never met your brother."

"I'm speaking the truth. I have no idea why he specified you or that he was into antiques."

"He isn't—wasn't, unless he's hiding them somewhere." She draped an arm over the top of her open door, gaze narrowed. Now the pieces were falling into place. "This is why you offered five grand a week. You had to entice me."

"Yes. Roger requested you for a reason, and I need to find out why. The answer must be in that house somewhere." Scowling, he stuffed his hands into his coat pockets and stared at the house. "The cameras are another mystery to solve."

Muscles tense, she dropped her arm from the car door. "Another? How many do you have?"

"Quite a few, it seems." His shoulders slumped as his chin dropped to his chest. Then, he shook himself while lifting a hand to rub his jaw. A wry grin twisted his mouth. "That was a hard slap you gave me. I'd hate to see you throw a punch."

"I can defend myself." More than he'd ever realize.

"No doubt." A faint sparkle touched his gaze. In an instant, the glow disappeared as he leaned toward her. "Come to my house, Doctor. My family is there. No one will watch you while you sleep, and you'll have a peaceful night. Tomorrow, in daylight, we'll return and search the entire house. I need answers."

She shifted on her feet while shaking her head. "If the perpetrator is watching a monitor, he'll remove the cameras before we return."

"Maybe, but I don't think so. The cameras are probably following all of us, not just you." He pursed his lips. "Someone wants to see what we uncover."

That wasn't the answer she expected. "Who?"

His gaze narrowed. "If I knew who, I wouldn't be standing here arguing."

She should jump into her car and spin the wheels to thrown the driveway stones at his head. When he'd outlined the project, he hadn't mentioned a job full of mystery, and she wasn't in the mood to play Sherlock Holmes. "What are you hiding, Mr. Blandish?"

He watched the traffic pass on the street.

Either hesitating or ignoring her question, she couldn't tell. The light from her open car door shone on his face to reveal his determined gaze with jaw muscles twitching. Yes, he was hiding something. So, why not leave?

A curiosity maybe. Her entire career involved an insatiable nosiness. The trait had gotten her in trouble more than once, like in South America when she found herself being chased by a pack of wild dogs. One might think she'd have learned her lesson, but she'd become successful at her job, despite her impulsive behavior. And she understood men well enough to know when something bothered them. Like now. For some reason, he sounded helpless, as if whatever troubled him was beyond his comprehension.

Jonathan sighed heavily and gave her a sideward glance. "My brother left me with a lot of unanswered questions, Doctor. He had idiosyncratic ways and always did things to his liking, in defiance to advice from anyone brave enough to give it. He rarely dated and made no pretense of his distrust for women. That's why his note shocked me. My brother, of all people, giving me the name of a woman."

This was all too confusing. She toyed with the car door's handle. "I'd say about a half dozen Marina Cavanaughs reside in the Boston area." She met his gaze. "How do you know you picked the right one?"

His lips twisted to the side. "Your book, your name. What else am I to think?" He stuffed his hands into his coat pockets while his gaze burned through to her soul. "So, why you? Why not a male appraiser? What made you so special?"

A comment that couldn't pass without a response. She threw back her head and grinned. "I am special."

Finally, the granite face cracked. A half-smile curled his lips and stayed.

The gesture made him all the more handsome. The wind fluttered strands of his hair, flapping them against his forehead. Her fingers itched to comb them into place, to feel the softness of the strands. Hell, she'd even ignore his arrogance for a quick romp in a soft bed. Her gaze drifted to his left hand buried deep inside his coat pocket, the one with the wedding band.

"Now, you understand why I need you."

His voice broke her free of her bedtime vision. "Huh?" *Need me*?

"Something is in that house Roger wants us to find, and you're the only one who will find it."

Oh, not the same kind of 'need me'. She shook herself and looked into his determined expression. "That's a far-fetched theory I'm not willing to accept."

"Look, Doctor." He faced her and met her gaze. "I've based my career on strong hunches. Trust me when I say I've a real strong hunch about you. Stay with us tonight. Tomorrow, we'll investigate together."

Stay in his house? With a married man whose attractiveness drew her like a magnet? He was off-limits, no matter how tempting. But one night should be okay, right? Tomorrow, she'd make a decision whether to continue with the assignment. "I'll go under one condition."

"Name it."

"Show me Roger's note and a separate sample of his handwriting. I have an expertise authenticating signatures."

"Agreed."

Placing a hand on his arm, she stopped him from walking to his car. He turned with a curious lift to his brow. "What have you done with the camera in your hand?"

"On the end table. I've no intention of taking a camera home."

Satisfied with his answer, she stepped into her SUV.

The ten-minute drive moved through a neighborhood of swanky homes, the five bedrooms, three-and-a-half bath homes with dens and entertainment rooms. Every house had the grounds landscaped to perfection—some with tennis courts, almost all with three-car garages and security signs staked into the ground. Mercedes and BMWs lined the driveways along with Lincolns and top-of-the-line pickup trucks.

Jonathan drove a black Audi sports coupe, a car meant for a bachelor, not a family man…in her opinion anyway.

A wide circular driveway led to his house of gray stone and siding with a garage off to the side. Manicured bushes of various sizes surrounded the exterior with an interlocking brick walkway leading to the front entrance. Windows galore, each with a lit electric candle, welcomed all visitors. The house was in direct contrast to Roger's, and her heart lifted at the sight.

One of the three garage doors opened as he approached, and with a wave, he signaled for her to proceed to the front of the house. Seconds later, he walked to her side of the car and opened the door. "I called Mrs. Blandish. She'll have a guest room ready. Pop your hatch."

With her key fob, Marina opened the trunk.

Jonathan grabbed the suitcase.

She hefted the laptop. "Leave the guitar." Not like she'd be singing a happy little tune tonight.

As he slammed the hatch shut, he glanced over his shoulder with a raised brow. "Do you always travel with a guitar?"

"Oh, sure. I'm a regular troubadour." Something flickered in his gaze. She wasn't sure what. Surprise maybe at hearing of her musical talent. More likely, the candles in the windows caused a reflection on his cornea.

She entered a home, a real home—a place with flowers and bright lights, with cushiony furniture and soft rugs. She stood in the foyer area of a large living room where a roaring fireplace greeted them.

"Daddy's home!"

A little boy bounded down a spacious staircase while holding the banister so he wouldn't fall headlong to the bottom. He was a splitting image of his father. A little mini-Jon.

The boy ran straight into his father's arms who lifted and swung him around.

Jonathan lowered him to the floor. "My son, Tyler. Tyler, this is Doctor Cavanaugh."

The boy stepped back, pale brown eyes ready to pop. "She's not gonna stick me with a needle, is she?"

Marina laughed. "I'm not that kind of doctor, Tyler."

A blank expression stared up. "What kind are you?"

"I'm an antiques expert. I look at old things."

The little face smiled. "Oh, like Grandma. Okay then." He extended his hand. "How do you do?"

She bent over to take his hand. "I'm doing very well, thank you." He couldn't be more than six years of age, and already he had his father's good-looks, same color hair and eyes, same shape to the jaw. A heart-throb in the making.

A woman entered from the left archway wearing an apron over black slacks and a white blouse. She, too, looked like Jonathan, except for strands of gray peppered into her brown hair. She stood equal to Marina's height but had a good twenty more years of life under her belt.

"My mother, Mrs. Blandish," Jonathan said.

The woman's brown eyes twinkled as she surveyed

Marina and extended her hand. "My word, dear, you're as beautiful as your online photo. Call me Iris." She squeezed Marina's hand before releasing her grip. "Did you know Roger?"

"No, ma'am, and I'm sorry for your loss."

"Thank you, dear." She blinked away the moisture accumulating in her eyes. "Roger was always a bit secretive, even in death." She sniffed, threw up her chin, and smiled. "Jonathan can show you to your room. Will you be eating with us?"

"Yes, she will," Jonathan answered. He took Marina's jacket and hung it in the closet by the front door along with his overcoat and then grabbed the handle to her suitcase. "This way, Doctor." He headed for the staircase with Tyler zooming ahead as fast as his little feet carried him.

Thankfully, the staircase had the width to accommodate more than one body at a time, and the landing above was as bright and cheery as the rest of the house. A phenomenal difference between the two brother's homes, and Marina suspected marriage as the key.

"You may as well call me Marina. Doctor is a bit too formal."

He stopped mid-step and looked over his shoulder. "All right. I don't particularly like Mr. Blandish either. I hear enough of that at work."

"Okay, Jon, thanks."

"Jonathan," he corrected in a clipped tone. "I detest nicknames." Facing forward, he continued the climb.

Jonathan sounded as formal as Mr. Blandish. She kinda liked Jon. The name fit him.

They entered the guest room to see Tyler jumping

on the bed.

"This bed is for our guest, young man. Stop jumping."

Tyler landed flat on his back, arms and legs spread-eagle. "I like this bed, Dad. You can give it to me when I grow up."

"Yeah, well, get off before she throws a fit."

Tyler jumped to the floor and hopped over to Marina. "You're pretty."

"Why, thank you, Tyler. You sure are a precocious little man."

His eyebrows fluttered. "What's that mean?"

Smiling at the adorable expression, she bent over. "I like you, too."

"Yahhh!" He ran from the room.

Jonathan slipped her suitcase onto the bed. "You won't find any cameras in here. You have your own bath." He stepped around the bed and, with a slight wave, opened a side door. "No cameras in here either." He checked his watch. "Dinner should be in fifteen minutes. Join us in the kitchen."

"Hold on. Before anything else happens, I want to see Roger's note."

"Fair enough. Meet me in the living room."

"Yes, sir." She saluted.

He shot her a glance through narrowed eyelids. "I will apologize for Tyler's indiscretion."

"I don't care if he jumped on the bed." She placed her laptop by the dresser.

"I'm not talking about that. He called you pretty." He rested his hand on the doorknob and met her gaze. "Pretty is a gross understatement."

Chapter Four

Marina blinked at the closed door, her mind so blank she swore her brain took a walk. Was that a flirt? With his wife, mother, and kid nearby to overhear? She hit the side of her head to ascertain whether a plug distorted her hearing.

Absolutely brazen, as if being in his home offered an opportunity for a quick liaison while his wife ran to the store. He didn't know Marina Cavanaugh, the ultra conservative, moralistic idiot who'd never have a fling with a married man even if he paid her.

Not like she was a wonderful catch. *No, let's rephrase that.* She had a great-paying job which included free travel, a plus in any man's world, but a man like Jonathan Blandish would have a gorgeous supermodel on his arm, one who'd make a grand entrance as if posing for cameras. A ta-da moment.

Marina sighed heavily. *Just one night.* She'd eat dinner and be polite, avoid thinking of the bad memories from her own family dinner table, and at the earliest opportunity, escape to bury herself in her room. Tomorrow, she'd hunt for a hotel or commute from her condo. Better yet, tell Blandish to take a hike and hire someone else. Hell, she'd recommend a half dozen replacements.

She placed her suitcase on the floor without unpacking and scanned the bedroom. Pillows covered the queen bed along with a fluffy white comforter—all askew from Tyler's jumping—in neutral colors of grays, tans, and white to accommodate male or female. The room contained one window decorated with tie-back drapes and sheers and a large dresser with mirror. The bathroom was standard size with an enclosed shower, toilet, and sink. Nothing fancy. Lights galore. A bright and cheery look. Quite a contrast from the stark accommodations at Roger's, and the prospect of returning to such a gloomy residence gave her the heebie-jeebies.

Definitely a hotel after this stay. She refreshed herself in the bathroom, fluffed her mane, and paused at her closed door.

Oh, God, I don't want to do this. Her gut quivered from the vision of sitting with a happy family unit. She firmly believed the concept to be a misnomer and wouldn't know how to act or what to say, not to mention she hadn't an iota of appetite. After being raised in a house full of rules, she endured the occasional return trip for a holiday, but only if her brother and sisters visited. Without them, she'd laugh at the idea of sitting alone at the table with her parents. Unfortunately, dinner with Jonathan and his family might cause her butt to itch, especially since his wife had yet to make an appearance.

Okay, relax, I'll make the best of this. She opened the door and stepped out.

The hallway showed a total of six doors, all open. Framed scenery photos hung on the walls, carefully arranged to break the barrenness of painted wallboard. Plush carpeting stretched from one end of the hall to the other, giving the house the warmth that Roger's lacked.

She descended the carpeted staircase and stopped on the last step.

No one was about. The living room stood to her left with an inviting fireplace brightening the room. A sofa and four matching chairs faced the fire with an oval coffee table between. Family photos covered the marble mantel. She approached for a closer look. Jonathan and his wife. So young. Yes, the woman was supermodel perfect with long blonde hair and blue eyes shining at the camera. Another photo was Jonathan with his wife on a hospital bed, holding Tyler who couldn't be more than a few days old. Happy photos. The way families should be.

"There you are."

Marina turned to see Jonathan standing in the archway. His suit jacket was off, tie removed, and shirt unbuttoned at the collar. He looked relaxed and as handsome as ever, causing her heart to skip a few beats. She pointed to the mantel. "Nice pictures."

"Yes." He stared at the photos, his gaze empty. Then, he shook himself and held out some papers. "As requested, Roger's note along with his driver's license and credit card for signature verification."

Stepping to where he stood, Marina took the items and read the note.

My Dear Brother:

I have placed this rather obscure note within this book for a reason. By now, you are debating the validity of the supplemental notation to my Last Will and Testament and may very well deem me crazy. I assure you that I am completely sane and merely take these precautions because, quite frankly, the person reading this note may not be my brother.

I can't tell you how the beautiful Marina Cavanaugh has affected my life. Once you see her, you will agree. On the surface, she is a work of art, but underneath, she holds the key to a fortune. So, before you do anything, study her closely and let no one else touch her.

Your brother,
Roger

Marina looked at Jonathan with a blank stare. "This doesn't make sense." She compared the handwriting in the note to Roger's signatures. The curl of the R and B was distinctive. "All right, the note's authentic, but I don't know him."

"But he knows you, and we found the note in your book."

Her hands tensed on the papers. "Who's *we*?"

"Before packing, Mom skimmed through the book and found the note. You can understand why I'm confused."

He's confused? How could she convince him she hadn't met the man? And what had he meant by her holding the key to a fortune?

She studied the photo on the driver's license. Roger had a rounder appearance to his face, not oval like Iris or square like Jonathan's. He had the same brown hair but thinner on top. She handed over the documents. "I don't know your brother, Jonathan."

"Maybe not directly, but we'll drop the topic for the time being. Dinner's ready." He nodded toward the archway while folding the papers and slipping them into his trouser pocket.

Marine followed him past the foyer and through a large formal dining room boasting of a crystal chandelier and a heavy cherry dining suite, complete with matching china cabinet. The house smelled of money with top-of-the-line furniture, plush rugs, and fine china on display in the cabinet. Far beyond anything she could afford.

As she approached the kitchen, she experienced a quiver in her stomach. The prospect of meeting Jonathan's mate filled her with dread. The woman had yet to present herself, and that alone was odd. Marina stopped at the entrance.

Amid the onslaught of some fabulous aromas of beef and potatoes, she surveyed the kitchen to see Iris busy at the stove and only four place settings on a round table. Either the woman's math was off, or his wife had thrown a fit about his unexpected guest. *Talk about awkward.*

Iris turned from the stove and waved Marina toward the table. "Come in, dear. Tyler, where are you?"

Tyler ran in from a side entrance and showed his grandmother his hands, rotating them every which way. "All clean." With the back of his hand, he promptly wiped his nose.

Shaking her head, Iris clapped her hands. "All right, everyone at the table. Let's eat. Marina, sit over here."

She had yet to move from the entrance, opting instead to take in the modern appliances, all digital, and counter space around two-thirds of the kitchen.

Jonathan snapped his fingers to catch her attention and pointed to a chair, like a dog trained to obey commands.

She shot him a fierce look but kept quiet as she

took her seat opposite Tyler.

Throughout the passing of the plates, Tyler chattered about the girl next door and her lousy ball-throwing, boy-talk demeaning the uselessness of girls until age created a different depth of awareness. While placing roast beef and buttered potatoes on Tyler's plate, Jonathan listened with a half-smile, interjecting with comments of parental wisdom.

Marina sat rigid next to Jonathan, feeling about as comfortable as a chicken in a lion's den.

As Jonathan poured milk into Tyler's glass, he scrutinized her with a careful gaze. "You look like you're ready to bolt. Maybe I should tie you to the chair."

Too obvious. She wasn't used to the idle chit-chat at the dinner table. Her family had eaten quietly, as if a spoken word would cause the house to implode. She forced her rigid posture to relax.

Jonathan held up a wine bottle. "This, water, or iced tea?"

"I'll have the wine." A whole bottle at this rate, anything to calm her jittery nerves.

Iris claimed the seat opposite Jonathan and held her wine glass at arm's length, waiting as Jonathan filled it. She sipped before placing the glass onto the table then passed a bowl of peas. "So, Marina, you're quite well-known from what I've read. What made you start on such a career?"

Grateful for the distraction, Marina spooned some of the peas onto her plate before passing the bowl to Jonathan. "My grandmother was a collector. She took me to flea markets and mud sales and taught me the art of bartering. You don't learn that in grad school."

"What's a mud sale?" Tyler asked, his brows pinched tight.

"That's an auction in an open field. It takes place in the spring when the ground is all muddy. We have to wear boots."

"Hey, cool." He tugged on his father's sleeve. "We should go to one, Dad."

Jonathan twisted his mouth to one side as he cut Tyler's meat.

Iris leaned forward, knife and fork in hand. "Are you like those people on TV? They get excited at times."

Marina laughed at the woman's obvious interest. "Thrilled to death in some cases, even more so when a rare object is discovered." She picked up her fork. "Many of the antiques have a long history, and the whole process can be a lot of fun."

"I assume you're working on another book," Jonathan said.

"You assume correctly. *Antiques 102*. I'm almost done."

With a frown forming on her forehead, Iris buttered a piece of bread. "I never knew Roger was into antiques. He certainly never spoke of such a hobby. Yet, he left that note for us to find." Her head shook. "So odd."

"Odder still is its ambiguity." Jonathan tapped the table near Tyler's plate. "Stop thumping your chair. Marina will think you're a nervous Nellie."

"Nervous Nellie, nervous Nellie." Tyler stabbed his meat.

"And don't talk with your mouth full. You'll choke to death."

As curious as she was about Jonathan's absent wife, Marina refrained from asking questions. So what if the woman threw a snit and decided to hide in her room? Tyler and Iris seemed unconcerned, but Jonathan grew quiet, occasionally glancing toward Marina while taking an inordinate amount of time cutting his meat. Her once non-existent appetite had sprung to life when the aromas assaulted her nose, and she ate a sufficient quantity to appease Iris. So, the dinner hour wasn't entirely unpleasant. Tyler was funny in his little boy way, and Iris chatted about normal subjects, like the price of food and the traffic light being installed by the new supermarket somewhere outside the development.

After a dessert of apple pie and ice cream, Marina felt a tug on her sweatshirt. She turned to see Tyler standing by her chair.

"Wanna see my bugs?" he asked.

Marina cringed and shot a quick glance at both Jonathan and Iris. "Bugs?"

"Tyler's a collector," Jonathan explained with a smirk on his lips. To his son, he said, "Marina may not want to see bugs."

"No-no, I'm okay. I'll go see his bugs." *Oh, God, I'm out of my mind*! But Tyler had offered her a chance to escape. Despite the wedding band on his finger, Jonathan looked too damn stimulating in his open collar dress shirt, and his wife was a fool to allow Marina to sit in such close proximity with only Iris as chaperone.

Come morning, she had better make a beeline to the front door.

****

After Tyler and Marina left, Jonathan's mother stared at the kitchen entrance with an intense look on her face.

He had told her so little when he called, and the guilt crawled over his skin. She deserved to know every detail, and the unasked questions shot out of her gaze. "You showed remarkable restraint, Mother."

"To hell with restraint." She gushed the words as she hopped onto Marina's vacant chair. "I'm dying over here. I thought Patti prepared her a room. What happened?"

Jonathan corked the wine bottle. "Someone put cameras in Roger's house."

"Cameras?" With a loud gasp, she clutched his arm. "Who?"

"Well, if I knew who, I wouldn't be so concerned." He tipped his head to meet her gaze. "Marina only showed me one, but she found another in her bedroom and also the bath. She accused me of putting them in."

Her brown eyes widened, and she pointed to his chin. "She made that mark on your jaw?"

"Unfortunately, yes." He rubbed his chin, aware of the soreness that remained.

"Did you install the cameras?"

His eyes rolled. "Of course not."

"A peeping Tom then." She shuddered, gathered some plates, and headed for the sink. "You should inform Detective Farnsworth about this."

"Not yet." He stood to place the corked wine on the rack. "Whoever installed the cameras is obviously after the same objective. And if I tell Farnsworth, then I'll have to explain Marina."

"That's ridiculous." She stacked the remaining plates on the table and carried them to the sink. "She's an antiques appraiser. You've nothing to explain."

"Except for Roger's lack of antiques. Hell, Mother, even I see his house is full of junk." He grabbed a tie-wrap from the counter to close the bread bag. "Marina and I will head to the house tomorrow. I'll talk to Patti and see if she knows anything about the cameras."

His mother wiped the table with a dish rag and returned to the sink. "The cameras will be gone by morning."

"With the stakes as high as they are, I doubt it. I'm also guessing they're in every room."

As she stacked dishes into the dishwasher, she shook her head. "I hope Patti isn't behind this. She might not be as innocent as we think." She glanced in his direction. "What if the cameras are Roger's doing?"

His brows rose. "For what reason? To watch himself shit on the john?"

"Maybe to watch Patti, and don't be so vulgar."

"Sorry." The mental picture of Roger watching Patti turned his stomach. He hadn't pretended to know his brother well, but cameras were a perverted hobby.

His mother jammed silverware into the dishwasher holder. "I don't know what Roger got himself into, but I don't like how he's involved us and Marina. Maybe you shouldn't have her stay in his house. If I was in her shoes, I'd sleep with my eyes open." She pointed to her right. "Hand me those glasses, dear."

He slid them across the counter toward her.

She placed them in the dishwasher and poured soap into the holding compartment. "How much does Marina know?"

"Next to nothing. I removed the online details of Roger's death. We're safe for a while." Hopefully, he hadn't missed anything.

His mother straightened and cocked a quizzical brow. "How'd you manage that?"

He shot her a brief grin. "Money, Mother. How else?"

She closed the dishwasher and pressed the button to start the cycle. "Marina seems like a nice girl. Have her stay with us."

God forbid. She'd be a temptation far beyond his self-control. Jonathan placed the covered leftovers into the refrigerator. "I'm not sure she'll stay. She might be more comfortable in a hotel." He closed the door, leaned a shoulder on the cool metal, and faced his mother. "I'll talk to her tomorrow."

Frowning, she met his gaze. "Yes, Jonathan, please be sure you *talk*. All this brooding is aging you. You're only thirty-five, and you act like life is over. Talking to a beautiful woman might be the therapy you need since you refuse real help." With jerky moves, she wiped a counter that was already clean. "You're as stubborn as your father."

Ouch! She hit below the belt. "But unlike my father, I won't cheat on my wife."

She threw her arms in the air and jutted her head toward him. "What wife? You don't have a wife any more than I have a husband." She walked to the table and banged a chair under the table but stood clutching the backrest. After a few seconds, she turned toward him. "Tyler's off from school tomorrow. A special teacher's conference. Why don't you take him with you so I can go to lunch with the girls?"

An excellent suggestion. Tyler's presence would remind Jonathan to keep his hands off Marina, something he had struggled with from the moment they'd met. At the warehouse when he spotted her on the lounge sofa with her mane of auburn tendrils dangling from the hair clip, he wanted to unclip the rest and run his fingers through the long, silky waves and bury his face in its mass. Tonight, without the clip, he envisioned her unbound strands tickling his chest as they enjoyed a night of rapture. Her eyes, dark like the color of rich chocolate, gave him the impression she saw straight into his soul and recognized his need, but her furtive glances at his wedding band squelched any interest. And rightly so. The band was a visible symbol of attachment to another, and no woman was worth her weight in salt if she slept with a married man.

He shouldn't have thoughts like this, but Roger was right about her beauty. *Imagine that. My brother noticing a woman.* He was human after all.

"I don't appreciate Roger putting this cloud of mystery over our heads," his mother complained while wiping her hands on a towel. "Too much has happened, Jonathan, and I don't want Marina staying in that house alone."

Neither did he. If Marina knew the whole story, she'd pack her bags and leave, and Roger's mystery would forever go unsolved. But what could he tell her? He had no answers. Only questions. A hotel was an option, yet, none were close by. If not Roger's house, then she must stay with him or commute. How in heaven's name could he concentrate on the mysteries surrounding Roger's death with the stunning Marina Cavanaugh sleeping under his roof?

Chapter Five

Marina tossed and turned all night. New bed. New surroundings. New man creeping into her dreams. Jonathan Blandish of all people. A married man with a family. Totally unavailable. Instead of counting sheep, she conjured mental images of her parents' so-called happy union to remind herself about the reality of married life. Then, of course, the alarm clock blared her out of a sound sleep.

By eight o'clock, Marina entered the kitchen to see Iris sitting at the table with a cup of coffee in hand, her focus intent on an open newspaper. No one else was about. "I hope I haven't slept too late."

Iris looked up, her face brightening. "Well, good morning! If you mean Jonathan, he's in the den calling his office. What can I make you? Eggs? Toast? How about a muffin from the box on the counter?"

"Nothing, thank you. I'll stick with coffee." She headed to the coffee maker while hiding a yawn. The smell alone helped shake the fog clouding her brain.

Iris folded the paper with a rustle and pushed it aside. "Did you sleep well?"

"After I wiped Tyler's bugs out of my thoughts." She sipped the wonderfully strong brew and faced the older woman. "He has quite a collection."

"And thankfully, all dead. I make sure he's well supplied with pins." She slid the sugar bowl toward the center of the table. "Cream's in the fridge. I have artificial sweetener if you don't want sugar."

"Cream's fine." She strolled to the refrigerator, took out the cream carton, and poured. As with her luck, she yawned mid-pour, and the coffee resembled milk with some brown color. So much for a nice jolt of caffeine. She slipped onto the chair opposite Iris. "Why does Jon—nathan live so far from work?" She had stumbled over his name and silently cursed the slip.

Never had she met a Jonathan who wasn't called by another name. Mr. Jon Alberts in Charlotte, for example, her high school math instructor. Her college roommate's boyfriend was Nate. Maybe she should stick to Mr. Blandish to avoid any inadvertent mishaps. She cleared her throat. "Surely, he can afford a house in the city."

Iris waved aside the comment. "This house was picked by his wife. He won't sell."

"But an hour commute one way is tiring and probably twice as bad on a Friday evening. I'd want to hurry home to my little boy."

"I made the same statement. If his wife was a little more considerate, she'd have searched for a house closer, but he left the house-picking to her." She lifted the cup to her lips and shrugged. "Ah, well, who am I to complain? I'm living rent free." She sipped her coffee then tilted her head forward to attract Marina's gaze. "You know, Marina, you're welcome to stay with us while you work at Roger's. I hate the notion of you alone in that place." After exhaling a long breath, she lowered the cup to the saucer. "Jonathan told me about the cameras."

Marina leaned on her elbows to hold the cup closer

to her lips. The steam tickled her nose, but the cream weakened the coffee aroma. "I won't stay at Roger's, Iris. If a decent hotel isn't nearby, I'll commute." She sipped and lowered the cup. "The problem is the more distance I travel, the longer I'll take to finish. And despite your kind offer, I won't stay here either. Once I start, I work long hours." *If I continue at all.*

Iris's gaze twinkled over her cup. "I hope you don't mind me getting personal, dear, but you have the beauty of a Greek goddess with an Irish name."

Although the compliment was lovely, Marina laughed. "I'll disagree on the goddess part, but you're right on both counts. My mother is Greek, my father Irish. I'm the oldest of four siblings."

"Do you miss your family?"

Marina almost choked on her own saliva. How could she explain the tyrant and his slave, a house where words of opposition met with punishment, where love flowed only from her grandmother's arms?

Wondering how much to reveal, she shifted on the seat cushion. "You can't miss what you never had." She stared into her cup. "My father was a totalitarian in the truest sense of the word. He set a time to eat, to play, and to study. Rigid rules carved in concrete. Any deviation resulted in punishment, both mental and emotional." She sipped her coffee, contemplated sugar, but sweet cream with hardly any coffee taste would make her puke. She lowered her cup.

"Most of the time, we behaved like little soldiers, always waiting for the words of dissatisfaction, or the rip-it-out, do-it-over speech." She glanced at Iris who held her coffee cup close to her nose, gaze vacant. "My grandmother was the godsend. She kept us kids sane and encouraged me to go away to college. After she died, I had no real reason to stay home."

Iris lowered her cup onto the saucer, one brow raised. "What about your mother? Where was she, and why didn't she put a stop to his abusive behavior?"

Shrugging, Marina gave her a sad smile. "No guts."

Iris shook her head while muttering inaudibly before pushing her cup and saucer to the side. "Sometimes a wife doesn't want to rock the boat and finds life easier to agree with the husband. I was one of those wives." She leaned forward on the table, her arm outstretched, finger waving. "Not that my ex abused the boys. He was a man used to getting his way, and anyone else's feelings weren't considered." She sat back and stared at her lap. "I thought I was doing right by keeping the peace, but he left me for a younger woman."

Another woman's ego shattered because of age. Men were so friggin' cruel. "I'm sorry."

"Don't be." She shot Marina a quick glance and folded her arms across her chest. "I suppose if I argued more, I wouldn't have been his doormat." Then she sighed heavily and dropped her arms. "Sad to say, both our boys developed his bad habits."

"You mean always expecting to get their way?"

"Yes. Roger, being the oldest, was awful, and I suspect he stayed single for that reason. No woman with any self-respect can tolerate his constant orders. Jonathan's a little more pliable, but that's Susan's doing."

"Susan, his wife?"

She nodded. "She was a regular hellion, more head-strong."

Was? *Jonathan tamed the shrew*?

"Who's head-strong?" Jonathan entered the kitchen and moseyed to the coffee maker.

Iris grunted. "You. Your father. Roger. Three bossy men."

"I wouldn't be where I am today without some bossiness, Mother." He walked to the table, loaded his coffee with sugar, and then ambled to the refrigerator for the cream.

Marina's gaze followed him. The man wore blue jeans and a sport shirt. Both emphasized a build fit for a fashion magazine—slim, trim, and attractive. His hair had the look of being towel-dried on top and finger-combed on the sides, not messy, simply relaxed to go with the casual attire.

He caught her scrutiny and smiled. She diverted her gaze and stared into her milky-white coffee.

After closing the refrigerator door, he returned to the counter for a spoon to stir his coffee. "Is Tyler down yet?"

Iris pushed her chair from the table and stood. "He's watching *Sesame Street*. Don't run off without some breakfast. What can I make you?"

"We have food at the house and can eat when we're hungry."

"Good because I'm heading to the mall with the girls. I don't know what time I'll be home." She put her cup and saucer in the sink then turned toward the table. "Marina, it was a pleasure to have another woman in the house." After a quick nod, she hurried out.

Another woman? He wasn't married to a woman? A man then? An orangutan? *Oh, good grief, get real.* The photos on the mantel showed a happy, beautiful woman…*who's refusing to meet me.*

Was. Iris had used the past tense.

"I see your suitcase is by the door."

His voice broke into her thoughts. She glanced his way to see him watching her and the uneasiness from last night returned. She had so many questions, but her strict upbringing squelched the growing curiosity. "I agreed to one night, Mr. Blandish."

"Jonathan."

"Right…Jonathan."

"You're welcome to stay here. I'm sure my mother extended the offer."

"She did, and I refused. The invitation should come from the woman of the house." She stood and slid her chair under the table, resting her hands on the backrest. "Shall we go?"

"No. I'll finish my coffee."

"Then maybe I'll wait for you outside."

"Again, no. You wait for me." He turned to grab a white bakery box from the counter and extended it. "Have a muffin. I buy them from a baker near my office."

"I'm okay, thanks."

He placed his cup on the counter, opened the box lid, and passed the contents under her nose. "They're the best in Boston."

The muffins smelled of cinnamon and apples, rich butter and blueberries. She salivated and looked away. "No, thanks."

"Are you in a hurry?" His gaze sparkled with amusement.

She wasn't sure what he found so amusing. An inner joke perhaps. Certainly not her clothes. She wore her usual work attire of sweatshirt and blue jeans and, after a fitful night's sleep, definitely wasn't in a humorous mood. "I feel like I'm wasting time."

"You are, but I'm the boss. Have more coffee." He slid the open box onto the table, grabbed the coffee pitcher, and poured coffee into her cup.

She frowned at his delay tactic, but, at least this time, the liquid resembled coffee. Then her gaze drifted to the muffins. One with a golden rounded top had protruding blueberries. "Since I haven't planned on a second cup of coffee, I'll eat something." She reclaimed her seat and reached inside the box to grab the only blueberry muffin. The small cake had no weight. That meant no calories…in her book.

He leaned against the counter while watching her over the steam from his cup. "You look rested. Sleep well?"

"Ummm, okay."

"I haven't slept a wink. I kept thinking about you."

Her head snapped in his direction. *Please, don't do this to me*!

"More specifically, why Roger involved you."

Okay, breathe. She bit into the muffin to taste a light, buttery flavor. She died and went to heaven. "At the moment, I'm more concerned about the cameras and the who and why questions." She lifted a napkin from the table holder and wiped the corner of her mouth. She met his steady gaze. "What's going on, Jonathan?"

"I can't tell you yet because I don't know. How's the muffin?"

"Delicious, and you're changing the subject. I have fifty million questions that need answers."

"That many, huh?" A smile slipped onto his lips. Then, in a flash, the corners of his mouth dipped downward as he stared into his cup. "I don't have answers, Marina. I'm hoping between the two of us, we'll uncover a few." He placed his cup in the sink. "Ready?"

"No." *Damned if I'll hurry now.* She savored the last of the cake, washed it down with the coffee, and patted her mouth with the napkin, making all movements slow and deliberate. She stood, threw her napkin into the trash, placed her empty cup in the sink, and returned to the table to tuck her chair under the table. She faced him with a half grin. "I'm ready."

He stopped her from leaving the kitchen by resting a hand on her shoulder. "I can answer one of your questions." He dropped his hand.

His simple touch caused her spinal cord to melt. She inwardly shook herself and faced him. "Which one?"

"My mother is the woman of the house. My wife died."

"Oh." Their gazes locked, and her breath hitched. The attraction between them was powerful, like he tugged on a rope to draw her closer. *So damn wrong.* She stepped back. "I'm sorry."

He turned toward the entrance. "I'll get Tyler."

Well, that explained the four place settings. Now, all she had to do was steer clear of a man in mourning, a very handsome man who suddenly changed to single status, and one who stimulated her juices with a simple look.

Her feet itched as an uncontrollable urge to bolt swept through her. No way could she stay under

Jonathan's roof. The last thing she wanted was to entice a man still hurting from his wife's death. She was a professional with standards. Jonathan Blandish was a client. Nothing more. She fully intended to maintain that relationship, no matter what.

Except for one gnawing observation. As a woman with an anthropology degree, she understood the rituals of mourning by different cultures. Sadness had passed onto Iris' face when she talked about Roger, but the expression dissipated within seconds since his death occurred several months ago. At the mention of Susan's name, Iris revealed only irritation, but chalk that up to a mother wanting the best for her son. Marina got the distinct impression of no love lost between the two women.

Tyler was the puzzle. Everything about him displayed a happy little boy with his bugs, toys, and everything else he showed her. He hadn't mentioned his mother once. Only Jonathan revealed an underlying unhappiness…no, not even that. Perhaps a contemplative state of mind.

More questions of which she had no business asking. Marina followed Jonathan out of the kitchen.

****

Jonathan glanced into the rearview mirror to see if Marina still followed. For a change, traffic was light. No school buses and the rush hour over and done. Even so, he drove slowly to prevent her from getting lost.

His late wife, Susan, had chosen the area for their first home. The development was a bit more upper class than most, a look-at-me-I've-arrived type of community where people flaunted their possessions, even though they were in debt up to their eyeballs. Hardly anyone socialized with their neighbor, always preferring to stay within the confines of their own yard, never venturing out except in separate cars. An illusion to peaceful wedded bliss.

Financial difficulties destroyed several marriages on his street, and on many occasions, he debated whether his marriage to Susan would last with her enormous need to shop. Before her illness, they were happy enough, but their years together were short-lived. Since her death, he hadn't so much as looked at another woman nor had he the interest until Marina came along. Her presence forced him to think twice about sex and family, and just as quickly, he'd shake away the thoughts because Roger's death hung over him like a snow-filled blanket ready to split from the weight. After today, more questions might surface, and he'd be no closer to solving the many mysteries surrounding Roger's life.

He stopped for a red light and peeked at Marina through his rearview mirror. She had turned her head to the left to look at the construction site for a new car dealership. Her exquisite profile took away his breath. Straight nose, well-defined jaw, and even a cute ear popping through her hair.

A car horn blared from somewhere behind Marina. Jonathan jerked his gaze forward to see the green light waiting and hit the gas.

"We look like a train, Dad. Woo, hooo!" Tyler pulled an imaginary train whistle. "We're the engine, and Marina's the red caboose. Woo, hooo!" Tyler twisted his little neck to see out the rear window from his buckled-in position in the backseat, his plastic container with lid carefully balanced on his lap. He waved to Marina for the umpteenth time.

She merely shook her head, smiled, and waved back.

"You could have left your bug container home, Tyler."

"Can't, Dad. We got show-and-tell this week. I want to catch a live bug to gross out all the girls."

"The weather's too cold for bugs."

He grinned. "I'll find one. You'll see."

How Tyler had gravitated toward such an odd hobby was another mystery, especially in a neighborhood full of prim and proper kids playing on their cell phones. At least, Tyler had an interest in the world, even if he centered on the bug variety.

If truth be told, he'd rather do something more pleasant with Tyler than to spend the day hunting for cameras. The dreariness of Roger's house, garage, and everything in between had always depressed him. The exterior had the openness of the nearby fields, but the house sat alone on the hill with hardly any bushes to give one the appearance of ownership. A sick-looking tree here and there. Tons of weeds dried for the winter, ready to sprout to life whenever spring decided to come. The interior was no better with its oppressive darkness. Roger wouldn't allow Patti to add a woman's touch, like Susan had done to their home. Jonathan stopped to wait for traffic to pass before making a left turn into Roger's driveway.

"Someone's at Uncle Roger's," Tyler said, straining to see over the front seat.

Indeed. An unfamiliar blue sedan was parked in the horseshoe drive. Jonathan pulled behind the vehicle, and his gut tightened when he recognized the man staring at the house. *Of all people.* He cut the engine before rotating to unbuckle Tyler who immediately opened his door and ran in the direction of the garage with his plastic container, unconcerned about the stranger by the porch steps.

The man turned and stared after Tyler, pointing. "Was that my grandson?"

No hello as usual. His appearance hadn't changed much over the years. Hair a little thinner on top but still dyed a dark brown. Sideburns growing more onto his cheeks, also dyed. He wore a leather biker's jacket and dressed in tight jeans because he liked to display his balls. Over the years, they'd become two strangers, and Jonathan saw no reason to improve the situation now. "Why are you here, Father?"

"Is that any way to greet your old man?" He started and stared beyond Jonathan's shoulder. "Hello, who do we have here?"

Marina's red SUV pulled in behind his Audi. She stepped out and hesitated with the driver's door still open.

Jonathan watched his father eye her like a hungry wolf.

The old man hurried toward her, hand extended. "Duke Blandish, Jon's father." He took her hand even though she hadn't extended it.

Muscles twitching, Jonathan forced his legs to move. The sight of his father so close to Marina caused his blood to boil. With choppy strides, he joined them. "Dr. Cavanaugh, meet Brandon Blandish."

His father never removed his gaze from Marina. "Duke, honey. Remember that." Smiling, he shook Marina's hand vigorously while scanning her from head to toe. "You're the prettiest creature I've seen in a long time." He released her hand and tugged on his belt. "A doctor, eh? Do you make house calls?"

With a narrowed gaze, Jonathan stepped between them to force his father to give her some air. "Why are you here?"

His old man backed away. "I need a place to stay for a few days, and Roger's place being empty and all is perfect. I'm sure you won't mind."

"I mind a great deal. Dr. Cavanaugh is here to appraise the contents of the estate. You'll be in the way."

"Nonsense." He flicked up the collar to his leather jacket. "I won't be any trouble, right, little lady?"

This was not a time for manners. Jonathan grabbed his father's arm. "Can I talk to you privately?" Without waiting for an answer, he shoved his father to the side, away from Marina and out of earshot. He released the old man's arm. "Tell me why you're *really* here."

"I told you. I need a place to stay." Brandon adjusted his jacket sleeve.

He recognized the all-too-familiar clipped tone. "Why? Has your girl-toy thrown you out?"

"Nay. I realized how much I missed your mother. I'd like to get reacquainted, and this house is perfect as a command post."

Command post? Like Iris Blandish was a strategic spot on a map. His father still had a regular move-in-and-conquer attitude, unchanged even after so many years. Jonathan's back stiffened. "And why do you believe I'd let you stay here?"

While glancing at Marina, the man wiggled his eyebrows. "I'm your father, that's why. Besides, I'd like to meet my grandson."

His fists clenched. "Unfortunately, I don't want him to meet you. You broke Mom's heart by walking out like she was yesterday's fling. What makes you think she'll want to get reacquainted?"

"That's where I need your help."

"Bullshit!" His nostrils flared, and he invaded his father's space. "You only come around when you need something, never a call to see how we're doing." He stepped back in an effort to contain his anger and ran a hand through his hair. "I don't know who you are anymore, except a man reliving his youth by dying your hair and wearing clothes meant for a twenty-year-old. Hell, your last girlfriend was younger than me!"

"Made you jealous, eh?" He chuckled and puffed out his chest. "I like 'em young, full of experimental sex and low morals." He nudged his son with an elbow. "Like that beauty by the SUV. She makes me hard with that sexy hair blowing in the wind."

Jonathan glanced toward Marina, and his anger disappeared. She did indeed look sexy leaning against her car, her attention on the passing traffic, auburn hair fluttering. Trim and fit physique. Everything a man could want. He wouldn't give his father the satisfaction of agreeing, however.

"You two humping?"

Jonathan bristled at the inference, and he shot him a glare. "God, you are crude." With the use of his hand, Jonathan goaded his father toward the sedan and swung open the driver's door. "You're leaving. And FYI, Daddy dear, even if you reconcile with Mom, you're not staying in my house. Plan accordingly. Got it?"

"All right, all right. Take it easy. I'm leaving." He

shrugged off Jonathan's hand and stepped into the car.

While using his body to prevent the door from closing, Jonathan extracted his wallet from his rear pocket, opened the billfold, and tossed several hundred-dollar bills onto his father's lap. "The nearest hotel is in the city."

Chapter Six

Marina leaned against her car door and watched the traffic zip by as if on a raceway, the thirty-five mile an hour speed limit ignored. Clouds lingered overhead, obscuring the sun to make for another cold, blustery morning. If she had half a brain in her head, she'd sit in the car with the heater on, but nothing beat the smell of fresh air intermingled with car exhaust.

An electric company utility truck stopped alongside the pole across the street. The driver hopped out and placed orange cones by the rear, which accomplished little to slow traffic. The man took an inordinate amount of time strapping on his tool belt before climbing into a white bucket for a hoist to the top of the pole.

The slamming of the car door drew her attention to Jonathan and his father. They exchanged words through the open window, both voices angry, and neither letting the other have the last word. In appearance, they were equal in height and build but that ended the similarities. Jonathan had well-trimmed hair and the complexion of a tanned outdoorsman. The older gentleman hadn't seen a barber in months with hair unnaturally dark and wide sideburns to match. The color washed out his pale complexion and emphasized the wrinkles on his face. Definitely not the type to turn a woman's head.

As Duke Blandish steered the car around the

horseshoe drive, he slowed to wink in her direction then plastered a smile on his lips that was more lecherous than friendly, his gaze undressing her in a single sweep.

She shuddered at the image of his hands on a woman, and even worse thoughts entered her mind about him with Iris. *Ugh*! She cocked her head as Jonathan approached. "Well, that was interesting." His jaw was like granite, hard and unyielding, brown eyes blazing. The man looked angry enough to punch concrete. "Trouble in paradise?"

He eyed her through narrowed slits.

"Iris told me about him."

He mouthed the word "oh" and stuffed his hands into his jacket pockets. "My father is a self-centered bastard. I'm ashamed to call him my parent." With a hard swing of his leg, he kicked her front tire then shot her a quick glance. "Don't tell my mother of his visit."

"I wouldn't think of it, but you better calm yourself before you grind your teeth to a powder." She peeked at her tire to ascertain the rim seal hadn't broken on impact.

Shoulders tight, he stared into the distance. "That man never showed for Roger's funeral nor acknowledged the death of my wife and, even worse, the birth of my son. He left my mother penniless and in debt." He hissed through tight teeth. "He had brass balls to think I'd let him stay. All he wants is his own selfish world of partying and screwing around." He dropped his gaze but avoided a glance in her direction. "Sorry."

"Don't be. I have issues with my father, too."

Shaking his head, he faced her. "Do me a favor, Marina. Don't let that man near you. If you agree to stay, keep him out of the house. I don't trust him."

"No offense, Jon, but your father gives me the creeps. I'm glad you sent him away."

"Jonathan."

She mentally kicked herself for the slip and started for the house. "I see Tyler ran off with his bug container. He doesn't know his grandfather?"

"No." He followed. "I won't introduce him either. My father gave away that right a long time ago." He stopped on the step to look around. "Tyler's probably out back somewhere in his never-ending quest for bugs. He wants to be a beekeeper, too." A faint smile curled the corner of his lips. "Can you imagine beehives in our neighborhood? The neighbors would throw a fit." He joined her on the front porch and took a key ring from his pocket, sighing at the front door. "I never liked this place. Roger bought the property at a nice price, but he never bothered to brighten the inside." He flipped through the keys until finding the one he needed. "Big deal, a coat of paint on the ceilings. I'd have ripped out the dark paneling before moving in."

Hell, several big buckets of white paint would do wonders. "The house definitely needs more lights."

He inserted the key in the door. "Patti tried, but Roger liked his house dark."

"Maybe your brother had an aversion to bright lights. You have to admit the house has history and probably hidden secrets...the cameras aside." Her gaze scanned the ceiling of the porch. "I wonder if a camera is watching us out here?"

"We need to uncover who's watching the camera feeds." He opened the door and waved her inside. "I've seen this stuff in electronic stores. They transmit via wireless to a monitor so the perpetrator can sit with his feet on a stool and a beer in his hand miles from here."

Like the FBI on a stake-out. She frowned. "That's not encouraging." She stepped into the house. The gloom of yesterday slapped her face, despite her leaving all the lights lit. "I'll open the drapes." As if *that* would do any good. The front porch overhang blocked the daylight.

After throwing their jackets on the coat rack, Jonathan peered into the lampshades by the sofa. "The first item of importance is to change all the light bulbs. He's using forty-watt bulbs in these sockets."

"Not what you call a reading lamp." She looked around, hands on hips. "How do you want to begin?"

"Show me the camera in the bathroom. That one alone unnerved me."

They climbed the stairs to the second floor and entered the bathroom. She pointed to the overhead light.

He stared upward. "I'll need a stool or ladder to reach it. That means whoever placed the camera also used something." His jaw tightened. "Our intruder had time. Let's head to your bedroom."

Yeah, time to create his own porn show. She shuddered and then led the way to the artificial flowers in the corner, pointing. "I turned the camera toward the wall."

"Smart move." He stood with his back to the flowers while his gaze scanned the bedroom. "The camera angle covers the entire room. Someone definitely wants to see something." He pursed his lips and turned to look at the flowers. "I don't think this is Roger's doing. I can't see him spending money on expensive camera equipment while struggling to read under a forty-watt bulb." He plucked the camera from the flowers and slipped the device into his breast pocket. "You don't deserve a room like this, Marina. You're staying in my house."

"No, I'm not, but we'll discuss that later." To avoid any argument, she turned and headed for the hall.

He followed. "We will assume the cameras are in every room including the hall. Obviously, your discovery hasn't caused any need for concern since they're still here." He took out his cell phone and touched the display. "Let me call Patti. Hopefully, she's got her phone working by now." After a brief question about her arrival to the house, Jonathan headed downstairs.

"Patti doesn't have any set hours, Marina. She'll check on the house every day, do a few things, and then leave. Maybe she can be of help with the inventory."

Not a bad idea. She'd finish faster with a helper. *Assuming I stay.* She hurried down the steps to catch up.

They waited in the parlor, neither venturing to try the stiff-backed furniture. He stood by the front windows, watching for Patti, one hand on the window frame, the other on his hip. She leaned against the sofa, arms crossed over her chest while marveling at the comfortable silence surrounding them. Not like she had trouble with men, but Jonathan Blandish was a trifle autocratic, and if anything, she should feel uneasy in his presence. After being raised by a totalitarian father, she spontaneously clicked into a defiance mode whenever a bossy man spoke. Probably why she worked so well with Mrs. Billingsley.

Hating to be idle, she picked up an ashtray and read the bottom. Made in Japan. Another piece for the recycle bin. She placed the tray on the table, walked to the mantel, and pointed to the portrait. "Is she family?"

Jonathan stepped alongside and followed her gaze. "She came with the house." He glanced her way. "Worth anything?"

"The frame, yes. Regrettably, the painting is folk art, a bit amateurish. The signature's too high for me to see, but, as a rule, these types of paintings are often done by local artists." The poor woman, left with strangers. Marina gave a sad nod. "She's definitely early nineteenth century, not worth much at auction, but the money's in the frame." She faced him and tilted her head. "Tell me about your brother. I find all this formal furniture unusual for a man."

He wandered away from the mantel, hands stuffed into his jeans back pockets. "I don't know what to tell you. Roger was set in his ways, had a good job with a hedge fund, made a lot of money, but obviously never spent a dime. I once asked him why this house and not a condo in Boston, where he worked."

"And his answer?"

"The property has potential for development." He returned to the front windows and stared out. "My stockbroker brother realized the area was growing and took a gamble." He gave her a weak smile. "He won. This piece of land doubled in value overnight."

A stockbroker? What had he dealt in, horse manure? "Brokers usually earn a decent salary. Why'd he live like Mr. Scrooge?"

Jonathan moved away from the window. "Good question. He has no noticeable comforts." He pointed to the hearth. "I don't believe he ever lit the fireplace."

Marina stared at the cold grates. Black soot stained

the bricks, probably from eons ago. "I guess no one knows if the chimney's okay."

"Patti maybe."

As if on cue, Patti rushed through the front door, breathless.

Marina turned toward the noise. Patti looked a little disheveled as if she simply rolled out of bed and ran, despite the ten o'clock hour.

Glancing between them, she threw her coat on the rack. "What's up?"

Jonathan stepped toward her. "Do you have any idea who put the cameras in the house?"

Patti's mouth gaped, eyes fluttering to focus on Jonathan's face. "Cameras, sir?"

He extracted the two small devices from his pocket. "I took these from the fireplace mantel and Marina's bedroom. Marina found two more. I'm guessing they're in every room, maybe two to a room if one can't see all the corners. Who else has a key to the house?"

"Only you and me, Mr. Blandish, and of course, Dr. Cavanaugh." She scratched her temple and frowned. "Roger could have given a key to someone without telling me, but that doesn't sound like him." The frown deepened. "I know he didn't give Karl one. Karl uses the bathroom off the kitchen but only if I'm here to let him in."

"Does my father have a key?"

Her gaze flickered. "Your father, sir? Not to my knowledge, but again, I can't be sure."

Brows wrinkled, Jonathan turned to Marina. "If no one was here, how did my father expect to enter the house?"

Marina shrugged. "Maybe he was waiting for Patti."

"More likely, he'd have checked the perimeter for an unlatched window." As if to test his hypothesis, he stepped toward the front windows and tugged on one and then the other. "Locked." He faced Patti. "Is this one of Karl's workdays?"

"He was here yesterday, sir. He's doing twice a week with the weather being cold and all." She wrung her hands while widened eyes darted around the room. "Who would put in cameras, Mr. Blandish? And when?" Her mouth fell open with a gasp. "Ohmygosh, if they recorded—"

He coughed loudly. "Calm down, Patti. We'll get to the bottom of this."

Patti turned those wide eyes on Marina. "Doctor, your bedroom!"

"I stayed in Jonathan's guest room, Patti."

The blood drained from her face.

For a second, Marina swore the woman would pass out from fright. Why? And what had she meant by recorded?

If Jonathan hadn't cut her off... Or was the interruption on purpose? If so, what were they hiding?

Jonathan clapped his hands. "All right, ladies, let's approach this systematically. Patti, go into the kitchen and search the area including the mudroom. The cameras may be high so look good. Marina, cover the rest of the downstairs. I'll search upstairs. Pull the cameras as you go. I've no doubt whoever installed them is watching. If he doesn't want us to destroy his equipment, he'll show himself. As a precaution, check all the windows and doors as you work. I want everything bolted shut."

Tyler burst into the parlor from the dining room. "Marina, look what I found!"

Oh, joy. More bugs. She peeked into his opened container to see two spiders crawling over each other.

Patti shuddered and retreated toward the kitchen.

Marina strained a smile. "That's nice, Tyler."

"I got both of them by the mudroom door. Look, Dad!" He held up his prize.

"How'd you get in?" Jonathan demanded, not in the least interested in the container.

"The sunroom door is open."

Well, that answered the question of access into the house.

Patti ran in from the kitchen, eyes bright. "I found two, Mr. Blandish!" She opened her palm to show him.

Jonathan grabbed a tin can from a side table and dumped the contents of hard candies into an ashtray. He extended the can for Patti to toss in her cameras while he dug into his pocket for his two and closed the lid. "Whoever is watching is minus four cameras."

Tyler tugged on his father's pant leg. "I know who's watching."

Chapter Seven

Marina, along with Jonathan and Patti, stared wide-eyed at Tyler. The little boy had the attention of three adults, and his face beamed.

"Who?" Jonathan asked.

The boy stuck out his parka-covered chest. "Karl with a K. He's in his white van watching a monitor filled with tiny squares. He didn't see me, Dad, honest. I snuck close real quiet-like."

The groundskeeper? What reason had he to place cameras in a dead man's house? Seeking answers, Marina glanced from Jonathan, who stood stiff, to Patti who clutched her throat. *What the hell is going on here?*

Jonathan shook himself. "Good job, Tyler." He ruffled his son's hair then grabbed his jacket from the coat rack. "Everyone stay here. I'll confront Karl."

Marina stepped in his path. "I'm going with you."

"No, you're not." He glowered. "You won't leave the house."

She'd be damned to allow him to order her around like a child. "Either I go with you, or I hop into my car and leave. Your choice." Lifting her coat from the rack, she slipped her arms into the sleeves and faced him. "You're keeping secrets from me, Blandish, and I don't like it. I want to hear why Karl found cameras so necessary in a dead man's house."

Jonathan's gaze narrowed while one lip arched

78

with a silent snarl.

Not a pleasant look, more like a dog ready to defend his food. But Iris had warned her the Blandish men expected their way. *Well, tough toenails, Jonathan Blandish.* She had refused to cower as a little girl and sure as hell refused now.

He stepped toward her, shaking his finger in her face. "You're blackmailing me."

She thrust her face close to his, her gaze matching his intensity. Too close before she realized her mistake. His spicy cologne struck her nose, and she nearly swooned. Despite a strong desire to wrap her arms around his neck, she grabbed his pointing finger and held firm. "You need me, Blandish, and you don't know why. I suggest you level with me." Before she did something stupid, she released his hand and zipped her jacket.

A spark flew from his gaze. An amused spark, and she swore up and down he suppressed a grin. *Mental note. Get eyes checked.*

He threw on his jacket. "I'm not usually challenged."

"Noted and rejected." She headed for the front door and glanced over her shoulder. "Are you coming?"

Jonathan turned to his son. "Where's the van?"

His little arm flew into the air, finger pointing. "By the lake. Can I come, too? I found him."

Frowning, Jonathan jerked his jacket collar closer to his neck. "You know you're not supposed to wander that far from the house."

Eyes wide, he backed up at his father's tone. "I didn't mean to, Dad, but when I climbed the old tree out back, I saw the van. Can I come?"

"No, stay with Patti. She needs a man with her." He winked at Patti and opened the front door. "All right, Marina, let's go."

He had accepted the defeat, which wasn't a surprise. The man hadn't made his millions by being stupid. Once outside, Marina lifted her jacket hood to cover her hair. The clouds had drifted away and a bright sun glowed in a clear sky, but the wind robbed any radiated warmth.

They hurried from the front of the house to the far side of the garage and out into the open pasture. At this time of year, the grounds had hardly any green to brag about, the grass mostly brown, the scattered trees without leaves. She followed Jonathan through a wide stretch of pasture, over a small hill, and then downward toward another hill. He moved with long strides, which she struggled to match. "Yo, wait up!" Her voice had blown away with the wind. "Shouldn't we call the cops?"

"I want to make sure Tyler's right. For all we know, Karl's playing games on his computer." Jonathan increased his pace.

Hurrying to catch up, she ran, walked, and ran again. *Damn him.* Now, more than ever, she was convinced he harbored secrets. For a brief second, she pitied Karl. Jonathan, with his set jaw and a gaze as cold as ice, had the look of a man ready to kill with his bare hands. If their confrontation came to blows…

She patted all her pockets to ascertain the location of her cell phone. In her damn purse back at the house, of course.

Jonathan arrived on the peak of the second small hill. Surprisingly, he waited for her to come alongside.

Before them, the ground sloped downward toward a small lake. The van, a big, boxy kind with no side windows, sat on a barely discernible access road that ran parallel to the water. Catching her breath, she snorted. "We could have taken your car."

He stared aghast, eyes wide.

The horrified expression looked as if she committed a mortal sin by suggesting they dirty his precious vehicle. "All right, *my* car. I have a four-wheel drive, you know." Not like it mattered...now. "If Karl is watching the cameras, he knows we're on to him, not to mention he heard us talking. Why wait for us to come knocking at his door?"

"Arrogance, Marina, plain and simple. Shhh."

Yeah, shush the weeds. They crunched beneath their feet, making quiet movements impossible.

Jonathan motioned with an open palm for Marina to stay to the side while he crept to peek into the front compartment. He gave her a thumbs-down then tiptoed toward the rear panel doors and peeked. After a thumbs-up, he motioned for her to approach. They simultaneously grabbed a panel door handle and swung them open.

Karl leaned back in a chair with his feet on a plastic crate. A laptop was positioned on a small shelf in front of him. Tiny squares covered the screen as Tyler said. Without so much as a blink, he closed the laptop and swiveled his chair to face them, not in the least surprised by the intrusion. His mouth twisted into a sneer. "I saw you coming."

Well, duh, no kidding.

Jonathan leaned against the open door while lifting a foot onto the bumper, his manner nonchalant, but his gaze remained hard.

Both men sized up each other in a split second, a male power play she'd seen often enough between her father and brother. Jonathan had youth and the strength of a man who kept in shape. Karl had age but exuded experience, a cockiness for such, which intensified Jonathan's fire-and-brimstone glare.

Jonathan nodded toward the laptop. "Care to explain yourself? I'm a phone call away from notifying the police. Is that what you want?"

Karl released a harsh chuckle, more cynical than humorous. He unplugged the laptop and handed it to Jonathan who growled something inaudible as he opened the lid and watched the little squares pop onto the screen.

Cameras were in every room, even rooms Marina hadn't seen yet. Six squares were black. She pointed to the screen. "We plucked four cameras from their hiding spots." With one brow cocked, she looked at Karl. "Why are the other two squares black?"

"Basement and attic," he answered. "They're in place, waiting for a light to go on."

She cringed and glanced away. "They're that dark?" *God, help me.*

"How many total?" Jonathan asked, his words clipped.

"Twenty. I'd appreciate having every one of them returned."

Jonathan tapped on a square to see it expand in size.

As expected, the camera angle covered a broad section, in this case, the upstairs hall. The clarity was remarkable. Marina could see every detail.

A curse escaped from Jonathan's throat. "I knew I should have fired you. How long have they been in position?"

"Long enough."

Jonathan's face changed to stone. "Why, Karl?"

"You know why." Karl zipped his jacket and stepped from the van, his weight rocking the vehicle to and fro. He faced Marina then jerked his chin toward Jonathan. "This guy's not being honest with you, Doc."

Yeah, no shit. "Then someone needs to fill me in." She glared at Jonathan. "Should I hear the story from Karl or from you?"

Karl nudged her arm. "I don't suppose Blandish told you how his brother died?"

Stomach fluttering, she snapped her gaze to Karl's smug face. "I only read a brief obituary. The article gave no cause of death."

Karl crossed his arms over a thrust-out chest. "Well, little lady, Roger Blandish was murdered in the garage. Jonny boy is pretty high on the suspect list. I'm sure he paid handsomely to have his brother's info removed from the web, more than likely because of you."

A sudden coldness shot across her skin and caused every hair follicle on her body to rise. Staggering, Marina faced Jonathan, eyes wide. "Is this true?"

Jonathan's gaze cut Karl in two, but he immediately softened the look once shifting it to her. "Yes, it's true." He closed the laptop and tucked the computer under his arm. "My brother was stabbed with a screwdriver and bled to death on the garage floor. And contrary to Karl's accusation, the police cleared me." He stepped away from the vehicle.

"Then, his killer is still on the loose?" The news was mind-boggling, and she shuddered. While researching, she'd found nothing with any inference to murder. How could he keep such a secret, particularly when he expected her to work alone? She squared her shoulders and faced him. "When were you planning to tell me? You have me working in a house where a murder took place, and you kept the fact a secret? What if the murderer returns?"

Karl squared his shoulders. "Yeah, Blandish, what's the woman gonna do?"

Jonathan ignored Marina and faced Karl. "You haven't explained the cameras. Are you working for the police?"

"They can't afford me."

Marina's mouth fell open. *Afford him?* The man dressed like a pauper living on the street with his tattered clothes and scuff-worn boots. The van wasn't new, but the vehicle wasn't old either. She had liked him when they first met, but now, he made her skin crawl.

As for Jonathan…

The man had his nerve, placing her in an ignorant situation. *Who does he think he is, the king of Boston*? She almost turned on her heel had Karl not reached into his back pocket and handed Jonathan a business card. Resisting the urge to snatch the card from Jonathan's hand, she leaned toward him to read. *Karl Towson, Private Investigations.*

Jonathan shot him a glare. "Who hired you?"

"Your brother's hedge fund. They want me to find the forty million he embezzled."

Staggering, Jonathan stared while his brows arched

halfway into his hairline. "I don't know of any embezzlement. What proof do you have?"

"The fund has the proof. Your brother made systematic wire transfers that they traced to a Bermuda bank account. I was hired to follow the trail." He closed the rear doors with a bang.

"And obviously, you have no idea where the money went, and that's why you installed the cameras."

Karl turned with a wry smile. "Oh, I have a good idea all right. The money transferred overseas and disappeared, but somewhere in that house is the clue to the whereabouts of forty million dollars. I'm guessing a bank account number or an overseas security box."

Jonathan narrowed his gaze. "Did you record the murder, Karl?"

"Maybe."

"No *maybe*. Either you recorded it, or you didn't...unless you plan on a little blackmail to supplement your income." He matched Karl's steady gaze. "You knew we found the cameras. Why'd you stick around?"

Karl shifted on his feet. "Because I've gotten nowhere, Blandish. I've followed your brother's wire transfers and found nothing."

Holding the laptop outright, Jonathan debated whether to slam it to the ground. Then he hissed through tight teeth before, once again, tucking the computer under his arm. "The embezzlement changes everything about my brother's murder. The police labeled it a crime of passion. We need to tell them."

Karl stretched to his full height. An intimidating technique which Jonathan ignored since he was of equal height. Marina felt like a midget between them and stepped back—just in case fists flew.

"You can't go to the police, Blandish. If the embezzlement becomes public, the clients will create a run on the fund. That's what I was hired to prevent. I'll remove the cameras if you hand over the money."

Jonathan stepped into Karl's space and growled. "I have no idea where my brother hid the money—*if* you're telling me the truth."

Stunned beyond words, Marina glanced from Jonathan to Karl, her gut twisting into a tight knot. A man was murdered, possibly for the money he stole, and these two men argued over whether to tell the police. She turned on her heel and retreated toward the house, having no desire to be privy to their scheme.

"Marina, wait!" Jonathan caught up and grabbed her arm. "Doctor, please."

She whirled. The wind caught her hood and blew it off while whipping her mane into her face. She tucked strands behind her ears, but to no avail. "You're keeping too many secrets from me, Blandish. What else will I find out *later*?"

Karl joined them. "Time to come clean, Blandish, so she can help us."

She stuck out her chin and took a stance before them. "I'm not helping either of you. I'm heading home." Again, she turned to leave.

Moving swiftly, Jonathan blocked her path. "Marina, wait…please."

"Why should I?" She tilted back her head in defiance.

"Because I have too many unanswered questions. I'm sorry I kept secrets, but if you wait, I'll tell you both what I know."

Jonathan looked shattered. His shoulders had slumped, and he turned away to stare into the pasture. For the first time, she saw a man who stood alone with no confidant by his side, like little Marina Cavanaugh defending her brother and sisters. An ache formed in her throat with the unmistakable urge to reach out and touch him, for she knew from her childhood how helpless she felt to fight a battle alone, but common sense kicked in. He wasn't such an innocent bystander, opting instead to withhold information for reasons only he could explain. Curiosity more than anything kept her feet still. Hunching her shoulders against the chill, she stuffed her hands into her jacket pockets and waited.

Clearing his throat, Jonathan faced her. "My brother's will specifies the distribution of an estate worth forty-two million. I can only account for two million, and that sum includes the house and property. I searched everywhere for some clue and discovered nothing until Mother found the note with your name." He paused to look skyward.

She wasn't sure why, but she also glanced upward, half expecting to see birds overhead.

"I explored every page of your book, Marina, hoping he left a clue as to what he meant." Lowering his chin, he met her gaze. "I assumed he put the money in antiques."

Hearing the despair in his voice, she swallowed her anger. "Your brother doesn't have forty million in antiques in that house, Jonathan. If he dumped the money in one or two objects, I'd have heard the news through the grapevine. Maybe he buried his stash in the backyard."

"Then I'd have found the loot," Karl said.

"Unfortunately, nothing on the property has been disturbed. No loose floorboards anywhere, and no overturned dirt."

A shiver traveled through her spine. She'd come with the intention of evaluating antiques. Instead, she found herself involved in a mystery as dangerous as quicksand. Murder and embezzlement. A hell of a motive. A hell of a prize, too, for the winner.

Marina sniffed. The damn wind was making her nose drip. She met Jonathan's pleading gaze. Could she trust him enough to continue this assignment? But like many men before him, he'd withheld so much. "I asked you earlier to tell me about your brother, yet you kept silent. Why?"

He scuffed his shoe at the dirt. "I was afraid to scare you off." Reaching forward, he touched her arm. "You're the key, Marina. Somehow, someway, you will be the one to unlock the riddle. If it helps, I can assure you that Patti and I were cleared."

Gasping, she jerked away her arm. "Patti, too?"

"Yes. Both our alibis checked out."

Marina faced Karl and lifted an eyebrow. "And you?"

Karl flashed a crooked grin to go with his crooked teeth. "I'm a lowly groundskeeper who works two days a week. Poor me." He chuckled at his own joke.

She narrowed her gaze. "Don't give me that. The police should have uncovered your identity."

The grin widened. "I'm the best in Boston, Doc. Being the best means I operate under a shroud of secrecy. That's why the fund hired me."

"But in light of the missing money, you have a good reason to kill Roger." She faced him and glared.

"How do we know you haven't taken it?"

The man put a palm over his heart in mock shock and stepped back. "Do you think I'd be standing here making nice talk with you two?"

"Why not?" Jonathan interjected. He straightened his shoulders. "If you disappear, you'll raise suspicion, and the fund will have no choice but to notify the police. Either that, or swallow the loss in silence. I don't think they'll do that."

"The police need to hear this," Marina argued, her thoughts racing. "Both of you concealed vital information, and I resent being dragged in. If the police don't hear the facts, they'll never solve Roger's murder."

Like scolding two little boys. Jonathan, a successful businessman, a man who gave orders and expected them to be followed. Karl, a man who played by his own rules, right or wrong. And Marina Cavanaugh smack in the middle, an antiques appraiser whose most dangerous assignment had been a sandstorm in Egypt.

Karl stepped close and invaded her space. Her gaze snapped upward, defying him to come closer. *If he so much as lays a hand on me…*

"I can't let you call the police, ma'am. As I said, I was hired to keep the embezzlement quiet. If and when we find the money, no problem."

Jonathan wedged himself between Karl and Marina. With one hand, he shoved Karl back. "This woman is here to help us. My brother told me her name for a reason. She is not to be threatened, coerced, or intimidated in any way. Do I make myself clear?" His gaze cut Karl in two. "I can still kick you out, or better yet, tell the cops everything. I'll let them tear apart this house."

Hands raised in surrender, Karl backed off. "Whatever you say, Blandish."

"Now, drive your van to the house. I'll keep the laptop. We will pull every camera, and you're helping us."

Karl returned to his vehicle while Marina and Jonathan headed for the house.

A powerful sense of foreboding hit. Roger was murdered, and his killer was still on the loose. Forty million at stake. The police had no idea of the new developments, and two men involved her in a conspiracy of silence. What universe had she slipped into to change her life from everyday ordinary to cut-throat dangerous?

She had no reason to stay, no need for extra money, nor a clue why Roger recommended her. Her anger at the man walking alongside fermented with each step. He'd gotten her into this. Every fiber in her body wanted to get the hell out and away from him and his problems. But this time, he matched her strides, being in no hurry to rush ahead and leave her behind. *He's probably afraid I'll bolt.*

"I'm sorry I wasn't forthright, Marina." He tilted his head toward her to force her to look up from the ground. A faint smile touched his lips. "I hope despite everything, I can convince you to stay."

"I resent being tricked into this, Jonathan. If you were honest from the beginning—"

"You'd have refused outright. Roger implicated you. I don't know why, but you can help me find the answer. Please, stay."

Oh, damn. Her anger rose and fell with this man, and now, he was asking her to be his comrade-in-arms. Maybe not in so many words, but she'd taken the implication as such. How could she possible side with him? "Ask me after the cameras are removed. At the moment, I don't trust you or Karl, and I'm not feeling happy about Patti and Iris. All of you kept this horrible secret."

She stopped.

Four strides later, he jerked to a stop and faced her. His gaze pleaded.

The impression of him standing alone intensified. She managed a faint smile. "You had no reason to step between Karl and me. I can handle myself."

"I don't like men who bully women."

She stifled a laugh. "Then you better not meet my father."

Chapter Eight

Marina's muscles tensed as she stood by the dining room table with the open laptop in full view. One by one, the little squares turned dark as Jonathan and Karl collected the cameras. Karl had them strategically positioned in every room, including one covering the front yard and drive, and two angled to show the rear acreage. Not a speck of privacy anywhere. She'd also glimpsed the attic and basement as Karl turned on a light. Not pretty sights, and as expected, not a whole lot of light either.

"This is awful," Patti murmured. She stood alongside Marina, biting her cuticle.

Jonathan had explained Karl's purpose to Patti and how Marina now knew about Roger's demise. The round housekeeper hadn't stopped biting her nails since.

"I wonder how long Karl had his little spy game going? Did he say, Doctor?"

I'd like to strangle all of them, Jonathan first. Marina shoved her sweatshirt sleeves to the elbows. *Maybe flog them to death if I can get my hands on a whip.*

"Doctor?"

Marina jumped and glanced to the woman. "Huh?"

Tyler's face came into focus in a square. "Hi, Marina!" He waved happily.

Oh, God, that little guy is so cute. He had been following his father throughout the camera retrieval, hopping and flying over furniture as he ran.

Damn, what a dreary house. Even without the forty-two million, Roger had enough money to renovate the interior to his liking. Instead, he had kept the dark paneling, stark furnishings, and lived like a pauper. The man had a screw loose.

Patti fidgeted. "Roger hired Karl because he looked like a man in need of a job. If Karl recorded us all this time…"

"Karl admits to nothing, Patti. I'm guessing he's had the cameras in place since his arrival."

Patti wrapped her pudgy arms around her chest, not quite making half the circumference. "Do you think he witnessed the murder?"

"He won't say, but look at the camera angle in the garage." She pointed to a still-lit square. "He had a good view of the workbench and door. If the camera was in place, then he recorded the murder, and the police should be told." Another square darkened. "Karl strikes me as a man with no scruples. He'll keep quiet until he foresees some profit."

Her mouth gaped. "You think so? I always liked him."

"He surprised me, too, but the man's playing with fire if the killer finds out."

"Unless Karl *is* the killer." Patti shot Marina a sideways glance.

The idea had entered Marina's mind as well. Actually, several scenarios flashed through her mind, one of which she hated to believe. What if Karl and Jonathan had formed an alliance, and the scene by the lake was for show? Forty million made for one hell of a motive, and Jonathan sucked her into their game to help find the money. She had no trust in Karl, and only a smidgen for Jonathan in light of all the omitted details. How could she possibly stay?

Because I don't believe a word I'm thinking. She faced Patti and adopted a stern look. "You should have told me about Roger."

Patti's face paled. Her arms fell to the side while she took a step back, her posture stiff. "I'm sorry, Doctor. Mr. Blandish ordered me to keep quiet, and he's the man paying my salary."

What excuse did Iris have? No guts to defy her son? "What I don't understand is why the police didn't find the cameras."

"The police concentrated their attention on the murder site and only took a cursory look in the house. They called it a crime of passion, being done with a screwdriver and all." Her stance relaxed, and she shot a look around the room. "You have to admit this house isn't loaded with technology. They had no reason to look for cameras." Her gaze returned to the monitor. "Besides, I'd like to know why *I* missed them. All right, some are pretty high, and I reach those spots with a dust wand, but I'd make a bet they weren't in place while Roger was alive."

Patti sounded desperate to believe what couldn't possibly be true. Why would Karl place cameras *after* Roger's murder? For that matter, would the hedge fund pursue the investigation even after Roger's death? Karl could be acting on his own. Marina studied the woman then turned again to the monitor. "No, I think they were in place from the beginning, Patti. He's after the money, whether for himself or the fund." She chewed the inside of her lip. "He left the cameras to see what I uncovered." And then what? Bop her on the head and run with the prize?

Heat flushed her skin at Jonathan's blatant disregard for her safety. *Friggin' men and their conniving ways.*

"Please don't leave, Doctor. Mr. Blandish needs you."

Yeah, like a hole in the head. Marina glanced at Patti, at the pleading look on her face. "I'm angry enough to walk out."

"I don't blame you, but I'm sure he had his reasons." She bit another cuticle while staring at the computer screen. "I can't believe Roger embezzled money. He always told me he had enough."

"That's probably what he meant." He hadn't spent a dime either. A few more chairs in the parlor along with flowery pillows would be nice. Definitely more lamps. Marina waved an open palm at the computer. "The money is probably the real motive for his murder, and here, we're just finding out. With all the time that's passed, how do we know the murderer isn't lounging on a beach in Belize with forty million in a Central American bank account?" She stuffed her hands under her armpits and clamped her arms tight, making every effort to control the unmistakable urge to hit something. Instead, she stared at the screen. "Jon needs to tell the police."

"Jonathan."

"Right. Jonathan." Marina rolled her eyes. The man even had Patti trained.

Twenty minutes later, all the squares turned black.

The three males re-entered the dining room with a tray full of tiny cameras.

Tyler ran ahead and hopped onto a dining room chair. "Did you see me, Marina?"

"Yes, I did. You looked very handsome." Her anger softened just from this little boy's smile. Would Jonathan jeopardize his son's adoration for his brother's stolen money? Her gut said no, and damned if she could figure out why. They hardly knew each other, but the very idea of Jonathan killing for money felt so wrong. *Although, what do I know*? One man she'd thought was special had fooled her completely. He suckered her into a relationship with the promise of forever.

Karl turned the laptop toward Jonathan and pointed to the dark squares. "Satisfied?"

Jonathan's lips twisted into a sneer. "Just don't reinstall them when we're not looking, or I'll smash every last one." He shoved the tray into Karl's hands.

"Thank goodness that's settled." Marina slapped her hands together as if brushing off dust. "Now, I can get to work without feeling my skin crawl."

Jonathan jolted then whirled, brows high. "You're staying?"

Surprised by the hopeful tone in his voice, she held up a finger. "I will do a preliminary evaluation, nothing more. A few hours, tops." With that finger, she closed the laptop. "What do you say we eat something? We skipped breakfast."

"Good idea," Patti chimed. Turning, she extended her hand toward Tyler. "Come on, little man. Let's go to the kitchen and make some sandwiches."

Karl tucked his cameras into several cushioned boxes. Once finished, he placed the boxes along with his laptop into a large canvas bag. "I'll tell my boss you're cooperating, Blandish."

Jonathan stiffened his back. "You also tell him I'm paying a visit tomorrow. I want to see what proof exists that Roger took the money. Tell him not to balk, because I'll go straight to the police."

"He won't balk." He turned to Marina with his thumb jerking toward Jonathan. "Watch this guy, Doc. He inherited his brother's estate and might be tempted to hold onto the money."

With posture rigid, Jonathan confronted the groundskeeper. "By the way, Karl, you're fired."

The older man sneered, lifted the bag onto his shoulder, and left. Marina stared after him. "He's a cocky SOB."

"I don't like him either. After I talk to his boss, I'll call Detective Farnsworth. He's the man in charge of Roger's case."

A wave of relief swept over her. "Good. I prefer an open dialogue with the authorities. The longer you keep quiet, the longer you'll stay at the top of the suspect list, not to mention implicate me in your dastardly plot."

A smile tugged at his lip. "Dastardly?"

All right, not the best word choice. Especially for a man she didn't know. With a cringe twisting her mouth, she faced him. "You didn't kill your brother, did you?"

His brows lowered into a frown. "That isn't a good question, Marina. If I killed Roger and told you, I'd have to kill you, too." He took a deep breath. "As it stands, no, I had nothing to do with my brother's murder."

Michael Corleone had made a similar statement to his wife in the *Godfather* series. She shuddered. "You'll tell Detective Farnsworth about me and the note?"

"Everything, Marina. My brother's immersed us in a mystery, and I don't like it. Maybe Farnsworth can search through Karl's videos and see if the PI is hiding the killer. He's dead meat if he is." He inspected his dirty hands and frowned. "I'll wash first and join you in the kitchen."

After a lunch of sandwiches and coleslaw, washed down with iced tea, Marina shooed everyone out the door. Jonathan had given Patti a handful of money to purchase light bulbs and some cheap lamps with the hope of better lighting—probably as an inducement for Marina to stay. More lights wouldn't influence her decision, but whoever followed her in evaluating the estate needed light, too.

As was her habit, Marina strolled leisurely through the house, clipboard and pen in hand, estimating a time for each room or jotting notes if any particular piece caught her eye. She needed *something* to keep her here. A rare find. A priceless jewel. Anything to help pique her interest.

Dining and living rooms were ordinary...and dark, furnishings meager and of poor quality with the exception of the dining suite. The den, off to one side of the dining room, had floor-to-ceiling books and would take the longest to catalog. The sunroom, off to the other side of the dining room, had more light than the entire house combined. A wall of windows along with two skylights helped.

Nothing remarkable struck her eye in any of the downstairs rooms. Pretty much the same on the second floor. Roger's brass bed stood polished to perfection, reflecting what little sunlight the dark draperies allowed. The bed was of good quality. Heavy. And new. Regardless, the house still reminded her of a convent, which was a small step above a Benedictine monastery.

At the opposite end of the second floor hallway, she opened a door to a narrow staircase leading to the attic and flipped the light switch. Like the basement, one bulb for illumination. If both held untold treasures, well, too bad. She'd find out later…if she stayed. She headed downstairs.

Should she persevere despite Jonathan's questionable honesty? The doubt gnawed at her gut. Five grand a week to create a house inventory tempted any working woman, but an unsolved murder hung in the air. The whereabouts of forty million dollars remained a mystery with a possible clue hidden somewhere in the house. *I'm the clue.* Why had Roger requested her when she'd never met the man, never even heard the Blandish name? And why an antiques appraiser?

So, she returned to the same question. Why continue on the job? Judging from the house contents, she'd face tedious work, but Mrs. Billingsley, who'd been such a great employer, deserved as much profit as possible. Jonathan was paying Marina's salary, so whatever the house contents received at auction, seventy percent would go to Mrs. Billingsley.

But was her loyalty to a wonderful lady her only reason? She had this unfathomable desire to hug Tyler to death, but why wasn't that cute little boy the least bit down-in-the-dumps over losing his mother?

She stopped by the sofa and stared at the list on her clipboard. Roger's estate, not Tyler, was the issue.

Jonathan had hired her to appraise the contents of the house with the secret hope of her uncovering a clue to the embezzled money. Unfortunately, this hell-hole of a dwelling with its dark corners tested the stability of her nerves. If nothing surfaced, she'd waste a lot of time working in a dungeon.

The doorbell rang. Without Patti in the house, she debated answering, but she peeked through the front window nonetheless.

A man in a heavy overcoat stood on the porch. A silver Lexus sat in the drive behind her car. She turned to ignore him when the doorbell rang again. *All right, it could be important.* She opened the door.

He stared with raised brows. "I'm sorry. I was hoping to catch Patti." He jerked a thumb in the direction of the driveway. "That must be your SUV."

A leeriness surfaced. Down south, the comment about her SUV would be construed as friendly, but up here in the northeast, she'd learned early to be wary of a stranger's attempt at conversation. "Yes, that's mine. Patti's at the store. Can I take a message?"

"I'm Henry Ladner, a close friend. I stopped by to see how she was getting on."

He wasn't a bad-looking man, certainly not tall but a good height for Patti. A head of thick black hair drizzled with gray matched his mustache and beard, perfectly trimmed. He wore a business suit under the black overcoat with spit-polished black shoes, his air that of a confident business man. With her hand on the door, she waited.

He adjusted his overcoat. "I don't remember meeting you at the funeral. Are you family?"

"Estate appraiser." She nudged the door as an

indication she was about to close it in his face. "I'll tell Patti you stopped by."

His palm stopped the door. "I'll wait."

Company was not what she needed at present, and a stranger to boot. She stood her ground, blocking any entrance on his part. "Mr. Ladner, I can't let you inside. Come back in an hour. I'm sure she won't be long."

He forced a smile, but a scar through his upper lip gave him an unintentional sneer, only partially hidden by the mustache. "Roger and I worked together for many years, so naturally, I recommended Patti as his housekeeper. We're old school chums—Patti and I. She needed a job, and I thought the fit was perfect." Stretching to the side, he looked beyond Marina into the living room. "So sad what happened." He met her gaze. "I suppose you know."

"Yes." *Enough of this*. She'd never get anything done with his stalling. "Look, Mr. Ladner, not to be rude, but I'm on a timetable. I'll tell Patti you were here."

"Right. I'll stop by on my way back. Cheerio."

Cheerio? She closed and, as an afterthought, bolted the door.

Henry Ladner's interruption had cleared up one internal debate. Marina decided to complete the job—for Mrs. Billingsley's sake. Brighter lights were coming to help alleviate the gloom, and why not earn five grand a week?

After several minutes had passed, she looked through the front windows to assure the Lexus was gone before heading for her SUV. Popping the hatch, she grabbed her laptop along with a small case that contained several different sizes of magnifying lenses, a small flashlight, her trusty utility knife, digital camera, and, of course, six pairs of store-bought eyeglasses and three hair clips. Back inside, she arranged a little workshop area in the parlor by placing everything on the sofa, slipped her utility knife into her back pocket, clipped her hair off her shoulders, and began the process of snapping photos before starting the inventory.

By late afternoon, she had finished with the parlor and carried her gear onto the dining room table. While standing, she busily typed on her laptop when the doorbell rang.

"Hello!" Jonathan called.

"In the dining room."

With a clumping of feet, Tyler ran through the archway, his blue jeans covered with dirt. "We got pizza! I'm starving!"

Jonathan followed equally covered with dirt. He carried a large pizza box. "I see Patti bought the lights."

Marina looked around with a smile. "She bought lamps and extension cords for every plug in the place, and now, with brighter bulbs, I can actually see what I have in my hand."

After changing the light bulbs from forty-watt to LED fifty, the home took on a whole new appearance. The shadows in the corners disappeared, and the dark paneling lost some of its ominous appearance. "She also bought extra flashlights and batteries. Smart girl." But Patti left before Marina had a chance to tell her about Henry Ladner.

Standing at her side, Jonathan waved the pizza box near her nose. "Can you eat?"

Who could refuse the aromas of tomato sauce and

cheese topped with mushrooms? Her mouth salivated. "I can always eat pizza." The whole box in most cases. "I've got a fresh pot of coffee on."

"Good. I need a cup. Tyler wore me out in the park." He faced his son and nodded toward the archway. "All right, young man, hand-washing time."

Tyler ran from the room, and his footsteps echoed all the way up the staircase.

Jonathan placed the pizza box on the dining room table and pointed to the top of her head. "I like the glasses."

After reaching up, she tossed them on the laptop. "What about your mom?"

"She had a late lunch with the girls." He leaned over to read the screen on the laptop. "How's it going?"

"I've itemized the parlor." She took a position beside him and pointed to the figures on the screen. "The auction amount may reach four thousand, with the frame over the mantel bringing in the largest chunk. Nothing impressive so far. The majority of the figurines in the house are junk." She turned to look at him. "Shall I smash them in case Roger hid a key inside or a clue to a safe deposit box?"

He shrugged. "Won't bother me none." He held up a finger. "As long as you don't run off with whatever you find."

Standing close, she couldn't ignore a whiff of his spicy aftershave intermingled with sweat. He smelled all man, and the scent was enough to drive her to distraction. She dared not take in a deep breath. Otherwise, she couldn't be responsible for her actions.

Jonathan grabbed the pizza box. "Time to eat."

Thank God for the diversion. She concentrated on

the wonderful aroma of the pizza and followed him toward the kitchen.

He slid the box onto the table and glanced over his shoulder. "Are you staying, Marina?"

The inevitable question. "Yes, I won't cheat Mrs. Billingsley out of an easy profit. Besides, I inherited my grandmother's curiosity and might find that lucky piece to make everyone rich." *Yeah, dream on.* She stepped back to rearrange the loose hair strands that had fallen from the clip. Her hair had a mind of its own. She could tie the locks into a ponytail, but waves always managed to find a way to break free. "I haven't investigated the attic or basement yet. They might surprise me."

His gaze followed her movements and relayed his fascination at her struggle to control her mane. She'd tried a short haircut years ago. The bob looked great until the first wash. After that, she resembled a wavy mop.

A slow smile formed on his lips. "I can't tell you how happy I am to hear you won't leave, Marina. You'll be much more objective than my mother or Patti." He stepped to the sink to wash his hands then called over his shoulder. "Tyler, come on! Time to chow down."

Tyler appeared out of nowhere. "Chow down, chow down. Look what I found, Dad." He put on a pair of eyeglasses.

Jonathan wiped his hands on a towel. "They're Marina's. Did you take them from her laptop?"

"I found them in the upstairs bathroom. See, I'm clean." He rotated his hands for his father's inspection.

"Give those glasses to me before your eyes cross," Marina said while suppressing a chuckle. She slipped the glasses onto the top of her head and took her turn at the sink to wash and dry her hands. "Plates anyone?"

"We're men and don't use plates. Right, Dad?"

"Right."

"Oh, brother," she mumbled and grabbed two mugs and a glass from an overhead cabinet while desperately hiding the smile tugging on her lips. Jon and mini-Jon. So cute. She joined them at the table.

Tyler dominated the conversation, rambling about their day in the park. Then, he shifted to a bug topic that was about as appetizing as rolling in mud. She and Jonathan exchanged amused glances, which struck her as so unlike her own childhood where she and her siblings ate with their gazes downward, never to speak unless addressed by an adult.

Tyler was one lucky little boy.

After last night's initial awkwardness passed, she had enjoyed the company of the Blandish clan at the dinner table, although she preferred not to make sharing a meal a habit. Even more surprising, a warmth surfaced by simply observing the closeness of father and son, and feelings of regret filled her chest at the distance her parents placed their children. Why bother with children at all if they weren't loved and cherished?

Releasing a heavy sigh, Tyler flopped back and rubbed his tummy. "I'm stuffed." He leaned toward his father. "Can I play in the sunroom?"

Since Jonathan's mouth was full, he waved his son out of the kitchen.

Marina grabbed her second slice of pizza and smiled at Jonathan. "He'll be an entomologist one day."

"I hope so." He swallowed quickly. "I hate to think those bugs gave their lives for nothing."

She rose to retrieve the coffee pot and refilled their cups. "Why the sunroom?"

"Roger kept coloring books and toys in a cabinet for him." He waited until she reclaimed her seat before his gaze drew hers. "Was your decision to stay more than Mrs. Billingsley, Marina?"

What could she say when she wasn't one hundred percent sure? She pulled off a sliver of mushroom until the cheese beneath snapped free then popped the piece into her mouth. "I don't have a clear-cut answer, Jonathan, just a gut feeling." Which was the truth. Not like she had any desire to find a forty-million-dollar fortune, but Roger involved her, and she'd like to know why. Jonathan's innocence was another matter, but her inner voice said to trust him. She bit into her pizza. "Your five grand a week, I guess."

"I was hoping for a different excuse, but I'll take it." He wiped his mouth. "I keep my mother out of the loop because Roger's death upset her enough. With you here, you can help me control my sanity."

Her belief about his no comrade-in-arms was true. But what was the different excuse he expected? Surely, nothing personal.

Jonathan grabbed Tyler's half-eaten slice of pizza and took a bite. "You're to sleep at my house, Marina. Regardless of our three-week agreement, I want you to take as much time as you need."

Her chest tightened. "A hotel would be wiser."

"Don't be ridiculous. My house is ten minutes away. A quick commute." He swallowed and washed it down with coffee. "And you're not to work late. I want you in my house by six. Do you understand?"

Surprised by his demands, she stared, wide-eyed,

and flopped back in the chair. "That's too early. I'll never finish."

He waved away her protest. "I don't care. I want you locked in and safe by six. I'm usually home by six fifteen. Listen to me."

Was he crazy? He expected her to eat with the family like she was a replacement for his dead wife? *No way, Jose.* "Daylight is getting longer, Jonathan. I'll waste too much time leaving at six."

"I'm still your employer, and you'll listen."

Her back stiffened. His orders flashed her to a childhood full of stipulations. She was her own woman now and old enough to defend herself with a vengeance. Like now. She pushed her plate to the side. "Look, Mr. Blandish, if you expect me to continue, then stop treating me like a child. You should ask, not command."

With a napkin, he dabbed his mouth while his gaze studied her. "According to our contract, I'm paying for three weeks of your services with the option to extend the time as appropriate. I have no desire to work you to death just to remain within that timeline."

He had a point, but she'd rather get the job over and done. She glanced at the wall clock. "We still have several hours of light. You and Tyler go home. I'll leave when I'm ready."

His jaw twitched. "I'm not one to compromise."

Undeterred, she raised her coffee mug to let the steam tickle her nose. "I'll accomplish a lot more if we do things my way, Mr. Blandish."

He pushed himself away from the table and stood, his face like stone. "I'll let you do your job, Doctor, but considering the circumstances surrounding this house, I want you under my roof by six, even if I have to come over here and drag you out. Is that clear?"

She hadn't swung at her father, but this man might get her foot up his ass. Was her destiny to live a life fighting controlling men? Why couldn't she meet a more docile man, one who gave her flowers and asked her opinion?

"Is that clear?" he repeated, his gaze shooting fireballs.

"Oh, yes, perfectly clear."

He stormed out while calling for Tyler. Moments later, the front door slammed. The Audi started with a roar and drove away amid the sound of flying stones.

Sipping her coffee, she smiled. Jonathan Blandish was about to discover that no man pushed Marina Cavanaugh into submission.

Chapter Nine

When Marina rang the doorbell at seven forty-five, she'd expected to see Jonathan on the other side with froth pouring from his mouth.

Instead, Iris answered, chuckling. "My son isn't used to his orders being ignored. Come in, dear." She waved Marina through the doorway. "He fumed all through dinner, and I swore he'd go to Roger's to throw you over his shoulder." She shut the door, still chuckling.

Marina placed her luggage on the floor before hanging her jacket in the closet. "I almost stayed another hour, but I figured he'd throw a royal fit."

Iris glanced at the luggage, but her gaze remained on one piece in particular. "You have a guitar!"

"I hope I won't bother anyone."

"Honey, this house needs some music. We've been quiet too long."

Marina picked up her luggage and glanced casually about. "Where's the tyrant?"

Iris nodded toward the staircase. "Giving Tyler his bath. Take your stuff to your room then join me for some ice cream. Tyler already had his."

"Sounds good."

Midway up the stairs, she glimpsed an approaching shadow and knew instantly who stood in the way. She suppressed the smile creeping onto her lips, because he was probably mad as hell and in no mood for humor. When she glanced in his direction, she almost laughed. Jonathan stood on the landing, hands on his hips, and brows creased into a scowl. He resembled an angry Goliath ready to chop off her head for insubordination. And was that steam shooting out his ears? "I haven't achieved a doctorate because I was pampered, Mr. Blandish."

"Call me Jonathan, dammit!"

"I'd rather call you Jon, but you don't like that either." She stopped alongside him and met his gaze. "Were you always such a stick in the mud?" She slipped past him and entered the bedroom, placing her suitcase on the bed. The guitar she handled with care and leaned the case against a chair.

Jonathan followed but blocked the doorway. "I don't like being disobeyed."

"That's obvious." She put her laptop case on a small side table and confronted him. "Look, Blandish, I'm a grown woman and a professional. I expect to be treated accordingly."

"I can see you're a grown woman and a stubborn one. I don't want anything to happen to you." He peered. "You have a blatant disregard for authority."

"No, I ignore bossy men. So, Houston, we have a problem."

"Dad, I'm done!"

Jonathan glanced down the hall, his body stance rigid.

"I can still leave." She tilted her head and smirked.

His jaw twitched. "You know I can't let you do that."

"Right. You need me and don't know why." She

crossed her arms over her chest, gaze dancing. "Irritates the hell out of you, doesn't it?" *The man will blow a gasket if I keep this up.* She approached the door and stood directly in front of him. "If Tyler's in the water much longer, he'll resemble a prune."

The fire shot from his gaze.

He'd lost this round, and she envisioned the wheels turning for retaliation. He had no choice but to accept defeat, and she smiled.

He growled something inaudible. "I'll check on Karl's story tomorrow. Call my cell phone if you have any questions."

"Yes, sir." She saluted and stepped to scoot around him, but he remained stationary, his neck veins visibly pulsing. If he wasn't careful, he'd have a stroke right in front of her. She pointed to his throat. "Your blood pressure is too high."

"Understandably so. Do you intend to aggravate me every night?"

"I suppose it's inevitable." In one step, he completely blocked the doorway, stretching his frame as if he was a grizzly bear on hind legs. She wasn't afraid. Her old man had given her enough practice facing bullies. "Tyler's waiting, Jon—nathan."

With a glare, he whirled and headed for Tyler's room.

She hadn't had this much fun in a long time and smiled at his receding back. Not like she earned Brownie points by confronting him, but somewhere beneath the bossy facade was a kind man, confused perhaps at her resistance, but of no comparison to her father. Philip Cavanaugh hadn't a kind bone in his body—except in public. To strangers, he was an angel without wings. To his children and wife, he was the supreme ruler of Hell. He demanded everyone to cower and obey.

As for Jonathan, he yielded to Marina's stubbornness, something her father had never done. This made Jonathan the more fallible human and well worth her patience. *If he doesn't fire me first.* She ran down the stairs.

Iris sat at the kitchen table, chin in her hand, staring into space. She was a world away, oblivious to Marina entering.

"Iris?"

The woman shook herself and gave a weak smile. "Sorry. Daydreaming."

Marina rested her hands on the back of a chair. "About what?"

"Oh—you know—about this and that. Let's have some ice cream." She retrieved a carton of vanilla fudge from the freezer and spooned the contents into two waiting bowls.

Marina pulled out the chair and slipped onto the seat, debating whether to confront Iris. Not one to hold back, she took the plunge. "I heard about Roger today."

"Yes, Jonathan told me." She shot her a sheepish look. "I hated keeping secrets from you, but he insisted. Is this enough?" She held out the bowl.

"Plenty, thank you." Marina took the bowl. "I suppose he told you about the embezzled money."

Iris closed the carton and returned it to the freezer. "I can't believe Roger did something so stupid, but the news explains why we couldn't find any trace of the money." She retook her seat. "Roger was always the secretive one—like his father, always doing things his own way without explaining why." With her spoon, she pointed to Marina's bowl. "How's the ice cream?"

Marina shoved a large spoonful into her mouth in answer. The fudge burst on her tongue, and she swooned. "Yummy."

"The flavors taste better when you enjoy it with someone."

If only my own mother was this nice. Marina would have enjoyed sitting at a table with her mother for a woman-to-woman chitchat, but her father's strict rules had forbidden any waste of time. Even a sister-to-sister chat was frowned upon.

She peeked at Iris over her dripping spoon. "I must say you're holding up well after what you've been through."

Iris toyed with her ice cream. "I do wonder when life will normalize again."

"What was your daughter-in-law like?"

"Self-centered." She swirled her ice cream before taking a spoonful. "Jonathan loved her dearly so I never complained about how she treated me. I stayed in my own little apartment and let them be. And then, of course, she contracted ovarian cancer and died. The cancer took her so quickly." Frowning, she stared at her ice cream. "Jonathan was devastated. He still isn't over her death."

"That's understandable. He needs time to grieve."

"Hmmpf. I think six years is long enough." She shot her a quick glance.

Marina's spoon froze mid-air, and she gaped at Iris across the table. "His wife's been dead for *six years*?"

"Yes." She snorted. "He refuses to date, even refuses to take off that damn ring." She slid her half-eaten bowl to the side and sat back, gaze vacant. "The doctor found Susan's cancer while she was carrying Tyler. She pushed him to perform an abortion, but she was already seven months along. Then, she insisted on starting chemotherapy which, of course, would have killed the baby." Using her index finger, she made invisible circles on the table. "The doctor made a deal. He'd deliver the baby at eight months and then have the oncologist take over. She died before Tyler was three months old."

"That's so sad." Her heart ached for Tyler. No wonder he acted like a normal little boy. He hadn't known his mother.

Iris leaned forward and crossed her arms on the table, her gaze focused on the table top. "During her pregnancy, we went through a horrible time. I'd catch her cleaning with the strongest chemicals on the market. She even drank to excess and accumulated so many speeding tickets Jonathan threatened to take away the car." She paused to look at Marina. "Once, I even found her in the hardware store, staring at a can of rat poison. We only had a week to go before the doctor took Tyler, and she was doing everything possible to abort the baby." Shaking her head, she sighed heavily. "After Tyler was born, I left my apartment and moved here to care for him. He's now six, and I'm still here. I can't get on with my own life, because Jonathan won't get on with his. All this waiting is frustrating."

Finished with the last of her ice cream, Marina slid the bowl to the side. Unfortunately, Iris' half-eaten bowl tempted her self-control, but she'd had pizza for an early dinner, cookies for a snack before leaving, and now ice cream to top off her high-caloric day. "Maybe

Jon should seek professional help."

Iris straightened in her chair with a faint smile touching her lips. "Are you allowed to call him that?"

Oops. Slipped again. "No, sorry. I'm informal by nature because of my southern upbringing. Was he always like this with nicknames?"

"Oh, gosh, yes. He's named after his great-granddaddy who fought for the South in our country's Civil War, but Grand-pappy hated formalities, and no one dared use his formal name. My son is the opposite, and none of us can figure out why. He and Susan were a good match, because she hadn't an informal bone in her body. She was a bit of a prima donna." She clucked her tongue, leaned back, and folded her arms across her chest. "I shouldn't speak ill of the dead."

"Your son doesn't strike me as formal, Iris. This afternoon, he and Tyler walked in covered with dirt." She smiled at the memory. "That looks like a good father-son relationship."

"If Susan was still alive, she'd have both their heads." She uncrossed her arms and, again, leaned onto the table. "I sometimes think Jonathan will grieve forever."

"Then, you're the one who should change. You have no viable reason to put off anything." She met Iris halfway across the table. "What would you like to do?"

Iris's gaze twinkled. "I'd like to meet someone, have my own place, and be independent. I was divorced only a year when Susan became ill." She touched Marina's arm. "I love Tyler, but I really want someone to grow old with." She sat back and stared into the distance, her gaze dreamy. "If I had an apartment in the city, I could go to functions, travel, and maybe volunteer at a hospital." She refocused onto Marina. "I won't meet anyone stuck here."

"So, tell Jonathan." She tapped the table to get her attention. "*Tell* him, don't ask. You'll have to put your foot firmly on the ground, because he'll say no." She leaned back and drummed her fingers on the table. "Tell you what. I have a two-bedroom condo. We can double-up until you find your own place." *And Jon will kill me for such a bold suggestion.*

Iris' face brightened. "That's a wonderful temptation, Marina, but I'm sure you have men knocking down your door. You don't need an old lady as a roommate."

She reached across the table to squeeze Iris' hand. "You're still attractive and don't let anyone tell you otherwise." She patted the woman's hand and leaned back. "Besides, I travel a lot for my job. Sometimes I'm away for weeks. You'll have the place to yourself."

Iris' face brightened even more as a sparkle filled her gaze. She was clearly intrigued with the idea. Whether she acted on the offer was another matter.

"I'm not sure what Jonathan will do with Tyler." She bit her lip.

"He's a grown man. He'll figure out something."

"Figure out what?" Jonathan entered with evidence of water splashes on his shirt and blue jeans.

In an instant, Iris lost the sparkle in her gaze as she grabbed the bowls and hurried to the sink.

Was she afraid of her own son? Or was she so complacent, she let men use her for a rug? Marina had seen too much of this behavior in her life. No female should be subservient to the male, and if she gained any knowledge from her abusive father, she learned the purpose of self-defense, both physical and mental. She pushed back her chair and stood to face Jonathan, staring directly into his eyes. He'd lost some of the fire from earlier. Unfortunately, she was about to ignite it again. "Do you beat women?"

He staggered, brows halfway to his hairline. "What kind of question is that?"

"Just wondered. How angry do you feel when people don't follow your orders?"

"Extremely angry." He narrowed his gaze. "I usually fire them."

Marina glanced at Iris and smiled. "There you go. Get yourself fired." Chin up, she faced him again. "I'm sure he's debating such an action with me."

"As a matter of fact, I am."

"Well, say the word, big boy. I'll be out of here faster than your next breath." Her head cocked. "I never pretended to be an angel."

"And hopefully, I haven't let the devil into my house either." He slanted toward her, fisted hands on hips. "Have you been putting ideas into my mother's head?"

Undaunted, Marina met his gaze. "Your mother is a wonderful woman, and you should learn to appreciate her. Good night, you two."

****

Jonathan stared after her, desperately restraining a retort. Heat surrounded him, flushing from his shirt collar like a blast furnace, and all because this damn minx defied him at every turn. If he had known of her problems with authority, he'd have...done nothing. Except swallow patience pills. He still needed her assistance for whatever Roger's reason, but why must she be so cock sure of herself? Confidence radiated from her pores, and she wasn't afraid to challenge him. She forced him to recognize the brains, beauty, and guts all rolled into one attractive package. He wasn't used to assertive women on the home front. In business, yes, but this was *his* castle, *his* domain where women should be like his mother, docile and obedient.

"What are you grumbling about?"

He jerked his gaze from the archway. "I'm right. She's the devil in disguise."

"I like her." Iris turned from the sink to dry her hands with a towel. "I guess Roger liked her, too."

"She denies knowing him."

"And I believe her. She has a job where she meets a lot of people and can't possibly remember all their names." She folded the towel and placed it on the counter. "Roger may have been good-looking, but he wasn't the sort to impress people, especially women."

Jonathan stuffed his hands into his jeans pockets. "The least he could have done was given us a better warning. She's a bad influence."

"Why, because she speaks her mind? I admire a woman with some backbone." She opened a top cabinet and, stretching on tiptoe, grabbed a prescription pill bottle from the top shelf and read the label. "I need to get this refilled tomorrow." She returned the bottle to the top shelf and wrote a quick note on the counter notepad before facing her son. "You can't expect every woman to worship the air you breathe, Jonathan. That's too much like your father, and look what he's doing, chasing every filly who crosses his path." She walked to the table and shoved the chairs under.

He crossed his arms over his chest and peered at

his mother. "I am *not* like my father."

She met his gaze. "Yes, all right, that wasn't a fair comparison, but I don't know why Marina bothers you. You're not interested in women anymore."

The words jarred him, and he dropped his arms. "I never said that."

"Six years without a date? Ha! Actions speak louder than words, dear. You have this beautiful woman under your roof, and all you want to do is order her around." She stepped toward him and placed a gentle hand on his arm. "Explore the possibilities, Jonathan. Life is full of surprises." She smiled and patted his arm before dropping her hand.

His mother had never dared play matchmaker. Why now and with, of all women, Marina? "What possibilities, Mother? She has a problem with authority."

"You mean *your* authority. The woman has a doctorate. She's not a subordinate. Maybe you should ask instead of order." She headed for the living room.

He followed. Why, he wasn't sure. To continue the argument. Or for the sole purpose of not letting his mother win.

Approaching the sofa, she grabbed a pillow and punched to fluff the stuffing. "You're too much like your father. He wanted an automaton for a wife, and I acted accordingly."

"Dad was a good father early on."

"Yes, but he wasn't a good husband. He never treated me like a partner. That's what a marriage is, Jonathan, a partnership. You can't go around controlling your spouse. Hell, even Susan rebelled." She tossed the pillow in the corner of the sofa and retrieved another.

Unfortunately, his mother made a valid point. He and his wife fought constantly over her spending habits, and he had threatened to cancel all her credit cards. Then, of course, she announced her pregnancy, and the spending increased—for the baby. At seven months, the doctors informed her about the cancer. Since the law required his approval for a late-term abortion, they fought even more. For the first time in his life, he couldn't make a decision. Her life for the child, or the child for her life? He agonized for days until the doctors suggested taking the baby at eight months. Aggressive chemo followed, but Susan deteriorated too quickly. On her deathbed, she had made a last request, and he vowed to honor her wish for as long as he lived.

His mother pounded another pillow. "I thought you liked being married."

"I do, but to Susan, no one else." Was that true? At times, Susan was a royal pain-in-the-ass, but he loved her. And she'd given him Tyler.

Still holding the pillow, his mother turned, one brow cocked. "And you plan to live the rest of your life alone? That's a bit of a stretch, dear." Pressing her lips tight, she gave the pillow several swift slugs. "Think about the future, Jonathan. Tyler will grow up and leave. I'll eventually die of old age. And you? You'll work 'til you drop, because you won't have anything else to do." She cocked her head, her gaze steady on his face. "You're still young, Jonathan. I want you to fall in love again."

What was it with women and their damn romantic fantasies? He was happy enough without a wife and didn't need his mother pushing him out the door. He narrowed his gaze. "Why?"

"Because then I can have a life of my own, find a man for a little company, and flush your bastard father out of my mind forever." She placed the first pillow with the second and positioned them against the sofa arm. "My intention wasn't to live here permanently, you know. I planned to help you over the rough part, wait for Tyler to be out of diapers, and then find an apartment in Boston. I spent years raising two boys of my own. I don't need to raise yours." She grabbed a magazine from the center coffee table, kicked off her shoes, and flopped onto the sofa while adjusting the pillows at her back.

What the hell was with her tonight? His gaze bounced from the women's magazines on the table to the bouquet of flowers on the mantel then to his mother. "But you like living here."

She stretched her legs across the sofa cushions and met his gaze. "I do, but every night, I go to bed alone." She waved a finger toward the side chair. "If you want to sit, use that chair. I'm not moving."

Marina had said the same words the day he'd entered the lunchroom to see her stretched across a worn sofa. She had been dressed in those oversized coveralls that reminded him of a circus clown. She hid a nice shape beneath them.

The strumming of guitar strings snapped both their heads toward the staircase.

His mother gasped. "That's Marina!" She tossed aside the magazine and jumped from the sofa. "Let's go see!" She ran barefoot up the stairs.

He took his time. Music wasn't a part of his life anymore. They had a stereo in the living room but mainly for decoration. He paused at the top of the stairs to listen.

The guitar sounds flowed from Tyler's room. His mother was already standing in the doorway with her arms wrapped around her torso in a tight hug.

He stepped behind her to see Marina sitting on the cushioned window seat with Tyler in bed watching her. She still wore her jeans and sweatshirt and finger-picked the strings with an expertise that kept the boy mesmerized, her voice humming along with the notes, lulling him to sleep.

She winked at them but never broke rhythm.

His knees wobbled. He opened his mouth to speak, to protest her audacity to play in his house, but the words froze in his throat. He was wrong about Marina being the devil. A devil could never sing with the voice of an angel. Within a matter of days, Marina had turned his world topsy-turvy and unknowingly caused his body to ache for a woman. Maybe he was a fool to keep Marina under his roof. Yet, he'd be a bigger fool to ignore the emotions she stirred.

Jonathan kissed his mother on her head and forced his legs to carry him to his room. A tightness gripped his throat and caused him to gulp air into his lungs. He hadn't cried since the day they buried Susan, not even for his murdered brother, but tears burned behind his eyes, and he had no clue why.

Chapter Ten

Itemizing an entire house without help proved a daunting task. If Marina had half a functioning brain, she'd pack Roger's possessions and ship everything to the secondary warehouse. From that point, she'd have better lighting for a proper evaluation, maybe discover a surprise or two. *Like a forty-million-dollar treasure.* So far, Roger's house held only the typical stuff of flea market quality with the rest as curb-side trash.

She had to force herself not to skimp with an inspection. Roger could have hidden his clue anywhere and in any form. Had he, in fact, expected Marina Cavanaugh to uncover the whereabouts of his stash? Jonathan and Iris could have easily gone through every possession. So, why involve a total stranger, an antiques appraiser he'd never met?

At least, she hoped they hadn't met, but the possibility existed they might have run into each other at an auction. He'd remember her more if she stood by the podium holding up an object. To her, he'd be only another face in the crowd.

Marina had emptied the contents of the dining room's china cabinet onto the table when the click of the front door's latch froze her.

"Anyone home?"

The sound of the unfamiliar male voice sent a shiver straight down to her toes. Had she left the door unlocked? If so, who would be brazen enough to waltz into a house uninvited? Forcing herself not to jump to conclusions, she patted her back pocket to assure the whereabouts of her utility knife and peeked around the archway separating the dining room from the parlor.

Brandon Blandish stood by the front door, his darkened hair slicked with gel, casually dressed in blue jeans, flannel shirt, and short coat. He wasn't a handsome man but not an ugly one either. Average perhaps for a man in his early sixties reliving his youth. Nose too broad and red. Eyes sunk in with crescent shadows beneath. Jonathan certainly received his good looks from his mother.

Not wishing for Brandon to enter farther into the house, she joined him in the living room and immediately curled her nose. His acrid cologne overpowered the area. "You have a key?"

He smiled, showing sparkling dentures. "I recognized your SUV. Most people say hello."

"Not when someone walks in without an invitation. You were told not to return, Mr. Blandish."

"Duke. I don't like formalities."

A contrast to his son, for sure. She crossed her arms over her chest, not at all comfortable with his presence. "What do you want?"

He strolled around to her side of the sofa, his heavy boots echoing on the hard wooden floor. "As I told Jonny, I need a place to stay. Some time ago, Roger gave me a key and told me to make myself at home whenever I'm in town. Are you sleeping here?"

"No, sir."

"Ah, too bad. We could cozy up in Roger's brass bed." He winked and took several steps closer.

She took several backward steps toward the other end of the sofa. If that man so much as touched her, she hadn't enough soap in her possession to wash away his stench.

He followed, a twisted smile curling his lips. "I've come to reclaim Iris."

The statement sounded as if he walked into a Lost and Found. "Cozying up with another woman is not an encouraging sign, Mr. Blandish. And you can't stay."

One dyed brow cocked. "Why not? I can keep an eye on Roger's treasures." He looked around, and his smile waned. "If he has any."

The man caused the hairs on the back of her neck to vibrate. For one, he had slowly closed the gap between them, and with his long arms, he could easily grab her. As a precaution, she stepped around to the opposite side of the sofa, using the protection of the furniture to maintain some distance. "Your son doesn't want you here, Mr. Blandish, and frankly, neither do I. I have a lot of work to do, and you'll be in the way."

"Nonsense. I'll help you." He stretched over the back of the sofa to retrieve a pair of eyeglasses and dangled them between two fingers. "These yours?"

He flashed a smile that made her skin crawl— probably believing the look wowed the women into submission—then, with two fingers, swung the glasses from the ear piece like waving bait in front of a horse. No way in hell would she step close to his hand. "Just drop them."

His smile broadened. "Afraid of me?"

"I've work to do, Mr. Blandish."

He sighed heavily and lobbed the glasses across the sofa.

She caught them and slipped them onto the top of her head only to discover a pair already in position. Lowering her hand, she placed the glasses in her back pocket. What should she do? How could she toss out a man who had an open invitation to the house? "Mr. Blandish—"

"Duke."

"Mr. Blandish, please don't force me to defy your son's orders. He gave specific instructions not to let you inside."

"I let myself in. His order becomes null and void."

Obviously, the man didn't take no for an answer. *Persistent old devil.* "Please, sir."

He released a loud belly laugh. "And you, being the dutiful little female, must follow every command."

"For this request, yes." Even though his words elevated her blood pressure a notch.

Brandon chuckled while adjusting his coat. "Jon's a chip off the old block. All right, I'll leave, but not for long. Roger was my son, you know, and I consider *you* the intruder." He trudged toward the door but paused with his hand on the knob. "When will you be done?"

Relief swept through her just to see him close to the threshold. "I'm estimating five weeks, maybe longer." If she could get away with the exaggeration, she'd tell him two years.

"Five weeks? Hell, I'll be back with Iris by then." His gaze scanned her from head to toe, pausing too long on the vee between her legs. "Maybe we'll invite you to the wedding, and you and I can have a nice slow dance together." He winked and closed the door behind him.

Puke, puke, puke. Iris, you poor, dear woman.

Pulse racing, Marina whipped out her cell phone

and called Jonathan.

"He *what*?"

"You heard me. Roger gave him a key. I don't like it, Jonathan."

"Neither do I. I'll call a locksmith and have the locks changed, hopefully today. Will you be okay?"

"Yes, now that you know." She walked to the front window and peeked around the thin curtain to see Brandon standing by his car looking toward the street. "I pity Iris. He's here to get her back."

"He told me. I have no idea whether to forewarn her or not. She wants a man in her life, Marina, but I'm not certain my father is the answer. We'll talk about the subject later. I'll stop by on my way home." A short pause. "Is that okay?"

"Sure. See you then." Actually, she was thrilled. As a rule, she preferred to keep distractions to a minimum and usually told people to stay clear to allow her brain to focus, but today, she welcomed Jonathan's visit. Being in such a gloomy house and to have a man like Brandon Blandish waltz in eyeing her like a cheap whore waiting naked on a heart-shaped bed had unnerved her. She didn't like the man, plain and simple.

She returned to the china on the table and began the long process of sorting and labeling. She'd exaggerated the five weeks to Brandon, but the way things were going with the constant interruptions, the job could take that long.

Last night, she'd made a decision to wrap up the assignment in two weeks before her emotions overrode common sense. Tyler already tugged on her heart every time he ran into the room, and Iris, too, whenever they sat together at the table for chitchat. She'd spent a childhood on the defense, always waiting for the ax to fall, and in her house, the ax fell hard. Staying longer with the Blandish clan would cause irreparable damage to her psyche.

And then, of course, she had Jonathan to worry about. The man was into his sixth year of mourning with no desire to end the trend. Bad enough she stayed under his roof, but he crept into her dreams and disrupted her sleep. He, above everything else, was the reason to end the job sooner than later.

Finished with the inventory in the dining room, and after a quick lunch of a delectable chicken casserole, Marina grabbed her leather gloves and flashlight and threw open the door to the basement. Mustiness assaulted her nose along with the odor of damp dirt. *Not a good sign.* She stared at a blacker-than-black stairwell with a sick feeling settling in the pit of her stomach.

Beads of sweat formed on her brow as she fought the familiar tightness in her chest. Heart racing, she wanted to scream the muscle into a calm state, or better, to do this job another day, but she had yet to take a look at the dungeon. Maybe the basement wasn't so bad. Just because Karl's camera angle showed one light illuminating an area full of shadows didn't mean a second light wasn't hanging somewhere. She'd been in this predicament before and survived, free to come and go without fear of a locked door. No one could imprison her without a good fight.

She flipped on the light switch, which did little to illuminate the staircase. With a white-knuckled grip on the flashlight and gloves, Marina sucked in a deep breath and descended the wooden staircase.

Her heart pounded louder with each step and

caused her limbs to shake. Childhood memories flashed through her mind—the awful sound of the closet door slamming in her face, the silent prayers on her lips to help her see without light, the discomfort of sitting for hours on a coat from the overhead rack. She learned at an early age to put on a false bravado no matter what.

She stopped on the last step and shuddered.

One light bulb, hanging from a wire attached to the ceiling, lit the entire basement. Patti had discarded the forty-watt and screwed in a hundred-watt, but all four corners of the dungeon stayed in darkness. Marina swung her flashlight beam to check for a lost skeleton chained to the wall.

To this day, images of zombies creeping from the shadows clutched her throat, making air nearly impossible to pass. Sweat tickled her spine as it beaded under her sweatshirt, and she fought the urge to retreat, to leave the inspection of the basement until Jonathan demolished the house. Then, daylight would dissipate the darkness, and she'd give the area a proper evaluation.

Her stomach rolled, and she swallowed the casserole erupting into her throat. Squaring her shoulders, she stepped onto the floor and took a good look around.

The basement was exactly as she imagined—old and ignored, a return to the early nineteenth century with a packed dirt floor and ceiling low enough to touch. Her five-foot-six height enabled her to walk unhindered, but anyone over six foot needed to walk with shoulders and head hunched.

No windows, which wasn't a surprise. Lack of air flow created the musty smell and prevented the dampness from dissipating. Irregular stones formed the walls, a common cellar construction for a hundred and fifty year-old house. The stones, large and small, were of the field variety, gathered and mortared into place. Several areas showed evidence of repair with large patches of cemented chicken wire covering a bulge where the stones threatened to collapse inward. *Repaired to fix damage or to hide forty million in cash?* Well worth mentioning to Jonathan.

About a dozen cardboard boxes were piled on the floor, stacked two or three high. All had water stains half-way and looked about as sturdy as cheap paper plates. Against the wall, a disassembled motor cluttered a small workbench, its parts rusted beyond use. Underneath the bench was a metal bucket full of galvanized pipe pieces, worth nothing except in weight. Toward the left and in the midst of the ancient surroundings stood a sparkling furnace and hot water heater.

The area behind the staircase aroused her curiosity. Something had been stacked on a wooden table then covered with a sheet. She slipped on her gloves and threw the yellowed sheet to the side to see a pile of paintings, some wrapped in burlap and twine, others exposed to the open air. She picked up the first and stared at a horrible blend of colors and patterns, the signature obscured by grime. Lifting an arm, she reached for the glasses on top of her head but paused. Even with the flashlight, she hadn't enough light to see. *Best to wait 'til later.*

She returned the picture to the table and let out a heavy sigh. Paintings were not her strong point. They needed proper evaluation and cleaning by an expert.

For all she knew, she could be holding a Picasso. Everything required good lighting and room for labeling and rewrapping, and upstairs was the answer. She debated taking several paintings with her when the basement turned black.

Panic clutched her throat. Automatically, she swung the flashlight beam in every direction, searching for the zombies emerging from the walls. Had someone thrown the switch on purpose? No one knew of her phobia, but whoever had turned off the light should have called down first.

In her desperation to reach the staircase, Marina stumbled over her own feet, tripping on uneven dirt, and nearly colliding into one of the beams supporting the steps. Her heart pounded wildly, sending a surge of blood to pulse in her ears. *Whoosh-whoosh-whoosh.* Perspiration dripped into her eyes…or were they tears? *Calm down. Slow, deep breaths. I can do this.*

Something brushed her hair. She choked on a cry only to discover she'd walked into a spider web. Finally, the staircase stood before her, but her feet behaved like lead weights. She bumped the riser on every step until reaching the door and collapsing where the sunrays from the kitchen windows brightened the floor.

Sweat drenched her sweatshirt. Her breath gushed as if she had run a marathon in record time. For so long, she had endured the darkness in silence, with no tears, not even a whimper. She hadn't given the bastard the satisfaction. *And this is my payoff, a phobia too hard to shake.*

"Marina?"

She jumped half out of her skin. She hadn't heard

him come into the house.

Jonathan entered the kitchen and froze at the sight of her on the floor. With an incredulous stare, he knelt alongside, his hands reaching but not touching. "You're white as a sheet! What happened?"

She hated for him to see her this way, all weak and whimpering, like a child backed into a corner, but she blessed the air he breathed because of his sudden appearance. He'd scare off the zombies and protect her. She hung her head. "Panic attack. The light went out in the basement."

Standing, he flipped the switch, trying it several times. "Yep, the light's out. Don't tell me a grown woman with your credentials is afraid of the dark?"

Feeling like a fool, she gave him a weak grin. "Terrified is the word." With the use of her sweatshirt-covered arm, she brushed damp hair from her forehead. "You can blame my father for this. He locked us in the closet for punishment. As the oldest of four, he used me most often to set an example." She leaned her head against the wall and closed her eyes. "Whew! This is my worst attack in a long time." Ever since the lights snapped off in the Great Pyramid. Her guide had been beside himself helping her ascend the passageway. She tugged at her gloves, which were drenched and stuck to her skin. Successful, she slammed them onto the kitchen floor.

Jonathan again knelt alongside, his brows together in a scowl. "No child should endure such punishment. Where was your mother?"

"Not brave enough to intervene." She had endured torturous years in a house with a mentally abusive father. Had she not worried about her younger brother and sisters, she'd have packed her belongings and wandered the streets. But as the oldest, she suffered in silence until her brother grew strong enough to challenge their father and protect the last two. Unfortunately for her, the damage was already done.

Jonathan brushed his fingers along the upper part of her arm. "You need to relax and allow some color to return to your face." He stood and extended his hand. "Let's go to the sunroom."

She took the offered hand, and strength flowed through her fingers, but she staggered to her feet and fell against the wall with an oomph. Her knees refused to lock.

Without a word, Jonathan swept his arms under her and lifted her to his chest.

A slew of new sensations shot through her—not only a physical awareness of the man holding her so protectively, but also a feeling of weightlessness coupled with a warmth radiating throughout her body from the feel of his muscles rippling beneath his clothes. No man had ever come to her rescue, and of all people, Jonathan Blandish, a man still mourning the death of his wife.

A smile wavered on his lips. "You're lighter than you appear." With long strides, he headed for the sunroom.

Because of her father, she'd kept her distance from men, never rushing the relationship and always evaluating her beau's trust before allowing even a simple touch. Yet, she clung to Jonathan without hesitation, hardly knowing him, but wishing he'd hold onto her forever. She rested her head on his shoulder with her nose nuzzling close to his neck. His spicy aftershave was the perfect analgesic.

Entering the sunroom, the brightness of the afternoon sun was her light at the end of the tunnel. Like the strip of light seeping through the bottom of the closet door. Even as a child, she had known not to tell her parents about the light. Her father would have found a way to cover the opening.

Jonathan kissed her forehead. "This should help. How long were you locked in the closet?"

"Hours. I learned to control my bladder and my tears." To avoid looking at him, she toyed with his tie. "You can put me down." She hardly said the words with conviction since his arms eased every muscle in her body. For a split second, she hoped he'd gone stone-cold deaf.

"Marina, look at me."

She lifted her head. His light brown eyes blazed with an intensity that caught her off-guard, and she inwardly gasped. Was he about to kiss her? She wanted his lips more than she imagined, and her arms slipped around his neck. His mouth was only inches from her own, too tempting, yet, she couldn't look away.

His lips parted.

Well, I'll be damned.

She met his lips halfway, savoring the softness and the pinch of stubble from his lower lip. His kiss was gentle, a suckling with only a hint of exploration, a man unsure of how far to push himself. She let him take his time since her own feelings were a jumbled mess.

"Yoo, hoo, Mr. Blandish, Dr. Cavanaugh!"

Jonathan gave an audible gasp and pulled away before dropping Marina onto a worn divan.

What the hell...

He stepped toward the door, his body unnaturally stiff. His gaze darted, like an animal trapped in a corner. In an instant, he turned from hot to cold.

"In the sunroom, Patti." He stuffed his hands into his trouser pockets.

Bracing a hand on the sofa back, Marina struggled to sit up.

Patti ambled in and gave a quick glance at Marina, eyes widening. "Good heavens, Doctor, you look awful pale. What happened?"

Damned if I know. She managed a shaky grin. "Panic attack. The basement's a little creepy."

"I wondered why your gloves and flashlight were by the door. Roger never went into the basement much. Most of the stuff was left by the previous owners." She shifted on her feet. "Can I get you anything?"

"Yes, Patti, please, some water." And a sedative. And a cold shower.

Nodding, Patti hurried from the room.

Marina glared at Jonathan who stood like a board nailed to a wall. "Well, that was new. I've never had a man toss me before. Are you two an item?"

Her voice broke his stiff stance, and his widened gaze drifted toward her. "What made you say that?"

"You dropped me like your wife appeared." Eyebrows high, she scanned the sunroom. "I don't see her ghost anywhere."

"Don't be ridiculous."

Patti returned with a large glass of water.

Taking the glass, Marina thanked her and drank the fluid in four gulps.

"Maybe you shouldn't go to the basement unless one of us is here," Jonathan said.

"Actually, I'd like to carry all the stuff to the sunroom so I can do a better inspection."

"Not a bad idea." He removed his suit jacket and tie and tossed them both on a side chair. "What do you say, Patti? Are you up to a little stair climbing?" He rolled up his shirt sleeves. "Get me a light bulb first. I'll change the one that burned out in the basement."

"That was brand new," Patti said, her voice rising.

"Then perhaps the socket has a limit. We'll lower the wattage." With a furtive glance at Marina, he hurried from the sunroom with Patti close behind.

Marina stared after them, not in the least willing to move. Her legs were weak from her panic attack. His kiss weakened them further, and she wasn't sure how sturdy she'd be on her feet. *So, what the hell happened?* Patti's interruption was like a cold bucket of water, dousing a flame that barely sparked. She hadn't experienced such a stunned state since the day her brother stood up to their father.

Releasing the hair clip, she slipped all ten fingers into her hair and pulled. She yanked several times, mindful that her frustration levels might cause her to rip out her hair by its roots.

He has no right to confuse me like this.

Friggin' men.

She gathered her hair strands and replaced the clip before standing to check the condition of her legs. Satisfied they'd bear weight, she headed for the kitchen.

Chapter Eleven

Jonathan welcomed the distraction of a burned-out light bulb, a simple but effective task to help take his mind off Marina. His lips still radiated the heat of her kiss. She had tasted wonderful. Soft, luscious, and moist. The essence of a woman. She'd returned the kiss with a depth he hadn't expected, but now, guilt consumed him. She had been weak and vulnerable from her scare in the dark. But with her lips so close, he couldn't stop himself.

When he'd entered the kitchen and spotted her cowering on the floor, he reacted with a strong protective gene. The old damsel-in-distress scenario—a beautiful, frightened woman who gripped his heart and held firm. Unshed tears had moistened her eyes, and then, to carry her in his arms, to feel her soft curves…hell, he was a man after all and couldn't resist the flood of satisfaction at coming to her rescue.

"I had screwed in a hundred-watt bulb, Mr. Blandish. Do you want to try another wattage, like one of the LED kind?"

Jonathan jerked, not sure where he was. "What?" He had followed Patti into the pantry where she stored the bulbs and flashlight batteries. "Yes, Patti, I'll take a chance with a seventy-five or an LED equivalent."

"Hold on, you two." Marina rushed into the kitchen, the paleness gone, a plastic bag clasped in her hand. "We're using hazmat suits." She handed them out. "I'm not sure the length will fit you, Jonathan, but the suit should give some protection."

He dropped one to full length and held the fabric against his body. The hems hit a half-foot short.

Patti giggled. "Maybe you should let the doctor and I do this, Mr. Blandish."

"I'll use it anyway." He struggled into the garment, but the crotch cut deep into his balls, conjuring images of a career as a soprano at the opera house. With a frown, he met Marina's twinkling gaze and then tore off the suit. "I can afford to ruin my clothes." Grabbing a flashlight, he descended the staircase.

After Roger's burial, Jonathan hadn't bothered with anything but a cursory inspection of the house contents. Once he'd read the will, he expected Roger's fortune to be found among his financial records, not hidden in an obscure message about an antiques appraiser.

He descended to the last step and stopped, swinging the flashlight beam over the area. The place resembled a dungeon without bars. The lone light hung from a wire near the steps, an easy reach. He unscrewed the burned-out bulb and replaced it with a new one, but the seventy-five watt did little to alleviate the dark corners.

The low ceiling was an inconvenience. He could stand straight with his head between two floor joists, but to move around meant kinking his neck. If Roger had stripped another foot of dirt off the floor, he'd allow a normal-height man to walk around without feeling like Quasimodo.

Stacks of cardboard boxes flanked one wall. None

appeared strong enough to survive a trip upstairs. Several piles of wrapped pictures rested on a table behind the stairs, one completely exposed to show the worst art piece he'd ever seen. All of them looked as ancient as the house.

His foot bumped something on the floor. A pair of Marina's glasses. She was probably staring at this ugly piece when the light went out, and the image of a cowering woman returned to mind. How could any father lock his child in a closet for punishment? Her fear was phenomenal, but despite her father's cruelty, Marina had turned into a lovely woman. Smart, independent…well, too independent for her own good. And she had a definite problem with authority. He placed the glasses in his breast pocket.

The rear of the house had a metal coal chute built into the wall with the remnants of a square brick partition on the floor to catch the coal—the fuel of choice eons ago. A new oil furnace currently provided heat. The rectangular apparatus sat in the center of the basement floor with aluminum vent ducts resembling the legs of an upside-down spider, stretching outward to allow air flow into the upper part of the house. The steel oil tank hid in the shadows against the wall with a feeder line buried into the dirt floor.

The women descended, Patti first. Marina's steps faltered as if debating whether to continue. Both wore the white hazmat suits and gloves, looking like a crime-scene cleanup crew—one cute and cuddly with her auburn hair clipped in the back, the other resembling a snowman without the hat, leg sleeves rolled up to accommodate her short height.

Jonathan stomped his foot on the hard dirt. "Once

we carry everything upstairs, I'll give the floor a good inspection in case Roger hid his stash under the dirt." Not that he believed his own words. Roger wasn't one to pick up a shovel and do manual labor.

They managed to remove the contents of the basement in no time, in spite of three boxes falling apart at the seams. They piled what they could into the sunroom with the overflow inching into the dining room. Everything was covered with years of dust including their clothes. The women's white suits had changed to a smudged gray, and his pale lemon dress shirt was a goner. They gathered at the kitchen table for a break, sandwiches and iced tea before them.

"Why in thunder didn't Roger empty this house before he moved in?" Jonathan complained. "I can't believe he left so much junk."

Patti bit into her sandwich and chewed. "I asked him the same question." She swallowed. "He said one day, he'd go through the stuff and find a real treasure." She dropped the sandwich onto her plate and, with both hands, covered her mouth and nose to contain a double sneeze.

Marina downed a large portion of her iced tea. "I usually throw supplies in the rear of my SUV when I go on assignment, but for some reason, I forgot the masks."

Using a napkin, Patti released another double sneeze then rubbed her nose. "If you want, I can run out today and buy some."

"That's a plan, Patti, along with more hazmat suits. I'm afraid we'll need them." She took her fork and stabbed a sweet pickle from the jar. "By the way, Henry Ladner stopped by yesterday." She placed the pickle right into her mouth and bit down.

"Yes, he came by my house around dinnertime." She tilted her head toward Jonathan. "You remember him, don't you, Mr. Blandish?"

"Of course." He hadn't liked Henry from the second they met. He was Patti's old school chum and a man who had worked with Roger. Other than that, Jonathan couldn't care if the man took a long walk off a short pier. He tore into his sandwich like a starving Neanderthal.

"Henry said he will stop by later." With a napkin, Patti wiped her mouth. "We go way back, Dr. Cavanaugh."

Not far enough, Jonathan fumed. He wasn't sure why he disliked Henry. The man had never done anything to annoy him. Except breathe. He swallowed the contents in his mouth. "Patti, we carried about three dozen paintings to the sunroom. Were any of them Roger's?"

"Not to my knowledge. Like I said, I think they came with the house."

"They've been wrapped and tied for at least thirty years," Marina volunteered. "Maybe longer. I haven't checked the attic yet. We might find more."

Again, Patti sneezed. "If I'm done, Mr. Blandish, I'll run home and take a shower. Then, I'll go and buy the masks and suits." She slid back her chair and stood. "Do you need anything else?"

"No, Patti. Thanks for your help." Picking up the iced tea pitcher, he refilled his glass and Marina's.

The doorbell rang.

"I'll get it," Patti said with a wave. "It might be Henry." She hurried from the kitchen.

Jane Drager

Marina stared after her while sipping her tea. "I'm pleased Patti has a boyfriend." Cocking a brow, she looked at him and lowered her glass. "Is something wrong? You seem grumpier than usual."

"I'm not grumpy. Just irritable as hell and no clue why." What a lie. He knew precisely why. He had broken a promise to himself as well as Susan and had no way to rectify his error in judgment. He had kissed Marina. And to be alone with her again…

His own fault. He could kick himself for being so damn weak.

Patti returned, brow raised, a finger pointing over her shoulder. "A locksmith is at the door, Mr. Blandish. He gave your name."

Jonathan rotated on his seat to face her. "Yes, I called for new locks. All three doors are to be changed. And tell him only three keys. My father surprised Marina today by walking in unannounced."

Her mouth gaped, but she hurried to instruct the locksmith.

Marina helped herself to another pickle. "Thank you."

Leaning back, he grunted. "I'd like to know how my father obtained a key."

"Roger and your father probably got along better than you think." She crunched on the pickle. "Duke knows about Roger's brass bed."

My damn father and his stupid nicknames. "Duke isn't his real name. He likes to give the impression of being young and virile when he flits from one self-centered woman to another." He narrowed his gaze. "How'd the subject of the bed come up?"

"Take a guess." She sipped her tea, watching over

the rim.

His food instantly churned in his stomach. He dropped his sandwich onto the plate and stared. "Are you kidding me? My father hit on you?"

"I got the impression his flirts were a matter of habit." She lowered her glass to the table. "For the record, the man's a complete turn-off."

A sour taste developed on his tongue and, for damn sure, not because of the sandwich. Nothing had changed with his father. The man never knew when to keep his mouth shut.

Patti re-entered with Henry in tow. "Look who appeared right behind the locksmith." She jerked a thumb over her shoulder.

With one sweep of his gaze, Jonathan sized up Henry and remembered why the man annoyed him. At the gathering after Roger's funeral, Henry acted like a ladies' man and flirted with every female on two feet—married, single, young, and old. He commented on a dress or a piece of jewelry, all at embarrassing lengths. As if he was God's gift to women, when in fact he was a chubby little man who worked behind a desk for a living.

Henry approached Jonathan and extended his hand. "How's your mom doing?"

Not to cause a scene, he shook Henry's hand but remained seated at the table. "She's not complaining. You've met Dr. Cavanaugh?"

His dark gaze sparkling, Henry turned to Marina. "You didn't introduce yourself as a doctor."

"PhD."

Henry flashed her his god-awful smile that was more a sneer caused by the cut on his upper lip. Women had called it sexy. What a laugh! The smile was more lecherous than sexy.

With a quick glance at Marina, Jonathan studied her reaction. Non-committal. Polite was a good word, neither smiling nor expressing interest, no dilated pupils. A sensible woman. Even so, he wanted Henry out of the kitchen and away from Marina before he strangled the man. Which in itself was puzzling. Marina was another employee, nothing more.

Patti grabbed her plate and utensils and carried them to the sink. "I'll leave now and take Henry with me."

"Don't hurry in tomorrow morning." Jonathan wiped his mouth with a napkin. "You won't have the new key."

"Right."

Jonathan watched them leave but not without a silent good riddance. When he turned his attention to Marina, he found her watching him with an amused glint.

"You don't like him much, do you?"

"Very perceptive." He sipped his iced tea.

"Why?"

Before answering, Jonathan shoved the last of his sandwich into his mouth and chewed so he wouldn't choke to death. "It's a male thing. Every time we meet, the hairs on my neck rise." He swallowed what remained in his mouth.

Marina rested her elbows on the table, holding her glass to her lips with both hands. "Territorial response?"

"Don't be ridiculous." She could be right. A primitive gene destined to trigger no matter how civil a man. But, of all men, why Henry? Jonathan rotated his chair to face Marina, crossed his legs, and sighed. "I never knew Henry until Roger introduced us at a business luncheon for his clients. When Henry heard Roger needed a housekeeper, he recommended Patti who happened to live across the street."

"Convenient for Patti." She lowered her glass to the table. "Are you afraid he'll take her away?"

"She's an employee, no more."

"Like me."

"Yes, like you." The words irritated him. She might be a paid employee, but he couldn't quite place her in the same category as Patti.

Marina finished the last of her tea and wiped her mouth. "Why don't you admit you have feelings for Patti?"

He glowered at the suggestion. "Because I don't, not in the way you suggest. I like my women as good-looking as you."

Aw, shit. If he was standing, he'd kick himself in the ass for losing that vital brain/mouth connection. Moving hastily, he stood and nearly toppled the chair. "Do you mind clearing the table? I'm going into the basement to have a look around." He grabbed the flashlight and hurriedly descended the stairs, mindful of the woman with her beautiful mouth agape.

He was acting like a fool. Marina was more than an employee. She had awakened long-buried emotions that died with his wife, and her presence slowly chipped away his iron-clad willpower. He wanted to be with Marina every second of the day, and yet, he wanted her as far away as possible. She had a pull that was unmistakable, and distance was his best defense. *How can I keep my distance when I insisted she stay under my roof?* The internal conflict was enough to drive him mad.

Thankful for the gloominess of the basement, he glared at the ineffective light bulb before swinging the flashlight beam into the shadowed corners. The cellar stretched the full length of the house so its size was substantial, far too large for a single light bulb dangling by the stairwell. He expected to see rusted chains and maybe a noose or two to complete the dungeon look, but instead, he found several rusted eye-hooks screwed into the floor joists.

When footsteps echoed on the stairs, he turned as Marina descended and then settled on a step midway. She had removed the hair clip, and her lovely hair hung loose onto her shoulders. "You don't have to be here, Marina."

Gaze darting, she hugged her knees. "Yes, I know, but I need to conquer this phobia."

He admired her courage and cursed the man who caused her fear, along with the mother who hadn't intervened. Both of them should be stripped of their parental privileges and thrown into a locked cell.

After grabbing a metal pipe from a bucket, he pounded sections of the floor. "The dirt's packed solid." He hit several areas on the stone wall, half-expecting the rocks to tumble to the floor.

"How about the coal chute?" She pointed toward the rear of the house.

He walked over, gripped the latch, and tugged. "Rusted shut. This hasn't been opened in a long time." He wandered to the wooden workbench. Scattered pieces of corroded motor parts covered the surface, along with a screwdriver without a handle and pliers rusted in an open position. He moved the largest piece of the motor and spotted a folded sheet of paper, still white and crisp. He opened the paper.

Jonathan:

I have never been a demonstrative man, but when I look at the sleekness of Marina Cavanaugh, I become tongue-tied, like a boy on his first date. That is why I chose her to conceal my secret. Keep her cool to keep her safe but, above all, do not abandon her to this house. She's worth more than her weight in gold.

Roger

Doubts collided. This was Roger's second note mentioning Marina's name. Was she as innocent as she claimed? How could he be sure she wasn't playing him for a sap?

"Jonathan?"

He glanced up into her questioning gaze. "Another note from Roger." He hadn't become a successful businessman by being a gullible idiot. If she knew where Roger hid the money, would she endure the darkness of this forsaken house just to bide her time? He scanned the basement's shadows. With her phobia, he thought not. Besides, she could just as easily stuff the stash in her SUV and say *adios*.

No, every fiber in his being believed her. Roger implicated Marina for reasons unknown.

"What's it say?"

He considered her request then walked to the staircase to hand her the note.

She read quickly, her brows rising halfway into her hairline. With a shaking hand, she returned the note, meeting his gaze. "I never knew your brother, Jonathan.

You have to believe that."

"I do, Marina." He folded the note and slipped the paper into his breast pocket. "Why did my brother have to be so cryptic? What does he mean by keeping you cool?" He was talking to himself. She stared into the distance, her face as blank as the underside of the note. She looked vulnerable and alone, and her shoulders slumped as evidence, a direct contrast from her proud, confident persona. "How long have you had this fear of the dark, Marina?"

She focused on one of the dark corners. "I'm worse now than when I was little." She shifted her stare to her feet. "I never let my parents know how the closet frightened me. Even though I had a strip of light at the bottom of the door, I couldn't help developing this phobia. Sudden darkness is the kicker. My throat tightens, and then I can't breathe." She sighed heavily, glanced in his direction, and gave a weak grin. "By the time I was thirteen, I was strong enough to break open the door. Then, I'd break it open for my younger siblings. This resulted in more severe punishment with a chair jammed against the doorknob. Eventually, my brother grew in both height and weight and obliterated the closet door. From that point, he took over protecting the youngest two since I was on my way to college. As the oldest, I had the longest run of punishment."

What would possess a parent to punish a child in such a way? Discipline could certainly be obtained by other means. "Did your father beat you?"

She met his gaze. "No. Bruises show, and teachers are required to report stuff like that." She shook herself then scanned him from head to toe, one side of her mouth curling into a smile. "You made a mess of your clothes."

He frowned at the hand prints smearing his trousers. "You changed the subject quickly enough."

"I'm changing it again. I could use some fresh air. Feel like taking a walk?"

"I thought you'd never ask. I'll see how the locksmith's doing, and we'll head out when he's done."

Chapter Twelve

Marina snapped up her hood to protect her head from the chilly air. The afternoon was another typical March day with blustery winds and below-average temperatures, especially out in the backyard with the breeze whipping through the open fields. Despite the cold, she'd rather freeze to death than spend the entire time inside Roger's dreary abode.

They'd discovered another note as vague and meaningless as the first. What had Roger meant about *keep her cool to keep her safe*? Nothing made sense with that damn man. All right, Patti had mentioned about Roger's cool house temps and how she turned up the heat several notches after his death, but why Marina Cavanaugh? Why not Patti, or his mother?

Jonathan reached for her arm. "Watch the dip here."

They exited from the sunroom after testing their new door keys and walked straight out the back to the field. The view wasn't picturesque by any definition of the word, just a wide, open space full of dormant grass, stretching over small hills and valleys. From a dreary house into a dreary outdoors. Everything about this job was depressing. She turned to face the house.

The parsonage/farmhouse had a back view as devoid of habitation as the front. No covered lawn furniture or barbecue grill, no awnings, not even a potted plant. The block-like building had no personality whatsoever.

"I often questioned why Roger bought such a dump." Jonathan stepped alongside and stuffed his hands into his overcoat pockets, his gaze fixed on the house. "Now that I'm staring at the rear, I see how the place fits him." He sighed heavily and stole a glance in her direction. "My brother was a loner, like his house sitting in the middle of ten acres. I can picture him standing on a hill with no one around for miles and be perfectly happy."

"In comparison, your house is a palace."

"That's my mother's doing. And speaking of my mother—" He faced her, his brows drawing together into a scowl. "I'd appreciate if you keep your ideas to yourself."

Marina met his gaze with as straight a face as possible. "And what ideas are you talking about?"

"She wants to fall in love." He rolled his eyes and turned to continue their walk.

His pace was leisurely, unlike their first venture where his strides surpassed hers two to one. She matched his steps, unwilling to let the topic drop. "I don't recall an age limit to love, Jonathan."

He snorted. "She's sixty-one, past her prime."

Marina stopped, forcing him to look back. "I guess you'd rather put her in a rocker with an afghan around her shoulders and two knitting needles in her hands. And let's not forget the silver-rimmed glasses perched on the tip of her nose." While shaking her head, she continued up the hill.

Jonathan hurried to place himself before her and walked backward. "She's better off with me."

Oh, dear Lord, how archaic. "In other words, she can't have her own life, because you want her to take care of yours. That's a bit selfish."

"She's my mother whom, I emphasize, has no money of her own." He turned to face forward. "She couldn't afford her own place."

Marina stopped to stare. "You mean her millionaire son won't pay the rent?"

"I never said I won't support her financially." He glanced over his shoulder. "All I'm asking from you is not to put ideas into her head."

The man was impossible. She picked up a rock, half tempted to knock some sense into his head but, instead, hurled it across the field. "Iris had her ideas long before I came along, Jonathan. The woman feels life is passing by. Her husband dumped her for a younger woman, and she had her ego crushed." She kicked a clump of weeds to watch them scatter with the breeze. "She needs to know if she still has the capability to attract a new mate and live the happily-ever-after dream. As a woman, I understand her frustration."

"I don't. I thought she was happy enough."

"Maybe you should talk to her more. She's not happy at all."

Scowling, he held up a finger. "That's none of your concern."

"Then, fire me! I don't need this job." She stuffed her hands into her pockets. A safety precaution. Otherwise, she might take a swing at his handsome face. She stopped to close her eyes and inhale a large breath. Sensing his nearness, she shot him a one-eyed glance. "Obviously, you and I will continue to butt heads on a lot of subjects. I'm just surprised you show no interest in your mother's happiness." She hurried up an incline.

Under normal circumstances, she'd dismiss a family's personal problems and stay as far as possible from their squabbles, but right or wrong, she'd fight for Iris. The woman deserved a chance at a new life and to not grow old raising a grandchild. Whatever Jonathan planned for his own future was his problem, and if his agenda included mourning his late wife forever, then so be it.

They strolled side-by-side in silence, he more in step with her than the other way around. The wind blew his hair in every direction, and the effect gave him an appealing ruggedness. Despite her annoyance, she felt comfortable with the man. He might be bossy, but he was not unyielding and definitely not abusive.

He cleared his throat. "I paid a visit to Roger's boss this morning. He confirmed the embezzlement. Roger created an elaborate money trail that leads roundabout to Brussels. Then nothing."

One brow raised, she tilted her head toward him. "Was Roger planning to relocate?"

"Not to my knowledge. After the hedge fund office, I stopped by the police station. The detective handling the case was out so I left a message." He adjusted his overcoat.

They arrived at the crest of another hill. The lake stretched to the left where they had confronted Karl. To the right, an old, gnarled oak tree stood in mighty splendor to preside over the landscape.

Memories of fun times in her grandmother's backyard floated into her mind. Grandmama had an old oak that Marina climbed on every visit. She'd lie on the fat limbs for hours and wish for wings like the birds overhead, to fly away from her abusive parents. In the year of her sixteenth birthday, a lightning bolt had split the tree in two. A year later, her grandmother died. Saddest day of Marina's life. "How far does the property go?"

"Over the next hill." He pointed then cupped his hands to blow warm breath into them. "The air's cold. Want to go back?"

She jerked her gaze from the tree and sniffed. "I'm fine." Actually, the wind cut through her like a razor. Yet, she had no desire to return to the house nor end this casual conversation. She liked talking to him—if he wasn't ordering her around. "When you discovered your brother was worth forty-two million, what passed through your mind?"

"That he had a certifiable screw loose." He continued over the crest before glancing her way. "I stayed quiet for that reason, Marina. I couldn't find any evidence of where or what he was talking about." Taking her elbow, he guided her around a hole. "Have you discovered anything substantial?"

"Not yet." She looked down at the hole. Vole, more likely. They loved open fields. She tucked some loose strands of hair back into her hood. "I can use some help, Jonathan. Do you mind if I enlist Patti? She can pack as I go and save a lot of time. So far, most of Roger's stuff is destined for our secondary auction house, the one where common household items are sold. Anything worth more than a thousand dollars will stay with Mrs. Billingsley for a proper auction...oops!" Her hood flew off as her foot sank into a groundhog hole.

He caught her arm. "You okay?"

"I'm good. Hold still." She placed her hand on his shoulder to steady herself while she shook the dirt from her sneaker. His hand slipped to her back protectively, and she immediately felt the warmth through her jacket. Resisting the urge to fake a swoon, she stepped away and adjusted her jacket. "Thank you."

"No problem." He met her gaze then quickly looked away. "I'm sorry I kissed you, Marina." He returned his hands to his coat pockets.

She looked at his wind-blown hair and slightly red ears. "Are you really?"

"Yes." He stared into the distance, jaw tight. "I'm not ready. I loved my wife very much."

"I'm not here to seduce you. You're paying me to do a job, nothing more."

He met her unwavering gaze. "Then why did you kiss me back?"

This time, she looked away. How could she tell him she melted from the taste of his lips? He'd bolt like a scared rabbit. "I was under the impression that our kiss was a mutual reaction."

He stopped her by touching her arm, a smile flickering on his lips. "I enjoyed every second, Marina, but I can't let it happen again."

They reached the next crest where he jerked to a stop and motioned toward the left with a nod of his head. "That's Karl's white van."

She followed his gaze and spotted the vehicle parked along an access road. "I guess he didn't take being fired seriously. What's he near...oh, the cemetery." She gasped and gripped his arm. "Maybe he deciphered a series of clues and is digging out Roger's buried treasure!"

His jaw twitched. "What clues? I don't have any, and I doubt Karl does." With long strides, he headed toward the van. "I want to know why he's on the property."

Marina ran to catch up. "If he's looking at cameras again, what do you say we beat him to a pulp?"

He rotated his head and smiled. "I'm game."

She was all for charging down the hill and jumping Karl, but as they approached, Jonathan held out a finger and gestured for her to check the driver's front window. She peeked and gave a thumbs-down.

Jonathan threw open the rear panel doors, but the interior was empty.

Reaching with two fingers, Marina lifted a worn overcoat from the van's floor. "I don't see his laptop or the canvas bag for his cameras."

"The son-of-a-bitch is setting them up again." He pointed to an open tool box. "He shouldn't need tools." His gaze scanned the open pasture. "Where the hell is he?"

"Maybe he's in the woods taking a pee." She wandered to the edge of the cemetery. The area was eerily quiet with the wind creating soft whistles as the current blew through the tombstones. A makeshift stone wall surrounded the perimeter of the graveyard, most sections collapsing with age while ivy acted like a net to hold the rest together. The yard contained about sixty grave markers, some tall, others small. The names on two of the stones caught her eye, and she gasped. *Oh, my God.* "Jon!" She pointed.

"Jonathan, dammit." He hurried alongside and

froze.

They stared at the Cavanaugh name carved into the stones.Finally, an answer to Roger's cryptic messages. She almost jumped with joy. "That's why Karl's here. He found her!"

"Let's read the headstones, Marina. You take the left side of the cemetery, and I'll cover the other side."

"But where's Karl?" Squinting, she scanned the surrounding area. "If he found the treasure, why leave the van?"

"We'll deal with Karl after we inspect the stones."

Several of the carvings were weather-worn with lettering barely legible. A few markers had broken in two and collapsed into a heap. The cemetery was long forgotten, a plot in the middle of nowhere, slowly being buried by weeds and leaves from lack of care.

A dark shape caught her eye lying at the far end beneath a pillar. Curious, she meandered around several old stones until reaching the pillar and stopped. Her gut wrenched, and she clutched her arms tight to her chest. "Jon!"

He ran over. "*Jonathan*! Why can't you—" He stopped in his tracks.

Karl lay prone in the weeds with a steel file protruding from his back, his blood saturating jacket and ground alike.

****

Marina had a difficult time keeping down her lunch since the image of Karl's bloodied corpse danced in her mind and wouldn't leave. Once the police arrived, Jonathan handled the details while a female officer escorted Marina back to the house where she collapsed onto the sofa.

Shortly after, Jonathan entered followed by a tall, heavy-set man in a black overcoat. Glancing at Marina, Jonathan did a quick double-take. Probably because she looked as if a bucket should be by her mouth.

"Marina, this is Detective Nick Farnsworth from Boston PD." He touched the top of her head. "You okay?"

She shrugged in answer.

They stayed in the living room—Jonathan standing by a side chair with his arms folded across his chest, Marina still on the sofa, and the big man positioned between them.

Farnsworth reminded Marina of every cliché applied to a TV detective. Rumpled in appearance with wind-blown hair and wrinkled trouser legs, he lumbered more than walked with shoulders stooped as if the woes of the world rested on his spine. His face revealed the creases of a hard life, his nose broken at one time as evidenced by the twist to one side, and his skin held the color of a man who stayed indoors too often. Dark circles surrounded a pair of analytical gray eyes that sharpened substantially as Jonathan explained Karl's purpose, about the missing money, and the mystery of Marina Cavanaugh.

Jonathan uncrossed his arms. "I stopped by your office and left a message for you to call. Too much was happening around here."

While using a pencil hardly big enough for his hand, Farnsworth scribbled into a small notebook. "I haven't been to the office all day." He dotted a few i's with enough force to break his pencil point then glared at the tip. "You might think someone would let me know." He took another pencil from his suit pocket, not much bigger than the last one. More scribbling. "The money gives us a strong motive for your brother's murder, Blandish. I should throw you in jail for obstruction of justice."

"But I had no idea if Roger exaggerated his net worth until Karl's embezzlement story."

Farnsworth narrowed his gaze. "All right, I'll go with that excuse. Did you find a tombstone for Marina Cavanaugh?"

"After we found Karl's body, we stopped looking."

With a quick nod, Farnsworth glanced around the living room. "I'll have one of the officers check out the stones. And in the meantime, my men can scan the house and garage for more cameras. We have some sophisticated sensing equipment." He paused, a frown forming on his weathered face. "What I don't understand is why Towson's identity wasn't uncovered." He scribbled while gritting his teeth. "Damn rookies these days. No one's thorough."

His cell phone rang. After a short conversation, he replaced the phone to his pocket. "Negative on the laptop and canvas bag on the property. My guess, Towson recorded the murder of your brother and agreed to meet the killer for a blackmail payoff. Let me see your hands, Blandish, palms up."

With a quizzical lift to his brow, Jonathan followed the instructions.

Farnsworth studied his hands. "Your turn, Doctor."

After a quick glance at Jonathan, Marina rotated her hands, feeling like Tyler and his "all clean" statement.

"Where are your gloves?"

She met the detective's piercing gaze, and her gut

twisted. "My winter gloves or work gloves?"

"Both."

"Winter gloves in the SUV, used work gloves in the kitchen, new gloves in a tote in my SUV."

"All right. You, Blandish?"

His gaze narrowed. "Just winter gloves in my car. Why?"

Farnsworth opened the front door and gestured to the officer standing on the porch. "Have the lab boys bag their gloves." He turned back to Jonathan. "Because a steel file plunged into a man's thorax would rip hands and gloves alike. Your hands show no evidence, but the gloves might."

Jonathan's face flushed to the color of a cooked beet, and his gaze shot fireballs at Farnsworth. Marina wasn't thrilled at the detective's implication either. If her knees weren't so wobbly, she'd stand and confront the man.

"You think we killed him?" Jonathan asked through tight lips.

Farnsworth waved aside the comment. "Relax. I have to follow every possible lead." His gaze surveyed him from head to toe. "Explain why you're so dirty."

Forcing out a large breath, Jonathan told him about the basement contents being lugged to the sunroom.

The detective lumbered into the dining room to confirm the story before plodding back. "Where's your hazmat suit, Doctor?"

The question startled her, and she glanced up with a slight lift to her brow. "In the trash bag in the kitchen along with Patti's."

"And where's Miss Gleisberg?"

Jonathan ran his fingers through his hair. "She took

off with Henry Ladner, her old school chum. He also worked with Roger."

"Is that right?" With his tongue, Farnsworth wet the tip of the pencil.

Marina shifted her butt on the uncomfortable sofa. She should stand like the two men, but a dead body wasn't a common occurrence in her line of work, especially one with a heavy-duty file in his back. She glanced at Jonathan. "Is it too late to quit?"

Farnsworth bent to place his face close. "You're involved, Doctor. I don't want you to leave the area until I clear you, understood?"

Scowling, Jonathan stepped forward. "Surely, you can't suspect Marina."

"Everyone is suspect, Blandish." Farnsworth straightened. "As for the doctor, she has strong hands and could have easily plunged the file into Towson."

Great. She envisioned finishing *Antiques 102* in a jail cell. Marina tucked a strand of hair behind her ear while looking at Jonathan. "You want to tell him about Duke?"

Farnsworth's gaze darted to Jonathan. "Who's Duke?"

Shifting on his feet, Jonathan scowled. "My damn father. He showed up today with a key."

The detective's eyebrow twitched. "That's interesting." He examined the nub of his pencil and frowned. "Where can I find him?"

"I haven't a clue. I told him to rent a hotel room."

"What's he driving?"

"A black sedan." He stuffed his hands into his trouser pockets. "I was too aggravated to notice more."

Marina cleared her throat. "Mercury Marquee,

older model black, one hubcap missing from the rear wheel driver's side. License plate SXYLVR."

The two men stared.

She lifted one shoulder in a half-hearted shrug. "I have a trained eye for details." Like Farnsworth hadn't polished his shoes in months while Jonathan's still shined despite the dirt in the basement and the walk in the pasture.

While writing, Farnsworth snorted. "Sexy lover plate. That's rich."

The detective had yet to smile. Of course, he had no reason to, but a show of sympathy would be nice. Unless, of course, he had the worst dental care ever, and half his teeth were rotted.

"Well, Blandish, forty million is a hell of an inheritance." He met Jonathan's glare. "Don't look at me that way. You stand to gain the most from your brother's unfortunate demise. For all we know, you killed Karl, disposed of his equipment, and then came in here to help the doctor unload the basement. A clever plan, but I'll wait for the medical examiner to give me a proper time of death before I make more accusations." He flipped a page on his notebook while giving them both a stern stare. "If I uncover evidence that you two knew each other prior to this, I'll put you both behind bars." He locked his gaze onto Jonathan. "I want to see your brother's note so our lab can authenticate the handwriting."

Jonathan slipped two fingers into his breast pocket. "Here. We found this note today." Holding only the edges, he handed him the paper.

Farnsworth extracted a latex glove and small plastic bag from his coat pocket and, using the glove, gingerly took the paper by the corner and read. Finished, he slipped the note into the bag then placed both bag and glove into his pocket. "And the first note?"

"In Roger's legal papers at my house."

"Oh? Why didn't we find such an important piece of evidence when we skimmed through his papers?"

"Because my mother found it tucked in Marina's book, *Antiques 101*."

"Ah, so your mother found the note. I'll need her statement." More scribbling. Sighing heavily, he slapped shut his notebook then slipped the tablet into his breast pocket. "I planned on retiring soon, but I won't leave the Roger Blandish murder unsolved. Unlucky for me, I have Towson's on the list. If this continues, I may die at my desk." He faced Marina, an eyebrow quirked. "Are you staying in this house, Doctor?"

"No. Jonathan insisted I stay at his place."

Eyeing Jonathan, Farnsworth twitched his jaw. "Why's that, Blandish?"

Jonathan paced behind the sofa. "I won't have her stay alone with everything that's happening. I want her safe in my house with my family. You have a problem with that, Detective?"

"Not at all, son, but I could also say you don't want her to find the money without you."

Marina gasped. The thought hadn't entered her mind! She whirled on the seat to stare at Jonathan. "Is that true?"

"Oh, good grief." The pacing stopped, and he stiffened, his gaze hard. "I've no intention of keeping the money. I already told Roger's boss."

Farnsworth adjusted his overcoat. "At least I'll know where the doctor is. I suggest you make sure nothing happens to her, Blandish. This whole case smells worse than rotten eggs." He strode toward the front door. "Stay here until I return, and then I'll follow you home."

Jonathan frowned at the closed front door. "I'm sorry I dragged you into this, Marina."

After struggling to her feet, Marina rubbed her butt. Her buns had fallen asleep from the hard cushions. *Like sitting on a rock.* "You and Karl withheld vital information from the police and made the trail go cold. You deserve to be a prime suspect."

Without a word, he wandered to the front windows to stare through the opened curtains, his face an emotionless mask. Her image of him standing alone intensified—a man with no one to confide in, protecting a son too young to understand and a mother from needless worry. Not like she felt sorry for him. He chose to conceal the information and brought the solitude on himself.

After a few minutes, he turned his head to give her a wan smile. "I didn't kill anyone, Marina. You have to believe that."

Looking away, she wasn't sure what to believe anymore. Two murders. Missing money. The questionable use of her name. Too many unanswered questions. And she had become part of the suspect list.

Chapter Thirteen

Jonathan drove home feeling like a locomotive pulling the rest of the train. Marina followed in her red SUV with Farnsworth hugging the rear in his black Ford. If Tyler was in the back seat, he'd have a field day playing engineer.

As he pulled into his driveway, he activated the automatic garage door button on his dashboard and waved to Marina and the detective to continue toward the front door. Since he hadn't warned his mother about the extra company, he hurried from the garage to the front to open the door.

Upon entering, Farnsworth caught Marina's elbow and spoke softly close to her ear.

She nodded with a quick glance toward Jonathan before hanging up her coat and heading toward the kitchen.

"I'll see that note now, Blandish."

"Do you mind if I hang my coat first?" He took his time, mainly because he hated to be ordered around in his own home. Bad enough he was grinding his teeth into a powder, but a headache threatened to pound the hair off his scalp. After closing the closet door, he led the detective to the den. Not bothering to sit, Jonathan opened a desk drawer and extracted a manila folder. He found the first note and extended the paper. Farnsworth repeated his routine with latex glove and plastic bag. A deep frown creased his face as he compared the two notes. "Looks like the same handwriting, but I'm no expert."

"I've another of his letters in this folder somewhere." He rummaged through bank statements and probate waivers.

"No, thanks, Blandish. I'll let our lab compare a sample that hasn't been in your possession. Who handled this note?"

"Me, my mother, and Marina."

"Good. We already have yours and your mother's prints on file. I'll have one of our tech guys get the doctor's." He slipped the bag into his coat pocket and patted the material. "I'll let myself out."

Alone at last, Jonathan ran all ten fingers through his hair. Nothing but problems had surfaced since the murder. Business had become a tedious chore and Marina an unprecedented distraction. His mother talked about independence, and with two murders and no solution in sight, his life was out of control.

Jonathan flopped onto his desk chair, his energy drained. His back ached from too many trips from the basement with a load in his arms. *I really should exercise more.* Resting his throbbing head on the back of the chair, he closed his eyes.

Karl's murder compounded the problems. Why pick the cemetery for a blackmail payoff? All right, the area offered isolation and an easy access road, but without thinking, he set himself up for ambush.

So much for Karl's declaration about being the best PI in Boston.

Feeling the need for a distraction, Jonathan reached across the desk and turned on his computer to access his emails. After an hour of steady work, he could no longer ignore the headache throbbing inside his skull. He stood, stretched, and followed the aroma of coffee. His mother's laughter stopped him in the kitchen doorway.

Detective Nick Farnsworth sat opposite his mother at the table, coffee cup before him, his overcoat draped on the chair alongside. His mother's face was about as bright as a light bulb, and her gaze twinkled as she leaned forward on the table, hanging onto the man's every word.

The entire scene tightened his chest. Farnsworth had the note and should have left an hour ago. Jonathan cleared his throat. Both turned their heads simultaneously, and Jonathan frowned at their animated faces.

His mother leaned back, her mouth twisting to the side. "He's just having coffee."

Jonathan's frown deepened as he strolled to the coffee maker and poured a cup. "Are you sure he isn't digging for dirt, Mother? I am his Number One suspect." He sipped the hot fluid and nearly burned his throat. Seeing the two of them together did nothing to improve his headache. Now, he had a scorched mouth to treat. "What's next, Farnsworth? You want to become chummy with my son?"

"Jonathan!"

Chuckling, Farnsworth stood with a stiffness and grabbed his coat. "Relax, Blandish. Your mother extended her hospitality." He took her hand and leaned over to kiss her fingers. "Thanks for the coffee." He turned to Jonathan. "I want a word with you in private."

With pleasure. Jonathan slammed his coffee cup

onto the counter, ignored the mess of sloshed liquid, and led Farnsworth through the house and onto the front doorstep. Outside was private enough. He had no desire to keep the older man in the house any longer.

Farnsworth slipped on his overcoat. "I can't make any move while the case is active, but afterwards, I want to ask your mother for a date. I don't often have a normal conversation with an attractive woman."

"Assuming you don't lock me away, you mean." He peered at the older man, hoping to get his point across. "I know how you guys work. I don't want you near this house unless you're in an official capacity."

The detective's full lips curled into a smile. "I liked your mother from the second I set eyes on her. I'm sorry we met because of her son's murder, but I'd never have met her otherwise."

Well, hard cheese. A cold breeze cut through his dress shirt as if he stood naked on the doorstep. He stuffed his hands into his trouser pockets and clamped his arms close to his sides. "If you don't mind, I'm keeping my father's visit quiet from my mother. He caused enough pain."

"I can't make that promise, Blandish. The fact that your father had a key to the house puts him on my suspect list." He adjusted his overcoat. "FYI, my boys found no Marina Cavanaugh tombstone in the cemetery."

He had hoped for a better outcome to ease Marina's mind, but they were back to square one.

"I want you to come to the station in the morning for an official statement."

Jonathan's arm hairs bristled. Because of the cool air or Farnsworth's serious tone, he wasn't sure. "What about Marina? We found Karl together."

"I caught her after I finished with you in the den. You, however, have a lot more to put in writing."

His back stiffened, and little warning bells clanged in his head. No cop requested a visit to the station without a good reason. Jonathan eyed him through narrowed lids. "Should I have my lawyer present?"

He waved a hand. "Just a simple statement. What you saw, what you heard, your first confrontation with Towson. That sort of thing." With a nod, he headed for his car. "Nine o'clock in my office."

"Make it ten." He was no dummy. He'd make a quick call to his attorney and follow his advice. "One question before you go, Detective. Is Marina in danger?"

The man placed an open palm on his car roof and swept an unfocused gaze on the surroundings. "I don't know for sure." He met Jonathan's gaze. "I'd like to reassure you, but I can't."

"She's the key to the money, isn't she?"

"Of that, I am certain." He opened his car door but paused, his gaze intense as he scanned Jonathan from head to toe. "For the record, I'm glad she's in this house. Keep an eye on her, Blandish."

The statement eased the knot in his chest. Farnsworth wouldn't have made such a comment if he believed Jonathan Blandish to be a murderous thug.

After a detailed conversation with his lawyer, Jonathan returned to the kitchen to see his mother wiping the table with a towel. She had the look of a new woman with a gleam in her eye and a smile tugging both corners of her mouth.

She glanced his way. "I cleaned your cup and the

mess you made on the counter. You can finish the last of the coffee."

"No, it's late." He stuffed his hands into his trouser pockets. "What did you and Farnsworth talk about?"

She stopped wiping and stared blankly at the wall. "Well, I found out he's divorced. His wife left him, because he was too boring." The wiping continued.

"He does appear that way." Although, the detective had become quite animated after talking with his mother. The man almost looked human.

"I didn't find him boring at all. You, sad to say, are another problem."

What the hell caused *that* comment? He jiggled the change in his pocket. "Explain, Mother."

"You have no life, dear." She hung the towel on a hook. "At least Nick goes to a movie once in a while. He's a big sci-fi fan." She headed for the living room.

Nick? Since when was she on a first-name basis? He followed. "I'm satisfied with my life. I have you and Tyler, a successful business, and the best employees Boston offers."

"But no social life." She flopped onto the sofa, kicked off her shoes, and stretched her legs onto the cushions. "Face it, Jonathan. Roger's death put a kink in your eat-work-sleep routine. Once everything is settled, you'll fall right back into the pattern."

And he couldn't wait. All this disruption got on his nerves. He strolled to the fireplace and rested an arm on the mantel. "I make time for activities with Tyler."

"But that's not a social life." She rotated her head to see him. "You can't tell me you're not intrigued by Marina. She's beautiful, Jonathan. If you let her leave, you'll turn into Mr. No-Life again."

His mother's words hit like a stone. He didn't agree with the Mr. No-Life title, but the vision of Marina walking out the door felt as if a vise gripped his chest. He wanted to know so much about the doctor—her likes and dislikes, her favorite foods, her joys and accomplishments. How could he uncover any part of her history without seeming interested? Which he was. But he had a promise to keep, and he would not follow in his father's footsteps and break a vow, despite the tempting allure of an antiques appraiser.

His mother pointed to his legs. "I haven't seen you so dirty since you were ten years old."

He dropped his arm from the mantel and looked down at his clothes. The layers of filth plus cobwebs caused his skin to itch from the top of his scalp straight down to his toes. He headed for the staircase. "Time to hit the shower."

****

The strumming of Marina's guitar strings floated through the house again. He showered and shaved throughout the soft concerto, humming along to a song from one of Tyler's favorite animated movies. Five minutes later, the music changed. A soothing melody from another classic.

What happened to the music in this house? All during high school and college, he had listened to every folk song and knew quite a few of the words. Not anymore. His whole life had stopped after the death of his wife. He buried his mind in work, because the pain of losing her ran too deep.

Mom's right. He had become an eat-work-sleep man. When was the last time he viewed a good movie or strolled through a shopping mall? He ignored party

171

invitations and social gatherings as if they were the plague. He'd even refused bar-hopping with his brother.

After slipping into a pair of pajamas, he threw on his robe and followed the music to Marina's room where he paused in the open doorway.

Tyler sat cross-legged on the bed in front of her, his attention riveted to her finger-picking on the strings. She leaned against the headboard propped with pillows.

The scene was a powerful one, filling him with...something, as if all the worries of the past several months disappeared into a puff of smoke. A woman and a child. A guitar between them. The music angelic, her voice like a purr. Tyler wore his space pajamas while Marina looked lovely in her sleep attire of T-shirt and shorts, her hair freshly washed and falling in gentle waves onto her shoulders. She cradled the guitar as though the instrument was a part of her body, her voice in perfect harmony with every note. After the discovery of Karl's body, she had paled to the color of snow, but now, a pink glow flushed her cheeks. The guitar, no doubt. Her companion. A godsend for the woman fighting memories of an abusive childhood.

He should send her home. How in good conscience could he let her work in a house with the mystery of two dead bodies unsolved? But she was the riddle key. Without her, he might as well bulldoze Roger's house and fill in the hole.

He stepped into the room. "You're way past your bedtime, Tyler." Not like the boy would fall asleep anytime soon.

"Aw, Dad, please." His shoulders slumped. "I like listening to Marina."

Marina leaned forward and flicked a finger under

Tyler's chin. "Tell you what. You get into your bed, and I'll keep playing. You can hear me through the walls."

"All right." Tyler kissed her cheek, hopped off the bed, and then ran from the room.

After removing the toys covering Tyler's bed, Jonathan tucked his son under the blankets. The sound of Marina's soothing voice brought a smile to Tyler's lips.

"I really like her, Dad."

"Well, if you want to enjoy her playing, you need to close your eyes and listen."

Tyler clamped his eyes shut.

The tone of her music changed as Jonathan left his son's room. She no longer sang with the cheeriness of a child's song, and the words had something to do with a jilted love...no, a stolen love, love given freely but stolen anyway. A strange choice of words. He listened through her open doorway until she finished. "Who was he, Marina?"

Without removing her gaze from her fingers, she picked softly on the strings. "The first love of my life. He's gone now, of course. This song reminds me to keep everything in perspective."

"And are you?"

Their gazes locked.

Frowning, she looked away. "No. My heart isn't hard enough."

Unfortunately, he wrapped his heart in an iceberg. After Susan's death, he'd slipped into a deep depression that lasted for months. Until Marina, he had little feeling for anything, even the death of his own brother. Without realizing the fact, Marina had chipped away at the ice surrounding his heart. He had cried the other night, a first in many years. And the other day, he saw Tyler and his bugs with a pride he couldn't explain. The hobby had irritated him for so long, yet the image of his son as an entomologist made him smile.

Marina was the cause. That auburn-maned woman had activated so many dormant feelings. Why? What magical touch did she possess? Or was he, like his mother, tired of sleeping alone?

An undeniable yes. Marina had stirred a longing too emotional to ignore—the desire to hold a woman, to love her, and experience the oneness so inherent for a man and a woman. He took a step into the room. "You're not working at the house tomorrow."

One auburn brow cocked. "Why not?"

"Farnsworth's men aren't finished. I told Patti to stay home, too. I'll stop by her house and give her the new key so she can secure Roger's place when they're done."

"Are the police searching for the money?"

"That and any of Karl's cameras." He pointed to a small light plugged into the wall socket. "Nightlight?"

She gave him a shy shrug. "I have one in the bathroom, too. I never travel without my guitar or my nightlights."

With such a profound fear of the dark, he wasn't surprised. "Detective Farnsworth wants me at the station tomorrow for an official statement. My lawyer's meeting me."

Her fingers stopped picking. "Since I won't work tomorrow, I'll drive home, pack fresh clothes, check my mail, and then, call the auction house to make arrangements for pickup."

"That's fine. After my meeting with Farnsworth, I'll head to the office. Over the past several months, I've put a lot of work onto my vice-president. Hopefully, he hasn't pulled out the rest of his hair." He adjusted his robe. The damn material had shrunk. Or he grew bigger. He wasn't sure which.

He tugged on the belt. "The police confiscated Roger's computer. They want to dig deeper for any hidden accounts. If you need to print anything, you can use my computer in the den."

The finger-picking resumed. "I'll make a printout while I'm home. Just two rooms so far."

He should move on and let her have some privacy, but his feet wouldn't budge. "By the way, I found Farnsworth flirting with Mom. He plans on asking her out once the case is settled."

"If he solves it, you mean."

He grunted in answer.

She stopped playing. "I suppose you'll accuse me of matchmaking?" With a twinkling gaze, she leaned forward. "I didn't encourage her. I want you to know that."

Another grunt. Too many changes too fast.

Marina slipped off the bed, rested her guitar against the dresser, and faced him. "Good night, Jon—nathan."

She looked beautiful in simple sleep shorts and T-shirt. Her feet were bare and her legs long and tanned. Her shape showed a healthy lifestyle, a woman with meat on her bones, one a man could hold without fear of breaking her into pieces. When he held her in his arms, he'd enjoyed her softness, and the memory caused him to ignore how she stumbled over his name.

Yes, he was tired of sleeping alone.

She approached and placed her hand on the door. An indication that she intended to close it. She stood so close, watching him with a steady gaze, her flowery scent enticing his nose. *The vow. Don't forget the vow.* He stuffed his hands into his robe pockets. "Good night, Marina." He turned and headed for his room. Without debate, he was the biggest jerk on the entire eastern coast.

Chapter Fourteen

In the morning, Jonathan met with Farnsworth, and as expected, the detective had turned their meeting into an interrogation. Farnsworth accused him of plotting the death of both men, stealing the money, and coercing Marina to participate—all conjectures, of course. After one too many pointed questions, Jonathan's attorney, Marvin Silver, took control, citing one law after another to protect his client's interests. The meeting was frustrating and aggravating as hell. And Farnsworth wanted to date his mother? Ha! *When hell freezes.*

Back at his office, Jonathan endured the briefings from his management team, shifted through a mountain of paperwork, and throughout, struggled with a lack of focus. His thoughts drifted to a certain woman with a mane of auburn hair, the same one who'd kept him awake at night and caused a whirlwind of indecision. She had become the spark in his otherwise staid existence. He *had* to see her...no, *wanted* to see her. By now, she'd be in Boston. He double-checked his watch before calling her cell phone.

She answered on the third ring. "Hi. This is a surprise."

He surprised himself even more, but the sound of her voice lifted his sagging spirit. Until today, he'd never have made such a call. "How about a late lunch?"

"Funny you should ask. I've a strong hankering for

a hot dog at Tony's."

"The shop on the harbor? I haven't eaten at the place in years. I'll meet you in thirty."

"Make it forty-five. My laundry is almost done."

He arrived at Tony's in thirty minutes anyway. The place was a popular little mom-and-pop cubbyhole, squeezed between a live bait shop on one side and an outboard motor repair shop on the other. No dine-in accommodations, but nobody cared. Some of the best hot dogs in the city passed through its window.

His motivation to beat her to the harbor had a two-fold purpose. He wanted to watch her walk toward him and see her in some place other than Roger's. Most of all, he treasured every second in her presence. Meeting Marina had made the world feel right again. The sky was bluer and the air cleaner. Traffic was tolerable, people polite. A delusional world for sure, and he laughed at the whole picture.

He shouldn't do this. So many years had passed without a hitch with his vow intact and resolve firm. Until Marina, no woman had tempted him, and he couldn't for the life of him figure out why. She was disobedient, opinionated, and too damn independent for her own good. Yet, she showed a vulnerability that gripped his heart. Despite her abusive childhood, she was no patsy and stood on two firm feet, a woman ready to challenge any man. On the flip side, her tenderness toward Tyler revealed the natural connection between a woman and a child, and the boy had responded with a wide, adoring gaze. If Jonathan wasn't careful, he might do the same.

Determination. That's the key. Marina is merely a woman piquing my interest. Nothing more. Nada. Zilch.

Zip.

He hated arguing with himself, but his internal battle to keep her at a safe distance conflicted with the need to draw her into his arms. *Too much on my mind, that's the problem.* Roger's murder, Karl's, embezzled money…Marina. Always Marina. He leaned on the steel rail overlooking the boat docks and stared out into the harbor.

The salty breeze filled his lungs while the smell of rotten fish assaulted his nose. One pleasant, the other repulsive, balancing out so that neither dominated. A few boats bobbed against their docks as gentle waves disturbed the water. Canvas covers protected the majority of the small boats, but some of the larger ones were ready to sail. Too cold, though, the water was like ice. Only a diehard fished at this time of year.

The city had done a great job of rejuvenating the harbor area. A large red brick walkway ran adjacent to the water with a concrete abutment and steel rails to prevent an idiot from toppling over into the bay. The water was calm despite the closeness of the Atlantic Ocean, mainly because the harbor contained so many inlets where boat docks, restaurants, and warehouses made their home.

Fifteen minutes later, Marina ran toward him, and his breath hitched. Her hair was askew, her cheeks flushed, but she could roll in mud and still be beautiful. He smiled. "How far did you run?"

"From my condo. Three blocks. I didn't want to keep you waiting in case you had a busy schedule…whew!" She bent over, hands on her knees to catch her breath. "I am so out of shape." She straightened while pushing away the hair from her face.

He bit back the words to deny her out-of-shape comment. She had, without question, the most enticing shape to feast a man's eyes—proportioned at chest and hips, long legs, beautiful neck. He'd love to see her dressed to the nines, but she looked just as good in sweatshirt and blue jeans.

"Have you been waiting long?"

His gaze snapped away from her hair, all wind-blown and lovely. "Nope. Just got here." A bold lie, of course. Seeing her run toward him swelled his heart with an indescribable pride, and the vessel thundered within his chest. He pushed away from the rail. "Ready to eat? I can go for a foot long."

"Me, too, with sauerkraut and mustard."

After ordering, they carried their purchase to a nearby bench where Marina spread several napkins between them for their sodas and curly fries. The bench faced the boat docks where a succession of splashing thumps served as background noise, a peaceful sound broken only by the squawk of an overhead seagull eyeing their food.

Jonathan stared into the distance with a strange sense of melancholy filling him. "I don't come here much." With his hot dog, he gestured toward the docks. "Years ago, my father rented a small dinghy and took Roger and me fishing. I haven't done that with Tyler yet." He bit into his wiener and chewed, again focusing on nothing as his thoughts wandered. "I always believed my mom and dad had a solid marriage. Not until later did I see the changes occurring in my father. He treated my mother like dirt, as if he wanted her to walk out. She never did." Using a napkin, he wiped his mouth with a quick glance in her direction. "I had just gotten married, and whatever happened in her life was not my concern. But when she received the divorce papers, Mom called with the news, and for the first time, I heard my mother cry." A painful memory. He had no words of comfort, just anger at his father. He munched on a few curly fries before meeting her steady gaze.

"I don't want to be like him, Marina. To me, a vow shouldn't be broken." He tore his gaze from hers and once again stared into the harbor. "My father said he's come to get her back." He smirked and flicked off a crumb from his overcoat. "Maybe he discovered he let go of a good woman."

Marina sipped her soda. "Don't let him fool you. All he wants is a woman to cook and clean for him until the next fling comes along. Look how he propositioned me without a thought." She lowered her soda to the bench and picked up a fry. "I hope Iris is sensible and doesn't make a rash decision just because she's lonely." She bit into her sauerkraut-covered hot dog.

His father had guts propositioning Marina, and at the memory, the hot dog stuck in his throat. He quickly gulped a mouthful of soda then offered her a strained smile. "This job is turning into one memorable assignment for you."

"One for the record books, I'll admit." She rotated slightly to face him while tucking one leg under her butt. "How'd your meeting go with Farnsworth?"

He grimaced. "Terrible. I think he's in a hurry to retire and wants to throw the book at me. My lawyer stopped the meeting."

A bullhorn blasted for a yacht entering the docking ports. He and Marina watched the captain maneuver the bow into the slot while crew members jumped onto the wooden dock to tie ropes around hooks. *The showoff.* Not like Jonathan Blandish couldn't afford a yacht, but a bullhorn to announce his presence was out of the question. "I can't believe how my entire life has turned upside down since the death of my brother."

Marina wiped mustard from the corner of her mouth. "Farnsworth thinks we're sleeping together, and we've connived from the beginning to steal the money."

"He said something like that to me, too." The detective's words were a little more on the explicit side, as if Marina was trash picked off the street. Jonathan had almost swung at his old face…almost.

Marina shook her head. "I hate all this uncertainty. Your brother should have explained my purpose."

"He should have explained a lot of things, like why he embezzled money. Mom thinks he was jealous of my success." He shoved the last of the hot dog into his mouth and brushed his hands of the crumbs.

While chewing, Marina nodded. "Sibling rivalry is a possibility. Maybe he had to prove something to himself, like in that movie where the rich guy steals expensive art work for the thrill." She snapped her fingers in rapid succession, her gaze distant. "What was that called?"

"*The Thomas Crown Affair.* Great movie." He patted the crumbs from his overcoat and grabbed a fry. "Did you talk to Mrs. Billingsley?"

She bit a large chunk of her hot dog, chewed while holding up a finger, then swallowed. "Yes, I told her what to expect. When I'm ready, I'll order a truck and ship the stuff to our secondary site. Patti and I should handle the load okay."

"Yeah, well, keep the house doors and windows locked. Thankfully, the weather is still cool enough so you won't need to open the windows. The house doesn't have air conditioning." He wagged a finger. "You're to call me every hour on the hour."

Her shoulders slumped. "Oh, please, Jonathan, I'll never accomplish anything if I have to watch a clock." She licked sauerkraut from her finger. "Tell you what. I won't touch the garage contents unless you're with me. Otherwise, Patti and I will stay indoors."

The woman displayed common sense like any good woman in business, one able to make decisions and plan a course of action. She was such a joy to be with—when she wasn't insubordinate. But was that such a bad trait when she made him feel light and happy? Hell, for the first time in years, he'd stopped to smell the roses sitting atop his executive assistant's desk. Shocked her into a near faint.

If only he could show Marina how she'd changed his life. But not today. Maybe not ever.

Marina cocked her head. "Are you okay? Hot dog backing up?"

He gave her a slow smile. "Thinking of things, that's all." How could he tell her that she was the object of his thoughts? That she'd thrown his world into a tailspin with feelings he shouldn't have? He cleared his throat. "I'll help with the garage. In the meantime, remember to keep your wits about you. Don't get self-absorbed and forget to keep your eyes and ears open."

"Right." She shoved the last of the hot dog into her mouth, but a smidgen of sauerkraut landed on her chin.

With his napkin, he brushed off the piece, and that

simple touch shot a surge of awareness straight through his fingers and to his core.

Their gazes locked.

He had the unmistakable urge to wrap her in his arms and kiss her senseless, to taste those luscious lips again in a deeper, more meaningful way, but his hands froze in his lap.

Inviting her to lunch was a bad move. Marina, more than any woman, had a way of crushing his willpower. Six years, he had remained true to his vow. Why her, and why now?

She broke their eye contact by jumping to her feet and gathering the trash to toss into the bin.

Time to end this before I sink too deep. He followed, but since his arms itched to hold her, he resisted temptation by stuffing his hands into his coat pockets. "You said you live three blocks away? I'll walk you." Not like he had any idea why he offered. Perceived duty perhaps. Protect-the-woman, keep-her-safe routine. He should have his head examined.

She brushed the seat of her jeans. "You don't have to walk me. I'm sure you need to return to the office."

As if he had any idea what the hell was going on with the business. Even the briefing this morning flew right over his head. "I'm the boss, Marina. Come on…unless you'd rather I didn't."

Her gaze sparkled. "I'd like your company very much."

He strolled alongside on the wide, red brick pathway, keeping to her pace—a nice slow, leisurely walk.

Several runners zipped by, nodding in greeting. An old woman, with an equally old dog, stared out into the harbor. The dog stretched his neck to sniff as Jonathan and Marina passed.

Despite the comfortable silence surrounding them, Jonathan couldn't contain his curiosity. He wanted to know so much about the beautiful anthropologist and waited until the dog-walker was out of earshot. "How long have you lived in this area?"

"Two years. When the weather's perfect, I ride my bike to work."

"Sounds like fun. I haven't been on a bike since I was a kid. Tyler's had his training wheels removed and now rides all over the neighborhood."

"Then you should buy a bike and ride with him."

He envisioned the three of them riding together, laughing and having a good time. The image was a fleeting one, and he shook it away. Susan should be the one riding, not Marina.

She cocked her head toward him. "Can I ask you something personal?"

"Depends on the question."

She nodded toward his left hand. "Why do you still wear your wedding band?"

He held out his hand, as if to confirm the ring still circled his finger. On multiple occasions, his brother had advised him to resize the ring to fit the pinkie finger, but he saw no purpose. "I'm not interested in marriage anymore, Marina. My wife died from ovarian cancer, and I don't want to go through the experience again."

"What, the marriage or the cancer?"

His jaw twitched. "The cancer."

She nodded. "We go through life losing the ones we love."

"Like the guy you were singing about?"

She grunted as she stuffed her hands into her jacket pockets. "I found out he had a girlfriend on the other side of the city."

"You can't judge all men by that ass."

"And not all women die from ovarian cancer."

He met her steady gaze. "Touché."

They walked another block in silence.

"I'm staying in my condo tonight, Jonathan. I've no reason to drive to your place when I can sleep in my own bed."

"Except I'm getting used to having you around." *Aw, shit*! He shouldn't have been so blunt.

She arched a brow. "Are you?"

More than he believed possible. He smirked. "It's odd, I know. We've only known each other a short while."

"Here we are." She pointed.

And not a moment too soon. Any farther and he might blurt something he'd regret. He already told her he wasn't interested in marriage, and Marina deserved to be married to a good man who gave her beautiful children.

He stopped and craned his neck at a five-story brick building with an array of windows. "This is one of those renovated warehouses. We recently bought several depressed properties like this and have two more under renovation on the south end of the harbor."

"Well, as you can see, my condo has lots of windows. I'm on the top floor. Want to come up?"

An overwhelming hunger swept through him. A hunger for her taste, touch, and scents. His thoughts of savored sex and luscious softness bordered on the obscene, and a part of his anatomy erupted with anticipation, a part he'd sworn shriveled and died eons ago. Nice to know he was wrong.

"No, I better not." Despite the conflict churning in his gut, he couldn't have Marina in his life. *A vow is a vow, and one never to be broken.* With his hands still in his pockets, Jonathan formed tight fists to control an unexplained anger. "I'll see you tomorrow."

Using both hands on his lapels, she gripped his overcoat and plastered his back against the brick face of the building. Her lips connected to his—greedy, sensual, and the best dessert ever. Blood raced through his veins, and he suckled with equal greed, purposely thrusting his fists deeper into his pockets.

Releasing his coat, she pushed away.

He stared wide-eyed at the sudden disconnect. "Why the kiss?"

"Because *you* wanted to and wouldn't. Thanks for lunch."

The woman was a friggin' mind reader.

Chapter Fifteen

Rejuvenated after sleeping in her own bed, the next morning, Marina joined Patti in the dining room. Together, they worked with the contents from the basement starting with the boxes ready to crumble. Marina unpacked while Patti wiped away the dust and dirt with a damp rag. They wore oversized hazmat suits with facemasks to shield from the never-ending clouds of dust.

Patti sneezed anyway, her notorious double-sneeze.

Dust had never bothered Marina. Over the years, her nose developed a tolerance since her whole career involved dusty, old objects found in barns, attics, and abandoned storage lockers. She rarely handled a sparkling object.

When everything had a semblance of cleanliness, Marina removed her facemask, gloves, and suit and began the long process of itemizing.

Patti also removed her protective clothing. "I noticed you take pictures before you catalog. Is that for insurance reasons?"

Marina checked the back of her digital camera for battery life. "Insurance for the client *and* the auction house. Sometimes, items disappear or become damaged, and sometimes, a client claims he had such and such. At that point, he has to prove it." She turned and snapped a picture of Patti then smiled. "I love these cameras. They're small and hold tons of photos." She slipped the camera into her opened briefcase and lifted the laptop lid. The inventory page popped onto the screen. "So, tell me about Henry. He seems like a nice guy."

Patti scratched her nose. "Oh, he is. We've known each other forever."

"He never married?"

She smirked. "He says he's waiting for me." She glanced around the room. "Should I pack the stuff from the china cabinet?"

Marina looked at the stacks of dishware on the dining room table. Nothing matched. A hodge-podge of pieces, none pretty enough to use for a dinner party. "Yes, start packing. The china and figurines haven't any value so I wouldn't fuss. We should also start a box for curbside trash, because half the junk from the basement belongs in the dump. Does this neighborhood have a recycle day?"

"Thursday. Roger kept a container in the mudroom. I can put it on the front porch."

"Good idea. You do that, and I'll tackle the paintings."

They'd stacked at least thirty paintings from the basement, none of which struck her as valuable. The same for the frames, just typical pieces of wood nailed together and lacquered.

A short time later, Patti returned and tossed an empty box and a pile of newspapers onto the dining room table. "Here, Doctor." She handed Marina a pair of eyeglasses. "I found these in the mudroom."

Marina slipped them onto the top of her head. "What do you mean Henry will wait for you?"

Jane Drager

"Oh, he's always had a crush on me." She wrapped a plate with a sheet of the newspaper. "The problem is I don't have a crush on him. He's a friend I've known for a long time." She shot Marina a sheepish look. "He keeps telling me I'll come around one day."

Marina studied her. "Like when you're tired of being alone?"

"I don't mind being alone." She wrapped another plate.

Marina took out her utility knife and cut the twine on several paintings before returning the knife to her pocket. "I grew up in an abusive environment. I like being alone."

"But your face brightens whenever Mr. Blandish walks in."

Eyes wide, she turned sharply. "No, it doesn't."

Patti smiled. "If Tyler's with him, your gaze grows even brighter. You like them both."

Did she? Certainly Tyler, little mini-Jon. And Jonathan's house was a home, a place of comfort and security…unlike her parents' house with plastic slipcovers on every upholstered piece, even the dining room chairs. God forbid anyone should dare sit.

"Admit it, Doctor."

"I admit nothing." Granted, some odd sensations had surfaced around the Blandish family. They'd made her feel welcomed from the start, and warm feelings bubbled to the surface every time she entered their house. After a day in Roger's stark and dark monastery, she needed the hominess of the Blandish clan. One of these days, she'd thank Jonathan for the invitation.

As for the big man himself… Well, okay, she was attracted. So was he to her, but he resisted at every turn.

Still married, of course, to a ghost.

Oh, hell. If she'd lost a deeply-loved mate, she'd understand better. Right now, six years of mourning seemed downright unreasonable.

Once finished with the contents in the dining room, Marina and Patti took a lunch break before heading upstairs. The objects on the second floor were much cleaner than the basement's so no hazmat suits…yet. Marina headed first to Roger's bedroom.

The room contained furnishings expected for a man. A wide armoire for suits—the assemble-it-yourself kind. Marina opened the double doors to find the interior empty. A tall chest of drawers was another piece, also empty, some quality to the wood but worth no more than a couple hundred bucks. The piece that surprised her—and one she hadn't expected in a bachelor's room—was a vanity table and chair with a three-panel mirror, decorated in typical feminine style of white with pink trim and flowers on all three sides.

She ambled toward the brass bed, running her hand along the smooth metal headboard. "Nice bed."

"Roger bought it two years ago." Tears filled Patti's eyes as her fingers traced along the brass. "I found Roger in the garage, you know. The cops told me he had been dead for at least eighteen hours." She sniffed. "Worst experience of my life." She yanked a tissue from the box on the vanity and blew her nose. "We were engaged to be married."

Marina's mouth fell, then she quickly snapped it shut. Patti had answered the question of the feminine look to the vanity, but an engagement? The news that Roger had an interest in women shot Jonathan's opinions all to hell. "I'm sorry, Patti. Obviously,

Jonathan doesn't know."

"Nobody knew." Patti lowered her butt onto the bed. A tear rolled down her cheek as her hand glided across the bedspread. "We made love on this bed many times and talked for hours into the night. On that fateful day, I left early to take my niece to a school concert and hadn't returned until the next morning. I should have been here." Her shoulders slumped.

Poor Patti. From the sad tone of her voice, she truly loved the guy. Marina sat alongside. "Whoever killed Roger could have killed you, too, Patti. But why the secrecy? Iris would have loved to hear about the engagement."

Her shoulders slumped. "He convinced me to wait on any formal announcements." She held out her left hand and wiggled the fingers. "No ring either."

Men who kept secrets did so for a reason, and Roger definitely kept some whoppers. Of course, Patti could be delusional, another woman suckered into sex for promises never intended. On the other hand, bedding an embezzler might give her some privy information. Suppose Roger had mumbled in his sleep? Or sleep-walked? Maybe led her to the treasure without realizing? *Tread lightly.* With as nonchalant an air as possible, Marina surveyed Patti. "I'm sure you and Roger talked about a variety of subjects. His work perhaps?"

She wagged a finger. "Never business. He was always careful about that. We always talked love."

How does one talk love? People either performed the act, or they slept. Hell, all Marina's partners had left by the midnight-pumpkin hour…except for the last one, the two-timing, no-good SOB.

Patti gazed at the ceiling. "Roger was so sweet. He'd come home from work with a magazine or a bag of goodies, and we'd read and munch together until everything was finished." She sighed heavily and lowered her gaze to the floor.

Flowers would have been a better option. They would have added color to the damn place.

Patti clamped her fingers together on her lap, her lips tight. "I don't believe Roger embezzled anything."

The little housekeeper sounded as sure as the neighbor back home in North Carolina. The woman swore up and down her thirty-eight cats never left her yard when, in fact, the farmer across the street had most of them buried in his field. "Jon checked out the fund's proof, Patti. Roger has forty million somewhere."

"Jonathan."

"He…eh—huh? Oh, right. Sorry." She shouldn't apologize to Patti for flubbing Jonathan's name. What could Patti do, tell the man? Have her fired? *I should be so lucky.* "Embezzlement is a big secret to keep. He was probably afraid to tell you." And Patti had a hell-of-a motive. What if she already had the money stashed in an overseas account? What if she killed Roger, then Karl, destroyed the cameras, and simply stood aside to bide her time? Was Marina sitting next to a cold-blooded killer?

God help me. She shook away the heaviness that settled in her chest.

Marina slapped her knees and stood. "We don't have much to pack in this room. Maybe as we go, we'll find a key to a lockbox."

"Roger doesn't have a lockbox."

Shot that idea to smithereens. "How about a wall

safe?"

"That's in the den. Mr. Blandish already emptied it."

She was fresh out of ideas. Marina examined the bed. Could the brass tubing possible contain a forty-million-dollar fortune? How about the mattress?

Oh, good grief.

She tapped the rail with her knuckle. "This isn't an antique, Patti. If Jonathan doesn't want the bed, maybe he'll let you have it."

Patti jumped to her feet, her face bright. "Dr. Cavanaugh, that's a wonderful idea! Do you think he'll agree?"

"I don't see why not. The sentimental value is far greater than the monetary one. You can't put a price on that. I'll talk to him."

Patti wrapped her short arms around Marina and squeezed. "Thank you, Doctor. You don't know how much this bed means to me."

Assuming Jonathan wouldn't drop dead after hearing about Roger and Patti.

They worked a while longer then quit for the day. Patti had a dental appointment, and as per Jonathan's orders, she pushed Marina out the door, never to be left alone.

Marina arrived at the Blandish house as Tyler, wearing a backpack too big for his slight body, hopped from the school bus steps.

With her arms tight around her chest, Iris stood in the middle of the driveway waiting, as if freezing to death in her light cardigan.

Tyler ran to Iris first then made a beeline for Marina who stood alongside her closed car door. She squatted for a hug.

"Marina's here!" He wrapped his arms around her neck. "I knew you'd be back. Your guitar is still upstairs."

She kissed his cheek then held him at arm's length, gazing into his beautiful brown eyes. "That's right. I won't leave without taking my guitar."

Iris stepped alongside. "You're early today. Anything new at Roger's?"

"Not really." Except the news about Roger and Patti. For another time—when Tyler wasn't around.

They entered the house. Marina slid off her jacket and hung it in the closet as Tyler yanked his arms free of the backpack's straps. He was about to remove his coat when Iris waved a hand.

"Leave on your jacket, Tyler." Iris threw off her sweater and slipped on an overcoat. "We'll make a quick run to the market." She buttoned the coat to her neck. "The weather wasn't supposed to be this chilly today."

Tyler kicked his backpack onto the living room rug. "Aw, Grandma, can't I stay with Marina?"

"He can if he wants," Marina said. This would give Iris a chance to stroll the aisles without a six-year-old snatching everything off the shelves.

"Yeah, yeah!" Tyler tugged on his grandmother's coat.

Iris released a heavy sigh, but a smile curled one side of her mouth. "Okay, I won't be long. I'll pick up a few things and return shortly. Tyler usually has a snack when he comes home."

"Take your time." She could go for a snack whether Tyler wanted one or not.

Tyler sat at the kitchen table, munching and chatting about school. First grade. New experiences. New friends.

After their snack of milk and cookies, Marina followed Tyler into the living room where he spread his books on the coffee table. She stood by the fireplace and stared at the cold hearth.

Tyler ran to the side of the fireplace. "I can turn on the flames. Wanna see?"

Without a match? "Show me."

He flipped a switch. The fire started with a puff.

A gas igniter! *Perfect.* Marina kicked off her sneakers and stretched out on the sofa with a magazine while Tyler started his homework. He chatted as he worked, mostly to himself or his pencil. She wasn't sure which.

The entire scene felt foreign. Even though her earlier life was anything but ordinary, a strong sense of normalcy swept over her. This was how the average person lived. No fear of being thrown into a closet for the duration of the day. No one screaming in her ear while she cleaned her room. Just her and a little boy sharing time together with a fire to warm the air. A house that was lived in. Nice...and scary. Her gaze wandered lazily toward Tyler.

He was a lucky little boy. She, her brother, and two youngest sisters had constantly lived on the edge of fear. No one listened to their cries because, in appearance, they were well-cared-for children—clothed and fed, always clean and polite. Never the picture of abuse. Her grip tightened on the magazine at the memory.

Tyler jumped to his feet and thrust his paper in her

face. "Is this right?"

Grateful for the distraction, she checked the math problems. "Yep. You're a smart little cookie."

His lips pursed. "I'm not a cookie. I'm a man."

She stifled a laugh. "Sorry. I hadn't meant to insult you."

The little man who'd grow to be as handsome as his father. He even had the same haircut, the same tilt of the head to toss the hair from his forehead. And, of course, the same gorgeous brown eyes. In a few more years, he'd develop the inevitable sexy smile and melt a girl's heart.

After watching Tyler drop onto his knees to return to his homework, Marina tossed the magazine to the side and let her gaze wander about the room—at the array of framed photographs strategically positioned on the mantel, on the wall, and on the end tables, none hidden by another. Almost all were pictures of Jonathan's wife.

"I never knew my mom," Tyler said without glancing from his paper.

"She's pretty."

"That's what everybody says. I wish my dad would get me a new mom."

Judging from the number of photos, she doubted Tyler would receive his wish anytime soon. "Your father loves your mother, Tyler. Sometimes people struggle to move on." Yeah, real words of wisdom. Her PhD was in anthropology, not psychology. Still, her heart ached for this little boy. She'd like to erase the sadness in his voice. She'd also like to kick Jonathan in the pants, not to force him to marry again, but to acknowledge his son's needs.

The front doorbell rang.

Tyler jumped to his feet. "I'll get it."

Stretching, she grabbed his arm to stop him. "No, you won't. Stay here." She hurried to the door and peeked through the peephole. *Oh, dear. Certainly not pizza delivery.* She opened the door.

Brandon Blandish stood on the step. He wore tight blue jeans with a black leather jacket, hair slicked back into a dovetail, jacket collar up, and heavy black-leather boots. She looked for a motorcycle in the driveway but only saw his dark sedan.

His mouth twisted into a lopsided grin. "You again, eh? Over at Roger's and now, here." He crossed the threshold, forcing her to step back. "Where's Iris?"

Marina blocked any forward motion, even though he stood a good six inches higher and seventy pounds heavier. "She's not home but won't be long…if you want to wait in your car."

"No, I'll wait in here." He looked around, an eyebrow cocked. "Jon's got himself a swanky place."

Obviously, the man had not stepped into Jonathan's house before today. She squared her shoulders and thrust out her chin. "This is not my residence, Mr. Blandish. I'm asking you to wait outside."

"Geez, you're tossing me out wherever I go. These are my sons, you know. You're the hired help."

"True, but I'm looking at a man who never showed for his son's funeral. That doesn't put you high on my admiration list. If you want Iris, then you wait outside."

Bushy eyebrows rose. "I don't take orders from a woman."

"Then you'll take them from me! She told you to

leave!"

Marina turned to see Tyler standing with his fists on his hips, jaw set, and gaze piercing. He was three and a half feet of determination.

"We learned about bullies in school, and you're bullying Marina!"

Brandon faced Marina, a smile stretching onto his lips. "I can see my grandson is on his way to keeping his women in line. However—" He leaned over to put his face close to Tyler's. "You need to know when to shut your mouth, son. I don't like sass."

Tyler's face twitched, but he puffed out his chest and narrowed his gaze. "I don't know what that means, but you stop bullying Marina."

My God, the little guy was standing up to his grandfather! Her admiration for him soared.

Brandon raised a hand.

Back stiffening, Marina thrust Tyler behind her and stepped into the older man's space. "You touch a hair on this child's head, and you'll have a good fight on your hands. If you want to talk to Iris, you will wait outside." She'd had too much experience with her bullying father to submit to Brandon's tactics. She protected her younger siblings by stepping between them and her father and took the punishment rather than allow him to hurt the people she loved. Tyler deserved the same protection. She squared her shoulders and glared into Brandon's face.

Without moving, he matched the glare. "I don't take sass from a woman either."

"Trouble?" said a male voice.

Detective Farnsworth stepped through the open door and placed his bulk between Marina and Brandon.

"I don't particularly like men who pick on women and children."

Brandon whirled, eyes wide. "Who the hell are you?"

"I've been looking for you." He produced his badge. "Luckily, one of our patrol cars spotted your license plate and called me. How about we step outside, Mr. Blandish?"

"What do you want to see me for?" He took a step back. "I'm only waiting for Iris, and I have a right to see my wife."

"Grandma isn't home," Tyler shouted. "And she's not your wife!"

Farnsworth winked at Marina. "The man of the house has spoken. Let's talk outside, Mr. Blandish." He waved for Brandon to step out before him.

Marina released a long breath. Whatever Iris did with her ex-husband was her business, but Marina had spent a lifetime at the mercy of a bully. She'd be damned to let the man raise a hand to Tyler. After closing the door, she squatted to Tyler's level and took him by the arms. "I'm proud of you. You stood up to him."

His little chest puffed outward. "I'm not afraid. I'm a man, and a man has to protect a woman. Daddy said so." He stared at the closed door. "Was that my grandfather?"

Her heart broke to hear such an uncertain tone. Tyler *could* have had a grandfather—if the friggin' man wasn't so self-absorbed. "Yes."

The little face frowned. "I don't like him. I like the pol-lese-man more."

Marina gave him a quick kiss on the cheek. "What

do you say we forget about him and finish your homework?" Brandon's visit had unnerved her. What gave him the right to barge in like he owned the place?

Tyler grabbed her hand. "You need to relax, and I know how to help you." He led her to the sofa, urging her to sit. Then, without fanfare, he jumped alongside and wrapped his arms around her neck. "Grandma says a hug is the best therapy to lower blood pressure."

"Is that so?" She wrestled him onto the sofa and tickled his belly.

Squirming, he hooted with laughter.

"I think you're avoiding your homework."

"I like you, Marina. Will you be my mommy?"

Holy shit! How should a woman respond to such a question? She met his pleading gaze. "You can't pick a mother at random, Tyler. Your father has final say."

"Why?" His eyebrows squished together. "He has his own mother."

"True, but as a rule, your father picks your mother. Now—" *Before I dig a hole too deep...* "Let me see where you are with your homework. And for the record, I like you, too." In that moment, Marina fell in love with Tyler Blandish, hook, line, and sinker.

Chapter Sixteen

Warmth brushed Marina's nose, a familiar mix of heat and moisture, given with a whisper touch to tingle pleasure nerves. She stirred, and the warmth slipped to her lips, creating a breeze intermingled with the scent of a spicy aftershave.

An awareness emerged. Comfort certainly. A feeling of being loved and protected, of someone watching over her. Since her parents weren't the type to kiss their children while they slept, she deduced the sensations as nothing more than a dream.

Her eyelids fluttered open to see Jonathan sitting on a foot stool by her head, his elbows on his knees and a gentle smile on his lips. His gaze held an intensity so dark she blinked several times just to clear her vision. And then she felt Tyler who slept soundly in her arms.

Oh, my, how did this happen? The boy was finishing his homework when she had yawned. Then, he yawned and snuggled against her on the sofa, his hair smelling of shampoo. So trusting. Little mini-Jon. She'd hummed until they both fell asleep.

Grimacing, she shook herself awake. "Iris will shoot me. He'll never sleep tonight." She nudged Tyler. "Wake up, sleepy head."

Tyler rolled toward her and rubbed his eyes, focusing first on her and then on his father. "Hi, Daddy. Marina and I took a nap."

Jonathan straightened on the stool. "So I see. Dinner's almost ready. Think you can eat?"

"Yeah, but I hafta pee first." He rolled off the sofa and ran from the room.

She watched him disappear, guilt rising. "Iris should have awakened us." She moved to swing her legs from the cushions, but Jonathan stopped her by placing a hand on her shoulder. The maneuver surprised her, even more so when his fingers slipped from her shoulder to stroke her jaw. She nearly shuddered from the heat of his touch.

He tucked a strand of hair behind her ear. "My mother is in the kitchen, sniffling. Since she knows I come into the house through the garage, she told me to go see the most beautiful sight in the world." He gave another stroke along her jaw before dropping his hand. "She was right. You with Tyler in your arms."

With trembling fingers, she touched her lips. The warmth remained, and she met his gaze. "Did you kiss me?"

His brows wrinkled. "Why would I do that?"

Yes, why would he with his wife's photos staring at his back? But his gaze sparkled. She squinted. "You lied."

"Maybe." He leaned close, and with one finger under her chin, he lifted her lips toward his.

He suckled with a tenderness she hadn't felt in a long time. Visions of this handsome man naked activated a yearning deep within her core. Her heart thundered against her rib cage, the sound pulsing out her ears. If she died this second, she'd have no regrets, and she returned the kiss like they had only today to live, her tongue seeking his for a seductive dance.

Footsteps pounding, Tyler ran in.

Jonathan shot backward and used a hand to shove her against the sofa cushions, his gaze darting to the photos on the end table.

Sighing, Marina searched the room for the ghost of his late wife.

Like a properly starched soldier, Tyler stood by his father. "Dad, I want you to know I'm gonna do the right thing." He squared his small shoulders.

Jonathan snapped his gaze from the photos and studied his son with a guarded expression. "Explain yourself, young man."

"You always told me that when a man and a woman sleep together, the man has to stand firm and be the responsible one. I'll marry Marina."

Marina bolted upright to a sitting position, eyes wide, with her gaze shifting from son to father.

"Go on." Jonathan eyed the little soldier, his face dead serious.

Tyler swallowed, and he shot a quick glance in her direction. "We slept together, Dad, here on the sofa. That means Marina is pregnant." He jutted his chin high. "I'll find a job and support her."

Marina slapped a hand over her mouth to stifle a cry. The deluded boy was serious and meant every word.

Jonathan frowned, his lips in a tight line, but a twinkle of mischief emerged from his gaze. "A woman is a huge responsibility, Tyler. Have you thought this through?"

"I have, sir. I love her."

He patted his son's shoulder. "Then, that makes everything worthwhile. You have my blessing."

The next topic of discussion would be the wedding date. This had to stop before she exploded with laughter. "All right, you guys, that's enough." She placed her stockinged feet on the floor and took Tyler by the shoulders to gaze into his brown eyes. A precious kind of sweetness pierced her heart as he stared back. The boy was so damn cute. "A man and a woman have to be naked for that responsibility to kick in, Tyler."

His mouth opened, and he shifted his gaze from her to his father then back again. "They do? You mean you're not pregnant?"

"No, Tyler, I am not pregnant." She dropped her hands to her lap.

He turned to his father. "Is that true, Dad? You have to be naked?"

"Yes, son, a man and a woman have to be naked."

"Whew!" He wiped a dry brow. "That's a relief. I'm still in the first grade. Yahhh!" He ran from the room.

Marina burst out laughing. "He's adorable!"

Jonathan frowned while drumming his fingers on his knees. "I need to elaborate on the details of my sex lesson. I never told him about the naked part."

"You left out more than that."

He shot her a stern look. "He's only six years old. I gave him what he could absorb."

"Yeah, well, typical male. We slept together, and off he ran." She snickered. "That was so funny." She attempted to stand.

But he stopped her. "One moment, Marina. I want to explain something."

She cocked her head. "Like why you're riddled

with guilt every time your lips touch mine? You don't have to explain. I figured your late wife threw a few daggers at your back." With a wave of her hand, she indicated the photos around the room. "I guess her ghost follows you everywhere you go. If you remember, the other day, you dropped me on the divan like I weighed a ton." A possibility she hadn't considered. *Time to step on a scale.* She patted his hand. "Relax. You can't seduce a woman if you push her away all the time. You're safe."

"You're not offended?"

"Hell, yes, I'm offended. You're feeling guilty, and I don't understand why."

He rubbed his palms along his thighs. "I won't deny my attraction to you, but I need more time."

"More than six years? Maybe you should wait until Tyler graduates from college." She stood and ran a hand down the front of her shirt. "Do me a favor. Don't toy with my emotions. All right, yes, we're attracted to each other, but you're the one putting on the brakes. You either want to do something about this attraction, or you don't. I hate this middle-of-the-road shit. When you decide, let me know." She picked up her sneakers and turned to leave.

He grabbed her arm. "Don't go away mad."

"I'm not mad. I'm frustrated. There's a difference." If she were mad, she'd punch his handsome face until he blew up like a melon. She sighed heavily and faced him. He had the look of a man caught with his pants down, his gaze repeatedly drifting to the photos on the table. "Tell you what. Since I'm not in the mood for your games, let's return to our employer/employee status. I have a few things we need to discuss." She reclaimed her seat on the sofa and placed her sneakers on the floor, facing him.

Iris burst into the room, her face animated with wide eyes and raised brows. "Is Tyler telling me the truth, Marina? Brandon came?"

"What!" Jonathan bolted to his feet.

Marina stood. "Yes, it's true."

Her mouth gaped. "That means he's in town. What should I do, Jonathan?"

"What are you asking me for? I've no respect for the man."

Iris bit her lip and glanced toward the front window. "My gosh, what does he want?"

"You, more likely. His girlfriend ditched him."

She cocked a brow. "How do you know?"

With a heavy sigh, Jonathan explained his father's visit to Roger's, including his impromptu visit with Marina.

"Brandon had a key?" Iris glanced from Jonathan to Marina. "Why?"

Jonathan threw his hands into the air. "The big question is how? Roger never mentioned Dad's visits."

Marina cleared her throat. "I'm sure Brandon will return."

"I still don't know what I'll do." Iris stared at the front door.

Jonathan glowered. "Depends on whether you want to reconcile. Any thoughts?"

"None at all."

Tyler ran in, pointing behind him. "Grandma, your stuff's boiling."

"Oh, good heavens." She hurried to the kitchen with Tyler close behind.

Marina grabbed Jonathan's arm and practically spun him around. "What do you mean reconcile? The man will use her like a dishrag."

"Need I remind you that you're talking about my father?" He thrust his hands into his trouser pockets.

"Yes, I know he's your father, but he only wants a place to park his butt."

He shrugged. "Here's her chance to put a man into her life."

The argument could drag on for hours, and the situation was none of her business, even if she believed Iris deserved better than Brandon Blandish. "Let's return to the employer/employee part. Do you have any plans for Roger's brass bed?"

He cocked a brow. "No. Why?"

"Patti's expressed interest, as a memento of sorts. The bed isn't an antique, Jon."

His expression grew shuttered. "Why do you have such a hard time with my name?"

Oops again. At this point, the truth was the best answer. "I like Jon. The name fits you." She shot him a quick glance. "I don't mean any disrespect, but Jonathan is a little too formal. I'll try harder." *Not too much harder, you old stick-in-the-mud.*

"Thank you. I've been called Jonathan my entire life. I've no intention of changing."

No pet name for Jonathan Blandish. No sweetum, honey-bun, or darling. Just as well. Nothing fit him. Except Jon. She leaned toward him to force his gaze to meet hers. "What about the brass bed?"

He sighed. "All right, Patti can have it. I can't see why."

A now-or-never time. She sucked in a large breath

but took a step back—just in case. "She and Roger were lovers."

His back stiffened, and he stared, mouth ajar. "I find that hard to swallow."

"Why? Patti might be a trifle overweight—"

"Trifle?" He turned toward the fireplace.

She crossed her arms over her chest. "All right, she's overweight, but she's cute." She dropped her arms. "I don't know anything about Roger, but the possibility of a relationship between them is plausible. Single man, single woman, close proximity. Happens all the time."

He stared at the flames for several long seconds before glancing her way. "I find your news downright impossible. What proof did she present?"

Her mouth fell open. "Proof? She only wants the bed."

"Well, right now, we've got her word against a dead man." He chewed on his lip, his brows creasing into a frown. "Okay, she can have the bed, but make sure you inspect every inch thoroughly in case Roger stuffed his money in the brass tubes."

Marina slapped her mouth shut and gave him a long look. "Why is a relationship with Roger impossible? Every man I know seeks release once in a while...except maybe you."

Jonathan eyed her through narrowed slits. "We better go eat." He headed for the archway.

"Somebody's going away mad."

He shot her a look that cut into her soul.

Gotcha, big boy.

Chapter Seventeen

After spending the rest of the week and the weekend itemizing and packing the contents on the second floor, Marina began her Monday morning with a determination to tackle another dreaded task. She stood in the middle of the den with a disheartened lump settling in her chest. She couldn't put off the room any longer, and to see hundreds of books lining floor-to-ceiling shelves on three walls was enough to make her cry.

On her preliminary inspection, she discovered old books mixed with new. One lamp illuminated the desk of carved mahogany, and the leather sofa positioned in the middle of the room had an end table. Other than that, nothing but an ill-conceived reading room. An impossible room in which to evaluate books. Damn good thing she listened to her inner voice and asked Mrs. Billingsley for some floor lamps. She mentally patted herself on the shoulder for the foresight.

Patti walked in and stopped short. "What's all the cursing about?"

Marina straightened from her bent position under the desk and let out an exaggerated sigh. "Sorry. This house is too damn frustrating." From her kneeling position, she lifted her butt onto Roger's desk chair. "Do you realize this room has only one electrical outlet under the desk? Nothing in the walls at all."

"Well, sure. This is an old house. Roger had that outlet installed to give him light to read." She glanced around the room. "Only the kitchen has more than one socket. That's why I ran extension cords all over the place to connect the lamps."

After dusting her pant legs, Marina stood with the distinct urge to kick something. How could one man live with such darkness? Even more important, how had he expected a housekeeper to see the dust balls hiding in the corners?

She released a long breath as she glanced around. "One lamp for nighttime, and no windows for daytime. What purpose was this room for the original owners, mushroom cultivation? I thought building inspectors took care of problems like this."

Marina removed the clip holding her hair, shook the strands loose, and then gathered the fibrils to re-clip. The simple fussing with her appearance helped calm her frazzled nerves. She gave Patti a crooked grin. "I'll need the cords in here, Patti. Can you get me some?"

"Sure. I'll take a few from the dining room. Be right back." She hurried out, returning with a fist-full of electrical cords.

Marina had already carried the floor lamps into the den and positioned them at opposite ends of the room. After running a series of electrical cords, she plugged in the first lamp. "Let there be light!" She flipped the switch, repeated with the second lamp, and stood back. Two lamps with two hundred and fifty watts of power illuminated all four corners. "Isn't this wonderful?" With hands on her hips, she scanned the room.

Patti squinted at the brightness. "Hopefully, we

won't blow a fuse."

"The lamps have low amperage. We should be okay."

As Marina surveyed the room without the shadows, she experienced the ominous presence of Roger laughing his head off at the amount of books awaited her evaluation. With the help of proper lighting, a high percentage of the books revealed their age. Each would require careful and delicate handling. She had hoped to finalize the house inventory by the following weekend, but the den alone could take a week, and she hadn't yet inspected the attic or garage. Lord only knew what waited. She slipped on a hazmat suit and gloves. "Are all these books Roger's?"

Patti scratched her nose. "They came with the house, like the stuff in the basement. Roger sold some of the books, though." Her eyes teared as she looked around. "He loved this room. He spent most of his nights reading by that single lamp."

And probably getting eyestrain. Marina zipped her suit. "Without question, we're standing in a man's room. Dark furniture, dark wood, and even a musty cigar smell." Dreary and eerie. She pushed the floor-to-ceiling ladder to test how well the wheels moved on the thin, metal track. The rusty wheels screeched but rolled. She stepped onto the first rung and jumped to test its strength. The wood felt firm beneath her feet so she tested each rung to the top.

"We don't have enough boxes for all these books, Doctor."

Marina agreed. She looked from one top shelf to the next, and her heart sank. "I had hoped some of the top shelves were empty, but they're not. The books are lying flat." Her shoulders slumped. More work, more packing, more time in this dreadful house.

"Did you talk to Mr. Blandish about the bed?"

Marina grabbed an armload of books and descended. "He said yes." She stacked the books on the floor.

Squealing, Patti clapped her hands. "Oh, thank you, Doctor. I'll make arrangements to move it to my place."

"If you're not in a hurry, you can let the boys from the auction house handle the delivery. They won't mind." Again, she ascended the ladder. "Besides, Jonathan wants me to inspect all the parts in case Roger hid his stash." She collected more books.

"Yes, I can wait." For a second time, she clapped her hands. "Thank you, thank you, thank you, Dr. Cavanaugh."

"Thank Jonathan, and call me Marina." She descended with another armload.

Patti stared at the books on the floor. "Do you want me to start packing?"

"Not yet. I'll do a preliminary inspection of each and separate by value. I know enough about books to guesstimate, but our book expert from New York will have the final say." She ascended the ladder.

"If we quit early, I can go to the supermarket for more boxes. The guys on the loading dock told me to take whatever I need."

"That's a great idea, Patti." She descended with another armload and stacked the books. "With all the ladder climbing, I might need to quit early." Her legs already ached, but once she emptied the top two shelves, she'd have three less rungs to climb.

"Then if you don't need me, I'll continue packing

the stuff in the kitchen." Patti headed for the door. "How about some coffee?"

"Patti, that would be wonderful."

Some of the books were heavy journals ready to separate from the binding. Others nearly crumbled in her arms. The musty odor of old paper and dust filled the den, and the bright lamplights reflected the dust particles floating in the air. She should have worn a mask. *Ah, well, too late.*

Marina kept to her task until her arms and legs ached to the point of collapse. She placed her last load on the floor and stared up the ladder. What if Roger hid his stash behind a secret panel? Easy enough to create one with all the shelves.

After rolling the ladder to the end of its track, she grabbed her flashlight and climbed, thighs aching with each step. Nothing on the first two panels. No evidence of latches or a hook to grab. She tapped the back panel to hear a solid sound. Pressing accomplished nothing either. She inched the ladder to the next two panels and repeated the process from one section to the next.

"Careful up there."

Jonathan stood under the ladder, knees bent and looking like a man ready to catch a fly ball. Her, she guessed. "Well, this is a surprise."

Tyler ran into the room. He took one look at Marina at the top of the ladder and flew over. "Marina, can I come up? Please, please!"

"No, you cannot." She grabbed an armload of books from the next two shelves and descended. Placing the books on the floor, she turned to face them. They wore similar outfits. Khaki cargo pants and sport shirt. Jon and mini-Jon. Yes, something about the two of them always brightened her mood. "What are you two doing here in the middle of a school day?" She wrenched off her gloves.

"Daddy met my teacher, Miss Wingate. I like her." He rolled the ladder on its tracks. "Why can't I go up?"

"Because the ladder is old. I don't want you to fall off and hurt yourself."

Nodding to his son, Jonathan gestured with a thumb over his shoulder. "Why don't you see if Patti has any cookies?"

"Yeah, cookies, cookies." He ran from the room.

Marina unzipped her hazmat suit and slipped her arms from the sleeves. Jonathan's intense gaze followed every movement. "What?"

He flashed a wide, sexy grin. "When we first met, you wore a pair of oversized coveralls that looked big enough to fit King Kong. This hazmat suit is no better." His gaze twinkled. "I like the shape that emerges."

The damn flirt, always confusing her. "Was everything okay at school?"

"Oh, sure." He strolled over to the books on the floor. "The teacher noticed Tyler had a strong interest in science, especially after his bug collection on Show-and-Tell day. She's recommending him for advanced classes."

Marina scratched her nose. *Too much dust.* "He's only six years old. Is that wise?"

He stepped closer to the piles of books and tapped them with the edge of his sneakered foot. "She assured me the courses will hold his interest better." He met her gaze. "I noticed you changed the subject quickly enough."

"I'm changing it again. How do you like the lights?

I took advantage of my trip to Boston."

He narrowed his gaze. "You're good at changing the subject."

"That's because I never know whether I'm coming or going with you. I'd rather we keep everything business-like."

Patti walked in carrying a coffee tray and placed it on the side table near the sofa. "Thanks again for the bed, Mr. Blandish. I can't tell you how happy I am." She turned to Marina. "If Mr. Blandish plans on staying, he'll watch over you while I run out for the boxes."

He slipped his hands into his pants' pockets. "I'm not going anywhere. I'll leave when Marina leaves."

"Great. I'll clean up after Tyler and then scoot." She left the den.

Marina stared at the coffee tray with its array of cookies. "I might gain weight on this job." She headed for the door. "Let me wash first."

That damn man will drive me to drink. He should stay home. The more distractions, the longer the job. She had enough trouble maintaining a professional attitude when so much pleasure could be had…namely him, in a big bed.

She ran up the steps to the bathroom and splashed cold water on her face to squelch any further thoughts of pleasure. Even Tyler was a distraction. She wanted to hug and kiss him to death. Hopefully, he hadn't acquired his father's habit of pushing away his women. *That will be a total blow to my ego.* She returned to the den.

Jonathan held two leather-bound books in his hands, rotating both this way and that. He faced her, brow cocked. "These books are ancient literature. Look at this." He turned the cover toward her. "*The Parables of Gropolis*, whatever that means. And here, *Electric Current and Its Possibilities*. This room is a museum."

That wasn't the word she had in mind, but she let the statement pass. "Some of these books might be worth money." She poured coffee into two cups as Tyler ran in, arms outstretched like the wings of an airplane.

He snatched a cookie and flew out.

"Stay in the house, Tyler!" Jonathan frowned at Tyler's vapor trail. "I sometimes wonder if he's eating too much sugar."

Marina laughed. "He's normal. Don't worry about him." She grabbed a cookie and took a bite. The flavors of oatmeal and raisins burst on her tongue. "Patti was my helper, you know. I may have to put you to work."

"I already ruined a dress shirt and trousers helping you. Any more wreckage and I'll have to deduct the cost from your salary. Sit and drink your coffee. You're not on a time clock."

She was indeed on a clock. The longer she stayed, the harder to leave. She had become too comfortable with the Blandish family, far more than she'd ever been with her own.

They lounged at opposite ends on the leather sofa that resembled a piece of furniture picked up at a curb. The cushions—if she could use such a general term—were dried and flat. Even worse, her knees rose higher than her butt. To compensate, she tucked one leg under, but the position put too much pressure on her tired knees. Moments later, she slipped onto the hardwood floor.

Jonathan grabbed the coffee tray and followed. "I considered the sofa in the parlor uncomfortable, but this one wins by a mile." He set the tray between them.

She sipped the wonderfully strong coffee and caught his gaze. "Your brother lived like a pauper." She threw a thumb in the direction of the desk. "Forty-watt bulbs. Someone else's leftover furniture." She elbowed the sofa then pointed upward. "One television in the bedroom that I swear is black and white. I guess his salary sucked."

"On the contrary, Roger made excellent money." He bit into a cookie and chewed. "He had a bank account containing three-quarters of a million and also a brokerage account worth over a million. He wasn't a pauper by any stretch of the word."

She nearly choked on her coffee. Hell, if she had that kind of money, she wouldn't pick up curbside trash.

He shoved the rest of the cookie into his mouth and chewed. "Any luck with the books?"

Glancing at the piles, she sighed. "I haven't gone through them. All these on the floor are from the top two shelves. I was checking for secret panels when you walked in." Not like she had any real hope of finding one. "After my break, I'll start sorting and packing in what boxes we have, but this room will take a while." She glanced over her steaming cup and cocked her head. "Are you serious about not helping?"

"Of course not. What do you need?"

"I'd like you to clean out Roger's desk. He still has a lot of paperwork in the drawers." She glanced at the mahogany desk and mentally calculated the people interested in such a solid piece of furniture. "The desk itself should fetch a nice price at auction, and while you're pulling out drawers, tap around for any hidden compartments."

His gaze sparkled. "I already tried that." He stared into his steaming cup then gave her a sideways glance. "Marina, do you honestly believe we can be employer/employee anymore?"

"You alone want the status quo, Jonathan." The words shot his brows halfway into his hairline. She pointed to his left hand. "You're wearing a wedding band. Your commitment to your late wife is commendable, but to another woman, the ring is a symbol of a relationship that will go nowhere." She lowered her cup to the tray before meeting his gaze. "For the record, I don't date married men, and you, my dear, are still married. A woman can't compete with a ghost."

His left thumb flicked the gold band on his finger. "The ring reminds me of a vow I take seriously."

"And every time we kiss, you feel like you're cheating on her. No, don't try to refute something so obvious. Freeing you from your guilt trip is not part of my job description. Hell, I've enough emotional scars of my own." She picked up the coffee carafe and refilled both cups. "I want you to keep your distance while I'm working. Don't steal kisses or flirt, and above all, don't insinuate promises you've no intention of keeping."

His mouth twisted at one end. "Stolen kisses, stolen love. Words from your song."

She lifted her cup in a form of salute. "I'm surprised you listened so closely, and yes, the words are appropriate. I won't fall in love again because men play emotional games, like this so-called attraction we share. You aren't ready to move on, and I accept that. What I need from you is to let me do my job so I can return to the auction house."

Raising a brow, he placed his cup on the tray. "You want me to stay away?"

Yes, as far as possible. She nodded. "I also want to work longer hours."

He shook his head. "I disagree with both requests. I'm here because this house gives me the creeps. I worry about you and Patti, about the unsolved murders, and the missing money. I can't concentrate on my own work, so for a time, I feel like a bodyguard." He shot her a glare. "You have a problem with that?"

Men and their damn egos. She managed a faint smile. "I'm not used to men acting like my knight in shining armor. This maiden always fought the dragon on her own."

His face softened. "Just call me the dragon slayer."

Their gazes held. Something fluttered in her stomach. The coffee more likely. Acid reflux.

Tyler burst through the doorway, squealing. "I found a secret room!"

Chapter Eighteen

A secret room? After enduring two months of nothing but setbacks, Jonathan welcomed good news for a change. His pulse quickened at the prospect of a breakthrough and followed an excited Tyler to the parlor with Marina close behind.

Tyler stopped before the cold fireplace and pointed to the left wall. "There!"

Jonathan pushed along the dark paneling until one press created a click. A thin door opened on rusty hinges.

Well, I'll be damned.

Musty air wafted from the interior, and he sneezed into his shoulder before peering inside. "I need a flashlight."

"I have one on the dining room table." Marina ran through the archway and then hurried back. She handed him the light.

Clicking the switch, he waved the beam in all directions inside the open panel and illuminated water-stained wood and cobwebs. His heart sank.

Marina leaned over him. "Well?"

He squatted to shine the beam upward. "Not very wide. Tall enough for one adult but only narrow enough for small children."

The outside wall had a mass of rusty nails sticking through wide planks of wood, nails that tacked the exterior tar paper used to insulate a nineteenth century home. Standard two-by-four's supported the wall, unevenly spaced as was the norm back then.

"Any hidden treasures?"

He snorted. "About an inch of dust and the remains of a dried-up mouse. Doesn't look as if anything hid in here for a long time." He stuck his head into the opening and flashed the beam to and fro. "The fireplace blocks one side, the dining room wall the other."

"I found it! I found it!" Tyler hopped alongside his father.

Jonathan eased back and straightened. "Yes, you won the prize. Congratulations." He snapped off the flashlight and shut the panel then clicked it open and shut again. "Why does a parsonage need a hidden panel? Even though the house was built prior to the Civil War, this is Boston. We had no need to hide slaves." He glanced at Marina. "Can you think of anything?"

"Several things. Prohibition for one." She stepped around Jonathan while lifting a pair of eyeglasses from her front pocket. She placed them on the tip of her nose as her fingers traced along the paneling. "The seams are cut perfectly to hide the opening. Since the paneling style is from the early nineteen-sixties, the panel was used from that time forward." She met his gaze. "Maybe even by Roger."

He shook his head. "I don't think so. No disturbance shows in the dust on the floor."

"I'm gonna find more panels," Tyler declared and ran from the room.

Jonathan smiled after him. "I hope he does."

After sliding the glasses to the top of her head,

Marina stared at the sofa, her gaze intense. She wagged a finger toward the cushions. "You know, Jonathan, this is an odd position for a sofa in a living room. The den I understand because of the metal tracks for the ladder, but not here. Why place such a large piece in the center of the room?"

He hadn't given much thought to his brother's furniture arrangement, but since she mentioned it... "Let's move the sofa." Together, they slid the piece two feet to the side. He pounded the floor with his foot. "Nothing sounds loose." He squatted and used the flashlight to tap the wood. "Everything has a hollow sound from the lack of insulation." He glanced at the sofa then up at her. "How about in the sofa lining?"

Each grabbing an end, they turned the sofa onto its front.

Marina whipped out her utility knife and cut the thin sheathing to expose the underside of the cushioning. Nothing but the standard lattice metal to provide firmness.

They righted the sofa.

She slipped the knife into her back pocket. "Of course, you can wait until we ship the house contents to the auction then rip out the entire floor."

Jonathan hardly gave a damn anymore. Hell, the embezzlement was the hedge fund's problem, not his. He rubbed the nape of his neck. "I'm sorry, Marina. I know how anxious you are to finish the job." He handed her the flashlight.

She took it. "I'm more anxious to exonerate myself, and we haven't found a clue to help." She shifted the light from hand to hand, her gaze in a squint. "I think your brother was delusional."

The same prognosis had entered his mind. He ran a hand through his hair. "In a way, I'm glad you're here. Even if we find the money, I want you to stay."

Questions shot across her expression faster than lightning. Her eyebrows flicked. Her beautiful mouth twitched. Perhaps she needed clarification. "To finish the inventory, of course."

Their gazes locked.

"Oh." Shaking her head, she looked away. "You're a contradiction, Jonathan. I don't think you know what you want." She dropped the flashlight onto the sofa and headed for the den.

He wasn't sure what he wanted either. Bad enough he acted like a fool half the time. He wanted her to go then to stay. He wished the job was over and then wished it would last forever. All his life, he prided himself on his quick-thinking decisions, but now, he experienced nothing but confusion.

Jonathan returned to the den to see Marina sitting cross-legged on the floor sorting the books, eyeglasses perched on the edge of her nose. Several strands of hair had escaped from her clip, and he had the urge to loosen the rest, to bury his fingers deep within the curls. Visions of slithering nakedness on cool sheets flashed before him with her hair tickling his chest. Hours of ecstasy waiting to be had. To taste, to touch, to love a woman again. He wasn't sure he remembered what to do.

Discouraged at himself, he stuffed his hands into his pants pockets. "What else will we discover to make me hate this house more?"

She chuckled softly. "Old houses are full of secrets." She pointed to the desk. "In case you forgot."

"No, I didn't forget." He lied. Only one thought clouded his mind, and she sat a mere ten feet away. Grateful for the distraction, he flopped onto the desk chair and yanked open a drawer.

Alphabetized folders swung on a metal file rack. Utilities, taxes, deductible receipts. Roger's life in neat segments. The papers had revealed nothing on Jonathan's first inspection, but this time around, he adopted a save-or-destroy mentality.

Throughout, he watched Marina as she inspected each book then placed it in one of three boxes alongside. The woman had forced him to question his rock-solid feelings. For six long years, never a stray thought entered his mind despite the beautiful women who had crossed his path. What was Marina's special spell? Her close proximity? Or perhaps an unending curiosity created by Roger's notes?

Arrows had shot straight into his heart to find her cowered on the kitchen floor. Like a child, vulnerable and afraid. And then, to hear her guitar with her lovely voice purring the words of a lost love. She had awakened an appreciation of music that died with his wife. And, of course, to see Marina and Tyler asleep on the sofa, he damned near melted on the spot. Marina made the world feel right again. What to do about her was the problem. He sighed heavily and dumped the entire contents of the drawer into the trash bin.

"Oh!"

He looked up as Marina unfolded a piece of paper. "What is it?"

"This paper fell out of this book." Her eyebrows arched as she read, her complexion draining of color. She jumped to her feet to hand him the note.

The sheet contained a list in Roger's handwriting.

32 Pearl
60 Marquise
80 Pavilion
20 Rectangular
30 Square
45 Cabochon
30 Rough

Their beauty matches the intricate curves of Marina Cavanaugh. That's why I chose her to hold all.

"What in the world is he talking about?" she complained. "He has to be talking about another Marina Cavanaugh, because I haven't the slightest idea what this means." She paced the room, one hand on her hip, the other in her hair.

Three clues, all pointing to Marina. He pursed his lips. "Which book was it in?"

She whirled to grab the book and read the binding. "*The Art of Marquise Gelt.*" She flipped the pages and gasped. "Jon, he's talking about diamonds! The book's dated 1907, but look, Roger's note mentions the cuts." Extending the book, she showed him the page. "That's what this list means, diamond cuts!"

He flew around the desk, took the book, and flipped to a page illustrating the cuts. "Well, I'll be damned. The money's in diamonds, and Marina Cavanaugh holds all." He turned to her and peered.

In a gesture of surrender, she elevated her hands, palms up. "I do not know anything about your brother or diamonds."

Jonathan reread the note. "I'll show this to Farnsworth." He looked upward. "The book came from the top shelves, right? Why hide a note so high? Why not in his safe?"

"Because a safe can be broken into, but no one will take the time to search through all these books." After waving at the stacks, she tore off her gloves. "I'm part of a dangerous game and have had enough." She stuffed her gloves into her back pocket. "Find yourself another appraiser." She left the den.

His throat tightened. *She can't leave.* But she had paled to the color of a white sheet. *What the hell can I do?* "Marina, wait." He followed her into the dining room where she tossed her eyeglasses into her briefcase. "I'm sorry I dragged you into this, but you see my dilemma. This is the third time Roger mentioned your name."

She stiffened and faced him, her chin high. "You don't know if Roger means me. You can't be sure he smuggled diamonds. In truth, you don't know shit, except two men were murdered, and I refuse to join them." She slammed her briefcase shut and reached for the handle.

He laid his open palm on the case to stop her. "Look, our assumptions are all we have. Once Farnsworth sees the note, he can let his men tear apart this house, but I need you to stay."

Her chin jutted as she glared. "Why do you need me, Jonathan? From where I stand, I see a man who needs no one."

"That's not true." He placed his hands on her shoulders. They gave under his touch. "I can't force you to stay, but I've gotten used to having you around. I don't feel so alone in this mess."

One brow arched, she shot him a quick glance. "I don't think you meant that the way it sounded."

He wrapped his arms around her and drew her close. She melted against him in a way that sucked the resistance out of his heart. "I won't let anything happen to you. I promise."

"Men break promises," she mumbled into his shirt. Her fingers gripped the flap to his breast pocket.

"I'd like to prove you wrong." Her softness sent him reeling. He hadn't held a woman like this in six long years, and the sensations shooting through his veins were enough to force a groan from his throat. She had to feel his maleness pressing against her abdomen, his building need. "I want you so much."

Tyler ran from the kitchen, his fist full of eyeglasses. "Marina, I found these!"

Jonathan shoved her aside while taking two steps in retreat, thrusting his hands deep into his pants pockets. As her expression changed from wide-eyed to glaring, she threw her head back and stiffened. The look she shot his way said the words. He'd done it again, dammit!

****

His concentration sucked. All through dinner, food entered his mouth and rolled around on his tongue, but every morsel lacked flavor. His mother surveyed him with a raised brow since he shook salt and pepper over his plate like no tomorrow. More than anything, he wanted to leave the table to think about why Marina had refused dinner and what he should do about her. For so long, his constitution had remained rock solid, but he could only blame himself. He had invited her to stay in his home and created an unavoidable close proximity. At first, his motive was to find out as much as he could in relation to his brother and the missing money. Even after three notes mentioning her name, he truly believed in her innocence. She not only had a professional integrity but a personal one as well, and he'd never met anyone like her.

After shooing Tyler out of the kitchen, his mother shot him a sideways glance. "You were unusually quiet tonight. Has anything happened besides the secret panel Tyler gushed about?"

As he placed dishes in the sink, Jonathan explained about the note and the possibility of a fortune in diamonds. "The note rattled her, Mom. I'm thinking of sending her back to the auction house."

His mother placed containers of leftovers in the refrigerator. "Sending her home is the sensible course. I'd hate to see her go, though."

"Me, too."

She shut the refrigerator door and studied him. "Really? You're doing a great job of keeping her at a distance."

Not good enough. Whenever he stood close, he wanted to wrap his arms around her and never let go. Unfortunately, he had pushed her away one too many times. No woman would tolerate such an insane maneuver, but his promise to his wife flashed into his mind like a curse, and he reacted instinctively whenever he held Marina. If he couldn't keep his hands to himself, he'd continue to confuse Marina, and she deserved better.

He secured the bread bag with a tie-wrap. "I wish Farnsworth would talk to me more. I haven't got a clue how he's progressing."

After rinsing the washcloth, she wiped the table. "He can't talk to you, dear. You're still a suspect, as am

I." She returned to the sink and stacked dishes into the dishwasher. "Did you inform him about the note?"

"Not yet." He took out his cell phone and called.

The detective answered on the second ring.

Jonathan explained the note. "Right. See you then." He replaced the phone to his pocket. "He'll stop by in a little bit."

"Oh…good. Let me check my hair." She slammed the dishwasher shut, pressed the On button, and hurried from the kitchen.

This time, the image of Farnsworth and his mother hadn't flustered him. Nothing would become of the relationship while the case was active. At the conclusion—whenever that would be, his mother would realize her life was with her son and grandchild with Farnsworth nothing more than a passing whimsy. Life in the Blandish household should shift back into neutral.

He hoped.

Farnsworth arrived, looking a trifle downtrodden with shoulders hunched and sleep clouding his eyes— both of which disappeared when his mother approached. Jonathan had no intention of inviting the man inside, but his mother gushed and fussed while ushering him into the living room.

Despite her efforts, Farnsworth refused to sit, claiming a long day of dead-end clues.

Jonathan handed him the note. "Maybe I should send Marina home."

Farnsworth read quickly then met Jonathan's gaze with a cocked brow. "Even after a note like this?" He waved the paper in the air. "Sorry, Blandish, but the doctor takes center stage in our investigation. I have to keep both of you at the top of my suspect list." He pulled his earlobe while his brows furrowed tight against the bridge of his nose. "I can't find a connection between the doctor and your brother, but maybe the diamonds will be a better path. She does travel extensively, you know." After a directed stare, he patted Jonathan's shoulder. "Until I give the okay, you keep everything status quo, hear?"

That answered the question of whether to send Marina home. Deep inside, he had no desire to send her anywhere.

Jonathan left his mother and Farnsworth with the excuse of putting Tyler to bed. While passing Marina's closed door, he listened for the sound of her guitar. Nothing. Perhaps she was already asleep. He continued on to Tyler's room.

Tyler performed the classic bedtime shenanigans of doing everything possible to delay getting into bed—too long putting on his jammies, brushing his teeth, and suddenly tidying his room.

Even his last-minute trip to the bathroom took forever. Suspicious, Jonathan knocked and entered to see Tyler leaning over the sink with his hands covered in soap bubbles. "Okay, enough washing. Dry your hands and hop into bed before I fall asleep on my feet."

Like any little boy, he accomplished some strange feats with a bar of soap. One time, he had plugged the laundry room drain, because he wanted to see how far he could stuff the bar into the hole. Even with the crossbar intact, he squeezed the whole bar inside. How he achieved such a difficult task was beyond any comprehension. Jonathan had struggled with an ice pick and a lot of hot water to clear the opening.

Tyler sped from the bathroom, down the hall, and to his room then did a flying leap onto his bed. He tucked his legs under the blankets.

Marina's soft guitar picking flowed through the walls.

She was awake after all, and a smile tugged on Jonathan's lips. He'd grown accustomed to her nighttime music ritual. Sometimes she sang along with the guitar, but more often—like tonight—she simply picked the strings.

"You should learn how to play the guitar, Dad. Then you and Marina can play together."

If they played together, they wouldn't bother with guitars. He tucked the covers to Tyler's chin.

"She has night lights. How come I don't?"

"Because Marina is in a strange house. She doesn't know her way around." No sense telling Tyler the real reason.

Despite the trauma caused by a cruel father, Marina exhibited none of the outward signs of an abused child. She showed warmth and compassion whenever she and Tyler were together. Yesterday on the sofa, for example. She'd held Tyler against her breasts like he was her own, and Jonathan couldn't look away. Yes, he'd kissed her because her soft lips were too hard to resist.

"I like Marina, Dad. I want you to marry her so she can be my mom."

A thickness swelled in his throat. Tyler hadn't known his mother. She died so young, but her photos were a constant reminder of the little boy she'd given him. Tyler remained Jonathan's only link to the vow he'd promised to keep.

"You should date, Dad."

Since Tyler's had *dates* with the girl next door, he understood the concept of a boy/girl pairing. Although, carrying a box full of bugs on one date hadn't won him any special privileges. Jonathan sat on the bed. "You sound like your grandmother talking."

"You won't get anywhere with this." Tyler tapped the wedding band on Jonathan's finger. "You have to take it off."

Jonathan rotated the band.

"I never had a mommy." His little hands gripped the bed covers. "Don't you like Marina?"

Oh, God, what a question! "I like her very much. But I made a promise to your mother, and a man should always keep a promise."

"Marina likes you."

Jonathan leaned back with a jolt. "How do you know?"

"I can tell. I see how she looks at you."

An astute little man. Marina's dark eyes had a way of glowing like hot embers whenever their gazes met. Any man with a normal hormone level would drag her to a bedroom. But not Jonathan Blandish. He had a vow to keep.

Tyler held out his little hand, palm up. "You don't need the ring anymore, Dad."

Oh, God help me. Tyler was asking him to remove the shield that had protected him for so many years. Without the ring, what would stop him from ravishing Marina? Yet, if he held onto the memory of his late wife, he might lose Marina forever. Her inventory was progressing rapidly, and once finished, then what? She'd return to the auction house and forget they'd ever met. Could he bear that? And what about his commitment to Susan? Would she forgive him?

She hadn't verbalized any details.

At the realization, he inwardly gasped. How true! Susan had made one specific request of which he honored from the moment she asked. Only *he* had chosen to live a celibate lifestyle. No one forced him or twisted his arm. Since he made the rules, then he'd break them—all save one.

Jonathan twisted the wedding band one last time, eased it off his finger, and dropped the ring into Tyler's small hand.

Chapter Nineteen

Another three days passed before Marina finished the den. She and Patti had piled the book boxes against the wall, stacked for easy access onto a dolly. Their days started early and stretched late into the evening, breaking for breakfast, lunch, and dinner. Patti cooked throughout with every dish as delectable as the last. As a consequence, Marina had spent little time with the Blandish family, preferring instead the casual nighttime conversations with Iris and Tyler before running to her room. Never Jonathan, which was just as well.

Her feelings toward him were a jumbled mess. He might believe they'd lost the employer/employee relationship, but every time he pushed her away, he restored her place in their business association. For her sanity's sake, she wanted the job over and done with.

Aside from tearing apart the house, the police found nothing. A police expert examined Roger's diamond list and calculated a possible worth of thirty-seven million if the diamonds were of high quality, and depending, of course, on size.

Marina knew very little about diamonds—except she'd like to have one some day, preferable on her left hand. Nothing big or extravagant. The way her life was going, she'd have to buy one herself.

On Friday afternoon, Marina joined Patti in the kitchen for a light lunch before tackling the next task on the list.

"Sandwiches or casserole?" Patti asked with her head in the refrigerator.

"Sandwich sounds good."

Patti took wrapped luncheon meat from a drawer along with mayo, lettuce, and tomato while Marina grabbed the bread from the counter, glasses from the cabinet, and paper plates. Patti had packed the china—with the exception of a few mugs and glasses—and stacked the boxes near the mudroom door. They ate on paper plates for every meal.

"If you don't mind me asking, Marina, why are you doing antiques appraisals when you have a degree in anthropology?" She unwrapped the packages and spread them on the table.

Marina passed Patti a knife. "Anthropology took me around the world to some exotic places. Whenever I had free time, I'd wander through antique shops. I became so good at identifying pieces, I decided to specialize since antiques are a big part of various cultures."

Most of the credit belonged to her grandmother. The woman had taught her so much, and Marina wandered through the shops always with her grandmother's voice whispering in her ear. Her reputation as an astute buyer for several museums had prompted a visit from Victoria Billingsley who'd made an offer Marina couldn't refuse—main acquisitions expert with a great salary and unlimited expense account. The woman was a gem of a boss.

The doorbell rang.

Patti hurried from the kitchen and returned with Henry Ladner as Marina poured iced tea into two glasses. "Hi, Henry. We're about to have lunch. Care to join us?"

"Actually, I stopped by to ask Patti to dinner." He faced Patti and gave her a smile. "How about it?"

Patti turned to Marina. "That depends on how late the doctor is staying."

Marina slapped a sandwich together and took a bite. She chewed then shoved the food to the side of her mouth, bulging one cheek. Patti and Henry watched her expectantly, and she inwardly smiled. "You know, Patti, let's stop right now and take off for the weekend. I'll go home to my condo, and we'll start again on Monday."

"Really, Doctor?" Her face brightened. "That's a great idea. I have so much to do."

Henry beamed. "I hope some of your time is with me."

Patti and Henry made a cute couple. Henry wasn't quite as round as Patti, but he was close enough to give the appearance of two roly-polys standing together. His height matched Marina's, but even so, his stature against Patti's gave him a superior air, especially in his tailored suits and expensive overcoat.

Marina shoved the rest of the sandwich into her mouth, surprising herself by not choking to death. She chewed then swallowed. "I'll clear our short reprieve with Jonathan first." Whom she hadn't spoken to since Monday. *This will be awkward.* She hurried toward the parlor for her cell phone.

The idea of going home to her own bed thrilled her to no end. Over the past couple of weeks, she had become too attached to the Blandish family—above all, Tyler. Every night, he'd run into her room in his jammies to give her a hug and beg her to play a song before bedtime. When Jon and mini-Jon stood together, the sight overflowed her heart with a love never believed possible. Yes, she had fallen in love with both of them…with *all* of them but not the love experienced between a man and a woman. That she considered to be a deeper love, a more profound effect on her emotions, one she believed incapable of achieving, in particular, with Jonathan. So, a weekend on her home turf would do wonders for her confused psyche.

Jonathan gave his okay without an argument, which surprised her. Marina then made a quick call to Iris, who sounded thoroughly disappointed. Since Marina had already thrown her dirty laundry in the SUV with the hope of using Roger's washing machine in the mudroom, she had no reason to return to the Blandish house. She'd leave directly from Roger's without wasting a second of freedom and use her own machine. She returned to the kitchen to see Patti and Henry munching on potato chips. "We have the weekend off!"

A sense of independence hit as she drove through the thick Boston traffic. Nothing could destroy the elation of the mood, not even the two traffic jams that forced her to re-route. She'd gone through a trying couple of weeks, what with Karl's murder on top of the dreariest working environment ever encountered. She longed for the spaciousness of her warehouse-converted condo with its array of windows overlooking Boston Harbor.

Maybe this is the time to call it quits. Pack my belongings and say I can't handle the assignment anymore.

But she had never quit any job, big or small, regardless of conditions. The trait stemmed from a stubbornness cultivated by her forced confinement in a dark closet. The same obstinate characteristic had helped all the way through graduate school when money was tight. And besides, Roger's house was almost finished. Only the attic and garage remained. Another week, at best. *And then I'm outta that hellhole*!

Marina arrived at her condo and parked in her assigned spot, sucking in the cold sea breeze before heading into the building. She ran up the five flights of stairs, laundry bag bumping over her shoulder, in no mood to wait for an elevator. The excitement of being home powered her legs, adrenaline at an all-time high, the same elation experienced every single time she finished an assignment.

Once inside the condo, her first order of business was to open the drapes to stare at the boats bobbing in their slots. Fishing boats, yachts, and weekend cruisers quietly waited for owners to glide them into the open sea. On warmer days, she'd open the windows, but today, the condo needed some heat. She hurried to the thermostat by her bedroom door.

She loved her condo, with its array of windows to let in the northern light. Not a dark corner in the place. The main living area was a combination kitchen-living room with a cushioned sofa facing the windows, separated from the kitchen by an L-shaped island. An office corner with a desk computer and shelves covered with antique reference books stood to the side. At the far end opposite the windows were the only walls in the place to separate the two bedrooms and one large bath/laundry room. An abundance of open space, the perfect condo to keep her phobia in check. Unfortunately, she loved Jonathan's house just as much, along with Iris and Tyler.

The feeling was so wrong, but how could she squelch her growing affection with visions of Tyler bounding the stairs to greet her, or Iris always answering the door with a cheery hello and a hug? Marina had become the daughter Iris never had as Iris had become the mother Marina desired. The big thorn in the picture was Jonathan.

In the beginning, he had looked so stern, a man used to obedient women, but over time, the sternness eased. The tyrant had disappeared, and she envisioned a man who exemplified stability and strength, one confident of his place in the world.

Despite her conflicting feelings toward Jonathan, Marina empathized with his unending love for his deceased spouse. Her grandmother was the same way after the death of her husband. But age factored into the equation. Her grandmother was in her seventies and had no desire to hook up with another man. Jonathan was in his thirties, a virile, handsome man capable of sweeping any woman off her feet.

But every display of tenderness on his part resulted in a sudden disconnect because of guilt. If he only knew how much she wanted to feel his arms around her and to wallow in the maturity of a successful man...an anchored one, unlike any she'd ever met.

As time passed and she got to know him better, she understood the difference between a controlling man like her father and a caring one. Jonathan was definitely the latter. Everything he said and did was to protect her from harm, even though she argued each step of the way. He watched out for her more than any man she'd ever known.

After stepping from a long shower, she heard the persistent buzz of the intercom. She quickly wrapped a towel around her wet body and headed to the double doors covering the elevator. After pressing the intercom button, she leaned close to the box. "Yes?"

"It's Jonathan. I hope I'm not disturbing you."

Her heart performed a quiet, little flip within her chest, and she stared at the intercom as if not believing the voice on the other end. Thoughts scrambled together, but one persistent notion took hold. He hadn't liked her leaving after all. She stole a glance at the wall clock in the kitchen area. Five-thirty. What could he want besides drag her to his house? "Press button five, Jonathan. You're using a freight elevator that won't move unless you close the gate."

She ran to the bedroom for clothes and threw on a pair of sweats, ignoring the necessity of underwear since he probably wouldn't stay long. Her thick hair would stay damp for hours so she finger-combed the strands to tame the wild look and hurried barefoot from her bedroom as the elevator dinged its arrival.

He'll turn into his demanding self, order me back on the job, and say he isn't paying for comp time. Nothing else explained his sudden appearance. Yet, somewhere within her troubled thoughts, she hoped this was a personal visit, and her heart rate accelerated. Before opening the door, she fluffed her hair again.

Jonathan entered carrying a white shopping bag and a large bouquet of flowers, his business suit covered by an open overcoat. His hair was slightly windblown, but he looked as handsome as ever.

Without a word or a smile, he stretched out his arm to hand her the flowers.

The gesture was akin to a teenager going on his first date, slightly shy and definitely endearing, in complete contrast to the man she'd grown to know. With some hesitation, she took the bouquet and sniffed. "What's this for?"

"I thought we might have dinner together, so I hope you don't have plans. We haven't had a chance to talk this week."

With good reason. Being near him was too hard. More than any prior man, he jumbled her feelings into a knot. She wanted to keep her distance and, at the same time, wanted him close. She liked looking at him yet constantly averted her gaze, afraid he'd catch her staring. Why such an internal conflict?

Because she loved him. She was through arguing with herself. He was everything she wanted in a man— successful, feet firmly on the ground, strength in character. A family man without question. Naturally, hers was a one-way love, to be silently endured forever.

Jonathan placed the bag on a side chair and removed one sleeve of his overcoat but stopped, his head tipping to the side. "Am I staying?"

The shy tone of his voice relaxed her jumpy gut. She smiled. "You're staying. Hang your coat on the rack by the doors."

He obeyed and then turned to look around, nodding his approval. "Nice place. You have one giant room."

"That's what I love and, you'll notice, lots of windows for light." Again, she sniffed the flowers. The arrangement was a mixture of whites and blues with the hyacinth's fragrance dominating. "I'll put these in a vase." She headed for the kitchen. "Were you at the office when I called?"

"Yes, trying to concentrate. Your voice shot that idea to hell." He grabbed the bag from the chair and extended it into the air. "Where do you want this?"

In need of a flower vase, she opened a cabinet and shifted several glasses to the side before finding the perfect container for the arrangement. "On the counter is fine. You saved me a trip to the market."

She spread the bouquet within the vase then added water, all the while keeping her back to him. Her hands shook. Nerves, of course. Was he here for a briefing? A when-will-you-finish speech? "I haven't had a chance to make a printout of the den's contents, Jonathan." She stole a glance in his direction. "I'll run a copy off while I'm here."

"No problem." He approached the array of windows. "You have a great view of the harbor."

"That's why the sofa faces that way." She placed the flower vase on the kitchen island and watched him standing by the windows. He had a strong profile with a square jaw, straight nose, and hair perfectly trimmed. She had once dated a man with hair covering half of his back. During sex, the stringy strands fell in her face, and she spent the entire time spitting them from her mouth. Never again. "Take off your suit jacket, Jonathan, and loosen your tie. I assume you're done working for today."

"I am." He turned from the window and removed his jacket and tie, tossed both onto the side chair, and loosened the top button on his shirt.

He looked awkward, not uncomfortable, just…awkward. Like he hadn't a clue what to do with himself now that he was here. An amusing situation. This was her castle. He was a visitor who had entered the gates. "What's in the bag?" She opened the flaps and peeked in.

"Chinese." He sauntered toward the kitchen. "I bought four different entrées so you should find something you'll like."

"I love Chinese." She lifted each container from the bag and set them on the island. The aromas of shrimp and chicken made her salivate.

He approached the counter. "I'm glad you weren't busy. I was hoping to catch you before you made plans."

"Why?" She sniffed the white carton in her right hand. Lo mein. Yum. Then the container in her left hand. Orange beef—yes!

He stepped close and, with a feather touch of his finger under her chin, tilted her head toward him. His lips slid across hers, moist lips, warm and tender, suckling from one end of her mouth to the other. Surprise clouded her brain. The what-was-he-doing thoughts flooded her mind until pleasure took hold as she responded to the gentleness of his kiss.

Lifting his head, he gazed into her eyes. "Put down the cartons, Marina."

Startled, she stared at the two cartons swinging from their metal handles then set them on the island.

His arms slipped around her and drew her close, pressing her body against his so that no space existed between them. His lips sought hers, still gentle, like an exploration, brushing back and forth until his tongue separated her lips and probed. As his kiss intensified, he squeezed her tighter, causing her knees to wobble. To prevent a quick slide to the floor, she wrapped her arms around his neck with one hand slipping into his hair.

She was in heaven. His hard chest pressed against hers, and she leaned against him in a way she hadn't done to a man in years. The power and strength of his arms and the pressure of his arousal against her abdomen sent her reeling. Sensations, all hot and carnal, shot to the surface of her skin, and she greedily kissed him back. Only a hint of his spicy aftershave remained, but with heightened senses, she sucked in the scent as if she sniffed from a bottle. Yet, doubts emerged. He'd pushed her away so often she expected to be thrown across the room at any second.

As his arms relaxed, he sighed into her mouth, and she looked up to see a slow smile stretch onto his lips.

Her heart thundered at the sight of this handsome man and his sexy smile. She stroked a fingertip across his lips. "I don't make a habit of kissing the boss."

"I don't kiss my employees either." His voice reverberated with emotion as he placed his forehead against hers. "Marina, I don't want to rush into anything. I need time to assimilate how I feel."

His arousal was plain enough for her. Regardless… "I'm not rushing you." Hell, her own voice shook. The man had too much of an effect on her, and with her luck, his kiss was his experiment in emotional self-control.

She broke free from his arms to continue with the cartons of Chinese food, aware that she could barely keep her knees locked. "You bought an awful lot for two people." Her voice sounded foreign, like a spirit possessed her soul to give a voice deep and seductive. She cleared her throat and reached for plates in the cabinet, her hand pausing near the glasses. "What do you like to drink? I can make tea."

"Tea will be perfect."

Marina placed the plates and mugs on a serving tray while Jonathan opened the cartons and sniffed.

With his left hand, he held the open carton under her nose, but she neither sniffed nor glanced at the contents.

Her eye caught something much more obvious, and she grabbed the carton and turned his hand to stare at the band of white skin on his ring finger. With wide eyes, she met his gaze.

He smiled and gave a slight shrug. "I feel undressed."

Her breath hitched. "Not because of me, right?"

"Yes, because of you. Your presence in my house ate away at my resistance. I...need time."

"Oh—kay, thank you, I guess." Talk about confusion. Rather than question his motives, she filled the teapot with tap water and set it on the stove. While waiting for the water to boil, she placed the cartons and plates on a tray, added serving spoons, and handed everything to him. "Put this on the coffee table. We'll sit on the sofa." She followed a few minutes later with a pot of tea and two mugs.

Dusk had settled over the harbor. Tiny lights lit the walkways to the boat slots, hiding the imperfections that were visible in daylight. Some of the yachts were illuminated with brighter lights since many held parties on Friday night. Marina often relaxed on the sofa and counted how many people fell overboard in a drunken stupor. She handed him a plate, barely controlling the shaking of her hand. "Chopsticks or fork?"

He chose the chopsticks. She selected the same, and they served sufficient amounts onto their plates.

Not like she would taste anything. She had never met a man who turned her on with a simple touch. Turning him off was the problem. The searing heat remained from his kiss, and her hands ached to glide along the hard body beneath his clothes. An avaricious feeling for sure…for more of him…for love.

Maybe she should follow his lead and learn to flip a switch. "I found several rare books." *May as well keep the conversation light*. "I don't know if you noticed the blue vase on one of the shelves behind Roger's desk. The value is at least sixty thousand."

He paused while dumping half the carton of fried shrimp onto his plate, brows raised. "No shit?"

At his wide-eyed look, she smiled. "Ch'ing dynasty. The stuff in the den is worth more than the entire contents of the house unless the paintings from the basement surprise me. I'll have the boys from the warehouse stop by for the books since they'll need to be evaluated by our specialist." She poured the remainder of the shrimp onto her plate. "Any news from Farnsworth?"

"Nada." He shoved in a mouthful of noodles and chewed. "He isn't telling me much. I suspect he's at a dead end."

"He might not tell you anything for a reason. Cops like to keep an ace in their pocket." She spooned out more rice. "What made him consider Roger's murder a crime of passion?"

He chewed then swallowed. "Choice of weapon. The murderer used a screwdriver, probably from Roger's workbench. Roger had on no jacket so he went to the garage for a reason. No one knows what. Roger took the screwdriver while facing his assailant. No resistance, no fight."

She mixed the shrimp with the rice and glanced his way. "An argument then?"

"That's the logical conclusion. About what and with whom are the questions. Whatever transpired got out of hand and end of Roger."

She studied him, her brows furrowed. "That was a cold statement."

"Reality, Marina. I've gotten over the pain." He dunked an egg roll into mustard sauce, and his eyes immediately watered. "Whew, mustard's hot." With his chopsticks, he pointed to his plate. "I like these noodles. Try some."

She did—grabbing several from his plate.

"Hey, not mine!"

His tasted better. "This stuff's good. Where'd you buy it?"

"That's my secret. This way, I can treat you every once in a while. I'd like to see you when this blows over." He grabbed the orange beef carton.

Wow. His statement caused butterflies in her belly. Unless the shrimp came alive. She smiled. "I'd like that, too."

The carton paused mid-air. "You would?"

With two fingers, she lifted the hair away from his forehead. "Yes, Jonathan, I would."

He took her hand and kissed the palm.

The conversation drifted to casual topics. Movie reviews. His construction projects. When the subject shifted to Tyler, Jonathan spoke with a pride that caused a warm glow to rise inside her heart. "Jon and mini-Jon," she murmured.

Leaning forward, he looked at her with a mouthful of food. "What?"

"Sorry. I was talking out loud."

He mocked a frown. Instead of a reprimand, he slipped his hand into her damp hair and pulled her toward him. The mustard sauce on his tongue tingled her lips, but she probed for more, giving him a taste of what he denied himself for six years. Would this kiss finally push him over the edge, or must she wrestle him onto her bed with her bare hands? *How much time does he need?*

He lifted his head. "I'd better go."

Obviously, the man needs a whole lot of time.

As he hurried to his feet and slipped on his suit jacket, he gave her a cursory glance, a kind of half-fast apologetic expression.

Sighing, she rose from the sofa to retrieve the silver tie he dropped on the floor. Pure silk from the feel. "Thanks for dinner."

"You're welcome." He took the tie from her fingers, rolled the material into a ball, and stuffed it into his jacket pocket. "Will you be on the job Monday?"

"Without fail."

"And in my house Monday night?"

"Yes." She'd spoken the word softly to hide the hesitation in her voice. She wasn't sure Jonathan's house was a good idea anymore. A knee-weakening kiss had a way of killing the employer/employee relationship. Most of all, he incited yearnings of love and protection—of someone who cared. A big void in her life right now.

Marina escorted Jonathan to the elevator doors

where he lifted his overcoat from the coat rack. He paused before activating the elevator button, his gaze searching her face.

Her heart somersaulted. "You don't have to go."

He dropped his overcoat onto the floor. "I don't think I will."

Chapter Twenty

Jonathan crushed Marina against the wall, seeking her mouth like a man starving for human flesh. He shouldn't have come yet he couldn't stay away, his internal arguments unheeded. Despite the vow to his wife, he found his hormones begging for this gorgeous woman. Marina made him lose all sense of place and time…and promises, her temptation proving too great.

Now, she was here in his arms. His fingers caressed the damp strands of her hair while the freshness of a recent shower seeped through her skin and tantalized his nose. Her lips, so moist and delicious, returned his kiss with equal fervor. How could he not ravish her? He wanted this woman, and judging from the heat of her body, she wanted him.

His suit jacket slipped off. The garment fell in a heap next to his overcoat. Her doing. She had deft fingers, like a thief lifting a priceless jewel. His hands slid under her sweatshirt to feel the firmness of her breasts, and then, her sweatshirt disappeared. Her doing again. With her breasts fully exposed, he traced his thumbs across the hard nipples then lowered his lips to suckle and lick. Arousal robbed his ability to corral his need. A primitive response, but he had lost the ability to turn on the brakes.

"Jon—bedroom."

Yes, the bedroom. Disorientation stole his sense of

direction. He lifted her in his arms, feeling her hands cupping his face with her lips giving feather kisses across his cheek. "Which way?"

"First door…on the left."

Her voice spoke with a deep, raspy pitch, a woman full of want, breathless with chest heaving. Hell, which way was left? With leaden steps, he aimed for a door, any door, and miraculously entered a room with a big bed. Cool sheets. Perfect. He lowered her to the bed, and reality froze him. He lowered his head to her chest and groaned.

"Don't lose it, Jon…please!" She jumped to her knees and grabbed his belt buckle.

"I'm so friggin' out of practice, Marina." His fingers wrapped around her wrists to stop the lowering of his zipper. He met a pleading gaze. "I didn't bring any condoms." She stared, wide-eyed, pupils in full dilation, gaze dark with desire, for him, for what he could provide.

"Oh, Jon." She bit her lip. "I might have one in the nightstand." She rolled across the bed, yanked on the nightstand drawer, and rummaged. "Please be here." She tossed the drawer contents to the floor then whooped, whirled toward him, and held up a packet, victory glowing from her face.

They tore off their clothes.

Her greed for emotional release matched his own, and she lunged. Hands roamed and stroked bare skin. Goose bumps rose. Foreplay became an afterthought. Six years of frustration poured from his core. Six long years of denying the pleasure of a responsive woman. No woman had tempted him like Marina. Tonight would never be enough.

"Jon—now!"

He slipped on top and thrust himself deep, and as she tightened around him, the most mind-boggling sensations shuddered through him. Simultaneously, chills and heat. A rush of adrenaline. His mind cleared of all troubles with only one thought—Marina. Her release hit first then he humped to increase her pleasure until he muffled a cry of pure bliss.

What a woman!

He had absolutely no desire to free himself from her body, but in time, he rolled onto his side and held her close, his fingers toying with the long strands of her silky hair. Her face had such a beautiful glow he almost cried. This was what he had craved from the moment he stepped into her lunchroom. Every night, he'd dreamt of her in his arms, loving her, and sniffing the multitudes of scents from the flowery shampoo to the soap on her skin. How could he have denied himself for so long?

Lying under his arm, she kissed his nipple then looked up with a smile. "You performed exceptionally well for a man out of practice."

He pretended to polish his nails. "Male instinct. We never forget how to perform." He kissed her forehead. "Our heat dried your hair."

"Can't ask for a better drier." She placed her cheek against his breast.

Sex had deepened her voice, and the tone tingled his nerves into action. An erection rose under the sheet. With hope that she was blind as a bat, he slid a hand the length of her spine to her cute butt. Round as a baby's bottom. He massaged.

"I only have one condom," she purred.

All right, so she noticed the rising sheet. "Yes, I realize. Obviously, I never expected this to happen."

"That's evident since you arrived without protection."

Her fingers walked across his chest and hardened an already-raised part of his anatomy. "You keep this up, and I'll have to reuse the condom, which isn't recommended."

She put her chin on his chest and met his gaze. A mischievous imp sparkled back, and her mouth twisted with a grin.

"We can make a quick run to the drugstore."

Or ask them to deliver. What would he do in the meantime to control the mounting heat? He took her wandering hand and kissed the fingertips one by one. "As much as I'd love to, I can't stay. Tyler plays soccer tomorrow, and his team has a good shot at the championship. I'd hate to miss it."

The grin faded. "Another time then." She placed a palm on his cheek and turned his head while stretching to brush her lips against his.

A tease, he knew, for what could have been.

A warm gaze searched his face. "Tyler has a great dad."

Her words were kind, but she couldn't hide the disappointment in her voice. He drew her close and kissed her nose. "You called me Jon again, but I'll forgive you since the heat of the moment ruined your manners."

She propped onto one elbow. "I like Jon even if you don't." She withdrew slightly, a brow raised. "You're sorry we did this?"

"Not for a second." *A bold lie.* Guilt consumed

him, and he had no one to blame but himself. He rose to a sitting position. "I should go." And have his head examined. He dressed.

She wrapped herself in a bathrobe, and they left the bedroom, no words between them.

He retrieved his suit jacket and overcoat from the floor before turning to take her chin in his hand. "Drive carefully Monday. I don't want anything to happen to you."

"Yes, sir." She saluted.

The first time she saluted, the gesture had irritated him. Now, she looked so damn cute.

Love was amazing. He inwardly jerked. Was he truly in love with Marina? *I can't be.* So much had died with the death of his wife, but being with Marina made him feel alive again. Would she accept the limitations in their relationship? He wrapped his arms around her for a kiss. "I want to keep quiet about this."

A cloud passed over her face. "Oh? Still hiding from your late wife's ghost?" She patted his chest and stepped away. "No, that's okay, Jonathan. You didn't toss me aside this time. I assume because she's not here in my condo." She grabbed his hand and gave a squeeze. "We're two adults attracted to each other. She'll understand. I'm sure she doesn't expect you to live the rest of your life with a vow of celibacy."

Damned if the words didn't rip apart his gut.

****

Monday came and went. Marina had stayed in Boston with the excuse of Mrs. Billingsley needing help with an evaluation. A total crock of bull. Despite her promise to Jonathan, she hadn't wanted to face him so soon. The uncertainty surrounding their relationship had robbed her of sleep and made her grumpy. Grumpiness destroyed reasoning, and her brain couldn't add three plus two without using her fingers.

Oops, red light. She braked hard.

Once, she had fallen in love. Like a fool, she believed his sugar-coated lies of the love-ever-after routine. Larry played her for a pawn in his game of sexual dalliances and broke her heart. After she'd tossed him out, she had questioned her own sanity, whether love had been an actual part of the equation, or perhaps she simply desired to belong to someone and to have a family of her own. She also wrestled with the biggest question of all. Was she looking for someone to come to her rescue if she called?

A car horn blared behind her.

Yes, all right. Green light. She turned onto the freeway.

She'd had no one growing up. As the oldest child, she took the abuse meant for her younger siblings and felt so all-alone until her brother—bless him—grew in strength and size and defied their father. But that took years. Grandmama lived across town and couldn't reason with her son-in-law or wimp of a daughter, and since the children looked healthy and clean, Granny had no legal recourse with the authorities.

So, yeah, Marina would love to have a man cuddle and protect her and to be an equal partner in life, but outward appearances were about as reliable as a man's love. She'd discovered that little tidbit of information from her last relationship. What a man said compared to his actions were two entirely different circumstances.

Jonathan was no exception. The whole liaison at her place had confused her. The man wanted her, and she gave willingly. He had no marital ties and no commitments to anyone else. So, why keep quiet? Was he ashamed?

He had removed his ring, but he could have easily left it on since he looked so damn guilty. From an anthropologist's viewpoint, she understood the complexities of cultures and the rituals of mourning the dead, and yes, some men loved so deeply, the idea of another woman in their arms was like cheating. The latter theory had made the most sense. Even so, she wanted to kick him for making her fall in love, and her confusion was the primary reason for remaining an extra day in Boston.

She had no excuse for Tuesday.

Marina arrived and set to work, full of determination to accomplish as much as possible. By midday, she stood in the center of the mudroom looking around while Patti fixed some lunch. The room itself was a return to the days of frontier exploration. Wide-slat wood planks covered the floor with indentations worn into the wood from years of foot traffic. Unfinished walls covered with bare wallboard showed age and rusty nail heads. Two window panes with the wavy glass of eons ago distorted the outside yard to make the view look like a scene from a horror movie. Only the door had entered the modern age along with the washer and dryer.

She joined Patti in the kitchen. "What will you do once Jon ships the house contents to the auction?"

"Find another job, of course." Patti placed paper plates on the table. "I'd like to work for Mr. Blandish, but with his mother available, he doesn't need me." She opened the refrigerator.

Marina laid out the napkins and silverware. "Iris is talking about getting her own apartment."

Patti jerked her head from the refrigerator. "She is? Then he'll need help with Tyler. That's great news…unless you don't want me."

Startled, Marina cocked a brow. "What do *I* have to do with anything?"

Patti loaded her arms with containers and placed them on the table. "Mr. Blandish is falling for you. He'll eventually make a move."

Yeah, he'd made a move, all right, and then shattered a wonderful experience. "Don't put too much stock into that, Patti. The man doesn't know what he wants." She grabbed glasses from the cabinet. "Did you know his late wife?" She placed the glasses on the table and poured iced tea from a pitcher into both.

"She was dead by the time I started." She snapped the lids off the plastic containers. "Roger called her a spoiled princess and complained about her excessive spending."

Roger would say that. The forty-watt man. Marina gathered the lids from the table and placed them on the counter. "Jon has pictures of his late wife all over the house. That's a bit excessive in my opinion."

"Maybe they're for Tyler's sake."

"Maybe." One or two photos should be enough for a little boy. Too many, and she's being jammed down his throat.

Patti paused with spoons in her hands, staring into space. "I grew to love Roger's idiosyncrasies."

Which were many. No rugs, no lights, no comfort. Would Patti have married such a miser? Marina wouldn't be surprised to hear Roger had plans to buy

Patti a butter churn.

"Roger wanted to rent a horse and carriage for our wedding day. He was so romantic." She released a heavy sigh.

Marina inwardly groaned. If this continued, she might puke all over the table. Romance wasn't in her cards. She was too practical and too centered on reality. Her parents had painted the world gray. Happy moments or career accomplishments were crushed. Any boy stopping by to say hello was scared off, never to return. Dreams of Prince Charming coming to the rescue were just that. She wasn't sure she'd recognize a romantic gesture if one fell on her with a big neon sign.

Jonathan's flowers?

A peace offering, no more. She'd be happy enough with pizza and beer.

She and Patti dug into their meal of chicken salad, reheated macaroni and cheese, and sliced tomatoes.

"By the way—" Marina forked some macaroni into her mouth and chewed. "Did you know about the hidden panel by the fireplace?"

Patti sipped her tea then nodded. "Oh, sure. The door popped open one day when I was cleaning. I told Roger, but he already knew." She salted her tomato.

Roger hadn't used his wall safe for the diamonds, but he could very well use a secret compartment. "Did he know of any more?"

"He never said. While I cleaned, I'd press on the walls but couldn't find any others. Some may be hidden behind the heavier furniture, but I wasn't curious enough to move everything." She ate a section of her tomato and made a face. "I can't wait for the summer tomatoes. These hot-house ones have no flavor." She shook on more salt.

Not curious enough to search for a forty-million-dollar treasure? Was Patti pulling her leg? Or perhaps she'd already found the loot and killed two men to hide the fact. A fanciful notion yet Marina had difficulty dismissing the idea. Patti had every opportunity to kill…and plenty of motive.

Oh, God, what am I involved in? Was Patti guilty? If not her, then who? Jonathan?

Marina swallowed her doubts with her iced tea.

"We're making good progress, Marina. The first and second floors along with the basement are done. That leaves the attic and garage." She spooned more cheese and macaroni onto her plate. "I can start carting out the stuff from the attic."

"That's a good idea, Patti. We'll empty one of the bedrooms and store the stuff there. I'll connect the floor lamps for proper lighting, and this weekend, I'll drag over Jon to shift through the contents in the garage. Men have a different mindset about garage junk. They view everything as treasures."

Patti chuckled into her tea. "Roger told me to stay out of the garage. He claimed he'd never find anything ever again if I so much as stepped one foot through the door." She glanced at Marina with a mouth full of macaroni. She quickly chewed and swallowed. "I noticed you still call him Jon. Is he okay with that?"

"Not by a long shot." *Only in the heat of the moment.* Which would never happen again.

Marina wiped her mouth with a napkin and slid her paper plate to the side. "That was good." She gathered her utensils and carried them to the sink. The plate she tossed into the trash. Through the kitchen window, she caught a movement out in the yard and lifted the frilly curtain for a better view. "Well, look who's here." She motioned with her head for Patti to see for herself.

Hurrying alongside, Patti stood on tiptoe and peeked out the window.

Detective Farnsworth stood in the middle of the driveway, staring at the closed garage door.

Marina nudged Patti. "Is the garage unlocked?"

"No. A switch in the mudroom lifts the door."

"Then I'll use this opportunity to take a better look inside." She ran for her jacket and hurried back, flipped the switch in the mudroom, and stepped outside as the garage door creaked open.

Farnsworth turned with a smile. "I thought I said open sesame too loud."

She zipped up her jacket. "Jonathan doesn't want me out here alone so I'm taking advantage of your escort."

"Glad to oblige."

Since the man had expressed interest in Iris, perhaps he was a little more human than originally believed. Marina's first impression was a man with a lackadaisical air, who'd throw any suspect in jail so he could sit with his feet elevated, beer in hand.

At the moment, she wasn't so sure. His gaze blazed with an unusual sharpness, like a laser cutting everything in two as he scanned the garage contents. He had a determined set to his jaw, which earlier was believed to be irritation, but in truth, he looked every bit a man unwilling to accept defeat. Detective Nick Farnsworth would solve Roger and Karl's murders, of that she was certain. She turned her attention to the garage.

On her preliminary inspection of the house and property, she had no idea how to open the garage door, so she had peered through the windows and formed a mental image by evaluating time and effort needed. As with the rest of this job, she had severely underestimated yet another room. Dust-covered boxes and crates lined one wall, piled high and collapsing onto each other. Planks of stacked wood rested against the opposite wall along with used doors in need of paint. A workbench had a pegboard tacked to the wall where only one rusty hammer hung. A table saw stood to the side, half the teeth broken from age. Overhead in the rafters piled in groups of threes were old wooden windows covered with cobwebs. The only new objects in the entire garage were a metal tool box on the edge of the workbench and an aluminum ladder. Everything else was junk. Lots of junk. She sighed audibly.

Farnsworth stood alongside. "Daunting?"

She gave him a crooked smile. "I don't usually do this type of work. Roger's stuff is more for a general auction or yard sale. The garage alone will take another week, and I wanted to be out of here by next Wednesday unless, of course, I toss everything into a dumpster." Which, at the moment, was damn tempting. She kicked a box full of scrap metal. The cardboard disintegrated on impact. "This doesn't look like a putter-around type of garage, more like a store-and-forget-it place." She paused while glancing from one side to the other. "I don't see a lawnmower."

"Karl used a shed on the other side of the garage. My boys fished through the stuff but found nothing but lawn equipment." Eyebrow arched, he glanced toward the rafters. "Anything strike you?"

"Yeah, depression." She opened a box to inspect the contents and had no idea what she was looking at. Parts of…something, old and rusted. "Roger told Patti to stay out of the garage. Do you realize the diamonds could be hidden somewhere in all this junk?" She let the box flaps drop and frowned while staring at a large stain soaked into the dirt floor.

"Where Roger was killed," Farnsworth explained.

She shuddered at the mental image of a man on the floor with a screwdriver sticking out of his thorax.

"My boys searched through here, Doctor. Found nothing but junk—in their opinion. You might have a different view."

Yeah, never agree to another estate appraisal. She wrapped her arms around her chest. "Garage contents amount to the price of scrap. Like those screws in the glass jars." She pointed toward the workbench. "Worthless except in weight. I might find an antique tool, but those generally don't fetch a high price at auction." She bent and opened another box. The flap fell apart in her hand. Dropping the disintegrating cardboard, she clapped her palms together to remove the dust. "Have you figured out why Karl was at the cemetery?"

He rubbed his nose. "Funny you should ask. We found a text message on his phone with a time and location and tracked the call to a prepaid phone. No name, of course." He approached a wall shelf lined with nothing but rusted spray cans. Shaking his head, he turned back. "Karl wasn't a man with a spotless record. I've no doubt his cameras recorded the murder, and the greed of easy money took over. He was lured to the cemetery, and wham! End of blackmailer."

But what other untold videos were filmed? A couple in a brass bed going full tilt? She gritted her teeth.

Farnsworth squinted. "Something on your mind?"

An astute man, or a mind reader. "I'm not the one to tell you."

"You're a smart woman, Dr. Cavanaugh. Even the tiniest piece of information can break a case." His face relaxed. "Tell me."

She explained about Patti and Roger's relationship.

As he stared at the floor, Farnsworth pursed his lips. "She never mentioned that." He shot her a quick glance. "So, we have two potential blackmail cases."

"You don't think she killed Karl, do you?"

In one quick sweep, his gaze scrutinized her. "Everyone is suspect, Doctor, even you. Granted, our research revealed you were in Greece at the time of Roger's murder. But who's to say you didn't create a rendezvous point after his trip to Belgium?"

Her throat tightened, and she whirled to face him. "You can't be serious!"

"I'm very serious. We have no viable explanation as to why he left your name. As for Karl's murder, no one has an ironclad alibi." His jaw twitched. "No one." He bent to open a box, scanned the contents, and then straightened. When he faced her, he gave a faint smile. "I don't consider you a strong suspect. My gut tells me your involvement is purely coincidental."

Well, golly gee, thanks so much. His words eased the pressure in her throat, and she released a long breath.

Wandering to the garage opening, Farnsworth stared up.

Marina followed his gaze, but nothing was above him except an old garage door.

"I want to tell you something, Doctor." He faced her and stepped close, his voice low. "This is not common knowledge, so keep the information to yourself. We never found the screwdriver."

She jerked. "It wasn't in his chest?"

"No. From the impression of the wound, the medical examiner listed several possibilities, and the long, heavy-duty type fit the best. If you find one or anything similar, keep the news to yourself but call me right away."

In the course of one conversation, she went from suspect to aiding in a police investigation. Either Farnsworth slipped a little off his rocker, or she wasn't really on his list of suspects. "A screwdriver is easy to hide, Detective. The lake, for example."

He adjusted his overcoat. "We dredged the lake and found everything *but* a screwdriver. The boys also used metal detectors around the property." He slipped a hand into his coat pocket and extracted a business card. Holding it between two fingers, he turned her hand, palm up, and pressed the card onto her skin. "Office and cell. Any questions, call me, day or night." His gaze softened as a slow smile stretched onto his lips. "You've already uncovered several clues to help the case. I suspect you'll find more."

With a nod, she rotated the card front to back then slid it into her coat pocket. "Jonathan told you about the panel?"

"Yes. Old house full of secrets." He opened another box, took a look inside, and released the flaps. "What can you tell me about Henry Ladner?"

The question threw her off-guard. Over the years, she'd watched enough cop shows to understand when someone was fishing for information. "I hardly know him."

"No woman-to-woman talk over lunch?"

Sneaky devil. But he wouldn't be a good detective without inquiring about all possible suspects. "Henry's always had feelings for Patti. She doesn't feel the same."

He turned from the boxes and faced her. "And have you figured out why Roger requested you?"

Not a night passed without her staring at the ceiling while mulling over that very question. She met his steady gaze. "I think Jonathan picked the wrong Marina Cavanaugh."

Chapter Twenty-One

Marina stood in the middle of the driveway after Farnsworth left, hands in her jacket pockets to protect her fingers from the afternoon chill. She looked at nothing in particular, just another busy road in the burbs.

Sighing heavily, she stared up at another cloudy sky. Like it or not, she was involved in this sordid mess. What surprised her was Farnsworth's willingness to tell her about the missing murder weapon. The police already searched the garage, and she seriously doubted the killer threw a screwdriver into the attic. Otherwise, she hadn't come across a heavy-duty tool of any sort. More likely, the weapon was tossed into a trash bin at a strip mall.

So many unanswered questions. So much speculation including doubts about Patti. The little housekeeper had sufficient time to discover the house secrets, make plans, and execute them. Suppose she lied about her relationship with Roger? Suppose she knew all along about the diamonds and used the first opportunity to kill her employer? She'd have to hang around to avoid suspicion. Then Karl, with his handy little cameras, recorded everything, and she fell victim to his blackmail.

A worthwhile scenario except for one gnawing inequity. Wouldn't Patti have used an easier weapon, like maybe a shovel to the back of the head? Marina was no expert, but wouldn't a woman need sufficient force to stab a man with a screwdriver or plunge a metal file into a man's back? Hell, she had enough trouble jabbing a fork into a large pot roast.

Jonathan's black Audi pulled in, the wheels crunching on the gravel drive. He cut the engine and stepped out wearing the most beautiful smile. Immediately aware of the tug on her heart, she mentally kicked herself for such a spontaneous reaction. Their relationship was so up in the air, she could get a nose bleed on the way down.

He approached. "I had doubts about your arrival today. Are you avoiding me?"

"No." *What a friggin' liar.*

"Tyler's guarding your guitar. He misses you."

And she missed him, more than she cared to admit.

He wrapped his arms around her waist but kept his hold loose. A simple public show of affection, a far cry from a lovers' embrace, but she understood his reluctance and kept her hands in her coat pockets.

Bending his head, he brushed his lips against hers.

Shock flooded her senses, but she resisted the urge to reach up and touch his face. His lips, full of softness and heat, tempted her, weakening her determination to maintain distance between their bodies. But he closed the gap by wrapping his arms tight and capturing her lips with a fierceness that turned her shock into pure joy. *A public display, after all.* She glided her arms around his neck and returned the kiss.

Sighing into her mouth, he lifted his head and met her gaze. "I'm going away on business for a few days. Do you think you can join Mom and Tyler for dinner?"

Oh…damn. His trip afforded the perfect opportunity to work late and get this assignment finished, but he had put her on the spot. Tyler probably knew already, and she wouldn't want to disappoint him. "Yes, I'll join them."

His body swayed against hers, a rubbing beneath the coats, and his erection swelled against her abdomen.

With the tip of his finger, he tapped her nose. "Don't break another promise. I don't want to worry about you while I'm concentrating on business."

An odd feeling surfaced. Not rebellion, her usual response to his demands. More a complacency. So unlike her. *What the hell is happening?* She had been independent since the age of eighteen and always watched her own back since no one bothered to watch it for her. Now, Jonathan was making requests that had everything to do with her safety. From day one, he worried about her, but she reacted in defiance because of lessons learned from her father. The two men were entirely different, and guilt surfaced for labeling Jonathan so quickly.

With a smile stretching her lips, she patted his chest. "I'll see you when you return." She broke free of his embrace, hooked her arm through his, and walked him to his car.

Nearing the vehicle, he swung her around and trapped her between the fender and his body. Leaving no time for a reaction, he seized her mouth, sinking his tongue deep, causing a flush of heat to rise from her core. For a man who hadn't bothered with a woman for six years, he was doing a hell of a number on her libido. She wanted to take him immediately, on the gravel driveway, in full view of traffic and anyone else in between. *Damn them all!*

However...

With open palms, she nudged on his chest and, with a gasp, met his dark gaze. "You asked me to keep quiet, yet Patti can easily see through a window."

"I know."

The man had a bad habit of confusing her. If she wasn't careful, she wouldn't tell up from down. "Then you want to prevent Iris and Tyler from finding out? Why?"

His gaze darkened. "Humor me."

She stiffened. "I can't, Jonathan. I'm not a toy to be played with then discarded. What aren't you telling me?" Annoyance replaced desire. From hot to cold within seconds. *Damn him.*

He broke away and straightened his tie. "I need to catch a plane."

And she needed to catch her breath, not to mention some semblance of common sense. What was wrong with this man?

After stepping into his car, he slammed the door and turned on the ignition. With only a half-fast wave, he drove away.

This was, without a doubt, the most emotional assignment she'd ever undertaken. She'd had Arabian sheikhs chasing her through the desert, diplomats inviting her to banquets, and countless professors and museum curators after her ass. Not once had she succumbed. *Why can't I control myself around Jonathan Blandish?*

Because Jonathan was the man who stole her heart.

After returning to the house and tossing her coat on the rack, Marina climbed the staircase to the second floor landing, threw open the door to the attic, and stared up into the gloomy darkness. A cold chill traveled the length of her spine as she struggled with a fight-or-flight dilemma. She flipped the light switch at the base of the stairs, grabbed the handrail, and purposely placed one foot on the first step to psych herself into climbing the rest. Like the basement, one light, dangling from a wire at the top of the staircase, illuminated a set of worn, wooden steps. But unlike the basement, these steps were narrower, creating a tunnel-like effect.

Time stopped. The steps grew right before her eyes, stretching higher and higher into oblivion, and her heart raced. Sweat dripped down the center of her spine and caused a shiver. *I'm a grown woman. I can do this.* Flashlight ready, she swallowed hard and ascended.

Once reaching the top step, she quickly swung the flashlight beam in every direction to inspect the shadows. The same dark paneling enclosed the longest wall while bare studs showed on the remaining three. No insulation, but like the cubbyhole by the fireplace, rusted nail tips protruded from the exterior walls. A lone light hung from the vaulted roof, the bulb too high to reach without a ladder. *Back to the forty-watt cheapo.*

The attic had two windows facing opposite the other. Sunlight struggled to pass through the dust, dirt, and bird poop covering the glass, making the view impossible to see but would allow enough light should the bulb burn out. The attic stretched the length of the house with solid floor boards throughout with ample room to stand except near the edges of the roof's vaulted beams. Tacked to the paneling, a disintegrating

Boston U school pendant hung in two pieces, the last remnants of human habitation.

Dust covered every object. Old lamps. A small desk. More boxes. An unassembled wooden bed frame. Luggage. Insulation still wrapped in store packaging. So much junk.

Footsteps on the staircase made her turn.

"What's the verdict?" Patti stopped alongside and looked around, eyes widening. "I haven't been up here much. I don't think any of this belongs to Roger." She released a double sneeze and crinkled her nose. "This place has an odd smell."

"The traditional attic odor." Marina swung the flashlight beam across the floor. "Most old homes used newspaper for insulation, and over time, the paper degrades. Mice gather the pieces and make little nests, and of course, let's not forget the bat poop." With a grimace, she pointed to the boxes littered with tiny black turds. "All that plus mold and mildew. Lovely, isn't it?"

Patti sneezed again. "That isn't the word I'd use." She vigorously rubbed her nose. "Where do you want me to start?"

"We've a lot to carry, and the staircase is narrow. So, we'll work in shifts." Leaning on the rail, she descended the stairs. "Time for the hazmat suits and masks."

After four days of steady work and crowding the bedroom with repacked boxes, the women took a soda break while sitting on the second floor landing, both with legs outstretched and backs resting against the wall.

"You're a good worker, Patti. I can recommend

you for a job at the auction house."

Patti's eyes grew wide. "Wow, that's tempting. I often wondered if I should sell my house and move on." She stared at the soda can in her hand. "With Roger gone, I may as well reconsider my life with Henry. He makes good money and says I won't have to work. I'm getting older and running out of options." She glanced at Marina and shrugged. "Henry loves me enough for us both. I think we can be happy together." She thrust out her lower lip.

Marriage without love? Hardly worth a second breath. She'd rather buy a dog. Marina gave Patti a faint smile. "Maybe you should make an effort and socialize. You're cute, Patti. Men will see that."

She grunted and tugged on her pant leg. "I'm overweight. Men like a woman with your shape, not mine."

After taking a long swig of her soda, Marina turned to face Patti. "That fact isn't true, you know. My youngest sister has always been overweight, and she found a wonderful guy. Give yourself some time. You'll see."

She'd also had the same pep talk with Janice, her youngest sibling. As the last child to leave home, she'd eaten with a frenzy to relieve the anxiety of living with an abusive father. On her high school graduation day, she packed her bags and moved to Rhode Island to live with Marina, found a job, and met the nicest man. She'd since relocated to Vermont while Marina prepared for her new job in Boston. "How often did Roger's father visit?"

Patti belched while thumping a fist against her breastbone. "Excuse me. Soda's too gassy." Another quieter belch. "Duke visited at least once a month. I was surprised he had a key, though. That would be so unlike Roger. He protected his privacy religiously." She drummed her fingers on the can. "Duke could have stolen a key, but I can't see why he'd bother."

"Unless he knew about the diamonds."

Patti gasped and rotated to face her. "You're right! Roger could have told him."

"The possibility exists." She shook the contents in her can. One or two mouthfuls, no more. She swallowed the remainder then stood and stretched. "I'm going through three more boxes, and then quitting for the day. Any objections?"

"None whatever." Patti stood and dusted the seat of her pants.

"We'll meet tomorrow, say around noon. If Jonathan's home, I'll drag him here to work in the garage."

Patti pursed her lips. "Tomorrow's Saturday. Tyler plays soccer on Saturday, and Mr. Blandish never misses a game."

Oh, right. She wouldn't mind seeing Tyler play, but she was already a little too chummy with the family. *And if Jonathan never misses a game, then he must be on his way home.*

The idea filled her with a mixed bag of emotions. Elation to see him again, anxiety for the same reason. Clear-minded when he wasn't around, confused with him nearby. Somewhere deep in her heart, she missed him. She doubted he'd say the same.

Several hours later, Marina arrived at the Blandish house to see Jonathan's car parked in the driveway. Her heart rate accelerated, and all kinds of thoughts shot in and out of her brain—like bedroom, naked bodies, and even sitting at a table staring dreamily into each other's eyes. Should she act as if they hadn't slept together?

If he can pretend, so can I.

Gathering her courage, Marina stepped from the SUV. As she approached the front door, she hesitated, her foot half-raised onto the concrete step. *So odd to be indecisive.* This wasn't like her. From the moment she decided on a career in antiques, she charged ahead and established an unprecedented reputation. Now, she had to force herself to ring the damn doorbell. *Here goes nothing.* She hit the button.

Jonathan answered wearing a full apron over an open collar shirt and blue jeans. Her breath stopped at the sight of him, and her heart sounded like a jackhammer pounding through her rib cage. *Oh, I missed him, all right.* The man caused too much stimulus merely by breathing the same air.

He ushered her inside and took her coat. "I left the car in the drive to let you know I was home. We're having pizza." He hung her coat in the closet. "How's the inventory going?"

"Almost done." She stuffed her hands into her jeans pockets. Otherwise, she'd reach out to grab him and kiss him senseless. "When did you arrive?"

"This afternoon. Join me in the kitchen when you're ready."

Tyler had not bounded in to greet her nor was he anywhere in sight. She looked up the staircase to see if he waited on the landing. Empty. She'd gotten used to his nightly hug. Fighting a wave of disappointment, she ran to her room for a quick wash.

Twenty minutes later, she descended the stairs,

again hoping to see Tyler, but the living room was empty. A bright fire burned in the fireplace. *And no one around to enjoy it.* She joined Jonathan in the kitchen. He was alone, working on the table shaping pizza dough onto two trays. "Where's your mom and Tyler?" She popped a piece of pepperoni into her mouth.

"They're spending the night at my aunt's house. A sleep-over birthday party for Tyler's cousin." He shot her a quick glance.

Marina stopped from reaching for a piece of shredded cheese. "We're alone?"

"All alone." He tilted his head toward her. "Is that okay?"

Her breath hitched. Was he serious? She'd be alone all night with this man in his house with his wife's ghost hovering? *Hold on a minute.* Pizza for dinner was a far cry from champagne and strawberries. With her luck, she'd be eating in front of the television while he hollered at a ball game.

With a finger, he punctured a bubble rising on the dough. "I'm making two different kinds of pizza. If you don't want one, you might like the other."

Marina eased onto a chair as Jonathan spread tomato sauce on two pizzas. Then, he tossed on the toppings with the skill of a pro, never skipping a beat, as if he was on a time clock. She grinned. "You're not just a pretty face."

He finished one pizza with pepperoni, careful to place the slices evenly. "I worked my way through college in a pizza shop. I wasn't always the well-to-do man you see standing before you." He slipped the two trays into the oven. Then, he removed his apron, worked a corkscrew into a bottle of wine, and popped the cork.

"I'm glad this wasn't one of your eight o'clock nights." He poured the wine into two glasses while watching her. "Ever since I told you to be home at six, you've been anything but." He smirked while handing her a glass.

She tasted the dark, red wine—a Merlot, a wine on her do-not-drink list. Too intense and peppery. She sipped anyway, because her nerves were a jittery mess. The what-was-he-up-to questions had surfaced. They were alone in the house with no chaperones to interrupt. Would he dare continue what they started at her condo?

Don't jump to conclusions. He might want to discuss the inventory or how long before she finished. A dozen topics floated into her mind, all neutral...well, except for humping him on the table while waiting for the oven timer to ding.

To force her mind from the impulse, she grabbed another piece of pepperoni. "If you're willing, we can clear the garage tomorrow." *May as well keep things light.* "I want you to go through the stuff before Patti and I send everything to the scrap yard."

He eyed her over his wine glass. "I have no interest in the contents of the garage, Marina. I'll be glad to join you after Tyler's game, however." He sipped.

"Then, do you mind if I order a dumpster? The attic has too much junk to place at the curb, and I suspect the garage will be the same."

"No problem."

The timer dinged.

Jonathan removed the hot pizzas and cut them into slices, combining both onto one tray. He handed her his glass, and with the tray in one hand and the wine bottle in the other, he nodded toward the doorway. "We're eating by the fireplace."

A wonderful idea. A change of pace from the kitchen. But as she entered the living room, she stopped at what hadn't been visible from the staircase. He had the coffee table draped with a linen tablecloth, set with plates and utensils, and pillows positioned on the floor with the sofa as a backrest. And more.

The room looked unusually bare, and she couldn't quite put her finger on the change. But her gaze drifted toward the mantel, and she gasped. The photos of his wife were gone! She swallowed hard. "Where's your wife?" Somehow, that hadn't sounded right.

He placed the tray on the table. "I buried her, Marina." He met her wide-eyed gaze and smiled. "I want to love again. Sit."

Instead, she backed away, too unsure to believe him. Her legs urged her to run. He'd only push her away once Tyler and Iris returned and deny their growing attraction to the two people who mattered the most. Then again, her heart hammered so fast she swore she'd die of a heart attack. *Oh, God, what should I do?* "I wasn't expecting this, Jonathan. You said you needed time."

"All I thought about was you on my business trip." He switched off the side lamps then stopped, a brow raised. "Is this too dark for you?"

Dark? When all she could see was him? She shook her head stupidly. Where was her argument now? How could she possibly avoid a man she wanted so desperately? "Maybe I'm the one who isn't ready."

"No problem." He took the wine glasses from her hands and placed them on the table. "The pizza's getting cold…or am I giving too much of an order?" He took her hand and pointed to the floor. "Which slice do you want first?"

Butterflies fluttered in her stomach. She hadn't room for food. She slipped a pillow under her butt. "Pepperoni and spinach."

He sat alongside and served the slice on a plate.

She took the plate with two hands in a valiant attempt to hide the tremors traveling from her elbows to her fingertips. *I'm acting like a schoolgirl on my first date.* But his spicy aftershave was enough to drive her mad, and his physical presence brought out an awareness nearly impossible to control. Hell, she was a woman with needs and desires, all of them for Jonathan. Would she be bold enough to tell him so?

Concentrate on the pizza. She took a bite, and the flavors burst on her tongue. "Wow, very good." *What should I do? Feign a headache? Hide? Jump on him?* Maybe she'd choke to death and solve all her doubts. *Oh, hell.* She placed her plate on the table and faced him. "Kiss me."

He chewed what he had in his mouth and swallowed, his gaze twinkling. "I advise against that. You should eat first. Once I touch your lips, I've no intention of stopping."

Her pulse quickened. "You're going that far? Here?"

"We went too fast at your place." With one finger, he touched her chin and smiled. "Tonight, I want to savor. So, eat. I can't have you weaken halfway through."

"I don't believe you."

"Believe me, woman. I told my mother to spend

the night at her sister's, because I won't accept any interruptions. Oh, and by the way—" He stretched toward the sofa's end table and dangled a string of condom packets. "I bought the large box."

Despite the pizza, a fluttery empty feeling hit her stomach. She stared, eyes wide. "Are you sure you won't have regrets in the morning?"

He swallowed a mouthful of food, sipped his wine, and then wiped his mouth with a napkin. He leaned toward her. His gaze burned so hot her breath hitched.

"I love you, Marina. You make me come alive every time I look at you. Tyler and Mom love you, but I'm at the top of the list, because I have never met a woman who could rekindle love the way you do." With two fingers, he lifted her chin. "Granted, you can be obstinate, hard-headed, and too damn independent, but I've grown to appreciate those traits. If you want me to back off, say so. Otherwise, eat." He faced forward and took another slice of pizza.

Well, I'll be damned. He loves me. He hadn't waited for her to return the words, probably because he sensed her hesitation. And rightly so. Doubts filled her heart, a reaction from being tossed aside one too many times. But she *did* love him, more deeply than she thought possible. And Tyler, and Iris. In so short a time, they had become her family.

He's not proposing marriage, dear. She'd helped him bury his wife, if temporarily. Tonight, she would let this man have her, regardless of his future plans.

In an instant, she became famished. For food. For him. Could she imagine a dessert more appetizing?

He wolfed down three slices of pizza in no time and simply leaned against the sofa, arm propped on the cushion with fist against his temple, and watched her. His gaze glowed as it wandered, warming her insides better than the jalapeños on her second slice.

This was, without a doubt, the most romantic dinner she'd ever had. No man had ever gone through so much trouble, a true wine-and-dine experience. The pizza was perfectly cooked, the Merlot still on her do-not-drink list but acceptable, and a crackling fire. The kicker to the evening was his devouring gaze, warm and glowing. *God, I am in love with this man*!

Yet, she still couldn't tell him. The last time she'd said the words to a man, she'd felt his boots stomp all over her back as he headed for the door.

A crumb hid in the corner of Jonathan's lazy smile. With napkin ready, she reached only to have him grab her hand and kiss the palm. The heat of his lips shot straight up her arm.

"Finished?" he whispered.

"For food, yes." She wiped her mouth. "The pizza was delicious. You can cook for me anytime."

Chuckling softly, he gathered the plates onto the tray and carried everything to the kitchen. When he returned, he lifted the table to the side and pointed to the hearth rug.

She cocked a brow. "Aren't you supposed to seduce me?"

"That's what I'm doing." He held up his hands in a gesture of surrender. "All right, I might be out of practice. Make sure you slow me down."

And who would slow *her* down? She wanted this man in the worst way and obeyed his command by wiggling onto the rug. His dark gaze caused more heat than the fireplace, and she did everything in her power not to yank him into her arms.

After positioning a pillow under her head and grabbing the other for himself, he settled alongside and lifted a lock of her hair. "Any ground rules?"

She stared into his beautiful eyes, and every nerve fired at once, on full alert, and most definitely aroused. "Only one. I don't think I can handle another push-away."

"You won't have another. I promise." Slipping an arm around her shoulders, he hovered, the fireplace flames to his back, forcing his shadow to dance. He appeared ominous, but his gaze was tender, glowing like the fire behind him.

He captured her mouth, slowly at first, suckling, tasting, until he drew her into a tender embrace. His kiss deepened, demanding control.

With both hands, she grasped the nape of his neck to hold him in place while slipping her fingers into his hair. Desire rose from her core, and as his tongue probe intensified, she nearly screamed with outright pleasure.

His lips left hers to travel toward her ear. "Allow me to ravish you."

"Do whatever you want." *I can't believe I said that*! But any follow-up thoughts shattered as his lips once again seized hers.

He inched his fingers under her T-shirt and brushed against the lace bra covering her breasts. Gaze twinkling, he smiled. "I envisioned you in lace."

His voice spoke with a huskiness that sent shivers scurrying across her skin. She fought the urge to strip herself naked to let him have her in any way he desired, but he was the man controlling the night.

He lifted her shirt over her head and smiled at the

black lace. "Perfect," he murmured and kissed both mounds of protruding breasts. "I caught you fresh from a shower at your place. You wore no underwear, and I had to have you."

"And now?"

In answer, he suckled the crease between her breasts while his fingers unsnapped her jeans and lowered the zipper. "I want you, more than you'll ever know." His hand slipped inside her jeans. "Lace panties, too. Very nice." He sat up to remove his shirt when, hands poised over the buttons, he glanced down and raised a brow.

Smiling, she shrugged. "You were preoccupied, so I undid your buttons. If I had another minute, I'd have your pants off." And enjoying another look at his lean body. She twisted an arm toward her back to undo her bra.

He grabbed her wrist and grinned. "Allow me."

With slow and deliberate movements, he brushed his fingers across her sensitive skin. She shivered from the sheer pleasure of his touch, and he stripped her naked in no time.

His gaze took her in. "I feel like the luckiest man alive, Marina." He muffled her response with his mouth and then stood to strip his clothes.

A magnificent man stood over her, allowing her gaze to wander and pause and wander again. This liaison was a far cry from their first where they had acted like two animals in heat. A savoring was the key, and her gaze took in every inch of his skin, all tanned with legs covered with light, curly hairs.

Lowering his nakedness alongside, he used his tongue to wet a trail around her breasts, nearly distracting her from his hand between her legs. His fingers were magic. They caressed to open the floodgates, and she groaned. "This is joyful torture."

He bit her nipple. "Call it what you will, but I'm having a wonderful time."

She shuddered. No man had given her such pleasure nor taken his time to drive her to the brink of insanity. "Jonathan—"

"Not yet, love."

His tongue sank deep into her mouth while his finger slipped into her moist heat. The simultaneous assault caused a flush of heat almost too intense to bear. *Oh, God! I'm about to die and go to heaven.* She gasped for air. "Jon—please, enter me!"

"Well, well, look who's giving the orders." He turned his back. A ripping sound followed.

She took several seconds to realize he had slipped on a condom and silently questioned if a large box was enough. She also hoped Iris and Tyler stayed an extra night.

In one smooth move, he braced his arms alongside her shoulders and hovered. While locking his gaze with hers, he placed himself between her legs and performed a gentle in-and-out movement.

She groaned from the pleasure he caused and closed her eyes. "Jon—please!"

"Look at me, Marina."

She did as a powerful orgasm shook her core.

Chapter Twenty-Two

A whirlwind of emotions rushed through Jonathan like a tidal wave crashing on a shore. Happiness, contentment, exhilaration, and yes, even regret for waiting so long. All because of this woman lying beneath him on the hearth rug.

The flames from the fireplace created shadows across her breasts, like the perfect blend of colors from an artist's paintbrush. He loved pushing her to the edge and to feel her nails dig into his back as her muscles tightened around his erection.

"You feel so good," she groaned.

She felt even better with her warm hands gripping his butt to hold him in place. Not like he was going anywhere. For too long, he denied himself the sexual gratification of a woman. One climax after another strengthened his desire to claim Marina as his own and never let her go. She was so beautiful that he almost cried the words aloud.

After the last mind-blowing orgasm, he rolled off and handed her his string of condoms. "We're going to my bedroom. I want to do this all night." Feeling like Tarzan claiming his woman, he lifted her into his arms and carried her up the staircase, two steps at a time.

Often, he had wondered if he remembered how to satisfy a sexual partner. Six years was a long time to deny such simple coupling, but Marina had helped guide his hands to her erogenous zones and encouraged him to experiment. He hadn't stroked a woman's sex in ages, and the heat she generated caused his libido to spiral out of control.

After a playful wrestling match on the bed, she met his gaze from her pinned position and smiled. "I hope you bought two large boxes."

Her mane of auburn hair spread across the bed's pillows, making her appear like a wild woman needing to be tamed. A flush colored her cheeks, and her gaze was so bright he swore he'd need sunglasses. "Honey, I bought the largest box on the shelf."

"Glad to hear it." She flipped him onto his back. "I'm gonna ride you until you see stars."

She was tender and adventuresome, had the physical prowess of an athlete, the agility of a cat, and the stamina of a marathon runner. She gave so much and filled a void he never knew existed.

She was the woman he wanted in his life forever.

As daylight brightened the bedroom, he opened his eyes to feel her still in his arms, her back to his chest, his hand cupping the softness of her breast. Even in sleep, her nipple had hardened from his touch.

Stirring, she yawned with a quick glance over her shoulder. Connecting with his gaze, she smiled. "We should clean up the living room."

He kissed her hair. "Already done. I ran down while you were sleeping and gathered your clothes. They're on my dresser."

Shifting on the mattress, she rolled over to press her softness against his chest.

With one finger, he lifted her chin and marveled at the long auburn lashes protecting her eyes. "How sleepy are you?"

Her brow arched. "What do you want?"

He handed her a condom packet. "I'd love to see you dance on me again."

"I believe the word is gyrate." She bit his nipple before taking the packet and jumping onto her knees.

Her fingers were magic, her touch gentle then firm, forcing a swelling of his erection to the point of near-explosion. He reached for her breasts, but she grabbed his hands and placed them to his side. He groaned in protest.

"Not yet," she whispered.

When she tantalized to her liking, she ripped the packet with her teeth, slipped on the condom, and guided him to her core. Her dance began—yes, gyrate—a slow, thrusting hump that escalated to a fervor pitch of which he could no longer control. He dared not ask who taught her the maneuver, but he thanked the man nonetheless.

"Any orders, Mr. Blandish?"

Words eluded him, but from the aroused gleam in her gaze and the sweat dripping down between her breasts, he knew she struggled to control her own orgasm. Gripping her hips to hold her in position, he released a cry as his climax hit. Her muscles tightened around his erection, and she threw back her head and shuddered. Never in his life had he experienced anything so powerful. He loved this woman. Without question, he was her eternal slave.

Too bad they would never marry.

"Daddy, we're home!"

Dear Lord, eleven already?

Jonathan tossed Marina off his body, threw the

condom into the waste bin, and shot out of bed while grabbing his clothes. "Hurry, get dressed!" He all but ignored the soft cry escaping from her throat.

Openly glaring, Marina struggled to untangle herself from the bed sheets. "Jon, you promised."

"Promised what?" He zipped his jeans. "Come on, Marina. I don't want Tyler to find us together."

"You know damn well what you promised, and now you've ruined a wonderful night." She drew the sheet to cover her breasts.

"Look, I don't have time for a discussion." He tugged a T-shirt over his head. "What we have is special, Marina, but Tyler has never seen me in bed with a woman. The experience will be new for him." With jerky movements, he tucked his shirt into his jeans. "Tyler's playing soccer this afternoon. Mom and I always go. If you want to come, you'll have to get moving."

She flopped onto the pillow while pushing the hair from her face, her gaze on the ceiling. "No, you go without me. Patti and I have things scheduled for today."

"Okay, but be home for dinner. I'm sure Tyler wants to see you." He slipped his bare feet into a pair of loafers then paused. "I'd rather Tyler not know about us, Marina."

She met his gaze. "What's to tell him, that his father's a jerk?" Looking away, she waved him on. "Go. He won't hear anything from me."

The pain on her face shot a surge of guilt straight to his heart. He hesitated with his hand on the doorknob, torn between his desire for Marina and his need to protect his son. Her words were harsh, but this was neither the time nor place for a debate. Marina wasn't aware of the truth. She'd understand once he explained. He rushed from the room and shut the door behind him.

****

Marina stayed in Jonathan's bed until the sound of Tyler's footsteps descended the staircase one last time. She would have loved to see him in his soccer uniform, but her frustration levels had reached maximum. She wanted to scream or at least hurl something. Once the front door slammed and the house fell silent, she grabbed her clothes and headed for her room.

How could such a special night and morning screech to a halt within the blink of an eye? *What the hell is wrong with this man*? Jonathan had removed his ring and wife's photos, but the gesture was nothing more than symbolic. He wasn't ready for another relationship, and damned if he hadn't made her feel like a cheap whore.

She showered then packed, contemplating a quick call to Patti to cancel their workday, but one last day shouldn't hurt. She'd had enough of the man who toyed with her emotions. How could he love her and still push her away? Thankfully, she'd kept her mouth shut about any declaration of her love.

With laptop, guitar, and suitcase in hand, she paused at the front door, feeling like Maria Von Trapp running off to the abbey after falling in love with the Captain. But enough heartache from one job. Her big regret was not saying goodbye to Tyler and Iris. She sighed heavily, took one last look around, and left the house.

Thirty minutes later, covered in hazmat suits and facemasks, she and Patti were hard at work hauling more of the junk from the attic. Like in the basement, several of the cardboard boxes had split open with a touch. They repacked the contents into newer boxes before carrying them downstairs.

After a half dozen trips, Patti straightened and placed a hand on her back. "I'm surprised the attic contains so much stuff." She looked around the bedroom. "We're out of space."

Marina dropped her box on the floor then tore off her face mask. She peeked inside the box at her feet. "Wow, look at this." She grabbed the eyeglasses on her laptop, slipped them on her nose, and rummaged inside the box to extract a section of newspaper. "This newspaper is dated 1922...oops!" The yellowed paper crumbled in her hand and floated to the floor.

Removing her mask, Patti stepped closer. "The parsonage still owned the house back then. The contents must be theirs." She leaned over for a look.

Marina shifted through the contents. "Mostly plates and glasses." More stuff for the secondary auction house. She closed the box.

Straightening, Patti checked the condition of her work gloves. "How about while you evaluate, I'll carry some of the repacked boxes to the first floor and make some room in here." She tapped on a box tied with twine. "Someone wanted to protect this one."

Reaching inside her hazmat suit for her jeans back pocket, Marina whipped out her utility knife, cut the twine, and opened the box. More books. And a surprise! Old black-and-white photographs. She flipped through them. Family photos of people long forgotten. "I hate to uncover a find like this. Unless identified, photos have no place to go but to a historical society."

One particular photo caught her eye—a snapshot of two teenagers, a boy and a girl. Lifting it out, she showed Patti. "This looks like you."

Patti took the photo, and a faint smile stretched onto her lips. "Well, I'll be. Yes, that's me and Benny Horner. His dad had just purchased a new camera and snapped us by the garage." With a finger, she stroked the image. "We dated in high school."

Marina peered at Patti. "Why would a picture of you be in this house?"

Her eyes teared. "Benny and his family lived here for a time. We were inseparable. Until he drowned in the lake on this property." She sniffed and met Marina's gaze. "Suspicious circumstances. His parents moved not too long after."

"Why suspicious?"

"He was a champion swimmer."

"Oh. That's a shame." But the photograph confirmed a nagging wariness buried deep in her mind. Patti had been in this house before Roger. She probably knew the house secrets, maybe suggested the secret panel as a hiding spot, then killed Roger for the diamonds, and bided her time as the ever-faithful housekeeper with no one the wiser. The thought twisted her gut into a knot.

"Can I keep the photo, Marina?"

What should she do? Allow her to keep what might possibly be evidence? Farnsworth needed to know Patti's connection to the house. Unfortunately, the pieces leaned in Patti's favor as being the prime suspect. "I guess you can keep it." When she returned to her condo, she'd give Farnsworth a call.

For a long time, Patti stared at the photo before

opening her hazmat suit and tucking the snapshot into her pants side pocket. Then, she closed a box and, with a foot, slid the carton toward the door. "After the Horner family left, the house had a series of brief owners. Henry told Roger about this property being for sale." She kicked another box toward the door, scraping the cardboard underside across the wooden floor. "Growing up, I lived in the development across the street, a few blocks from where I currently live."

"Then maybe you should take a look at all the photos. You might want some others." Marina released the box flaps and pointed downward. "Take the photos home with you. Otherwise, I'll see if the Boston Historical Society wants them." She hid a yawn. "I could use a cup of coffee." She hardly had any sleep last night. Maybe if she exhausted herself, she'd pass out tonight without the risk of Jonathan slipping into her dreams.

"I think we should take a break for something to eat." Patti grabbed the box full of photos and headed downstairs.

Marina watched her leave. Odd how Patti's men met an untimely demise. She either had the worst luck or…

Shaking away any further thoughts, she placed her glasses on the laptop before removing her hazmat suit and joining Patti in the kitchen.

Patti, also minus hazmat suit, was busy with the coffee maker but glanced over her shoulder. "Marina, I know your affairs are none of my business, but I spotted your suitcase and guitar in the trunk of the SUV. Are you heading home?"

Taking wrapped luncheon meat and bread from the

fridge, Marina placed the packages on the table while pushing aside two rolls of duct tape. "Jon and I had a big blowup. I'm done after today."

Patti whirled, her mouth agape. "He fired you?"

"No, I'm quitting. I'll return to the auction house on Monday and tell my boss to send someone else. I'll pass along the house inventory and tell my replacement what a good worker you are." For the first time, she would walk out on a job before completion. Over the years, she'd been on some messy assignments, getting covered with dirt, mud, and even cow manure, and never once thought of quitting. Mrs. Billingsley would put her through the inquisition, but Marina had the rest of the weekend to think of some plausible answers.

Patti sighed. "I'm sorry to hear that." Finished with the coffee maker, she turned toward the table with forks and knives. "I don't know what you and Mr. Blandish argued about, but Roger was unreasonable at times. The forty-watt bulbs, for example. I had to fight for brighter lights in the kitchen." She set the utensils on the table. "He balked until I gave him an ultimatum. Me or the lights. As for the rest of the house, I cleaned like I was wearing sunglasses. Probably why I didn't see Karl's cameras."

Patti's cell phone rang. She checked caller ID before answering. "Great! Give me a few minutes." She hit the End button and faced Marina. "My brother sent me a ham from Alabama. I have a note on my front door for the delivery man to call. He's at my house now. I should only be ten minutes. Come with me so I won't leave you alone."

Marina waved aside the comment. "Take your time. I won't do much more." She checked her watch.

Two-forty-five. "In fact, I'll pack up and head home."

"Not good enough." Patti jutted her chin. "Mr. Blandish doesn't want me to leave you alone."

"You're not." She replaced the food to the fridge. "I'll have coffee while I pack."

Patti hesitated while glancing at the back door.

"I'll be fine. I won't take more than five minutes to gather my stuff."

"Okay. I'll come back anyway. If your vehicle is gone, I'll turn around and go home." She shifted from foot to foot. "If you don't mind, unplug the coffee maker before you leave. I really enjoyed our time together, Marina."

"Same here, Patti." She forced a smile.

Patti hurried from the kitchen.

Standing at the counter, Marina gulped one cup of coffee—and burned the roof of her mouth in the process—but poured a second cup before turning off the appliance and heading upstairs. She hated to leave a job unfinished, but how many times in life must she mend a broken heart?

She entered the back bedroom where her laptop rested on a box along with her briefcase full of paraphernalia. The bedroom had taken on the smell of the attic, and she crinkled her nose at the musty odor.

Resting her cup on a small wooden table, she bent to unplug the laptop, disconnected the charger, and threw the cord into her briefcase. The magnifying glass was not in the case. She shifted several of the boxes and spotted a black handle protruding between two old lamps and the wall. Unable to reach it, she pushed several of the cartons to the side.

Something caught her eye on the baseboard behind

the old lamps. An odd-looking mechanism stuck out from the wood, covered with layers of brown paint. Senses alert, she squatted to inspect more closely. A small, metal latch! And someone had recently cut into the layers of paint, leaving tiny chips on the floor.

Pulse quickening, she reached into her briefcase for a pair of eyeglasses then slipped them onto her nose to examine the paneling. Yes, a seam. Using two fingers, she pressed. The paneling separated with her touch. Another secret panel?

With an adrenaline rush, she dropped to her knees and struggled to slide the latch away from the hook, forcing more of the thick paint to fall to the floor. With one final yank, the latch snapped free, and the panel popped open. Stale, cold air hit her face, and she rubbed her nose on her shoulder.

The cubbyhole was smaller than the one in the parlor, just as dirty with dust and pieces of plaster scattered on the floor. Nails protruded from the wood planks between the two by four studs, but no insulation. No dead mouse either. An object to the right caught her eye, but the darkness prevented her from seeing clearly. Again reaching into the briefcase, she grabbed her camera and aimed the eye inside the panel, snapping in every direction without the benefit of seeing the viewscreen.

Footsteps sounded on the stairs.

"Patti, look what I found!"

Giddy as all get-out, she felt like a kid who discovered the hidden treasure. She placed her camera to the side and stuck in her head to look to and fro and gasped at the blood-stained screwdriver on the floor.

No!

Who but a housekeeper would know the locations of secret panels? Who but a housekeeper recognized every little nook and cranny from cleaning year after year? Patti had dated the boy who lived in this house. She *had* to be the murderer. *I am not waiting around to find out.*

Throat tight and pulse racing, Marina shifted to jump to her feet when, propped against a wall stud, a white envelope caught her eye. Curious at such a clean object among so much dust, she removed the envelope, sat back on her heels, and extracted a photograph. With a gasp, she stared at a crisp shot of a naked Roger and Patti in the brass bed!

Chapter Twenty-Three

The crowd cheered. Jonathan broke from his trance to see Tyler intercept the ball and head for the goal. A teammate ran alongside, and they kicked back and forth until Tyler scored. *Not bad for a couple of six year olds.*

They were on the elementary school soccer field with a standing-room-only crowd, mainly because the school had no bleachers. Most parents took lawn chairs, but hardly anyone sat in them for long. The excitement of the game kept people on their feet as well as the slight nip in the air. Despite the bright sunshine, the early afternoon sun hadn't warmed the breeze.

His mother nudged his arm. "Are you paying attention? Tyler's playing a marvelous game."

"Haven't missed a kick yet."

Truthfully, his concentration sucked. He shook himself whenever Tyler's team stole the ball, but nothing helped. Every time his mind drifted, he would see Marina's dazed expression. He had indeed ruined their wonderful night, like she was a bing-bang-thank-you-ma'am pickup from a bar. Should he level with Marina and tell her about the vow that would always come between them? She'd understand once he explained. As much as he wanted her in his life, he had to make her accept the limitations of what he could offer.

More cheering. Everyone clapped. With a quick

glance in every direction, he joined them, although he had no idea why.

Maybe he should cut his losses, send her home, and ship the contents of the estate to the auction house. A sensible solution. Not heartfelt but logical. Except he had yet to uncover why Roger insisted on Marina Cavanaugh. Hell, nothing had a resolution, not the murders or the location of the diamonds. All he had was nonsensical clues involving Marina.

Again, the crowd cheered and applauded. Jonathan shook away his train of thought to see the soccer players congratulating each other with high-fives.

With a grin spreading from ear to ear, Tyler ran toward him. "We won, we won, we won! We're gonna be champs this year." He hopped in a circle, too hyper to stay still.

"You played the best game ever, Tyler." Jonathan darted his gaze toward the digital scoreboard. *Whoa*! A seven to six score. He had missed so much.

Traditionally, after every competition—win or lose—he and his mother took Tyler for a celebratory lunch of burgers and fries. Today was no different, and after settling into their booth, Tyler had chatted like a little motor-mouth, giving a blow-by-blow description of the plays. Then, on the drive home, he talked about his cousin's birthday party and sleepover and couldn't wait to repeat his news to Marina, but, as expected, Marina's SUV was gone.

"Aw, shucks." Pouting, Tyler slumped against the back seat.

Jonathan avoided the garage and stopped near the front door. "She's at your Uncle Roger's. Run upstairs and change out of your uniform, and we'll take a ride over." He glanced at his mother in the passenger seat. "She wants me to look at the garage contents."

His mother clucked her tongue. "She should have taken the day off and relaxed a little. Didn't you invite her to the game?"

"Sure I did." Haphazardly anyway. He should have insisted, but he was in a hurry to escape his own room, like a teenager sneaking from his girlfriend's bed, afraid to face angry parents. *My own house and I acted like a fool.* After his gaze followed Tyler up the stairs, Jonathan headed for the kitchen and grabbed a water bottle from the fridge.

His mother walked in, pushing away the hair from her face and gave him a cursory glance. "You seem far away. What's up?"

"Not a thing." He opened his water bottle and took a swig.

"Uh-huh." Her gaze studied him. "I don't believe you followed much of the game either." She opened the freezer and contemplated the array of frozen packages. "What should we have for dinner? Kumquats ala mode with a nice bug sauce?"

"Whatever you want."

A heavy sigh echoed from the freezer as his mother removed a plastic-wrapped package. "You haven't heard a word I've said." She threw the frozen pack on the counter with a bang and faced him. "So, what happened last night? I hope I didn't endure a night away from my bed for nothing."

"Marina and I had a wonderful night, Mother." How could he tell her that he behaved like a total jerk? The pained expression on Marina's face would be imbedded into his memory forever. He leaned against the counter and sipped his water, gaze focused on the floor.

"But what do you mean, Jonathan? A one-night stand?" She threw her arms into the air. "The woman is in love with you." She cocked her head. "Do *you* love her?"

With his free hand, he gripped the counter edge and avoided her glare. "I fell in love the second we met."

Her eyebrows rocked. "And I suppose you'll explain why that's a problem?" She folded her arms across her chest and gave him a one-eyed gaze.

He swallowed a large gulp of water. "Everything is happening too fast. I need to slow down."

"In your case, that means stop." She dropped her arms. "Six years is slow enough, dear." She tore the freezer wrap from a beef roast and placed the meat on a plate. "I suppose you're acting for the best. She'll have a chance to get over you."

Muscles tensing, he shot his gaze toward her. "I don't want her to get over me."

"Of course, you do, dear. That's the message you're giving, but don't worry about Marina. Whenever we chatted over a cup of coffee, she received one call after another from some Tom, Dick, and Harry, giving them all the same excuse of her being out on assignment." She opened the refrigerator and extracted a bottle of water. "Those burgers make me thirsty. Too much salt." She unscrewed the plastic cap. "She's beautiful, Jonathan. I hope you didn't think her as some old maid waiting in her condo for Mr. Right to come along." She drank several large gulps.

His stomach tightened into a ball. Marina hadn't

mentioned other men. She had sung about the one who broke her heart, and he hadn't bothered to question if another took his place. How many was she dating, and who were they? Jonathan peered at his mother. "How do I know you're telling the truth?"

She shrugged. "Doesn't matter. You're taking her s-l-o-w. For the record, Marina doesn't live in a convent." After tossing her empty bottle into the recycle bin, she opened her recipe box and rummaged. "I'm making Tyler's favorite dish tonight. Beef with sauerkraut and dumplings. I think we have a soccer star on our hands."

Jonathan placed his half-empty bottle on the counter. "Marina doesn't understand why I'm holding back. I have to tell her, because I'm not being fair."

His mother glanced up from her file cards. "You're not being fair with me either. I haven't the faintest idea what you're talking about. Tell me."

"I'd rather not." Using his fingertips, he rubbed his brow. His mother deserved to know. Hell, *Marina* merited the same courtesy, but for some reason, he couldn't verbalize the words.

She slammed the box shut and whirled with a glare. "I can't believe I raised such an idiot." She squared her shoulders, chin high. "You leave me with no choice, Jonathan. I'm leaving."

Here we go again. At least once a year, the woman demanded her independence when all she needed was a trip to the beauty salon. He chewed the inside of his lip, his gaze guarded. "You've no place to go."

"I've thought about Marina's offer. I'll use her spare bedroom until I find a place of my own."

His gut tightened. He had specifically warned

Marina about putting ideas into his mother's head. Once again, she failed to listen. "You won't be happy if you leave."

"Like hell! You'll never move on with your life, so I may as well get on with mine."

His thoughts raced. She'd always been so complacent and never argued or took a stand. This show of defiance was not her. *What should I say? How does a son demand a mother to stay?* "What about Tyler? You love him."

"Yes, I love him. He's my only grandchild, and at the rate you're going, you won't give me another." She placed her hands on her hips and kept her gaze steady. "I hadn't planned on raising him, you know, just help you over the hump after Susan died." She approached and poked a finger against his chest. "You need to take charge, because I am officially quitting. I'll talk to Marina tonight."

A surge of heat coursed through his body. This wasn't supposed to happen. His life had been status quo for six years, and Marina had no right to encourage an old woman to live a life of independence. Jaw tight, he pointed a shaky finger at his mother. "I warned her!"

With a scowl, she grabbed the finger and held on. "Don't point that at me, and Marina has nothing to do with my decision." She released his finger. "I've been thinking about moving for a long time, Jonathan. I want a man in my life. You and Tyler don't cut it anymore."

What should he do? *She can't leave*! Would Tyler adjust?

Once again, his mother opened the recipe box, took out a card, and placed it next to the roast. Maybe he should offer her a salary…no, too much money would encourage freedom. He squared his shoulders. "You can't force me to marry, you know."

"Whether you marry or not isn't my concern, but I want you to make a life for yourself and Tyler." She opened an under-the-counter drawer and lifted out a roasting pan. "I think peas and a salad will go nicely with this dish."

She seemed strangely calm. He'd expected a little more rant and raving before docility. He cocked his head. "Maybe you should wait a few more years."

"I've already waited too long." She placed the pan on the counter. "Hire Patti to watch Tyler. She's available."

A worthwhile consideration. Tyler liked her. And Patti could cook and clean. Maybe his mother leaving wasn't such a bad idea after all. He slipped his hands into his jean's front pockets.

Crossing her arms over her chest, she leaned against the counter and faced him. "Your father came to see me the other day. He made this big claim about inheriting money and wants to sweep me into a world of adventure."

He should have known she'd weaken once the old man returned. Jonathan curled his lips into a smile. "So that's where this is going."

She shook her head. "Get your head out of your ass, Sherlock. Your father—as do you—assumes too much. He thinks I'll drop everything for a chance to be with him."

His mind raced. *What the hell is wrong with this woman?* "But you said you want a man in your life. He's available. Maybe Dad's reconsidered his vows."

"Bullshit. His girlfriend left him for a man more

her age. He's fishing in the pond without a hook. I told him to find another whore to help spend his money."

He wagged a finger. "Vows are important, Mother."

"Not to your father." She walked to their floor-to-ceiling pantry. Shoulders stiffening, she whirled to face him with brows shooting halfway into her forehead. "Is *that* your problem, your vow to Susan?"

His chest tightened. "I haven't broken any vows."

"That's not what I'm talking about. 'To have and to hold, 'til death do us part' is the vow. And Susan has definitely departed. Yet, you act like you're still married." Sighing, she stepped toward him, her gaze tender. "I had high hopes when you took off your ring and removed the photos, Jonathan. Marina triggered that. She put a spark back into your eyes and a lift to your step. Now, you want to toss her to the curb." Leaning in, she stared into his eyes. "Why can't you let Susan go?"

Bracing for an argument, he fidgeted. "I've let her go, but I made a promise never to remarry for Tyler's sake."

Mouth agape, his mother took a step back and bumped into the counter, hand reaching to steady herself. "Was that your idea?"

With his hands in his pockets, he wandered to the kitchen window and stared into the back yard. Colorful childhood toys littered the ground—several balls, a pedal automobile, a red wheel barrel. Only recently, he'd given away Tyler's three-wheeler since he'd graduated to a small two-wheel mountain bike. Susan had missed so much.

Turning from the window, he met his mother's

wide-eyed gaze. "On her deathbed, Susan begged me not to allow another woman to take her place. I've sacrificed my own happiness to keep that promise." He dropped his hands to his sides.

He hadn't told anyone of that last conversation, and for the first time in years, the heavy weight in the center of his chest had lifted. Six years was a long time to carry such a burden, but he'd have promised Susan the moon to keep her with him.

His mother pushed away from the counter and approached. She touched his arm, stroking lightly. "You were twenty-nine years old, Jonathan, too young to lose a spouse, but you're not being fair to Tyler nor to yourself. Tyler has said more than once that he wants a mother." With her free hand, she touched his cheek. "Do you intend to spend the rest of your life alone because of a selfish deathbed request?" Shaking her head, she released his hand and strolled toward the table. "I know you loved Susan, but you're throwing away your life for an unreasonable promise." She stared at the table then looked up to meet his gaze. "You have so much to give, Jonathan, and Marina is available to receive."

With heavy steps, Tyler marched into the kitchen like a soldier on a mission with brows furrowed and small mouth tight-lipped. He thrust an envelope at his grandmother. "This is addressed to you. I found it on Marina's bed." He faced his father, his young eyes moist. "Marina's guitar is gone, Dad. That means she's not coming back."

His scalp prickled while a slight chill traversed the length of his spine. "Don't be ridiculous. Maybe she needs new strings."

"She's not coming back, Dad!" Tears flowed down his cheeks, and he ran from the kitchen.

His mother extracted a letter from the envelope and read. "Tyler's right. She's gone." She handed her son the letter.

Muscles tensing, Jonathan snatched the paper and read.

Iris—

I want to thank you for your hospitality over the past several weeks. I've enjoyed our many discussions, but despite your words to the contrary, Jon is not ready. He loves his late wife too much to move on, and no woman can compete with that memory. Please tell Jon I will return to Boston after today and send a new appraiser on Monday. He can work out the financial details with my boss.

As for the mystery of why Roger suggested me, that shall remain unsolved. I want no more to do with this assignment. My spare bedroom will stay open for you. Give Tyler a goodbye kiss. I will miss him.

Marina

His mother grunted. "Obviously, your wonderful night was a tad one-sided. What did you do that made her pack up and leave?"

He stared at the letter. "I tried so hard not to be like my father and break a vow, but every time I held Marina and someone interrupted, I experienced overwhelming guilt and pushed her away…this morning included."

"Oh." While scratching her ear, she grimaced. "Not too bright, son. Like any woman, she realizes a relationship with you is hopeless." She slid two kitchen chairs under the table but paused on the third chair to

306

look at him. "You can't cheat on a dead person, Jonathan. Susan's request to not give Tyler a mother was so friggin' selfish I could scream." She slammed the last chair under the table.

Using both hands, he scrubbed his face. "Marina will understand once I explain." Hell, his voice had a pathetic tone and hardly worthy of a man with his background.

"I got news for you. Despite her PhD, she won't understand at all. I certainly don't." She moved away from the table. "And what will you do about Tyler? He fell in love with Marina. He might fall in love with the next woman you take home. Then what?" She stood before him, gaze challenging. "Losing Marina doesn't faze you, does it?"

Normally, he'd have agreed with his mother, but uncertainty settled in his chest, like a piece of lead crushing his heart. He had no viable argument to change Marina's mind.

"Well?"

"I'm a grown man. I can handle disappointment."

"Then teach Tyler your tricks. He'll wonder why Marina left without saying goodbye." With one hand in her hair, she sighed. "You're like your father more than you want to admit. He let me go, and as a consequence, he's lost me forever. You're about to do the same with Marina."

The words stung. Marina was the spark that had returned life to his soul, filled the house with happiness, and forced him to question his own sanity. Before Marina, no woman tempted him, but now, he considered the validity of Susan's request. Staying true to his promise denied him the physical and emotional bond between a man and a woman, a bond he hadn't known was missing.

Gaze focused on the floor, he slumped against the counter. What if his mother was right? Susan had forced him to make a selfish oath, never considering Tyler's needs nor his own, and especially, the needs of his mother. How would he live knowing he let Marina pass through his fingers? She affected everyone, and the idea of losing her forever was a reality he couldn't accept.

Moving to the sink, his mother slammed the dishrag onto the counter loud enough to make him jump. "All these years, I urged you to date. Why didn't you tell me?"

He tapped a finger against his chest. "My vow, Mother."

"Well, Susan made an egotistical request, and you were equally as bad to remain silent. You may want to waste your life, but I've no intention of wasting any more of mine." Heading for the archway, she paused in the opening and glanced back with a fiery gaze. "Make your own damn dinner!"

Chapter Twenty-Four

Jonathan believed himself to be a successful man. He had a decent head on his shoulders with a worthwhile brain, a thriving business, friends and connections, and a nice home with money in the bank. Everything a man could want to mark his place in society. Yet, by every definition in the book, he was a jerk.

As he stood by the staircase staring up and debating what to do, he replayed his wife's final words. *"Please don't let Tyler forget me. Don't give him another mother who will never love him as much as I do."* Susan had begged him to honor her memory, and he, like a teary-eyed fool, agreed.

The words haunted him. And yes, they were selfish, but with his world crashing, he'd made the promise, and the soundness of such a vow was never questioned. He purposely scattered her photos around the house as a constant reminder. In all that time, he avoided any intimacy with a woman. He depended on his mother and, in turn, denied her the opportunity to develop a life after her divorce.

Marina hadn't caused his mother's quest for independence. All too often, Iris Blandish talked about moving out, and he passed off her words as a hormonal imbalance. She had a son and grandchild to occupy her time, and nothing else mattered. Then, of course, he ignored Tyler's countless requests for a mother, because his grandmother was the substitute.

With Marina gone, his world once again crashed. She was everything he wanted, yet he tossed her away. He shoved her right out the door.

Jonathan Blandish, despite his education, despite his wealth, was indeed a supercilious jerk.

He alone could right the wrongs made over the years—for his son's sake and his mother's, but most of all, for Marina. He loved her enough to push aside the vow and live again, make a new marriage vow, allow her to be Tyler's mother, and encourage his own mother to move on. He cupped a hand near his mouth and directed his voice up the staircase. "Mom, Tyler, I'm going after Marina!"

Without waiting for a reply, he grabbed his jacket from the closet and hurried to the car. He zipped through traffic without a hitch and pulled into Roger's driveway in record time, easing his Audi behind three vehicles crowding the U-shaped curve. Marina's red SUV wasn't among them, and his heart sank. An overwhelming urgency surrounded him, and he struggled with every ounce of self-control not to drive straight to the harbor, but common sense prevailed. Best to find out the time she left and her destination before driving all over the city of Boston. He stepped from the car and headed for the front door.

Of the three vehicles, one was Patti's compact sedan. The Lexus was unfamiliar. The third was a familiar dark car with the SXYLVR license plate. *Dammit, the man can't stay away.* And the thought turned his blood to lava. As was his habit, he rang the bell before using his key to open the door.

Patti hurried from the kitchen, chewing. "Mr. Blandish, this is a surprise." With a quick glance over her shoulder, she swallowed. "We're finishing a casserole. Want some?"

"No, thanks." He nodded in the direction of the driveway. "I see Marina's car is gone."

"Yes, sir. She said she'll pass on the information to the new appraiser."

Henry waltzed through the dining room, his cheeks loaded with food. He hurriedly chewed then swallowed. "What's going on?"

That answered the question of the unknown Lexus. "Nothing, Henry." Jonathan rubbed the nape of his neck before turning to Patti. "What time did Marina leave?"

"Probably around three. She was gone when I came back."

Eyelids narrowed, he dropped his hand to his side. "Back from where?"

"My house. I had a delivery that needed refrigeration. I wanted her to come with me, but she said she'd pack up and leave." She threw a thumb toward the front door. "Her car was gone when I returned."

Fidgeting, he checked his watch. Four thirty. "Okay. I'll drive to her condo. Maybe I can grovel at her feet."

Patti used her little finger to wipe the corner of her mouth. "Good luck, Mr. Blandish. She sounded more heartbroken than anything else."

Yeah, no shit. A heart he broke. She gave with the depth of a bottomless pit, only to be tossed aside in thanks. How could he be so stupid? *I need longer legs to kick myself in the ass.* "Where's my father?"

"Right here, son."

Duke Blandish lumbered down the staircase, clomping heavy boots on the uncarpeted steps and looking smug for reasons all his own. He meandered toward the small crowd gathered in the parlor.

The sight of him made Jonathan's skin crawl. He'd rather not be in the same room with the man but forced himself to be civil for the others' sake. "I'm glad everyone's having a party at my expense."

Patti cringed. "The food will go bad."

He didn't give a damn if the food fermented into wine. Jonathan rubbed his forehead. "That's okay, Patti. You and Henry go to the kitchen and let me have a few private words with my father." He waited for them to be out of earshot before squaring his shoulders and facing his old man. "Why are you here?"

"To see that pretty appraiser of yours, of course." He winked and tugged on his belt. "A man needs a little sustenance while he's waiting for another woman to change her mind. Namely your mother. She's playing hard to get."

His back stiffened. "Don't give me that. She threw you out."

"Nah. She was in one of her moods. She'll come around with a little sweet-talk." He crossed his arms over his chest. "You need to make them understand your point of view."

Just like he expected Marina to understand an asinine vow. *When have I become like my father?*

"Look, son, I'm glad you stopped by." He wandered toward the rear of the sofa and patted the backrest. "What do you say giving me this house? Your mother and I can live here real comfortable. We'll have all the furniture we need plus that nice brass bed upstairs. I might even keep cute, little Patti around."

Wide-eyed, Jonathan gaped. Did he hear right? What the hell kind of planet had his old man come from? He snapped his mouth shut. "Are you out of your mind? Mom hates this place."

"So? A little sex, and women agree to anything." He wiggled his eyebrows.

Jonathan clenched his fists. In two more seconds, he'd swing at his father and probably break a knuckle on his smug jaw. "You're a pig. I'm embarrassed to say I'm your son." He stuffed his fists into his jacket pockets and gave his father a stern glare. "For the record, Marina is off limits."

A bushy eyebrow arched. "Is she? You and her humping?"

Dear old dad, lewd and rude. "That's none of your business. Who left you an inheritance?"

With a one-eyed glare, he pointed. "And that's none of *your* business. The police already put me through an inquisition. I don't need another from you." With his head, he nodded toward the front door. "Why'd you change the locks?"

"Because I couldn't have you waltzing in on the ladies while they were working. Too much has happened in this house."

"Yeah, tough about Roger." He thrust out his lower lip.

Well, golly gee, he sounded all broken up. Jonathan turned on his heel. "I gotta go." The three of them could eat the refrigerator bare, including ice cubes and condiments. He had a more important task in mind.

He drove the hour to the harbor to find no red SUV

in the parking lot. He pulled into a slot on the opposite side of the street, cut the engine, and stepped outside.

The sun had set and left the area in gray dusk. No lights glowed from her windows, but he approached the main entrance and buzzed the unit anyway. As expected, no answer. He returned to his car to call her cell phone. For the umpteenth time, the device kicked into voicemail, but he left the same message. "Marina, I'm sorry. Call me." *She'll never call, unless I'm suddenly blessed with a bloody miracle.*

Ordinarily, he'd enjoy the peacefulness of a night on the harbor with the waves sloshing against the piers and boats thumping their docks. No moon overhead to create a romantic mood, but tiny lights illuminated the harbor walkway. The scene helped calm his frazzled nerves...until he checked the clock on the dashboard. Seven-fifteen. Still no Marina. Using the car's cell phone connection, he called his mother. "Has Marina arrived?"

She clucked her tongue. "Of course not."

"She wasn't at Roger's, and she's not at her place." He checked all the car's mirrors to be sure she wasn't approaching.

"You drove all the way to the harbor?"

If need be, he'd drive to Mars. "Yes, I've been sitting here for a while. She won't answer her cell phone. I'm getting worried."

"Maybe she's not heading to Boston. Maybe she stopped to cry on a girlfriend's shoulder."

Or worse, a boyfriend. His gut twisted with the thought. She'd be vulnerable. A man wouldn't hesitate to take advantage and initiate sex with the pretense of comfort.

Shoot me now, dammit!

"Call if you hear from her, Mom. I'll sit here for a little while longer."

"Wait a minute. I don't know what to do about Tyler. He's been so quiet. By now, he should be hungry."

A thickness formed in his throat. He squeezed shut his eyes then opened them, his resolve stronger than ever. "Go tell him where I am. If I have to crawl on my hands and knees, I'll get her back."

"Glad to hear. I'll tell him."

The connection ended.

Another hour wouldn't hurt. Hell, he might sleep in the car. With that consideration in mind, he reclined his backrest, flipped his jacket collar to cover his neck, and relaxed to await her arrival. He no sooner closed his eyes when his cell phone rang. Mother. *Marina's returned*! He bolted upright and tapped the phone connection on the dashboard. "Yes?"

"Jonathan—"

She gushed out the word, as if struggling for air. Alarm stiffened every muscle in his body. "Mom, are you all right?"

A sob. "Oh, Jonathan, Tyler's gone. His jacket and bicycle are missing. I think he rode to Roger's place."

Holy shit! "Those roads are too dangerous for a kid on a bike." Heart thumping, he repositioned his backrest and started the engine. "I'll head to Roger's."

"I can reach the house faster."

"No, don't leave in case Tyler returns. I'll call when I arrive."

Of all the stupid stunts. Tyler's behavior was irrational, even for a six year old. Fingers tight on the steering wheel, Jonathan hit the freeway and floored the gas pedal. He pulled into Roger's driveway in a record thirty minutes and eased to a stop.

The vehicles were gone. The house stood dark and lifeless. A gloomy place, maybe loved at one time, but not by him. He stepped from the car and cupped both hands to his mouth. "Tyler!"

No running footsteps. Only the sounds of passing traffic.

He clenched his jaw and had the unmistakable urge to kick something. Where the hell was he? Had the boy gotten inside? And more important, had he arrived here at all? Bending into the car, he reached across the seat and opened the glove compartment for his flashlight, clicked the switch, and breathed a sigh of relief. He couldn't remember the last time he'd checked the batteries.

Straightening from the car, he swung the beam over the grounds. No bicycle out front or on the porch. After a quick check for a secure front door, he hurried around the side, inspected the area along the mudroom, and tugged on doorknobs and windows, continuing until he inspected all four sides. Everything locked. Had Jonathan and his mother assumed Tyler would go after Marina, or had the boy gone somewhere else, all teary-eyed and mad at his father? "Tyler!" Since a full inspection of the exterior yielding nothing, he returned to the front yard and reached into his pocket for the door key.

His chest was so damn tight he could hardly breath, and his hands shook so bad he had difficulty finding the right key. *All my fault.*

A vehicle pulled in. The headlights snapped off,

and Farnsworth stepped into the beam of Jonathan's flashlight.

Jonathan clicked off the light and stepped off the porch. "This can't be a coincidence."

The detective gave a slight smile. "Your mother called." He buttoned his overcoat. "She told me what happened. I followed the route from your house to here with no sign of your son or the doctor's vehicle. Any word from the doctor?"

With a hollowness settling in the vicinity of his heart, Jonathan shook his head and turned toward the house. "I checked all the doors and windows. If Tyler's inside, then he locked everything behind him, but he can see Marina's car is gone. Where would he go?"

"At a guess, to sleep." He scratched his ear and heaved out a breath. "I dispatched a well-being check on the doctor. If a patrol car spots her SUV, they're to call. I also activated the missing child alert system in case your son took off for destinations unknown."

Jonathan lowered his head. "Thank you. I won't sleep tonight until I know where they are." Squaring his shoulders, he faced the detective. "I'm worried, Nick, and scared. I don't want anything to happen to either of them."

"Considering the history of this house, I'd say that's a justifiable concern. Of course, we've got to consider the possibility she found the diamonds and is on her way to South America." He gazed steadily at Jonathan. "Interpol discovered where Roger Blandish purchased the diamonds. In Brussels." His gaze intensified. "Not a week later, Dr. Cavanaugh arrived in Belgium. Stayed in the same hotel, too."

Jonathan's back stiffened. "I don't believe for one

second what you're implying."

"I'm stating a fact, son. Seems she's the right Marina Cavanaugh after all." He snapped up his coat collar to cover his neck. "Let's suppose your brother used the doctor's connections to ship the diamonds to the U.S. She handles a lot of expensive antiques that require special handling. So, why not smuggle diamonds within a shipment? She's the one who unpacks all the boxes, Blandish. I confirmed that with her boss."

His temper flared. No way in hell had Marina known Roger, smuggled diamonds, and then plastered on a false face from the get-go. He sucked in a large, calming breath before confronting the detective. "I don't believe a word out of your mouth."

Farnsworth shrugged. "I have to consider all possibilities. The diamonds may not be in this house at all, but over at her place, safely tucked away under some floorboard." He gazed at the passing cars on the street. "Since I have only circumstantial evidence, I can't obtain a search warrant, but, to ease your mind, she's not a killer." He shot Jonathan a quick glance.

How wonderful of him to think so highly of her. Unfortunately, Farnsworth's reasoning made sense. Why else would Roger leave her name, not once, but three times?

No, the detective is wrong. Roger would never take the risk of embezzling forty million dollars then exchange the amount for a fortune in diamonds only to transfer the lot into the hands of a woman. He wouldn't trust a woman to guard his treasure, not even Patti.

Farnsworth stuffed his hands into his coat pockets. "Human nature is full of surprises, Blandish. When you think you've seen enough to write a book, something new pops up."

But Jonathan *knew* Marina was innocent. A woman couldn't be so pure of heart while living a charade. Even though she hadn't verbalized the word, she transmitted her love with every touch and every kiss, more than he'd experienced from any woman—even Susan. Marina was as much in love with him as he was with her. She was innocent, dammit, and no one, not even Farnsworth, could change his mind.

Chapter Twenty-Five

Since neither man wanted to leave the premises without checking the inside of the house, Jonathan led Farnsworth into the dark parlor, slammed on the switch for the overhead foyer light, and then clicked the switches on the two flower-bellied lamps. "Tyler!"

The house was dead quiet, the smell musty, and in need of fresh air. He headed for the staircase while talking over his shoulder. "I'll check to see if he's in one of the beds." Not to mention throw the switch on every light he passed. But both beds were empty, totally stripped of linens. Again, he called with no response. What if he couldn't find him? What would he do? Jonathan hurried downstairs to the aging detective, still standing in the center of the parlor floor, staring at the array of cardboard boxes lining the walls. "He's not here."

Farnsworth shook his head. "Awful gloomy place. Hard to believe your brother left the rooms so dark." He faced him. "What pissed off the doctor?"

If he had only listened to the tone of Marina's voice or stopped to consider the shock on her face, he'd be home right now with both of them in his arms. Jonathan stiffened. "That's none of your business."

Farnsworth lifted a cushion on the sofa and inspected the underside. "Considering the developments in this case, everything *is* my business. Tell me." He dropped the cushion.

Feeling the heat rise from his collar, Jonathan unzipped his jacket. "Marina figured out I was a total ass. I drove to her condo to crawl on my hands and knees to beg for forgiveness."

Farnsworth's gaze twinkled. "In love with her, eh?"

"Big time." His posture relaxed as he stared toward the dark dining room. "I don't care why my brother asked for her and don't care if we find the diamonds. I want her back." On the floor near the dining room archway, he caught sight of a pair of Marina's eyeglasses. After walking over, he bent to retrieve them, and a surge of regret shot through his fingers as he envisioned the glasses perched on her cute nose.

Farnsworth stepped alongside and nodded his head at the glasses. "Are those hers?"

"Yes." He dangled them between two fingers. "The drugstore variety. She has a habit of misplacing them." The regret deepened. *She'll never forgive me.* He placed the glasses on the sofa's end table next to a half-used roll of duct tape. "She can't be here, Nick. She's afraid of the dark."

He joined Jonathan near the sofa. "Why don't you tell me what happened when you arrived this afternoon? A blow-by-blow, if you will."

An odd request. He stepped back, weighing the purpose of the question. "You think I hurt her?"

Farnsworth shook his head. "Easy, son. You need to answer questions without getting defensive. I'm a cop who appreciates lots of details. Start from the time you drove in."

Jonathan threw his arms into the air. "How can I

Jane Drager

not be defensive? I'm still your number one suspect!"

"Everyone connected with this case is still suspect, Blandish." He loosened his necktie and unbuttoned the top button on his shirt. "Tell me the sequence of events as you pulled in earlier."

Marina and Tyler missing and this guy wants details that have no bearing on anything. Jonathan ran both hands through his hair, his nerves on edge. He wanted action, not this bullshit to satisfy an old cop's curiosity.

"Put everything in order and tell me," Farnsworth encouraged.

Still, the detective had a good case record behind him, several commendations, along with an unprecedented reputation at Boston PD. Even the mayor had expressed his assurances the old timer was the man to find Roger's killer, relentless to the point of obsessive.

Jonathan sucked in a large breath and exhaled slowly. "I haven't much to tell. I arrived and saw Marina's car gone. Three vehicles were here—Patti's, Henry Ladner's, and my father's. Patti told me Marina left around three. After that, I drove to the harbor and waited then returned here when Mom called about Tyler. That's the story."

"What were the three of them doing?"

Oh, God help me. He glared at Farnsworth.

The detective held up a finger. "Patience, son. I have my methods."

Hopefully, one method was CPR. Jonathan's chest was so tight he could drop from cardiac arrest. He gripped the back of his head and stared at the ceiling. "They were eating. Patti walked out chewing, followed

322

by Henry with crumbs on his beard. My father was descending the staircase." He lowered his arms.

Farnsworth's gaze sharpened. "Why eat here and not Patti's place?"

Yes, why here? With Marina gone, why hang around? Patti could have easily taken a casserole and Henry to her house and left his father standing on the front lawn.

Jonathan groaned.

Farnsworth's attention snapped toward him. "What?"

"My father bragged about an inheritance." He thumped a fist against his forehead. "I can't believe I'm so friggin' dense. He probably found the diamonds."

The detective chuckled softly. "I already know about the inheritance, and it wasn't diamonds. He received a check from a late uncle to the tune of fifty thousand." His brows creased into a frown, his gaze askance. "What's your mother's opinion regarding his sudden reappearance?"

He stuffed his hands into his jeans front pockets. "She threw him out."

"Did she?" His face relaxed into a smile.

Jonathan dropped his hands to his sides and fidgeted. Marina and Tyler were missing, and in no way could he keep his legs still. He had to find them. "Look, Farnsworth, I appreciate your need for details, but I can't stand here and do nothing."

"Not a problem, son. What do you say we have a careful look around? Little boys like to hide when they're upset." The older man held up a finger, his gaze sharp. "You will stay with me, and we will search the premises together. Understood?"

A warning? Was Farnsworth afraid Jonathan would bolt? He narrowed his gaze. "Are we looking for more than my son?"

The detective tapped the side of his nose. "The police and search teams will work to find your son, but in the meantime, we'll look for evidence that your boy actually arrived. Let's thoroughly inspect the rooms. I'll start in the kitchen." He disappeared through the dining room.

Jonathan placed his fists on his hips and surveyed the living room. The entire house was in disarray with stacked boxes everywhere, each marked with bold red numbers and letters. But the detective was right. Tyler could be hiding. The house had several closets and...a cubbyhole!

With the latter thought, he strode to the fireplace panel and popped the latch. As expected, the hidden compartment was empty. Hadn't Tyler already done his search of the house? What if he'd found another?

As his new idea took hold, Jonathan pushed and pounded and continued into the dining room then the sunroom. He even tugged on the shelves in the den hoping something would open, like a hidden door. Nothing.

"Tyler!" Odd to say but every fiber in his being told him he was nearby. He couldn't shake the feeling or explain why. A father/son connection more likely. Ridiculous, of course. If he was so friggin' insightful, he'd have handled Marina differently.

Farnsworth joined Jonathan in the den. "I searched the outside. I found bicycle tracks."

Pulse quickening, Jonathan whirled to face him. "He's here!" *I knew it*!

"Or was. I called dispatch with the information, and they'll do a more thorough search between this house and yours." He patted Jonathan's shoulder. "Why don't you head home?"

Jonathan's jaw twitched. "First you tell me to stick around, and now you want to get rid of me. I'd rather stay here with you." He wasn't sure why, but a little inner voice said to hang around and keep looking. Tyler could still be on the premises. In fact, he was certain.

While pursing his lips, the detective pointed toward the wall. "Why were you pressing on the shelving?"

"In case Tyler found another hidden compartment and was hiding." While staring at the shelves, he fought the urge to tear off every damn piece.

Hurriedly lifting an arm to his face, Farnsworth sneezed into his suit jacket sleeve. "This place stinks. What the hell is the smell?"

Jonathan smirked. "Attic. The smell's worse upstairs."

Farnsworth scratched his nose. "Well, despite the odor, I'm heading up."

"I'll join you."

Both men climbed the stairs, and while Farnsworth proceeded toward the master bedroom, Jonathan opened the hall closet door only to find a completely empty interior. He pressed and banged the walls. The back bedroom was next. The two floor lamps were still connected. He flipped the switches.

The boxes were piled in such a way to create a path from one end of the room to the next, new boxes mixed with old. Pushing a box to the side, he caught sight of an earpiece to a pair of her eyeglasses, half buried beneath an old box. He lifted the edge to retrieve the lone piece and searched for the rest, moving several boxes until finding the glasses against the wall. Bent. No, mangled was the word with one lens missing. "Yo, Nick!"

Farnsworth hurried through the door. "Find something?"

Pointing toward the floor, Jonathan showed him the glasses. "I found the earpiece here, and the rest in between those two boxes. I haven't found the second lens yet." Just holding them in his hand filled him with apprehension. Had she broken them in anger? Perhaps at him? His gaze scanned the wooden floor. "This is the first time I've seen a mangled pair."

He and Farnsworth separated to search for the missing lens.

Once reaching the center of the far wall, Jonathan released a cry. "Here it is." He bent to retrieve two broken pieces of glass. For reasons that were more instinct than calculated, he pressed on the paneling. One section gave with his touch, and his breath stopped.

The two men locked gazes. Without a word, they lifted the boxes to the side.

On the floor, a brown paint chip drew Jonathan's gaze. He knelt for a closer inspection of the painted border. "Here's a latch!"

"Don't touch it! Let me in there, son."

Jonathan stood to allow the detective room.

Farnsworth squatted for a closer inspection. "Someone recently cut the paint to loosen the mechanism."

"Marina probably." Placing his hands on his knees, he bent to peer over the detective's shoulder. "She always carries a utility knife."

Extracting a pair of latex gloves from his overcoat pocket, Farnsworth hastily slipped them on, threw the latch, and used his finger to push on the paneling. The door clicked free.

The compartment was empty. *And too damn small, even for Tyler.* His hopes deflated.

Withdrawing a small flashlight from his suit pocket, the detective clicked on the switch and swung the beam inside the hole before sticking his head through the opening. "Well, well, what's this?" He leaned forward into the hole. "This is a blood stain, Blandish."

Heart racing, Jonathan waited for the detective to move aside and then stuck his head into the cavity. A dried, irregular rust-colored mark had penetrated the floorboards. "How do you know this is blood?"

"The voice of experience. Help me up, son."

Jonathan grabbed the man's arm and supported him as the elderly detective struggled to his feet.

Before straightening, Farnsworth rubbed his knee. "Maybe the doctor discovered the panel and found Roger's murder weapon." He glanced at Jonathan. "We never found the screwdriver, you know. I asked her to keep an eye out." His brows creased into a frown. "The broken glasses is an indication of a struggle, Blandish, and if that's the case…"

His gut twisted, and he fought the rising nausea. Marina wasn't answering her cell phone, because she couldn't! The killer came back and found her making the discovery, waffled her, and then what? Killed her? *Sonofabitch*! With the need to hit something, he slammed his fist into a cardboard box and immediately heard glass break. Who the hell would hurt Marina?

And where is my son? Scenarios shot into his brain like arrows, and one, in particular, seized his heart. He clutched Farnsworth's arm. "Patti!"

The detective shook his head. "Don't conclude without facts, Blandish. I'll have the lab dust for prints and do a DNA analysis of the blood stain. Hello, what's this?" He bent behind a stack of boxes. With a quizzical lift to his brow, he straightened while holding a digital camera.

Jonathan almost cried out, but the pain in the back of his throat stopped him. Her briefcase and laptop were nowhere in sight, yet... "The camera belongs to Marina." He met the older man's gaze. "She'd never leave it, Nick."

Hurried footsteps pounded on the staircase. Farnsworth slipped the camera into his pocket before Patti and Henry rushed through the door.

"What's going on?" Patti asked, breathless. When she spotted the opening in the wall, she gasped. "You found another secret panel!"

"That is so cool." Henry stepped around Farnsworth and stuck his head into the hole.

"Don't touch anything, Ladner." Frowning, Farnsworth faced Patti. "What brings you two here?"

Patti blinked several times before answering. "We were returning from the movies when we saw the house lights on. Has anything happened?"

"We can't find Marina or Tyler." Jonathan wanted to tell them to get the hell out since their interruption was about as welcomed as jock itch. Instead, he paced in the tight space between boxes.

Wide-eyed, Patti glanced from one man to the other. "What do you mean you can't find them? Why do you think they're here?"

Farnsworth nudged Henry to step away from the wall. "Did you know about this secret panel?"

Henry sneered. "No, of course not."

"How about you, Patti?"

She shook her head. "No, sir. A dresser sat in that spot before Marina and I carried everything into the hall. If she found the panel, she said nothing to me."

Farnsworth's shoulders slumped, and he gave a heavy sigh as he took out his notebook and flipped through the pages. "Tell me what happened today, Patti." He poised a worn pencil over a blank page.

Mouth ajar, she stepped back. "What do you mean? Nothing happened."

"Tell me what you and the doctor did today."

While biting her lower lip, Patti tugged on the hem of her jacket. "We didn't do anything special. Marina and I carried down more of the stuff from the attic. She wanted a cup of coffee so we took a break. I got a phone call for a delivery I was expecting, and she was gone when I returned."

Jonathan stopped pacing and whirled. "Wait a minute!" Eyes blazing, he glared at the little housekeeper. "How long did you leave her alone?"

Wincing, Patti's face drained of color. "About forty-five minutes. My brother sent me a ham too big for my refrigerator. I had to rearrange the shelving."

Jonathan's glare intensified. "So, for that time, Marina was alone in the house?"

Her gaze darting, Patti gushed out a breath. "I don't know that for sure, sir. I wanted her to come with me, but she said she'd leave instead." She wrung her hands. "I locked her in like always. When I returned, I pulled in behind Henry's car. Marina's vehicle was gone."

Farnsworth stepped forward. "Was Henry's car in the same spot as the doctor's car or behind it?"

Patti started and glanced at Henry. "I don't know."

"And where was Henry when you drove in?"

She bit her lip. "Coming around the side of the house."

Gaze intense, Farnsworth turned to Henry. "Why?"

Henry's mouth fell open. As his gaze drifted, he stuttered slightly. "I—um—wanted to see if Patti was in the kitchen and failed to hear the doorbell, that's all. You can't see her car from the driveway when it's parked around the other side. And besides, she walks here a lot." With a shaky hand, he stroked his beard. "I was about to head over to Patti's house when she pulled in."

Farnsworth nodded while scribbling in his notebook.

Unable to stand still, Jonathan resumed his pacing. He should be doing something—hell, anything but stand here and listen to Farnsworth play detective. If Tyler or Marina came to any harm, he'd never forgive himself. "When did my father arrive, Patti?"

Caught biting a cuticle, Patti dropped her hand and fidgeted. "Probably around four, looking for Marina."

Jonathan bristled at the image of his pig-of-a-father making another move on Marina. The damn man just wouldn't take no for an answer.

Farnsworth took Marina's glasses from his pocket and held the pieces on his gloved palm. "What can either of you tell me about these?"

With brows rising halfway into her hairline, Patti gaped. "What happened to them?"

"You tell me."

"I don't know, sir. They're the first pair I've seen busted."

Puffing out his chest, Henry positioned his body close to Patti. "Look here, Detective. Are you accusing us of something? Because I don't like what you're asking."

Farnsworth's lips stretched into a faint smile. "Developing a timeline, Mr. Ladner." He replaced the glasses into his pocket. "Has either of you seen Tyler? He rode here on his bicycle."

With her gaze shifting to Jonathan, Patti clutched her throat. "He did? When?"

Jonathan gritted his teeth. "That's what we want to find out."

"Not while we were here." Henry wrapped an arm around Patti's shoulders and gave a squeeze. "I'd say we left around five." He glanced down at Patti who nodded.

Farnsworth closed his notebook. "You two may as well go home. Blandish and I have other things to do...oh, and Patti, can you think of anything that was unusual when you returned?"

Her brows furrowed into a scowl. "No, I...wait a minute." Face brightening, she shook a finger in the air. "I left two new rolls of duct tape on the kitchen table. They were gone. I thought maybe Marina took them."

Still pacing, Jonathan watched Patti and Henry leave the room. Gut instincts told him everything was all wrong. Marina wouldn't take the supplies if she was sending another appraiser. She'd left the lamps. Why not the tape?

With a deep frown forming on his weathered face,

Farnsworth took out his cell phone and motioned for Jonathan to wait while he stepped from the room.

The hairs on Jonathan's scalp rose at Farnsworth's return. If given the chance, the detective's gaze, sharp and angry, would cut through steel. "What's up?"

The man pursed his lips. "First off, I wanted to make sure they left. My phone call was to headquarters. I requested a team to search the property." He shook a tight fist in the air. "She's here, Blandish, and I won't be surprised if Tyler's with her."

Jonathan's heart rate skyrocketed. He gripped the older man's arm. "How do you know?"

"This." He bent behind a pile of boxes and retrieved a nearly finished roll of duct tape. He dangled it on one gloved finger. "Another roll was on the end table in the living room."

Jonathan sucked in a sharp breath. They were bound and gagged with duct tape! Feeling helpless, he gripped his hair with both hands and pulled, gaze pleading at the detective. "Nick—"

"There's more, son." He reached into his pocket and handed Jonathan Marina's camera. "Take a look at the last two shots."

The first was an image of a white envelope propped against a wall stud. The second, a more angled shot, included the envelope and a blood-stained screwdriver.

Chapter Twenty-Six

Jonathan couldn't breathe, and for damn sure, the rock in his stomach wouldn't go away anytime soon. Thoughts collided. Marina and Tyler both missing. The murder weapon found. What happened after she snapped the picture?

He stuck his head into the open panel and scanned the alcove, in case Farnsworth was blind as a bat and missed something. *Dammit, Marina, I should never have let you leave.* Straightening, he faced the detective. "What should we do?"

The man's phone rang. He answered, said only one word, and quickly disconnected while waving a finger about the room. "You stay in the house and search every nook and cranny while I go organize the search team. We'll find them, Blandish." He hurried from the room.

Racing into the hall, Jonathan cupped both hands near his mouth. "Marina! Tyler!" Only the slamming of car doors answered.

An urgency strangled his heart. Jonathan banged and kicked the walls, not giving a damn if the paneling cracked into pieces. With adrenaline fueling unlimited strength, he tossed boxes like paper. *Where the hell is my son?* And Marina. He loved them both so much. And yes, he loved Marina, loved her more than any woman before her, including Susan. If he had stopped for ten seconds to analyze the expression on her face... But dammit to hell, he was too friggin' concerned about Tyler finding them together. Instead, he had hurt the one woman who filled him with indescribable joy. The realization forced him to pound faster.

What if they are hurt and bleeding to death in some forsaken hole? Or worse, what if they weren't on the property at all? The police would waste valuable time searching for nothing.

Tell me where you are, Marina.

She could be unconscious or somewhere else on the property. She might also be...dead.

No. His muscles tightened with the thought. She wasn't dead, and Tyler was with her. They were hiding or being held captive. Come hell or high water, he would find them.

A sudden thought struck. No one bothered to check the basement! That dark hellhole and Marina's worse nightmare. Hope sprang into his heart. He ran for the stairwell.

"Yo, Jon!"

"Jonathan," he corrected and turned to see Henry exit the back bedroom. Since Henry's reappearance caused a few hairs to rise on the back of his neck, Jonathan faced him with a narrowed gaze. "I didn't hear you come in."

"You won't hear anything with all the banging you're doing. I dropped Patti at her house and returned to help." He glanced to and fro. "Where do you want me to start?"

Jonathan's cell phone rang. He yanked the device from his pocket, fumbled, caught it, and answered.

"I'm by the lake," Farnsworth said. "We found her

car."

His heart thundered. *Found her car? And her?* Without asking any questions, he flew down the staircase. "She's outside, Henry. Follow me!" He dashed out the open front door with Henry close behind.

"What's going on?" Henry gushed the words, breathless.

"They found her car!"

Cops were everywhere. Their vehicles crowded the driveway, making a labyrinth to maneuver. If he'd thought better, he'd have used the sunroom door, but the front entrance was closest to the stairwell, and he'd raced through the opening without thinking. Once cleared from the maze, Jonathan sprinted toward the rear of the property where floodlights lit the pasture like a ballpark. He arrived at the lake in time to see Marina's SUV inching from the water.

A chain from a tow truck dragged the vehicle through weeds and mud, the operator working a lever in short bursts to allow the water to drain.

Jonathan spotted Farnsworth standing by the water's edge and hurried to his side. "You never said she was in the car!"

Farnsworth faced him. "Easy, Blandish. She's not in the car."

"So, she escaped?" Stepping closer to the water, he kept his gaze on the red SUV.

"No, I'm saying she's not in the car."

"Detective!"

Jonathan and Farnsworth turned toward the voice of the male caller who waved them toward the mud-covered vehicle.

Oh, God, she's in the car after all. Resisting the urge to vomit into the lake, he swallowed hard and followed Farnsworth.

A man in a rubber suit popped the hatchback. Marina's guitar, laptop, and suitcase were in the trunk along with Tyler's bicycle, all water-logged and covered with muck.

Unable to control his quivering gut any longer, Jonathan ran to the water's edge and heaved what little remained in his stomach. The bicycle was positive proof that Tyler had reached Marina. Now, both were missing. Where the hell were they?

"Dredge the lake," Farnsworth bellowed to several men, "and team up to cover the rest of the grounds. Blandish, you're with me. My money is still on the house." He approached the partially-bent Jonathan and slapped his back. "You okay, son?"

Nodding, Jonathan wiped his mouth on his sleeve and straightened.

The detective gave a faint smile. "Any objection to my crew busting a few walls?"

"I don't give a damn if we tear the house apart." But Farnsworth's reasoning created doubts. Jonathan clutched the detective's arm. "What makes you so sure they're not stuffed in the murderer's trunk?"

The older man nodded in the direction of the street. "The timeline, son. It was broad daylight and school bus time. After two murders up here, curiosity makes everyone nosy." He started for the house. "They're alive, Blandish. Otherwise, our killer wouldn't waste time wrapping them in tape."

The man made sense. Jonathan hurried alongside. "I was on my way to the basement when you called.

Henry and I—"

Farnsworth whirled, gaze sharp. "Henry returned?"

"Yes, he's—"

Nowhere to be seen.

Jonathan scanned the area. "He was right behind me."

"Was Patti with him?"

"No, why?" Farnsworth's expression had changed to stone. Even his gaze transformed into a cold, hard glare. The look was alarming and so boldly obvious that a vise gripped Jonathan's heart. He grabbed the detective's coat sleeve. "Are you saying Patti and Henry are in this together?"

Farnsworth quickened his pace. "Let me tell you a little story. Fifteen years ago, this house had another questionable death. A young man drowned in this lake. The coroner ruled the incident accidental, but the detective in charge had a strong suspicion of premeditated murder. His chief suspect was a teenager, the best friend to the victim. Unfortunately, the detective never found any definitive proof." He glanced at Jonathan who kept pace. "Murder is a habit, Blandish. Cops learn that early in their careers."

Jonathan jumped in his path and walked backward. "Which one's the murderer?"

"Which—eh, no, Blandish." He wagged a finger. "Only one killer. Patti's as innocent as Dr. Cavanaugh."

Jonathan gasped and stopped in his tracks. "Henry? What's his motive?"

The detective circumvented Jonathan and continued over the hill. "Patti's the motive. When I discovered for certain that Patti and Roger were a couple, I knew I was dealing with the same killer.

Henry was obsessed with her then and still is today."

Shaking himself, Jonathan hurried to catch up. "But why hurt Marina and Tyler?"

Slightly breathless, Farnsworth glanced his way. "I'm not sure yet, but I'll bet money their disappearance has something to do with Patti. Since Henry spends so much time with her, he probably took an impression of the new key to the house, let himself inside, and surprised the doctor. Then your boy shows up, and naturally, Henry had to do something with him." Farnsworth took out his cell phone but before dialing, stared at the display. "My original assumption of your brother's murder as a crime of passion holds true. He was killed out of jealousy and not the diamonds, but right now, I believe the doctor is alive because of her link to a fortune."

Too much, too fast. His mind whirled with all the new details. Were the diamonds Marina's lifeline? And had Tyler become the bargaining chip? "Nick, wait." Jonathan caught his arm. "Who was this detective?"

Farnsworth gave him a sideways glance. "Me."

****

Marina shivered awake, fluttering her eyes open to see nothing but black. A solid wall of black.

Panic choked her airway. A sob gurgled in her throat, muffled and useless. Tape not only sealed her mouth but wrapped her body as well, squeezing her arms and hands tight against her sides. Positioned on her back, like a mummy in a tomb, she rotated her head to search for that little gleam of light. Nothing.

Heart pounding against her rib cage, she struggled for some movement, pulling and twisting to no avail. Someone had made damn sure she wouldn't escape.

Clamping her eyes shut to ward off the rising hysteria, she stifled a cry and willed herself to calm down.

She cursed this phobia and cursed the parents who forced her into a dark closet. So many times, she'd fought to conquer the fear with the help of doctors and therapists. One doctor—a woman—had stated that a major catastrophic event, so monumental in nature, would cure her forever. *What could be more monumental than this*?

Marina yanked and twisted against the tape until breathlessness stopped her. *Take a minute to think.*

What had happened? She peeked into the hidden panel and spotted a blood-stained screwdriver. Then, she picked up a white envelope and extracted a photo of Patti and Roger. Something slammed against the right side of her head. The room spun, and she awakened in here…wherever *here* was.

She sniffed. The musty odor of the attic dominated the air, but the whole house now smelled like the attic since she and Patti had hauled everything into the bedroom. No sounds either, the silence making the darkness all the more eerie. And cold, so cold, like she was locked inside a freezer.

Determined to defeat the shiver raking across her skin, Marina rolled from one side to the other and bounced against a solid object in both directions. Was she inside the panel?

Coffins have solid sides, too.

That thought caused an uncontrollable tremor.

Enough! She squirmed to place herself in an upright position. An impossible maneuver with tape securing her entire torso. Instead, she raised her legs. No obstruction. That meant no lid. This wasn't a coffin but a tight spot nonetheless. A secret panel? If so, that meant a door and escape, but she couldn't see!

Another sob escaped from her throat. *I won't cry. I can do this.* But first, slow and deep breaths. Control the panic. Analyze the situation.

What's to analyze? I'm trapped in a hellhole.

Who could have done this? Why hadn't she been killed outright like Roger and Karl? Why was she the lucky one to be wrapped in tape and stuffed into a dark void? Only Patti and Jonathan knew of her fear of the dark. No one else. Would Patti be so cruel?

But, thinking back, were the footsteps on the stairs Patti's? Marina heard heavy footsteps scuffing on the uncarpeted steps. Patti always wore sneakers, and for a woman with weight, she was light on her feet. A man then? But who? Someone with access into the house…

Jonathan! Heat rose behind her eyelids. He *had* to prevent her from leaving, because she was the key to Roger's treasure. His declaration of love was nothing more than a ruse to keep her around. Why else would he push her away whenever someone entered the room?

No, her reasoning was flawed, probably because the right side of her head throbbed like mad. Whether his love was real could be debated at another time, but he *wasn't* the one who took a swing at her head.

Renewed optimism flooded her body, filling her with a determination to escape this dark hole. Drawing in a huge breath to expand her chest, she stretched and pulled the tape until her fingers wiggled into freedom. Inching them into her jeans' back pocket, she felt for her utility knife, and her heart performed happy cartwheels to find the tool securely in place. *Thank you, Lord.* Now, to get it out…

Creeping into a pocket was a lot easier than edging out with an object. Her fingers grasped the knife, but the tape left her with little ability to maneuver.

Having no other choice, she opened the knife inside her pocket and cut into the denim, not giving a damn if she removed half of her backside. Once freed, she snipped at the tape, little by little, a meticulous process in the dark with only her sense of feeling as a guide.

Ouch!

Too close to her hip on that one.

Maybe she should shut her eyes. She couldn't tell if they were open anyway.

Fighting a hand cramp, Marina manipulated and cut until loosening one arm enough to rip the remaining tape encircling her chest. She bunched the adhesive into a ball and tossed it before sitting up to tear the tape from her mouth, nearly yanking the skin from her lips. Mouth free, she gulped air, released a sob, and shook aside the relief. She wasn't free yet. Next, she cut the tape surrounding her ankles and, afterward, closed her knife and kissed the hand grip before slipping the tool into her front pocket. "Help!"

She cringed. That wasn't a bright idea. Whoever hid her could be close by and realize she was awake. *Oh, like I give a shit at this point.* She needed light to see, and someone coming to silence her would have to open a door. "Help!"

Reaching carefully, she lifted a hand overhead to feel an angled joist. A roof support? If so, then she had to be in the attic. She touched one side of the wall. Two by fours with protruding nails between them. Like the outside wall near the fireplace. She fingered the opposite side and traced along a wall of plaster lath.

Shit. Neither the fireplace panel nor the bedroom had a door backed with lath. Someone knew the house well enough to place her in a panel with no noticeable door.

Marina pressed on the thin strips of wood. One section snapped in two, and chunks of plaster fell to the floor. She froze, expecting the noise to attract attention, but only silence greeted her. With a flutter in her belly, she took out her knife and easily cut into the plaster between the lath.

With one hand guiding the other, she broke away pieces and busted the wood. A sizable hole greeted her fingers. She stuck her knife into the opening and hit something solid. Paneling. Only one wall in the attic had the same dark paneling. *Double shit.*

A door has to be somewhere nearby. She replaced the knife into her pocket and crept on hands and knees along the tight corridor. Her hips and shoulders bumped on studs along the way, and with one hand, she felt overhead for low-hanging rafters, all the while pressing the plaster lath walls in hopes something gave.

Her heart pounded wildly, and the cold air seeped through her sweatshirt as if she wore a thin cotton blouse. Every shiver caused her nose to run. This was way worse than being locked in a closet. At least, the closet contained hanging coats. She sniffed and wiped her nose with her shoulder.

All right, so where is the damn door? She couldn't be stuffed into a wall without access. Would anyone dare secure the door with a heavy object, like her father did with the chair under the knob? A violent shiver hit with the thought.

Still creeping along the floor and feeling her way with her fingers, she bumped something hairy and recoiled, her breath frozen in her throat. The panel by the fireplace had the remains of a dead mouse, but this hairy-something was much bigger. A cat, trapped for eternity? Or how about a rat? *Oh, God.* Her pulse raced. Should she continue or retreat?

She had no choice. With no idea where she was in the wall, she must crawl until she hit the end. If finding no door, she'd have to retrace her path to the other side. Swallowing hard, she reached toward the hairy object. The strands felt silky, and a solidness underneath paralyzed her fingers. A person? Using both hands, she traced along the face to the tape covering the mouth, and she let out an audible cry. A child. *Tyler*!

Anger, fear, and tears hit simultaneously as she gingerly removed the tape from his mouth. "Tyler, sweetie." No response. Warmth blew across her hand so he was breathing. *No more wasting of time.* She had to carry Tyler into the light to see if he was injured. "If I can't find how we got in, then I'll have to make another way out."

Moving away from Tyler and creating a fist like a hammer, she pounded the lath. The force cracked the thin wood, but the combined plaster and paneling produced stronger resistance. The power to break through was in her legs.

Placing her back against a wall stud, she struggled to her feet while feeling above her head for the rafter. Using a handhold to maintain her balance, she lifted her right foot for the first swing. *God help me if the person who locked us away is still in the house.*

Taking a deep breath, she kicked. Wood splintered.

More plaster cracked and fell in chunks to the floor. She kicked again and again, daring anyone to stop her from getting Tyler to safety.

A light snapped on.

Relief hit so fast, she felt giddy. Her rescuer had to be Jonathan. No one else would do. "In here!" She kicked harder, creating a hole big enough to see the interior of the attic. With the help of the light, she glanced toward Tyler, still motionless, his body wrapped in duct tape. No visible injuries, but his stillness constricted her throat.

"How the hell did you travel so far from the door?"

Pulse pounding out her ears, she froze. Now, she understood. The heavy footsteps on the stairs. A glimpse of a dark overcoat and spit-polished black shoes just before the blow hit her head. Patti's boyfriends mysteriously meeting an untimely demise. Henry! *Dear Lord, what will I do now*?

Stretching a hand through the hole, Henry grasped her sweatshirt, his gaze hard. "I should have killed you while I had the chance, but you're the key to forty million in diamonds." He yanked her between the two wall studs and slammed her face and shoulder against the unbroken lath.

The thin wood shattered into pieces, and she released a soft cry as pain shot through her left shoulder and down her arm.

He pulled again and again, using her shoulder like a battering ram to create a bigger hole. His frenzied jerks kept her off-balance, and as hard as she struggled to free his grip, she couldn't fight his greater strength.

One violent yank created a sharp pain that shot straight to her elbow, and she saw stars. *I'll be damned to let him win.* With her free hand, she grabbed onto a wall stud and used whatever power she could muster to resist.

"Oh, no, you don't!" His face flushed a deep red, and he repositioned his grip. "How can you suggest Patti work for Jonathan Blandish? The man's so friggin' good-looking."

What the hell? "I want her to work with me in Boston!"

"Liar."

The man was insane. Braced as best she could, she scanned the tight corridor for an escape but saw none. And then her gaze fell onto Tyler, oblivious to the ruckus. Anger consumed her. She'd protected her siblings. Come hell or high water, she'd protect Tyler. Henry would not touch another hair on Tyler's head! *I will rip out this man's heart.*

Grabbing onto his arm, Marina yanked Henry toward the hole, smashing his face against the paneling. "What'd you do to Tyler?"

He oomphed but his grip remained firm. "The kid's not hurt. The stupid shit was looking for you and complained about being thirsty. So, I dropped a few of my motion sickness pills into his water. The stuff works fast."

"How many pills? You might have overdosed him." *I'll kill him.*

He wrenched her into the opening. "Come out, Doctor. You tell me where the diamonds are, and I won't hurt him."

At the threat, she grabbed her knife from her pocket and flipped open the blade. "I'll see you in hell before I let you touch him." She stabbed his hand to break the grip on her shirt.

Screaming, he released her, and the sudden lack of resistance forced her back against the opposite wall, nails jabbing into her skin. "Ouch!"

He clamped the other hand over his wound, muttering curses. His wild gaze turned to fury as he searched the attic, tossing aside whatever was in his way. With a growl, he charged the hole with an old metal chair, slamming the paneling with one blow after the other, shattering lath and plaster, creating a rainstorm of debris through the hole.

She scurried to put her body in front of Tyler.

"You can't escape, bitch!"

No, they were trapped, but she had her knife and, if necessary, would fight to the death.

Lifting Tyler into one arm and using two knees and her free hand, she crawled along the tight corridor.

The madman followed her path, breaking through every section of the studs, bound and determined to reach her.

Her blessing was a too-narrow corridor for his wide body, but once the paneling was destroyed, then what? She reached the far wall and crammed Tyler behind her back before turning, knife ready to cut off Henry's hands. Then, she leaned back her head and screamed.

****

Jonathan's head snapped upward as he rushed through the sunroom door. The noise of crashing wood was nothing compared to a woman's bloodcurdling scream. He took the stairs two at a time, leaving Farnsworth and everyone else in the dust. Another scream. *The attic*! He flew.

Henry was on a rampage, smashing through the paneled wall like scissors through paper. He thrust his arm into the hole, cursed, and swung more.

Grabbing Henry by the shoulder, Jonathan swung him around and connected a solid fist to the man's jaw. Again, again, again. He couldn't stop. His own fury spiraled out of control. He wanted to make mincemeat out of Henry's head, but two police officers stopped him by tackling Henry to the floor.

Then, Farnsworth arrived, breathless. "Enough, Jon. It's over."

No, not until he had Marina and Tyler in his arms. He ran to the closest hole in the wall and stuck in his head. "Marina?"

She had cowered against the far wall, shielding Tyler who was wrapped in duct tape, unmoving. Her utility knife shook in her hand, held at arm's length, ready to strike.

Henry had gotten so damn close. She sat a mere three feet from his last hole. Shaking, Jonathan extended his hand. "We got him, honey. Put the knife down."

She stared at the bloody utility knife then, with a violent shudder, dropped it. Reaching behind her, she drew Tyler to her chest and, with a shaking hand, extended her arm.

Relief flooding his heart, Jonathan took her hand, her arm, and her body in that order as he helped her through the jagged opening, still clutching Tyler. Without wasting a second, he wrapped his arms around them both in a tight embrace. She did not return the hug. She felt frozen. "Tyler?" he asked, stroking his son's hair.

"Motion sickness pills. Henry put them in his water. I don't know how many."

He hardly recognized her voice, husky and strained without emotion, as if she had no power to propel out the words.

An officer knelt alongside to cut Tyler's constricting tape.

Marina watched with a blank expression on her face.

Farnsworth approached and, with hands on knees, bent over to study her face. "She's in shock. Help her downstairs, son. I'll have one of the boys take all three of you to the hospital."

When the last strip of tape had been removed from his son, Jonathan lifted Tyler into his arms and kissed him lightly on the forehead while blinking away the moisture behind his eyelids. Then, with a hand under her right armpit, he helped Marina to her feet. She was emotionless, her gaze far away and unfocused. He expected her to collapse to the floor, but her legs held.

A tall police officer took her arm. "I'll help her down the stairs."

Love exploded within Jonathan's chest as the image of Marina protecting his son took hold. She would have given her life, and tears dripped down his cheeks. What to do next was his dilemma. He loved his son dearly, but the boy was sound asleep and unaware of the horror Henry had caused. Marina, unfortunately, looked whiter than ice and ready to drop into a faint.

With outstretched arms, he turned to the officer. "No, you carry my son, please." He shifted Tyler onto the officer's arms and then reached for Marina.

She pressed an open palm on his chest, a feeble

attempt to assert some control.

But her gaze was so vacant he wondered whether she saw him at all. He put his face close to hers. "Sorry, honey, for a change, you're listening to me." He swept her off her feet and held her tight again his chest.

Chapter Twenty-Seven

Standing on the ambulance loading dock, Jonathan held his crying mother. She arrived at Massachusetts General Hospital's emergency room a nervous wreck and wouldn't take his word that everything was okay. She had to see for herself, touch Marina, kiss Tyler, and hug her younger son.

Tyler suffered no injuries but was left to sleep off the antihistamine effect from the motion sickness pills. He moaned and groaned during the doctor's examination, more in protest than pain, always instantly falling back into a deep slumber.

Marina endured the brunt of Henry's wrath and suffered a hard blow to the head, which left a whale of a lump. No broken skin, so no stitches. A dark bruise colored the left side of her face, and her left shoulder had already turned a deep purple by the time they arrived at the hospital.

While waiting for Marina to return from a CT scan of her skull, he'd escorted his mother outside to let her cry. He held her tightly and kissed the top of her head, realizing how deeply he loved his mother. She had always been available for him and Tyler and sacrificed so much after his squirm-of-a-father left. Her happiness at this stage of life was paramount, and he'd do everything possible to help her. If she wanted an apartment, fine. He'd sign the lease. Funds to travel?

He'd arrange a money transfer account with his bank. Anything she wanted, she would have. He kissed the top of her head.

She withdrew to wipe her eyes. "Let me get back to Tyler in case he awakens. I know the doctors told us he'll probably sleep until morning, but we don't know what he witnessed at Roger's." She urged him toward the automatic doors. "Go on. Marina needs you."

Since Tyler required the expertise of a pediatrician, he had been placed in a small room where his grandmother could sit and watch him. Marina was adjacent to the nurses' station in her own bay but hadn't returned yet.

With an effort to keep his mind occupied, Jonathan observed the sights and sounds of a busy emergency room. A woman wailed from behind one of the curtains. A baby screamed. Nurses conversed about everyday subjects while typing on a keyboard. Medics rushed in with a stretcher and headed into the trauma room. No one panicked or barked orders, and everyone remained professional and calm.

Several minutes later, two nurses wheeled Marina into the bay. He stepped aside to allow them room, grateful when they drew the curtain for privacy. They had Marina semi-reclined on the stretcher, but she stayed in an automaton state throughout all the jostling. Her smudged face remained devoid of emotion, her movements mechanical, and her beautiful voice a mere squeak in response to questions.

Attic filth covered her face and hands along with cobwebs in her hair and that awful musty smell. A hospital gown took the place of her dirty sweatshirt and jeans, and her garments draped onto a chair to await her return trip home.

Seconds later, a nurse hurried into the bay and pressed a wet washcloth into Marina's hand, but Marina simply fingered the material.

Jonathan took the cloth and cleaned the dirt from her face and then each hand. She never looked beyond the sheet covering her body.

His heart broke to see her like this and cursed Henry for being the cause. Then, he cursed himself for involving her in the first place. Right now, he didn't give a damn about the diamonds, only Marina. He wanted to whisk her off the stretcher and into his arms, never to let go.

The ER doctor stepped around the curtain. He was an older man with kind brown eyes who had handled Marina like a delicate flower. With a quick nod toward Jonathan, he took a position on the opposite side of Marina's stretcher.

"The CT scan revealed the presence of a concussion," he began. "No internal hemorrhage to the brain, and the skull hadn't sustained any cracks. Her mandible and shoulder are also intact despite the severe bruising." He watched her while twisting his mouth to the side. "Based on her physical state, I'd like to authorize her release, but her shock level is phenomenal. I don't understand the locked-in emotions."

Jonathan draped the washcloth over the handrail. "I do. We found her trapped in a dark, attic wall, and she's deathly afraid of the dark. Release her to me."

The doctor cocked a brow. "You're not family."

"No, her family is in North Carolina. She's been staying in my house with my mom and son."

"Then, I'll give her a mild sedative. The effect should be sufficient for a trip home and into the shower. Nothing to knock her out, just relax the muscles. She's to have two days of complete bed rest. If severe headaches occur, return her here at once. Understand?"

"Yes, sir."

"She might have nightmares."

"I'll be with her." Hold her for all eternity if need be.

The doctor glanced up at Marina's monitor then lowered his gaze toward Jonathan. "I'd like a reference before I release her to you."

A worthwhile request. Impressive. "Detective Farnsworth can answer your questions. He's been involved in the case from the beginning." He took out his cell phone and skipped through his contact list, found the number, and showed the doctor. "He's probably still at my brother's house."

According to the nurse preparing Marina for discharge, Farnsworth answered more than the doctor's questions. He had recommended Jonathan Blandish as the only man to care for Marina Cavanaugh. The recommendation filled Jonathan's chest with pride. *The old guy wasn't so bad after all.*

Since his car was still parked in Roger's driveway, Jonathan drove his mother's car home. Marina sat in the front seat, buckled in and motionless while his mother rode in the back with a sleeping Tyler in her arms. Once in the driveway, he parked by the front door and hurried around to open his mother's car door.

She stopped him from taking Tyler. "I'll handle him. Your responsibility is Marina."

He had no argument. Tyler would likely remember

nothing while Marina's memories could haunt her forever. "Marina's going straight to the shower, Mom. My shower, my bed."

Tears formed in her eyes. "I'm so glad." Lifting Tyler closer to her shoulder, she stepped from the car. "The doctor said Tyler might have a headache in the morning. Depends on how much of the water he drank. I'll sleep with him tonight, in case he wakes with nightmares." She motioned with a nod toward the front seat. "Go on. Help Marina."

Sprinting to the house, he opened the front door for his mother then returned to unbuckle Marina, who hadn't budged. "We're home, sweetheart."

A blank look stared back, but she swung her legs from the car.

Chest tight, he wished he had forced her to attend Tyler's game, then none of this would have happened. His heart ached to see her so distant. All his fault. He'd gotten her into this mess, but then again, he'd never have fallen in love.

As he guided her into the house with a hand on the small of her back, he felt a faint tremble course through her skin. This continued up the staircase and into his room, and after stripping her clothing and placing her in the shower, he wanted so badly to step in with her just to hold her in a warm embrace. Something told him to wait. She needed to return to the world on her own.

He stood and viewed her beautiful body through the shower doors, stiff and unmoving with her face turned upward into the stream of water. The automaton stayed in this position while the bathroom fogged with moisture. After a time, her head bent, her shoulders gave, and a soft sob filtered through the shower doors.

"Marina, I'm here." Would she forgive him? The trauma of confinement in a dark space could push her away forever.

The fact that he was a total idiot required rectification more than anything.

Before long, Marina turned off the water and opened the shower door.

Her gaze showed some life, confused perhaps, and tired. No hatred emanated—for which he was grateful. He held a towel ready. She stepped into his arms, and he wrapped the fluffy material around her body and drew her close. Pleasant fragrances of herbal shampoo and soap replaced the odors of the attic. She melted against him, her trust seeping into his pores, and he choked on a sob as a powerful wave of love filled his heart. To think he'd almost lost her brought tears to his eyes.

Her tears fell first. With loose fists pressed against his chest, she sobbed, and the tears along with her wet hair saturated his shirt. He'd never again let her go. He wanted to tell her, but his emotions were ragged, and he had only a choked-up voice to go with his tears dripping onto her hair. He blinked to stop them, or at least clear his vision, but they refused to stop.

Her damaged shoulder was right under his nose. Scrapes against the lath had cut into her skin, and the nurse doused the area with iodine. A brown stain covered the majority of purple bruising, despite the shower.

"I'm so sorry, sweetheart. For everything." He choked on the words. Whether she'd heard or not, he wasn't sure, but her sobs subsided, and trembling took its place. He lifted her towel-clad body into his arms and carried her to the bed. She clung like a frightened child, and he had never experienced such an overwhelming sense of helplessness. He could only hold her and offer the security of his embrace.

"Tyler?" she whispered.

"Sleeping like a baby. Mom's with him."

Within minutes, she fell asleep against his chest. The sedative. Exhaustion. With a two-finger touch, he brushed her damp hair from her face to expose the bruised skin. The purple discoloration traced along her delicate jawline and up to her left temple. Small wonder her cheekbone wasn't broken.

Unwilling to move but in desperate need to wash the attic smell from his own skin, he shifted her onto the pillow and slipped away for a quick shower. Afterward, the mustiness lingered in his nose, so he shaved and then splashed on a liberal amount of aftershave. The odor of Roger's attic would be embedded in his memory forever.

By morning, her warm hand stroked across his chest. He rolled her onto her back and gently captured her mouth, savoring what he'd wanted all night, mindful of her injuries to jaw, head, and shoulder. When she drew away, she gazed with an affection that collapsed his bones.

"I love you, Marina Cavanaugh." He gazed in the chocolate hue of her eyes, like melted fudge only he was the one melting. "Can you forgive me for being such a fool?" She said nothing, but he lowered his lips to meet hers.

Afterward, she broke away with a wry smile. "Depends on whether your mom and Tyler are in the house."

"They are, and for the record, they were both upset when you left." He touched her chin and gently lifted her face upward. "I don't ever want you to leave again." A smile tugged on his lips. "I'm asking, not telling."

"In that case—" She stroked his shaft.

A sensation of warmth flooded him faster than a dam bursting through a retaining wall. He grabbed her hand to stop the soft caress. "The doctor said you must go easy for the next few days. No brain activity."

"I wouldn't call this brain activity."

"But your shoulder—"

She rotated the cuff and winced. "I'm sore, but I don't have to do any heavy lifting, right?"

"You also have a head injury."

"Oh—well, okay then. I won't think about what I'm doing."

Grinning, she returned her hand to his shaft.

Her gentle caress caused him to harden beneath her fingers. She looked up with an impish smile since she knew full well what she did. Mocking a frown, he reciprocated by placing his hand between her legs. Moist heat greeted him. But no wild frenzy this morning. She deserved slow and leisurely with soft kisses on her injured shoulder and jaw. When her groan turned to a plea, she took his thrust with a satisfied sigh.

After a time wrapped in each other's arms, she lifted her head and rested her chin on his shoulder. "You kept on the light last night."

Containing an unbelievable king-of-the-world feeling, he lifted a strand of hair from her face and tucked it behind her ear. "You needed light to see where you were." He traced a finger along her neck and shoulder. "What happened at Roger's? Farnsworth will be over later this morning for a statement so if you can't talk, I'll understand."

She suppressed a yawn and replaced her head on his chest while a finger traced along his sternum. "Not much to tell. I found another secret panel in the back bedroom and saw a bloodied screwdriver along with a photo in an envelope. The next I know, someone whacks my head, and I came to in the attic wall. I figured whoever wrapped me in duct tape didn't know I always carry a utility knife." She took his right hand and traced her thumb over his skin.

Bruises covered his knuckles. "Henry's face," he explained.

Lifting his hand, she kissed each knuckle. "No man ever came to my rescue before." She rotated her head to meet his gaze. "I love you, Jonathan Blandish."

"You know how I feel, but I'll say the words again. I love you, Marina Cavanaugh. If the cops hadn't stopped me, I would have busted every bone in Henry's head." Never before had he felt so proud to be a man. He'd come to the rescue of a damsel in distress. His knuckles hurt like hell, but he'd endure any amount of pain to protect her.

He kissed the top of her head and cherished the feel of her soft hair strands tickling his nose. A lifetime with her wouldn't be enough. "Farnsworth arrived before you were discharged. He told me everything and how he'd suspected Henry from the beginning since he had a prior history with the house."

He toyed with her cute ear. Funny how he hadn't noticed how small they were. "Farnsworth's original assumption about Roger's murder being a crime of passion held true. Henry confessed. He killed Roger, because Roger fell in love with Patti. When he found out Roger proposed, he couldn't let any marriage plans happen. He knew nothing about the diamonds until Patti told him what we discovered."

She returned her head onto his chest. "Yet, Henry introduced Patti to Roger."

"Yes, irony at its finest. Henry viewed his goodwill gesture as a betrayal on Roger's part. Remember, Roger was a confirmed bachelor, and Henry believed Roger wouldn't change." He traced a finger up and down her arm. "I felt the same way. That's why I was skeptical when you told me about Patti." He sighed heavily. "Henry killed Karl, too. The PI caught him on camera. The envelope you found along with the screwdriver was a blatant attempt by Henry to frame Patti should she refuse his last proposal. Even though he claims he loves her, he'd rather she stay in a women's prison away from men."

She grimaced. "That's sick."

"I agree. Henry also took an impression of Patti's new key and spent every chance searching for the diamonds."

"I don't think he has them. He told me he kept me alive for that reason." She propped herself on one elbow, her gaze watching his face. "You may have been next on Henry's list, Jonathan. Henry believed Patti's new job was at your house." Her finger twirled his chest hairs. "I'm glad everything's settled. I can finish the inventory without looking over my shoulder all day long."

He splayed a hand on her back and nudged. "You're not going anywhere for a few days. Doctor's orders. Besides, your clothes from last night are filthy.

Mom will find you something to wear." Hell, she knew nothing about her car. Should he tell her now or later? *No time like the present.* He tapped her nose. "I hate to tell you this, but Henry drove your car into the lake along with all your stuff."

With a pained expression, she jerked back. "My guitar!"

"Laptop, too. The work you've done is lost."

She snorted. "Nothing is ever lost these days. I uploaded the inventory to Mrs. Billingsley's cloud account."

Snuggling against him, she brushed her soft breasts against his skin to shoot another surge of warmth to his core. He'd gone too long without the feel of a woman by his side. Never again. He lifted her head toward him and kissed her lips. "Did you know you were in the attic?"

"I wasn't sure at first. With all the stuff we transferred, the entire second floor smelled musty and old."

As gently as he could, he rolled her onto her back and hovered. "I will suck every last ounce of resistance from you and make you sleep the day away."

She smiled up at him. "Who's resisting?"

"Daddy, Marina's not in her room! Where is she?" Tyler threw open the door and burst inside.

Gasping, Marina grabbed the sheet to cover her nakedness.

Jonathan wagged a finger in her face. "Hiding behind a sheet is okay, but from here on, no more pulling away. Everyone needs to know you're mine." He turned to Tyler standing by the bed, dressed in his Superman jammies, mouth agape, and eyes wide to popping. "In the future, young man, this room is off limits when the door is closed."

"Why is Marina in here?"

"This is her room, too. She's sleeping with me." Tyler hadn't sounded sleepy, but his eyes had faint dark circles. He narrowed his gaze. "How do you feel?"

"My head hurts a little, but Grandma said food will help that. I'm starved." The little guy blinked, his posture rigid as his gaze scanned the bed. "Are you two *naked*?"

Jonathan almost burst out laughing. Marina's sex lesson left a much better impression on the boy, and she shook with suppressed laughter beneath the sheets. He cleared his throat. "Yes, Tyler, we are naked."

His cute mouth gaped even wider. "That means you have to marry Marina! I'm gonna have a mommy?"

"Maybe. If she wants the job." He waved toward the door. "All right, you've seen enough. Go find Grandmom and get something to eat. We'll join you shortly."

"I'm gonna have a mommy!" He jumped gleefully around the room. "A real mommy! Yahhhh!" Sustaining the yell, he ran from the room.

Jonathan leaped from the bed to close and lock the door. He slipped under the sheet and rotated her to put his face close. "I better make my proposal official. Will you marry me, Marina?"

With gaze sparkling, she smiled. "Well, we can't disappoint that adorable little boy." She stopped him from a kiss by placing a hand on his chest. "I intend to keep working, you know."

He pressed a finger to her lips. "Say no more. I've already decided to put the house up for sale. I'm spending too much of my life commuting to and from work."

A devilish grin twisted her lip.

He shot her a one-eyed glare. "What?"

"I have a strange feeling you'll cure me of night lights."

Heat radiated throughout his chest. She couldn't have given him a better compliment.

Epilogue

Finishing Roger's house involved another two months of Marina's time. Now, of course, she wasn't in much of a hurry. She started late every morning and finished early, always home in time for dinner and to help Tyler with his homework.

She and Jonathan were married in a quickie wedding with Tyler as the best man and Patti as maid of honor. In the meantime, Iris relocated into Marina's condo, Jonathan's house went on the market, and Marina and Jon bought a gorgeous brownstone twenty minutes from Jon's office, which they spent weekends decorating. The house had room for an expanding family since not a week passed without Tyler asking for a little brother.

Finally, moving day for Roger's house contents arrived. The auction house's van blocked the entire driveway while four men hauled boxes and furniture up the metal gangplank.

Marina directed the men on which box belonged to which warehouse. Men being men never bothered to read the bright red lettering on the lids.

Iris and Nick Farnsworth dated twice a week and were making plans for a cruise to Bermuda after his retirement. Patti put her house up for sale with plans to move in temporarily with Iris once Marina and Jon moved to the brownstone. She helped watch Tyler while Marina was busy at Roger's and worked weekends in the auction's warehouse. That would change to weekdays once she settled into town. She'd already met a man at the warehouse, and they'd clicked instantaneously.

"What about the portrait over the fireplace, Dr. C?"

Marina turned to Michael, a muscular young man with more shoulder than neck. "Everything goes. You'll need a ladder."

"Right. I've got one in the truck." He strolled outside.

Jon waltzed in from the kitchen and took a quick look around the near-empty living room.

The man grew more handsome with each passing day, and her heart filled with joy every time their gazes met. Like now.

He jumped aside as two men carrying boxes walked from the dining room. "The house looks just as gloomy without furniture."

"The place will forever look gloomy with all this dark paneling." Marina had believed total happiness would never touch her life, that she'd be destined to cower in the dark from a phobia too hard to shake. But Jon reminded her how she stood up to Henry to protect Tyler with her fear ignored. She walked toward him, pressed her body to his, and stretched up to capture his lips. Since no one was around, she grabbed his butt cheeks.

Smiling, he growled. "Careful, or I'll do you on the floor." He squeezed her tight. "Nick's retirement party is this Saturday. We're invited."

She sighed while smiling up into his face, aware of the hard press of his erection against her abdomen.

"Your mom likes him a lot. I've never seen her so happy." And they made a cute couple. Even Nick's ragged face eased. Although, his coming retirement probably helped. "Whatever happened to your father?"

"Nick told him to get lost. Mom was thrilled." He nibbled on her neck.

"Careful," she whispered, "I might do *you* on the floor."

He chuckled. "I'm amazed how everything turned out."

"Except we never found the diamonds. Do you think the hedge fund believes you?"

"Don't care. Someday, someone will uncover the stash and become rich. Of course, when I rip this place off its foundation, I'll be here every day. They could still materialize."

The peace she felt in the arms of this man was phenomenal. Even with the men coming and going and a few giving wolf whistles, nothing would pry her out of his arms. She kissed him again as Michael strolled back with an aluminum ladder, carrying it one-handed like a stick. Marina reluctantly released her husband.

"Need help?" Jon asked him.

"Just stand by in case the portrait is too heavy. I don't want you to dirty your clothes."

The mystery woman was finally coming down off the wall.

Marina tapped a finger on her chin. "You know, Jon, I never gave this portrait a thought because of the frame's worth." She faced him. "What if *she's* Roger's Marina Cavanaugh?"

Jon raised a brow. "A distinct possibility."

The poor woman had been ignored since Marina

Jane Drager

stepped through the door. What if the diamonds were hidden within the frame? Her pulse quickened at the prospect.

With two strong hands on opposite sides, Michael gave a grunt and lifted, carefully resting the frame on the top of the ladder. "The size makes for some awkward handling. Got her, Mr. B?" He lowered the portrait to Jon and jumped off the ladder. "Thanks, sir, I'll take her from here."

"No, wait." Marina stepped between the two men. "I haven't had a good look at the signature. Rest the frame against the fireplace, will you, Michael?"

Michael followed her order then clapped his hands of dust. "I don't think that picture has been removed ever." He sneezed in rapid succession. "Excuse me while I go find a tissue." Another sneeze.

"In the kitchen, Michael. Right countertop."

He left with a wave over his shoulder.

Staring down, Jon rested his hands on his hips. "This painting is awful."

She had to agree. The artist had little talent for detail. "This type of portrait was a common way of remembering someone before photographs, and what a crying shame. The subject had a family once, possibly a husband who loved her dearly. Now, no one is around to claim her." Marina took a pair of eyeglasses from her front shirt pocket and placed them on her nose as she knelt to study the right-side corner. "The signature is barely legible." She leaned close and peered. "The date is 1870. Let's turn her around so I can see the back."

Age took its toll. A dried paper backing crumbled where Michael had gripped the sides of the frame.

"I see writing in this corner." Jon pointed to the

upper right.

Standing, she followed his finger to read the writing then straightened with a shake of her head. "She's not Marina Cavanaugh. Her name is Cynthia Wainwright Cavanaugh. Age 42. 1870."

Jon ran his fingers through his hair. "So much for our last clue."

Michael returned with a red nose. "Want me to take out the mantel, Dr. C?"

"The mantel?" Running her fingers along the edge, she inspected the slate of stone. "Why?" With the figurines gone, she spotted holes along the brick face and gasped. Controlling her thundering heart, she waved the young man toward the door. "Michael, you can join the other men. I'll keep the ladder."

"Right, Dr. C." He grabbed a box and left the room.

She clamped onto Jon's arm and pointed toward the mantel. "I've seen this particular pattern of holes before. They signify the mounting of a long mirror. Did Roger have a mirror here?"

His eyebrows rose. "A long time ago, when he first moved in. Hardly any reflective material remained."

She hurriedly climbed the ladder and peered down at the stone surface. "Oh, my God, Jon!"

Jonathan clamped both hands on the ladder and stared upward. "What?"

"The mantel contains a stone etching of a tall ship." She stared down, mouth agape. "The name on the stern is Marina Cavanaugh!"

"Holy shit!" He stepped onto the first rung of the ladder to see around her. "You found Roger's hiding spot, Marina!" He dropped to the floor. "Do we have a mallet anywhere?"

"I remember seeing one in Roger's tool box." She jumped from the ladder and ran to the mudroom, rummaged through the box, found the mallet, and hurried back to the living room.

Jon stood on the ladder, studying the etching. He whistled. "This is beautiful!" He took the mallet and lightly tapped the underside of the mantel. The stone jiggled easily, and he slid the carving off the base. "Help me lay this on the floor, Marina."

Jumping off the ladder, he held one end while she took the other, and together, they lowered the stone to the bare floor. The etching of the tall ship with four masts was expertly carved complete with waves and even a whale rising from the water.

Jon hurriedly ascended the ladder and looked into the exposed crevice. "We've got them, Marina!" He lifted out two small cloth pouches and hopped to the floor. They exchanged glances as he opened one pouch and poured the contents into his palm. Diamonds glittered.

Heart pounding, she let out a cry. "They're gorgeous!"

He stared while spreading the precious stones with his finger. "I'll let Farnsworth know we found them. Then, I can return the gems to the hedge fund and restore Roger's name." His gaze misted. "This should give Mom some peace." He sniffed and leaned toward her for a kiss, his gaze tender. "All this time, I thought Roger meant you. He never said anything about a ship."

Just as well. Roger's cryptic notes gave Marina the job of a lifetime, and she would forever thank the man. She gained a husband, a son, and a jewel of a mother-in-law. Who could ask for anything more?

And, oh, yes. She called her husband Jon. She'd finally worn him down.

A word about the author...

With a growing backlist of books, Jane Drager continues to write cozy mysteries with a strong romantic element, always with a happily-ever-after theme.

An avid reader as well as writer, Jane has lived her life as diverse as her stories. She was a journalist, sports editor, office manager, firefighter, ambulance captain, caterer's assistant, but retired from her long career as a respiratory therapist and instructor.

She's married to a wonderful organic farmer who keeps her busy with canning and freezing.

~*~

Other Titles by Jane Drager
available from The Wild Rose Press, Inc.

Ask Nothing in Return
Infinite Choices
Secrets and Assumptions
Secrets By Necessity

Thank you for purchasing
this publication of The Wild Rose Press, Inc.

If you enjoyed the story, we would appreciate your
letting others know by leaving a review.

For other wonderful stories,
please visit our on-line bookstore at
www.thewildrosepress.com.

For questions or more information
contact us at
info@thewildrosepress.com.

The Wild Rose Press, Inc.
www.thewildrosepress.com

Stay current with The Wild Rose Press, Inc.

Like us on Facebook

https://www.facebook.com/TheWildRosePress

And Follow us on Twitter
https://twitter.com/WildRosePress